Falling for Mr. Darcy

KaraLynne Mackrory

Oysterville, WA

This is a work of fiction. Names, characters, places, and incidents are products of the author's imagination or are used fictitiously. Any resemblance to actual events or persons, living or dead, is entirely coincidental.

Falling for Mr. Darcy

 For information: P.O. Box 34, Oysterville WA 98641

ISBN: 978-1-936009-20-6

Graphic design by Ellen Pickels; cover images by Edmund Blair Leighton: "Off" (1900), "On the Threshold" (1900) and "A Source of Admiration" (1904)

To

My own dreamboat Mr. Darcy: my husband, Andrew, whose gentlemanly ways made imagining a hero an easy task.

Acknowledgments

Once upon a time, a girl fell in love with a boy who existed only in the pages of a book. I owe many thanks to those who, in small ways and great, helped me along this path.

To Michele Reed and Ellen Pickels at Meryton Press, for their faith, excitement, and support throughout this process; to Gail Warner, my wonderful editor, whose insight and shared love of swoon-worthy moments made for a memorable experience working together; and to Damon Larson who must bear the responsibility for first introducing me to one Fitzwilliam Darcy of Pemberley in his sophomore English class.

Undoubtedly, I also must thank my dear friends and family who excitedly giggled with me after each chapter. Together, we affectionately pretended every bit of the story was real.

Lastly, to Jane Austen, who first created these lovable characters and captured my heart so thoroughly with her books.

Chapter 1

Elizabeth awoke refreshed as she opened her eyes and looked towards her bedroom window. The great oak blew its colorful, autumn leaves in the breeze, beckoning her outside. While at Netherfield, she was unable to take morning walks due to the poor weather and her duty nursing Jane. Now that she was home, she was eager to return to the outdoors and her favorite walks.

Thinking of Jane, she smiled. Ever since returning from Netherfield, Jane had a look of contentment about her. She was always serene and docile in the display of her feelings, but Elizabeth knew her expressions better than anyone and could tell that she was truly lost to Mr. Bingley. Sometimes she would catch Jane's gaze becoming wistful from some remembered conversation, and a slight smile would steal across her face. Whenever Elizabeth caught her in one of these moments, her sister would blush, and before Jane could lower her eyes to her hands, Elizabeth would catch in them the love for Mr. Bingley that could not be hidden.

Elizabeth looked at Jane, asleep next to her in their bed. Even in slumber, the corners of her mouth turned slightly upwards. Yes, it had been good to be at Netherfield for those few days. Though she cursed her mother for her thoughtlessness in contriving such a plan, it had turned out well—well, except for that awful Mr. Darcy.

Elizabeth pondered Mr. Darcy for a moment as she carefully slipped out of the warmth of the bed, trying not to waken Jane. Sitting at her dressing table, she began to comb through her tousled chocolate curls. She thought Mr. Darcy a mystery. He always looked so stern—frozen like a statue. When he spoke, his Derbyshire accent commanded attention even when it was unwanted. He was very handsome—she had to admit to herself—with strong, broad shoulders and a lean, powerful stance. *It is too bad he cannot be as attractive in personality as he is in body.* Elizabeth sighed. *What am I doing pondering Mr. Darcy's features! He is ill tempered, and he certainly thinks himself more worthy than Mr. Bingley's country neighbors. And I am only tolerable, but not handsome enough to tempt him!* A laugh escaped Elizabeth's mouth before she could cover it with her hands.

Thinking she had better steal out of the house before everyone awoke, Elizabeth turned her attention back to the task of getting ready for her walk. She pulled her unruly curls into a simple, low bun and dressed in a rose-colored muslin walking-gown with yellow embroidered flowers at the sleeves and hem. It was one of her favorites, and it was bright and happy like her mood. After pulling on half boots, she grabbed her bonnet and quietly exited the room.

The smell of freshly baked sweet bread and tea brewing made her stomach rumble. Descending the stairs carefully to avoid the squeaky parts and not lose her balance, she came to the landing and saw light under the door to her father's library. She smiled; she should have guessed her father, at least, would be awake. He was an early riser like Elizabeth, and some of her favorite memories were of their private talks and discussions as they shared a cup of tea before the rest of the house arose. She decided to step in quickly and say hello.

After knocking softly on the door, she heard, "Come in."

"Good morning, Papa."

"Hello, Lizzy. I suspected it would be you. Are you not tired this morning?"

Elizabeth poured a cup of tea from the sideboard. "No, Papa, I feel quite refreshed and thought I would venture out on a walk this morning."

"Ahh yes, a walk—most refreshing," replied Mr. Bennet, smiling.

Elizabeth smiled inwardly as she savored the earthy taste of her tea. This was the game they played most mornings. Elizabeth would mention going on a walk, and Mr. Bennet would act as if he was interested in accompanying her. Then she would invite him to join her, but he would decline stating business that needed attending. It was their way of laughing at the notion of impropriety that some in society held about ladies walking out alone, as well as a way Mr. Bennet could express that he wished her to be safe. "Would you like to come with me, Papa?"

"No, Poppet, you go on by yourself. I should like to continue with my book. It is quite windy out today, though; take your wrap."

"I will be safe, Papa," she said, as she put her empty cup on the table and bent to kiss his forehead before turning to go.

Outside the library door, she smiled and shook her head at her father's way of expressing his love and concern. He never had been able to say exactly what he was feeling and would use humor or sarcasm instead. Elizabeth understood this, as she often used her wit as a defense. This was one reason she felt so close to her father and they understood each other so well. Donning her bonnet and wrap, she walked excitedly out of the house, anticipating a long, morning stroll. As soon as she was outside, she was pushed slightly as a gust of wind caught her off-guard. Laughing, she pulled her wrap closer around her, bent her shoulder into the wind and took off at a quick pace towards her favorite pathway.

Mr. Darcy had not slept well at all. Miss Elizabeth Bennet assaulted his every thought late into the night. He just could not determine what it was about her that captivated him. Having her at Netherfield had been dangerous; she was not only inside his mind but also physically in the room with him on several occasions. He tried desperately to chase away thoughts of her fine eyes by reading, riding his horse or writing letters. Nothing worked. He would just accomplish pushing those delectable eyes out of his mind, only to have them replaced by thoughts of her silky, dark curls. *What would they feel like in my hands?* he thought. *No! This will not do!* Agitated, he threw the counterpane off and got out of bed, ringing the bell for his valet, Rogers.

He was in serious danger of caring for Miss Elizabeth Bennet—really caring for her. When he saw her tenderly nurse her sister back to health, he thought of how his own sister, Georgiana, would blossom under the care of Miss Elizabeth. There was intelligence in her eyes that captured him and made him want to engage in conversation with her. Thinking of engaging with Miss Elizabeth induced thoughts of being engaged to her and holding her soft, delicate hands. Mr. Darcy shook his head violently. It could never happen. *Her family,* he groaned aloud, *was atrocious!* Mrs. Bennet was exasperating and completely inappropriate. Her sisters were serious flirts and lacked any proper decorum or intelligence. Mr. Bennet, he allowed, was well read, even interesting, but Darcy could not overlook the way Mr. Bennet ignored the behavior of his family. How was it that Miss Bennet and Miss Elizabeth were so different from the rest?

While at Netherfield, they were everything proper. Miss Elizabeth even bore the subtle insults of Miss Bingley with class and a gentle, rebounding wit. He smiled, remembering the many times she outsmarted and deflected Miss Bingley's slurs. He admired her, and it made him realize how ill bred it was of Miss Bingley to behave that way, especially to a guest in her brother's house. Miss Elizabeth was truly remarkable, especially when the sides of her mouth turned upwards slightly in a sly smile, her one eyebrow rising in challenge to him and her eyes alight with mischief... *Ohhh, I am undone!* Those eyes beguiled him at every turn. They beckoned him and drew him in.

"Mr. Darcy, sir?" Rogers opened the dressing room door to address his master.

Thankful for the diversion from his thoughts, he directed his valet. "Ready my riding clothes, Rogers, and inform the stables to saddle Salazar."

"Yes, sir. Anything else? Shall I order a breakfast tray brought up?"

"No, thank you, Rogers. I shall breakfast when I return."

"Very good, sir," replied Rogers, as he retreated into the dressing room to prepare the clothing.

Yes, a very long, hard ride is just what I need this morning to extinguish these persistent thoughts of Elizabeth. No! She is not Elizabeth to you; she is Miss Elizabeth. Get hold of yourself, man! he groaned as he chastised himself. *A hard ride and soon.*

In his dressing room, he leaned back in the chair and stretched out, closing his eyes as Rogers began preparations for his shave. He knew he only had to make it through another week or so before he could politely tell Bingley he had business in London to attend and could leave Hertfordshire and the bewitching spell of Miss Elizabeth. He had to stay for the anticipated ball at Netherfield; he promised as much to Bingley the night before over a game of billiards—the ball, where Miss Elizabeth would be laughing, smiling and dancing in front of his eyes; her soft figure arresting him at every turn. He could just imagine the gentle pressure of her hands in his as he took her down the set. She would look up at him and smile and tease him as they danced. *Danced! You cannot dance with her; it would betray your feelings!* Moaning softly, he tried to dispel his traitorous thoughts.

The sound alerted Rogers. "Is everything all right, sir?"

"Oh... of course, yes, Rogers. Carry on."

Trying to think rationally, Mr. Darcy focused his thoughts on his upcoming ride. He loved being out of doors and feeling the strength of his horse beneath him. He often beat out the stress of the demands of being the master of Pemberley or the worries he had over Georgiana by riding hard across a field. Only the sound of hooves beating into the soil and the exchange of air in his lungs seemed to work for him, pounding out his strain and doubts with each stride. It had not been easy becoming the master of Pemberley at a young age. Not infrequently did he long for the advice of his late father. His father would have known exactly what should have been done at Ramsgate with Georgiana—no, his father would not have made the mistakes that led to that situation in the first place. He had again been deceived by that dastard Wickham. Just thinking of him made Darcy's temper rise. His only consolation was that his father was also deceived by the character of George Wickham.

However, his father was not there anymore and was no longer the master, nor was he responsible for Georgiana. Darcy was, and it was a heavy burden as he worried about how despondent she had become since the summer and that horrible day by the sea when he discovered Wickham's scheme. Not for the first time, Darcy offered up a prayer of thanks that he arrived when he did. Still, the damage was done. His dear sister, the only family he had, was left hurting. He knew she felt remorseful and laid all the blame on herself, causing her to retreat even further into shyness. He tried to help her understand that she was not at fault and that he loved her, but she continued to hurt, and he did not know what to do about it. She needed some cheerfulness in her life. She needed liveliness and warmth. *She needs someone like Elizabeth.* If he allowed himself to be truthful, he knew that someone like Miss Elizabeth was exactly what he needed, too—someone to lift his spirits and help him to return to the Fitzwilliam Darcy that he was before the burdens of life weighed him down. She would do that for him and Georgie. Liveliness and cheer came naturally to her, and she radiated warmth. Thinking of her made him warm and contented when he allowed himself to do so without fighting it. His mind drifted to the time when she first came to enquire about Jane with concern after having walked determinedly to Netherfield. Her eyes were bright and her complexion was pink from the exercise. A few of her soft curls had escaped their pins, and they lay delicately at the nape of her neck. Her dress was splattered with mud and her shoes were caked in it as well. He remembered the way she bravely looked at the Bingleys when her arrival was announced—her eyes challenging them to reprove her for her impropriety and disgraceful appearance. Only he noticed the way her hands trembled slightly with uncertainty. He had never seen her look as beautiful as she did that day. It was all he could do not to cross the carpet and embrace her. He remembered how he had to hold on tightly to his teacup in a concentrated effort to will himself to remain where he was.

"Mr. Darcy, sir." Rogers called his master to announce his shave was finished, but Mr. Darcy did not move. His face held a calm and contented look that made his valet smile. Whatever he was thinking about was certainly doing him some good. "Mr. Darcy?"

The voice of his valet finally stirred him from his thoughts, and opening his eyes, he rose from the shaving chair and began to dress. Looking in the mirror as he adjusted his cravat, he thought, *it is for the best; my duty demands a lady from higher circles. Besides, she will never know my weakness, and one day she will marry someone else.* Darcy grimaced as he contemplated her being another's wife. Shaking the thought out of his head, he grabbed his riding crop and left his bedchamber with a determined stride in the direction of the stables. He did not pause to contemplate why he now had a bitter taste in his mouth.

Elizabeth drew in a deep breath of crisp, cool, autumn air. In another mile, she would be able to see the beginnings of an outcrop of trees. It was her favorite place to ramble, listening to the birds singing their morning praises as well as the rustle of the trees: those still half-laden with leaves bright with the color of fire—yellow, orange and red. This was her favorite time of year. She picked up her pace, eager to see the forest come into view. The combination of new saplings and old, dying ancients helped her to clarify her thoughts and make discernments almost as if the venerable trees gave her wisdom and the young ones gave her new life. Today the trees would talk to her as the strong wind bent them to its will.

As she walked, she held one hand to her bonnet and the other to her shawl to keep the wind from taking them. Her thoughts drifted back to her time at Netherfield. She felt mortified at the embarrassment Jane must have felt arriving on horseback on a day that threatened rain from its onset. Elizabeth knew the Bingley sisters and Mr. Darcy looked down on her family. When she arrived to ask after Jane, she noticed Mr. Darcy's teacup shook in his hand, and she was certain it was due to finding so many faults in her that he was trying not to lose his composure and turn from her with incivility. She had boldly stared straight into those dark eyes and had seen a fire there that she assumed was disapproval. When he drew in an unsteady, disapproving breath, she raised her chin in challenge of his censure.

Shaking her head as she walked, she wondered, not for the first time, why she could not get that man out of her head. He disliked her, and she disliked him, but she was still oddly drawn to him. He was brooding, dark and hostile, but she liked to challenge him and, in so doing, felt vindicated for his thoughtless comment at the assembly. She liked putting him in his place with her teasing remarks though there were times she detected a bit of amusement in his features. His eyes, which she always thought so expressive, would hold a trace of a smile and maybe even something more that she could not quite figure out. Occasionally, he would even smile. She was struck by the memory of his smile. *He should smile more often; it makes him look quite handsome, indeed!* The memory temporarily stopped Elizabeth's forward motion, and she stood still for a moment, thinking of the way his face softened with a smile. He had two teasing dimples that naturally drew her eyes to his smiling lips.

With color rising in her cheeks at these strange thoughts, she laughed out loud and resumed her walk. *All the better for Miss Bingley!* She laughed at what a pair those two would make. He certainly appeared not to desire her effusions, and she was too ignorant to notice.

Looking ahead, Elizabeth finally could see the forest and already felt its strength clear her thoughts. She quickened her pace, hoping the trees would serve as protection from the ever-increasing wind so she could rest a bit.

Darcy took his mount and, leaning forward to stroke and pat his horse's neck, could feel the animal's agitation at the blustery weather. "You and me, both, Salazar!" Taking a deep breath, Darcy kicked his horse into a steady trot away from the stable yard, heading for the open field directly ahead. It was the same field he and Bingley had raced across when they first came to look at Netherfield. Upon reaching it, Darcy set down his crop, and with silent agreement, horse and rider took off in full sprint. The wind made it difficult to steady himself as they sailed across hedgerows and fences at breakneck speed. At one point, a gust of wind came across Darcy so forcefully that his hat flew off. Looking back to where it landed, he contemplated going back for it, but after noticing it had fallen safely onto a mound of dry grass, he decided to leave it until his return trip.

It was unlike Darcy to be less than properly attired, but the feeling of freedom, of the wind in his hair, reminded him of the carefree days of his youth when he would ride across the grounds of Pemberley without a hat. He turned his horse towards a hill a short distance away and, upon reaching the summit, stopped briefly to take in the scenery. It was truly a beautiful county. The rolling hills and glens were quite different from the more rugged and untamed, natural beauty of Derbyshire. In the distance, he spied a grove of trees that reminded him a little of the forests at Pemberley. A gust of wind pushed like hands against his back, compelling him towards the grove. Taking a deep breath and one last look across the countryside, Darcy kicked in his heels and again raced across the fields.

Upon reaching the grove, he noticed a path leading through it. The peacefulness of the sound of leaves in the wind made the decision for him to ride on. Bringing his horse to a slow walk, he breathed contentment after the hard ride. As he rode leisurely along the path, he thought of Georgiana and their reliance on each other. Until recently, she had been the only person in whom he could confide his most personal concerns. He now felt she was too burdened with her own recovery to speak with her about the feelings stirred inside of him by Elizabeth. He was not sure she would understand his reasoning regarding Elizabeth's unsuitability. She saw good and never suspected ill will in anyone, which was why she was so easily persuaded by Wickham. She would not understand the pressure he was under to marry well nor the inappropriateness of the match. No, he could not tell Georgiana. Thinking of the improper match helped Darcy steel his emotions and that twinge of—*was it loss?*—that he felt when thinking of avoiding any connection with Elizabeth.

With his resolve in place, Darcy took in a cleansing breath to expel all thoughts of her from his mind and focused instead on enjoying the slight reprieve from the wind provided by the forest as he meandered through it.

A few minutes later, he came around a small bend and caught sight of a flash of rose-colored fabric about thirty yards ahead. Immediately drawing his horse to a stop, he retreated a few steps to avoid being seen as he was not in the mood to be civil. When his eyes focused on the patch of color, his heart stopped and then started beating fiercely at double time. *It is Elizabeth! She has not seen me; I will quietly turn around and go before she does.* He was thankful for the sound of the wind through the trees disguising the hoof beats, keeping Elizabeth unaware of his near approach.

But he could not move. He was frozen in place by the sight of her. She was sitting on a fallen log amongst a group of very old and frail oak trees. Her foot was tapping rhythmically and he just caught the sound of her humming as the wind changed direction and sent her song to him. Her head was tilted up, caught in a small patch of sun peeking down on her. Her eyes closed, and he noticed how her eyelashes splayed across her cheekbones, and in that moment, he wished he could kiss them. Adjusting uncomfortably in his seat, he noticed her dress had small, yellow flowers on the sleeve as one arm was peeking out of the shawl that had fallen temptingly off one shoulder. *She is so beautiful!* As she tipped her head further back to gain more sun, he noticed the wind brush softly across her features as a few tendrils of her dark curls blew out and around the side of her bonnet.

He was not sure how long he sat there atop his horse watching her. After a while, he felt embarrassed that he had spied on her for so long and decided to take one last moment to memorize the picture she made of pure contentment and then be on his way. Just as he was guiding his horse to turn around, a gust of wind tore through the forest, upsetting the animal. Darcy had to use all his skill as a horseman to calm his mount and bring him under control, lest he lose his seat. As he did this, a sharp booming crack caused Salazar to rear up in terror. He had barely calmed his horse when he turned to see Elizabeth. Another stronger gust of wind tore through, causing the old oak tree near her to break at its rotten base and fall. She screamed as she stumbled backwards, attempting to get out of the way. He watched in horror as she barely managed to avoid being crushed beneath the falling tree before her foot slipped, causing her to fall back on her hands. He froze as he heard her head hit the ground.

No! It cannot be, not her! were the only thoughts Darcy could manage as he kicked his horse to close the distance to her. In one fluid movement, he alit from his horse and was at her side, capturing her in his arms and holding her head to his chest.

"Elizabeth! Are you all right? Are you hurt?" Mr. Darcy cried in fear. "Elizabeth!" He was holding her so tightly that he did not notice she was fully alert, her eyes wide in surprise at his embrace.

She had closed her eyes only briefly in fear as she fell and hit her head when, in the next moment, she found herself in the arms of none other than Mr. Darcy! He was calling her name in concern—her Christian name—though she could not find the words to assuage his fear or to reprimand him for the familiarity of his address. Oddly, at that moment, her thoughts drifted to the feel of his embrace. He had such strong arms, and her head tucked perfectly under his chin as she listened to his rapid heartbeat. *He feels so warm too!* She noticed his scent was a pleasant mixture of lemon and leather. She felt his head as it rested against her hair, which meant she had lost her bonnet somewhere. Then she felt a gentle pressure on her head. *Did he just kiss my hair?* In the second it took for her to process all these thoughts and to firmly, if not successfully, push aside how that moment of pressure on her hair made her feel, she found her voice.

"Um... Mr. Darcy," Elizabeth mumbled against his chest where he was firmly holding her head.

She felt his body stiffen in realization of his rash behavior, and he slowly, but reluctantly, loosened his grip. With a feigned attempt at calm, he said, "Forgive me, Miss Bennet. I was riding and saw the tree fall, causing you to stumble, and I was concerned you were injured." He knew his actions could not fully be explained by his words, and he was unhappy at the cold sound of his voice.

He looked down and noticed that her hair had come out of most of its pins and was falling around her shoulders and down her back. His fingers ached with the desire to run them through the silken strands, but instead, he looked at her face, and their eyes caught. He stiffened as he looked into her brown eyes full of humor and not a little disbelief. The air around them thickened as his eyes moved down to her lips, which were turned slightly upwards at the corners. Elizabeth saw his eyes darken and wondered what it would feel like to kiss Mr. Darcy. She had not been kissed before, and the idea suddenly struck her as attractive. Startled by her bizarre thoughts and brought back to the strange reality of the situation, she heard him clear his throat in an attempt to speak.

She hastened to speak first. "Mr. Darcy, I thank you for your concern.

As you can see, I am quite well. I promise to forgive you, if you . . . umm . . . " She lost her words as she looked down at the arms still wrapped around her and nodded her head towards them. Darcy realized with great embarrassment that he still held her in his arms. He withdrew them slowly, stopping to rest his hands on her arms to steady her before releasing her completely.

They sat on the forest floor for a brief, uncomfortable moment, as neither knew what was proper to say next. Darcy was mortified at his rash behavior in his impulsive embrace of Miss Elizabeth and in using her Christian name in his anxiety of the situation. *Oh, heavens!* And then to find that she was unhurt and that he was still holding her! He tried not to dwell on the loss he felt after releasing her or the tingle of his lips from his thoughtless kiss on her hair. *Oh, it was so soft and silky! Stop it, man! You must get a handle on yourself this instant!* He chastised himself as he absently rubbed his jaw. A mixture of relief and regret simmered inside him as he thought about that brief, charged moment when he almost forgot himself and kissed her. Now he felt mortified, as he furiously fought for something to say.

Elizabeth was not much better off with her own thoughts. She was completely baffled by Mr. Darcy's behavior. He had brashly seized her into his arms, and his voice was shaky, yet tender, when he called her name. *And how is it that he could turn my name into a caress?* He seemed very concerned for her. And that slight pressure on her head — no, she would not dwell on what *that* could have been. *I had not thought he could be kind and tender, but he was for a moment. Then the cold Mr. Darcy came out as soon as he realized his impropriety.* She thought he must be quite ashamed of himself for showing concern to someone like her. *He must be congratulating himself that we were unseen here in the forest.* She did not allow herself to admit to the feeling of disappointment that coursed briefly through her when he withdrew his arms; it made no sense. A chill went down her spine as her thoughts turned back to how she had wished he would kiss her. She remembered the feel of his warm breath on her face and his rapid heartbeat against her hands where they had rested on his chest.

Mr. Darcy's thoughts were brought back to the present when he noticed her shiver. "You are chilled; forgive me for not retrieving your wrap." He stood and walked to where her wrap, which had flown off in the wind, had caught on a tall branch. He carefully detached it and came back to crouch next to her.

"Please, allow me." Carefully, and with as little contact as he could manage, he draped the wrap on her shoulders, bringing it together in the front. Then, his hands shaking, he pulled away and looked around in embarrassment.

"Thank you, Mr. Darcy, you are very kind." She felt no small amount of embarrassment herself. As she absently brought her hand up to her face in an attempt to cool her heated cheeks, a slight breeze blew her loose hair across her face and hand. "Oh!" she cried and colored with mortification, assessing the disheveled state she was in. "I apologize for my appearance, Mr. Darcy. The wind..." Her voice trailed off to a whisper.

"Do not concern yourself, Miss Bennet. I do not mind." His eyes widened as he realized what he had just said and saw her color again. "That is to say, I...um...understand the weather is quite at fault in this situation." *Idiot! If I could but disappear!* Darcy grimaced and gentlemanly turned his head away as she pulled her hair up and tried to replace her pins.

Out of the corner of his eye, Darcy could see her ministrations and was briefly fascinated with them. He had never before seen a lady set her hair, and he wished to watch her. He knew that, with each pin, the curve of her delicate neck would be further revealed and her femininity intensified. Instead, he looked around and, catching sight of her bonnet on the ground a few feet away, went to fetch it for her. He walked slowly back as she replaced the final pin in her hair. He bent slightly to hand the bonnet to her, and she took it and placed it on her head, tying the ribbons tightly under her chin. He extended his hand to her. "Please allow me, Miss Bennet."

She accepted his hand and attempted to rise, but when she tried to place weight on her left ankle, she whimpered in pain and sat back down. Mr. Darcy became concerned and kneeled next to her.

"Miss Bennet, you are hurt. Is it your ankle?" His hands floated nervously in the air around her foot as if attempting to will it to heal.

"Yes, sir, I am afraid I cannot walk on it. If you would be so kind as to go for help, I would be much obliged, sir."

"Please allow me at least to help you over to that log so you are not sitting on the ground." Mr. Darcy spoke with tenderness.

Elizabeth, caught by the look of concern on his face and the soothing sound of his voice, could not speak but blushed and nodded her acceptance. With that, he nodded and, hesitantly, as if he were afraid to touch or break her, moved closer. His mind reeled in nervous anticipation of touching her again. She awkwardly raised her arms, thinking he would lend his strength to support her in hobbling to the log. Instead, he paused briefly, then exhaled the breath he had been holding, and in one fluid motion, he put one arm around her back and the other under her legs and stood, scooping her up and carrying her towards the log. Her heart beat wildly in her chest at his sudden closeness and the realization of the ease with which he held her full weight as if she weighed nothing at all. In the suddenness of his action, she grabbed onto his neck in surprise, and her fingers felt the feathery softness of his brown curls just touching the top of his greatcoat. She looked up and noticed he was not wearing his hat and his hair was wildly windblown. A few wayward curls falling across his forehead drew her attention. He looked down at her, catching her scrutiny, and gave her a small smile, causing her heart to beat faster as she hastily turned her head away.

As soon as he reached the log, Darcy gently placed Elizabeth down and pulled his arms back as quickly as he could as if they were on fire—because in truth, they felt like they were. He used the excuse of wiping dust off his sleeves to massage the feeling from his arms caused by holding Elizabeth so close. When he had caught her looking at him with wonder in her eyes as he carried her, a smile appeared without his consent. He backed away a few steps to collect himself for a moment, and then concern for her again flooded his thoughts as he remembered the reason he had held her. She was injured.

"Miss Bennet. You have asked me to go for help, but I cannot. I fear leaving you unable to protect yourself should another gust of wind arise."

Elizabeth's face lit with a sly humor as she responded, "Mr. Darcy, I thank you for your concern, but I am quite certain the wind could not carry me away."

Mr. Darcy opened his mouth to protest but stopped as he realized she was teasing him and he smiled. "I do not doubt you, Miss Bennet." He was delighted with the smile she returned. An idea struck him as a solution. "Miss Bennet, if it would be acceptable to you, I have an idea to solve our current problem."

"And what is that, Mr. Darcy?"

"You can ride my horse, and I will escort you back to the safety of your home." He awaited her response to spending more time in his company.

"I see. Well, sir, I cannot accept—"

Mr. Darcy, becoming slightly agitated at her stubbornness, quickly cut her off. "Miss Bennet, I do not see another solution—"

With a slight smile, she stopped him and attempted to ease his discomfort by explaining that she could not ride his horse as she did not ride and it quite frightened her to do so.

"Indeed? Well then..." Mr. Darcy began to pace as he tried to figure out another solution and absently drew his fingers through his hair as he struggled. While he paced, Elizabeth smoothed her skirts, dusting off the dirt from her fall. She watched him curiously, seeing how much it bothered him not to be in command of the situation. She thought he must be used to having his own way. With a small amount of surprise, she found she was not as angry with him for his overbearing nature as she had been in the past. She had experienced his kindness and concern during the past half hour, and she realized, with some consternation, that at least some of her previous assessment of him was wrong. Yes, he was still arrogant, but perhaps his demanding nature was somewhat a result of habit. She knew he had become master at a young age and, from what Mr. Bingley had told Jane, his estate in Derbyshire was quite large. It occurred to her with sadness that he probably had few opportunities to be a gentleman of leisure, especially since he seemed to take such great concern and care of his young sister. *Maybe that is why he does not often smile. I wonder if I could make him smile again.* With that thought, she decided to put her fear of horse riding aside to ease his frustration.

"Mr. Darcy, if you can assure me that your great beast over there is quite safe, I will try to oblige you by riding it. But, under no circumstances, should you let go of the reins." Elizabeth was disappointed in the slight shakiness of her voice as she wished to appear more confident than she sounded.

Mr. Darcy stopped in mid-stride and turned towards her. He realized she was trying to make a concession to him despite her worries, and he was struck with amazement at her generosity. He smiled as he nodded his acceptance of her terms and assured her his "great beast" was capable of being very gentle.

Ahh, he does have a great smile. It really transforms his features. She felt quite happy with herself for so easily accomplishing her task to make him smile. Elizabeth then realized he was coming towards her, and her heart took off again. *What is wrong with me that he can cause such a reaction?*

"Miss Bennet, I must help you to the horse, if you will give your consent again." Mr. Darcy tried to sound as casual as possible even as his mind was screaming—*Yes, say yes! You belong in my arms, Elizabeth!*

She laughed, and the hair on his neck stood up at the musical sound. "Mr. Darcy, I cannot see any other way I could get there unless another gust of wind were to pick me up and place me atop your horse! You may assist me, thank you." Elizabeth realized she was using humor to cover her nervous feelings of anticipation at his touch. She thought, with a wry smile, that she was not that different from her father, trying to disguise her feelings with humor.

Mr. Darcy softly chuckled and, inhaling a deep breath in preparation, bent down to pick her up. As he walked the short distance to his horse, he noticed out of the corner of his eye that she was again inspecting his face. He tried to pretend not to notice and so pressed his lips together to keep from smiling. Despite his efforts, the smallest hint of a dimple began to appear on his cheek. He could see her eyes dart to it, and with a bit of mischief, he surprised her when he spoke.

"Miss Bennet, do I have a mole on my face or perhaps a bit of dirt that has caught your attention?" At seeing her color in embarrassment at being caught, he broke into a full grin.

Elizabeth, completely discomposed, managed to push her embarrassment aside in an attempt to tease him for his ungallant comment. "Mr. Darcy, you do not have a mole or dirt, I can assure you of that. However, I do see something at present on your face that I have not seen before, and it briefly caught my attention. I apologize." She paused, waiting for the response she knew he would give.

"Whatever do you mean, Miss Bennet? What is on my face?"

Chuckling to herself in satisfaction that he responded as she thought he would, she replied, "A smile, sir. Are you quite sure your face will not break?" She turned merry eyes to him with an eyebrow turned up in playful challenge.

His smile grew bigger and a soft baritone chuckle escaped his mouth as he realized her jest. He gave her a tender look that made the breath catch in her throat as he spoke with amusement, "No madam, I do not believe it will, but I thank you for your kind concern." As they arrived at his horse, he explained he needed to adjust her a bit, and if she would just use him as support, he would set her on the ground. "Just be sure, Miss Bennet, not to put any weight on your foot. Yes, that is right; hold my arm there. Good."

They stood for a moment with his hands on her waist and her arms on his as she tried to balance on her uninjured foot. Darcy looked at anything but her, as he was fully aware that if he looked at her right then, he would have to kiss her. With great effort, he reined in his thoughts and asked, "Miss Bennet, are you ready? I will lift you now."

She was breathless from their playful banter and close proximity and, so, did not think about her fear of actually getting on the horse until she found herself being lifted by strong hands into a sidesaddle position. Suddenly, she was quite high up on an extremely large animal.

Mr. Darcy could see exactly the moment she went from distracted to fearful as she stiffened and looked worriedly back and forth from the horse to the ground again and again. He raised his hand to hers and spoke softly and reassuringly. "Miss Bennet, it will be all right. Salazar is a good horse, and I will not let anything happen to you. You are quite safe."

Elizabeth could feel more than hear his words. She could see his concern and his attempt to comfort her. She looked in his eyes and, seeing the conviction in them, knew he would allow nothing to hurt her—not just then, but ever. A feeling of calm came over her, and she nodded numbly to him. He smiled reassuringly and, with a tender voice, indicated they would begin walking. While holding the reins, he prompted his horse to move.

Elizabeth's fear again rose at the movement, and she found her voice in panic. "Mr. Darcy—I cannot. It is too much—please!" she pleaded.

He could see she was trembling and wanted to take her in his arms and hold her, comfort her and help her to feel safe. *How is it, in just a couple of hours, she has become everything to me?* Thinking of holding her in his arms, he decided on another alternative. Without asking permission, because he was afraid she would not give it and he did not want to miss this opportunity, he grabbed the saddle, pulled himself up and sat behind her. He steadied her with his hands and, seeing her startled look, spoke softly.

"Miss Bennet, forgive me for my impulsiveness. I do not want to make you feel uncomfortable. I believe I can safely return you to your home more quickly this way, and you will be quite safe on this horse with me. You have only to protest, and I will dismount and try to find another way."

Elizabeth's heart was beating wildly but not out of fear; in fact, her fear had disappeared as soon as she felt his gentle hold and the deep timbre of his voice at her ear. Her face colored deep pink in the confusion of her feelings. *This is Mr. Darcy! How can his touch affect me so?* She thought of being terrified of riding horses since falling from one when she was nine. Never had she felt safe on one since—never until then.

Unsteadily she took in a breath and replied, "No, sir, you are right. I feel better now, and you may proceed. Slowly." She tried to relax as he nodded and prompted his horse to move again. "Very slowly!"

"Yes, madam." Mr. Darcy could feel her tension slowly ease after a few moments and he allowed himself to relax. Eventually, they set out at a comfortable pace that lulled them into a companionable silence as the gait of the horse's steps softly rocked them. After a while, they began to talk. It was a comfortable conversation about books, the theatre and landscape. He learned that she had similar tastes in books if not impressions of them. She learned that the formidable Mr. Darcy had a weakness for the theatre, especially Shakespeare. Before she realized it, the journey towards her home was nearly over as she spied Longbourn in the distance. She could not believe she had just spent thirty minutes on a horse and had enjoyed it! Seeing her home coming closer, she felt she must say something.

"Mr. Darcy."

"Hmm?" he replied absently, as he thought about how Elizabeth seemed to belong in his arms. He had one hand on her waist and the other around her holding the reins.

"Mr. Darcy, I must thank you for coming to my rescue and helping me. You have been most kind, and I am sorry for taking up your morning this way."

He was quiet for a moment as he contemplated how to respond. She could feel his hesitation and hastened to continue out of uneasiness, "I must also add that I appreciate your patience with my silly protestations about your horse. I can see that Salazar is quite tame."

He smiled down at her. "Yes, Miss Bennet, he is not so wild, and I must compliment you on your fine riding. You do not seem as afraid as you were earlier."

She turned to him with a smile. "No, sir, you are quite right. I am not very afraid right now."

He allowed her words to linger in the air and he savored them before speaking softly. "You have no need to thank me, Miss Bennet; the pleasure was all mine in, as you say, coming to your rescue." With mutual feelings of unhappiness at their upcoming separation, they rode quietly.

After a moment, Elizabeth said, "Mr. Darcy, I am aware of what improprieties may be assumed by my family spying us together on horseback, and I would not want you to bear the effusions that my mother will be unable to control. I understand you did only what any gentleman would do under the circumstances, and so, for your sake, I will try to manage the last bit of the journey on this beast by myself if you will hold the reins and walk beside. This way you are not put in an uncomfortable position with my family." She held her breath awaiting his response.

He could not help but again think how generous she was. At that moment, he did not care whether all of London spied him riding with Miss Bennet. In fact, the idea of being forced to marry her appealed to him in a most gratifying way. It pained him slightly that she would think he did not want to be connected with her, but he was touched by her concern for him, especially when it came to the behavior or conclusions her mother would make. He also could see that she was uneasy and perhaps worried about it herself.

"I thank you for your concern, Miss Bennet. I will just dismount here and walk with you the remainder of the way." He gave her a gentle squeeze, because he could not help himself and wanted to feel her pressed against him one last time, and then pulled his horse to a stop. Dismounting, he grabbed the reins and looked up to see she again had become a bit nervous on the horse.

"Are you all right, Miss Bennet?"

"Yes, Mr. Darcy, thank you," she replied, shakily. "I am just a bit unsettled. If you please, walk slowly."

"Of course, Miss Bennet."

He walked close to the horse and held the reins in his right hand, which rested near her legs. His occasional touch seemed to calm her and make her more relaxed in the saddle. Soon, they were at the gates of Longbourn, and as they walked into the garden, they could hear the concerned and relieved voices of her family coming out of the house to greet them.

Chapter 2

Elizabeth looked over at Mr. Darcy one last time before facing the members of her family. As they neared the house, she could see his shoulders stiffen and his posture mold back into the imposing wall he had always displayed anytime he had contact with the residents of Hertfordshire. The relative ease with which they had interacted over the last two hours was beginning to slip away, and he was reverting into the proud, aloof gentleman she found distasteful. Even now, she had the familiar stirrings of irritation over how quickly he seemed to set himself above those around him. She noticed now that his jaw was set into a firm line and his free hand rubbed rhythmically on the inside of his palm. As if sensing her gaze, he lifted his head to her on top of his horse, and she saw his jaw relax and his brows crease in anxiety. It struck her, then, that part of his proud visage was masking his real discomfort of the situation. She was not sure whether it was an uneasiness born from interacting with those below him or he simply did not like the attention others paid to him. She suspected the first, but then there was that look in his eyes that made her wonder. She had no time to ponder it as, with matching exhaling breaths, they turned to her family.

In a matter of seconds, Elizabeth assessed the entire feelings of her family. She knew them so well that it did not take long to see what each of them was thinking in seeing her—not only on a horse, but on Mr. Darcy's horse. She groaned inwardly at the glint in her mother's eye of suspicious excitement. It was as if she were already calculating the number of dresses and fine carriages Elizabeth would own as the future Mrs. Darcy. Her hands were even steepled together in anticipation of wedding bells. It was as if riding a man's horse was tantamount to being compromised by the man in a public square. She could not consider her mother any further and moved her gaze to her father. Mr. Bennet also had a suspicious look in his eyes at seeing her on a horse accompanied by Mr. Darcy. She knew her father would tease her about this and that her mother would be unbearable. With a sigh, she turned to the last member of her family. Jane's face held all that she needed at that moment. It was full of the most sincere concern and relief. Looking at Jane gave her a bit of comfort, and she took in a deep breath as the horse stopped.

"Mr. Darcy, how pleasant to see you this morning..." Her mother's sickeningly sweet words oozed out of her without the briefest concerned word for her daughter.

Mr. Darcy stiffened and turned to Elizabeth's family, nodding his acknowledgement. Addressing her father, he said with strangled civility, "Mr. Bennet, I came upon your daughter after she had taken a fall when a tree was blown down beside her. She has injured her ankle. If you could assist me, we should get her into the house."

"Of course, Mr. Darcy. I thank you for your assistance in coming to my daughter's aid." Elizabeth squeezed her eyes shut briefly and bit her lip at the amusement in her father's voice. *Oh, he is having fun with this!*

She had not noticed that her hands were shaking until Mr. Darcy turned and gave her a reassuring look before reaching up to help her off the horse. When his eyes caught hers, she could see his frozen features relax slightly. With his back to her family, he looked into her anxious eyes and winked. Elizabeth bit her lip to keep from laughing at the absurdity of the situation. *At least he sees some humor in this.*

Mr. Darcy did indeed see some humor in the situation, even through his discomfort at the scrutiny given by the ladies of Longbourn. He memorized Elizabeth's amused expression for future enjoyment, and securing her in his hands, he gently, and with as much dignity as he could muster under the circumstances, lifted her off his horse. He supported one arm as Mr. Bennet came to claim the other to assist her into the house.

Everyone cleared the way for them, and Elizabeth cringed at the giggles from her sisters walking behind. The gentlemen moved her as carefully as possible to sit on the sofa in the morning room. Jane rushed around them to lift her legs gently onto the sofa, ensuring her skirts were tucked modestly around her legs as she moved them.

As soon as Elizabeth was comfortably set, Mr. Darcy backed away from the crowding bodies of her family members and walked to the far end of the room. He brushed his hands through his hair and shook his arms out in an attempt to school his thoughts and regain his composure. All focus was now on Elizabeth, and he used the distraction to think about what he should do next. Mr. Bennet observed the gentleman surreptitiously as he feigned participation with his family over his second daughter's comfort.

Mr. Darcy's thoughts whirled in his head as if the wind from outside had broken through to his mind. His senses were coming back to him as, for the first time, he really thought about what had taken place that morning. Was he not trying to forget Elizabeth, only to come upon her in a moment of great need? He had truly enjoyed his time with Elizabeth, though. It was the only time he spent with her alone besides that hellish thirty minutes in the library at Netherfield. *That didn't count! She sat there reading so demurely the entire time, tempting me to distraction with the soft pat of her slipper on the floor as she tapped out the rhythm of the poem she was reading.* And he was sure she meant to torture him when she absently played with a small curl on her neck as she mouthed the words. He stopped his pacing as he remembered how his favorite chair in the library suddenly had become uncomfortable and his book about Wellesley's war chronicles no longer held his interest. Coming back to the present, Mr. Darcy looked around at the scene before him and turned towards the window to pretend interest outside.

Mary had just reentered the room with a blanket for Elizabeth's legs, and Kitty and Lydia were interrogating Elizabeth, huddling their shoulders together as they covered their mouths when they giggled. "Did he rescue you, Lizzy?" Lydia asked saucily and with definite implications. Her feet stamped excitedly on the carpet in her amusement and imagination. "His arms look very strong. I am sure you were very scared, Lizzy. Did he comfort you?" A fresh burst of giggles erupted from Lydia at this last inquiry, and Elizabeth colored in mortification as she tried to shush her sisters. She flicked her eyes towards Mr. Darcy and was thankful he seemed distracted by the prospect through the window.

Mr. Bennet observed both Lizzy and Mr. Darcy throughout it all with amusement at their discomfort. He had noticed Lizzy's tension and fear when she was on the horse and how Darcy's arm would occasionally brush her legs as he held the horse in check. He also noticed that both held their breath when Mr. Darcy lifted her from the horse, and he did not miss that Elizabeth tried to hide her smile by biting her lip. He had seen the humor in her eyes. Something was different there, and he was going to find it out. For now, he contented himself by smiling inwardly at the obvious disquiet in the previously impenetrable façade of Mr. Darcy. *If anyone could crack that shell, it would be my Lizzy. I wonder whether she is handsome enough to tempt him now?* That thought, though, turned Mr. Bennet's brows down in contemplation. He was not sure he wanted Lizzy capturing this great man's interest. He would miss her when she married, and although he knew she would someday, he did not welcome it.

Mrs. Bennet, having secured her daughter's comfort, began her own machinations. She sauntered over to Mr. Darcy at the window, swaying her matronly hips and skirts as she moved, and began spewing out her gratitude for him. "Oh, Mr. Darcy! You are so kind to come to my Lizzy's aid. She has the most patient of spirits and would have endured well, but we are so grateful that you came along and brought her safely back to our house."

Mr. Darcy bowed to Mrs. Bennet and stiffly replied, "It is nothing, madam. Your gratitude is not necessary." With that, he turned to the window again in hopes she would desist and return to her daughter. She did not.

"Oh, but Mr. Darcy, I am sure that it is! My Lizzy often walks out alone, although I swear she does it to tempt my nerves. As you know, I am a most doting mother, and I constantly worry about the comfort of all my children. Anyhow, she walks out often alone and is so headstrong sometimes." Mrs. Bennet's fluttering hands froze as she realized her words might not please a great man like Mr. Darcy, who would not be interested in a woman who would not bend to his every wish. She hastened to add, "That is to say, although she is headstrong at times, she has the most sweet, conforming nature, and I am sure when she marries, she will be the most proper and obedient wife."

Mr. Darcy drew from his years of practice and held himself back from dropping his jaw in appall at this woman's audacity. She was really quite insufferable. He knew she was trying to sell him on her daughter. For a moment, humor colored his disgusted thoughts as he thought of the reaction Mrs. Bennet would have if he replied, "*Mrs. Bennet, I am glad to hear it, as I was just considering what a lovely wife Miss Elizabeth would make.*" He schooled his expression and merely nodded. From the corner of his eye, he could see that Elizabeth had observed the interchange and was now squeezing her eyes shut as she lowered her head in shame. Seeing Elizabeth so mortified made his anger towards her ridiculous mother simmer, and he turned from her, bowing slightly, and went to Elizabeth.

"Miss Elizabeth, I hope that you are feeling comfortable now that you are home." *Stupid, stupid, stupid,* thought Darcy, cringing inwardly at the banality of his statement, but he smiled politely and awaited her reply.

Elizabeth drew in a deep breath and straightened her shoulders as she raised her chin and replied, "I am, sir. Thank you once again for your kind attentions to me." With this, her younger sisters burst into laughter and Elizabeth winced.

Mr. Bennet, although enjoying the entertainment the morning's turn of events had offered him, could see the discomfort of his favorite daughter and ordered the younger three girls from the room, ignoring Mary's protests that she had just been reading and not disturbing anyone. He then turned to his wife, who was at that moment walking towards Mr. Darcy for another round of flattery, and said, "Mrs. Bennet, could you please tell Hill that we will need some wraps for Lizzy's ankle? Some tea would be nice, too." He said this as he guided her out of the room, ignoring her whispered objections and the constant billowing of her handkerchief over her shoulder in an attempt to turn towards Mr. Darcy. Once she was safely beyond the door, he turned and, looking at Elizabeth, smiled and winked as he closed the door behind him.

Immediately, the three remaining felt a calm settle over the room. Jane, who had remained silent until then, turned to Mr. Darcy and said, "Mr. Darcy, sir, may I thank you again on behalf of my family for being so kind to Lizzy. I am sorry for the excitement you have witnessed here today. We were indeed very worried about my sister when she did not return as expected."

Mr. Darcy nodded. "You are welcome, of course." He turned back to Elizabeth as he thought about how kind Miss Bennet was and noticed how calm she remained. She never fawned or became excited like the rest of her family. She was tender and solicitous of her sister's comfort. Even then, he could see she was trying to placate his discomfort and, in a way, erase the distaste he felt for the behavior of her other family members. She would be good for Bingley. He needed someone to be a calming influence on his exuberance, but that someone needed to be kind and not commanding in doing so. It was the first time Darcy allowed himself to see the merits and good judgment in Bingley's attentions to Miss Bennet.

"Mr. Darcy, I must also say how shocked we all were to see Lizzy on top of your horse, sir. Did she not tell you she is afraid of horses?" Jane asked.

"Dear Jane," Elizabeth rushed in before he could answer and then paused with a glint in her eye. "I did tell him, but he was quite persuasive in his arguments and convinced me that his horse was not wild." Her eyes twinkled with hidden laughter as she said this to Jane but looked at Mr. Darcy.

Is she flirting with me? Mr. Darcy smiled. "Yes, Miss Bennet, I was fortunate enough to be able to help Miss Elizabeth see the merit in riding the horse, but she is being quite modest now. She did very well despite her fears, and I was quite pleased with her." He, too, spoke to Miss Bennet, but looked daringly back at Elizabeth.

Jane smiled to herself as she turned to remove Elizabeth's half boot and inspect her injury. "Yes, I am sure you are right, Mr. Darcy. Did she tell you why she does not like to ride horses?"

Mr. Darcy was keenly aware of the work Miss Bennet was now doing. Although he could see she was trying to obscure his view to allow Elizabeth some modesty, out of the corner of his eye, he could see as she slipped the boot off her uninjured right foot and then tucked it swiftly under the blanket. Unconsciously, he forgot all about being subtle and turned his head to get a better view. He held his breath as the left boot was unlaced and Miss Bennet began, with careful movement, to slip the boot from her sister's foot without causing her discomfort. *Here it comes, almost there. Ahhh, yes!* He breathed out. A small smile slid onto his face. He noticed the feminine curve of her ankle, slightly swollen on the outside, leading to the soft arch of her small foot. He could not believe how petite it was. *How does she stand without falling over?* He indulgently allowed his gaze to travel further to her pink, little toes just visible through pale ivory stockings. His hand twitched as he thought about reaching out and capturing her toes between his fingers.

Elizabeth had seen his distraction when Jane began to remove her shoes. She colored at the acknowledgement of the root of his attention. Then, when he turned his head to view the scene, she was amused at his total slip in propriety. *Mr. Darcy has forgot himself!* Although she was shocked and embarrassed at his uninhibited examination of her exposure, she found that, instead of being appalled at his ungentlemanly distraction, she was enthralled. Never before had any man given her more than the briefest of pleasantries in their compliments to her person. She was always hearing about how beautiful Jane was from her mother, too. *Could Mr. Darcy find me attractive?* The idea suddenly struck her that he might indeed, especially as she now saw that his face held a pleased smile. His gaze was quite intent, and she saw his hand move slightly. She suddenly felt very warm inside to witness his complete abandon at the sight. Elizabeth smiled to herself wickedly and decided to get revenge for his impolite acknowledgement of her scrutiny of his face when he had carried her to his horse earlier that morning. She eyed him carefully as she wiggled the toes on the foot he was watching.

Mr. Darcy stiffened when he saw her toes move and then heard a small chuckle come from Elizabeth. He quickly turned towards her, realized she had seen his lapse in manners, and colored deep red with embarrassment. She laughed this time, causing Jane to turn her head in question. Mr. Darcy allowed himself to laugh, too. He slowly raised his gaze and met her eyes, which were soft and tender and excessively amused. He breathed a sigh of relief that she was not upset with him as he returned a smile and mouthed, "I'm sorry."

Elizabeth adjusted in her seat and, sitting upright a bit more, smiled her acceptance of his apology before turning to Jane to say, "No Jane, I had not the chance to share with Mr. Darcy my most embarrassing reason for being afraid of horses. Thank you for bringing it up. I am sure Mr. Darcy is too much of a *gentleman* to ask me to tell the story though."

"Indeed, no! Miss Elizabeth, this story sounds too good to miss, and I am not so much the gentleman as you might think, so please—do enlighten me." He smiled cheekily at her jibe.

Elizabeth and Jane laughed together, and Elizabeth thought that she was not sure she knew this man at all. *He is so charming and playful. Who would have guessed stuffy Mr. Darcy had it in him to lighten up this way?* Her breathing quickened as she contemplated how she might be falling for him. *How absurd! After one morning? It cannot be; we are nothing alike.* The thought struck her with a bit of sadness. They were very different. He was rich and from circles in society that she could never touch, even if she cared to. She was an insignificant country gentleman's daughter. He was probably expected to marry an heiress or someone with impressive ancestry. *I have nothing to tempt him. He is out of my reach, and I cannot believe I am thinking about it at all. It cannot be.* She was surprised at how the realization of the difference in status, and the impossibility of a match between them, struck her with a pang in her heart. Unconsciously, her face drooped a bit in momentary sadness.

Mr. Darcy watched the play of emotions dance across her face. She had been happy—exuberant really—and then she seemed to be struck with something. When her face turned down with worry and sadness, he jumped in, "Miss Elizabeth, if it gives you discomfort to share the story, please do not. I was only teasing and would never wish to cause you distress. It was very impolite of me; please accept my apology."

Elizabeth glanced at her sister, who saw the change in her as well and asked about it with only an upturn of her eyebrow, the way only a sister familiar enough with her could do. She gave a silent promise to talk later and turned to deflect Mr. Darcy's concern.

"Mr. Darcy, it is nothing. I would be happy to tell you the story as it does not really distress me at all. I was only briefly distracted by an unpleasant thought. Please forgive me."

Mr. Darcy was relieved at her words, but his interest was captured by her reference to an unpleasant thought. He felt a wave of protectiveness flood him as he never wanted to see her face turn down so in sadness. He wished he could know that terrible thought and keep it from disturbing her ever again, so that her eyes would sparkle at him.

He nodded to her and, in hopes of making her eyes light up in laughter, displayed an uncharacteristic silliness as he found a chair and, moving it right up to her at the couch, sat down and leaned forward in eager anticipation of her story. His face expressed serious consideration for the tragic tale, and he brought his hand up to grip his chin in ready concentration. "Do begin then, Miss Elizabeth. I am ready for this terrifying narrative."

She sat back in delight at his mock seriousness and laughed, touched at his attempt to cheer her. *Oh, if you only knew, Mr. Darcy, how attractive you are right now, you would not continue in such a way.* She smiled and, taking a deep breath, forced her face into a solemn gaze as if to begin an account very tragic, indeed.

"It is a simple story, really, sir. My father had taken me out on my horse when I was nine, and we had ridden together to the far reaches of the estate."

"He used to take her occasionally on his inspections of the farms and tenant homes," Jane added.

"At one point, a particularly protective dog belonging to one of the tenants came to feel threatened by our approach and began barking excitedly at my pony's feet. Penny, my normally tame pony, became agitated and reared up. I was not an experienced horsewoman and did not know how to calm her. I flew off and landed very near Penny's excited hooves as they pranced around me."

Seeing Mr. Darcy's sudden frown, Elizabeth continued, "I was never hurt, and the dog and horse were soon calmed, but I could not persuade myself to remount ever again. Until today, I had not been on a horse in nearly eleven years."

During her narrative, Hill had come in once to give Jane some wraps for Elizabeth's ankle and again with a tea tray. Darcy found himself in a state of calm contentment to hear Elizabeth talk about her childhood. He enjoyed hearing her speak and thought she had a pleasant voice. He admired her even more as he considered just what kind of concession she made in allowing him to place her on his horse. Although he was not unaware of the fact that during the story Jane had uncovered Elizabeth's ankle from the blanket and had begun to wrap it tenderly, he could not find it as distracting as the thought of how brave Elizabeth had been earlier. Part of him realized with pride that she had allowed him to coax and comfort her in a way, and that he was the only one in over a decade who was able to help her set aside her fears and ride again.

Thinking of their ride reminded him of the feel of her relaxing against him, her head leaning on his shoulder as they talked. He was sure that her natural modesty would not have allowed that if she had been aware that she had done it. He remembered how he could feel the heat from her cheeks near his and could detect her scent was a mixture of lavender and what he could only describe as sunshine.

"So, you see, Mr. Darcy, it is not a very exciting story, but it is the reason I do not ride," Elizabeth finished.

Coming out of his reverie, he tenderly replied, "I am amazed at how well you did today considering your fears, Miss Elizabeth. You were very brave. Perhaps, one day, with the right mount and teacher, you will again be comfortable with the sport."

"Perhaps," was her only reply.

At that point, Jane offered Mr. Darcy a cup of tea. He took it and thanked her. "Will you not stay for breakfast, Mr. Darcy?" she asked.

Mr. Darcy turned his head to the window and, realizing how late the day had become, took out his watch. He had been with Elizabeth three hours now and away from Netherfield for four. "Thank you, but I have been gone a long time, and I am sure my party is now missing me. Forgive me for staying so long."

Mr. Darcy caught the disappointment in Elizabeth's eyes and chided himself. He knew he had feelings for her, and those feelings, he was willing to admit, were becoming strong. Yet he could not let her suspect his feelings any more than he had already. It had just been so natural with her. She lightened his mood, and he felt more himself than he had in years. *It is not fair to her.* He still could not be sure what his intentions were towards her or whether he even had any. *It would not be good to raise her expectations.* He had these same thoughts previously but with a different sentiment. Before, he felt he could not raise her expectations because she was so below him. He had considered it would be natural for her to wish for a connection with him. Now, he knew he could not raise them because he did not want to hurt her feelings should he decide he could not follow where his heart wanted to lead. She had become more real to him now that he knew a bit more. He had seen her momentary disappointment and had detected other moments of her regard, and that, combined with the still-vivid memory of her softness, made him realize that the idea of Elizabeth returning his esteem was delicious to him and exceedingly tempting.

"Mr. Darcy, please allow me to thank you again. Despite the many awkward moments we have endured this morning, I have had a most pleasant time with you. Thank you for coming to my aid," Elizabeth said with sincerity.

Standing to take his leave, he bowed to her and, taking her hand in his, gave it a quick, very proper kiss. "I wish you a speedy recovery, Miss Elizabeth." He bowed to Jane. "Miss Bennet."

Upon exiting the room, he recovered his gloves and his greatcoat from the footman and held out his hand for his hat. The footman looked at him in confusion and looked back to the sideboard for the missing item. Realizing that his hat was still in the grass near Netherfield, he laughed to himself and waved away the worries of the footman. "It is all right, man." And then to himself, he whispered, "It is all right." With that, he turned and exited the house with a sad smile.

Elizabeth and Jane listened for his exit from the house. They remained silent until they could hear the hooves of his horse as he rode away. Jane turned towards Elizabeth and gave her a huge grin. She grabbed her hands and, shaking her head, exclaimed, "What in the world have you done to Mr. Darcy, Lizzy?"

Mr. Darcy could hardly account to himself how he made it back to Netherfield. After leaving Longbourn and the presence of Miss Elizabeth, his mind was so caught up in the events of the past few hours that he could only credit the intelligence of his horse for his safe return, as it was by no means a measure of his own direction. He reached down and, thanking his horse with a pat, again contemplated what felt like a dream to him. Whether it was to be remembered as a nightmare or a pleasant dream was yet to be determined. He was sure he would suffer greatly if he were to turn away from Elizabeth now, as he knew he must. His duty demanded it. He could not decide whether or not he wished he had encountered her at all and, therefore, could avoid this further suffering. Whenever he started to wish that he had not spent the last few hours with Elizabeth, he found his mind would not tolerate it. It was anguish already to try to forget the heat of her skin through her muslin gown or the musical sound of her laughter as her sparkling eyes were turned towards him with a smile. How many times had he felt jealousy towards any man who could command that kind of smile from her? How many times had he wished he could prompt such a response? He had been a fool, indeed, to think she had been welcoming his attention at Netherfield. He knew the difference now, and he knew she barely noticed him then.

Nearing where he had lost his hat, Darcy turned his horse to retrieve it. Upon dismounting, Darcy took a moment to look at his hat. It was not like him to allow others to see him in less than pristine condition. He had not considered his appearance once during his time with Elizabeth. Darcy was surprised with himself at the relative ease he had felt with her those past few hours. It had not been that way before. He had always been so struck with her presence that it left him quite unable to speak with her at all. He usually only found enough command of himself to avoid gazing permanently at her or to say the merest civilities in response to her inquiries. He thought how frustrating it had been. After all, he was the master of Pemberley, a man of no small means and one of the most eligible bachelors in all England. So why was it his tongue had become tied at every turn in the presence of a mere slip of a girl from the country? The remainder of the ride back to the stables of Netherfield was spent in deep thought as to why that day had been different. The time did not afford him an answer, and all he could determine was that, for once, his consideration was more on Elizabeth's wellbeing and less about his own comfort, needs and duties.

After instructing the groom in the care of his horse, ensuring it would be well brushed and fed after the day's heavy exercise, Darcy headed for the side entrance to the house and up the back staircase. He was not yet fully in control of his faculties to appear composed to the Bingleys. Upon reaching his suite, he rang for his valet and ordered a bath.

"Darcy! I say, where have you been? It was very impolite of you to leave me to my sisters all morning. I should have liked an ally, man." Bingley's jubilant nature grated a bit on Mr. Darcy's ears as he came bounding out of his chair in the library to greet his friend.

"I apologize, Bingley, for my absence. I rode out early this morning and had intended on returning long before now." Darcy briefly considered not mentioning his encounter with Elizabeth and her family but soon realized it would be of no use. "While out, I came upon Miss Elizabeth Bennet after she had taken a fall. She was in need of my help, and I assisted her home." Darcy was pleased with himself for the coolness his voice held. He hoped he could appear as dispassionate about the encounter as possible.

"Miss Elizabeth! Heavens! What happened to her?"

"It is nothing. She merely twisted her ankle and could not walk home. I daresay she will be better in a day or so," Mr. Darcy replied as calmly as he could and turned to the side table to pour himself some coffee. He was trying desperately to appear calm even as his mind returned to the grove, remembering the pressure of Elizabeth's small hands on his chest when he held her.

"Well, it is good to hear it was not worse." Bingley mused for a moment. *Darcy is acting strangely, and I have a feeling he is not telling all.* "You say you assisted her home, Darcy? If she could not walk, how did you do it?"

Bingley smiled to himself when he saw his friend's posture become a bit more erect and heard him answer with feigned indifference, "She rode my horse." At this, Darcy swallowed hard and turned slowly to face his friend. He raised his coffee cup to his mouth in an attempt to disguise the slight, traitorous smile that threatened to expose him.

Bingley was a jovial man who loved a good joke. However, this was his friend, Darcy, and he looked to him in nearly all things. He would not push him to explain the smile he was obviously trying to hide with his cup—trying, and failing miserably. He had never seen him so discomposed, and it tickled his interest. Instead, he turned the discussion slightly and asked, "And how did you find the Bennets this morning?"

Darcy scowled in earnest now. Bless Bingley for finally bringing him to earth with that reminder. The family was every bit as horrible as ever. His jaw tightened as he remembered the effusions of Mrs. Bennet and the indelicate insinuations of the youngest girls. That was the trick to controlling his feelings for Elizabeth; all he had to do was remember her family and what a colossal mistake it would be to make them his own. With disdain, he answered, "The Bennets were all in good health and feeling quite themselves, I would say."

Bingley's good nature kept him from sensing the bitter sarcasm in his friend's reply and was satisfied with the response. A few quiet minutes passed in which Bingley was briefly lost in happy thoughts about the eldest of that family when the door to the library flew open and in walked Miss Bingley.

Mr. Darcy groaned internally as she moved directly to his side. She was shrouded in a noisy and stiff, mustard-colored, silk gown. Her red hair, clashing hideously with the color of the gown, was swept up into a pretentious knot at the side of her head. The top of her head held a matching turban adorned with a full six inches of brown feathers. As she swept closer, Darcy held his breath in anticipation as her fragrance wafted towards him a moment before impact. He quickly pulled his coffee up to his face, this time to block the assault of her nauseating perfume. Miss Bingley prided herself in the unique mixture of rose and musk toilette water that she used. She did not know, however, that when combined with the natural moisture of her skin, the two scents created an aroma somewhere between vinegar with eggs and decaying flowers.

Upon reaching Darcy, Miss Bingley laced one of her cold, clammy hands through his arm with a proprietary air as she looked up to him and spewed,

"Oh, my dear, Mr. Darcy! How worried we all were when we learned you had not returned from your ride in time for breakfast. It was not very gentlemanly of you to cause us such great concern." With this, she swatted his arm delicately with the end of her folded brown fan, stirring the air ungraciously up to his nose and causing the feathers in her headpiece to flick him in the face.

With stiffness, Darcy turned and braced himself as he looked down at her. She smiled widely, and he noticed she had a bit of stewed tomato from her breakfast protruding from her tooth. He feigned a smile that looked more like a grimace and said, "My apologies, madam, I was detained." He carefully detached his arm and walked towards the window in an attempt to find clean air to refill his lungs.

Bingley came to his rescue and began to explain the whole of the morning's excitement responsible for his friend's delay. With little grace, Miss Bingley's cold tone betrayed her as she asked with the barest civility after the health of Miss Elizabeth. She was not happy to hear that the morning was spent with Eliza. She had just gotten rid of the chit who was now tromping across the countryside after her Mr. Darcy. Caroline wished she were a better walker and could find herself somewhere in need of Mr. Darcy's assistance.

Her thoughts were interrupted as Darcy turned abruptly to Bingley and suggested they take the time before tea to look over some of the estate books. With his friend's consent, Miss Bingley was forced to smile pleasantly and leave the gentlemen to their work as she exited the room in search of her sister.

Elizabeth paused as she considered what to say to Jane's shocked outburst over the change in Mr. Darcy. She had no real answer to give except that he, indeed, had appeared different that day. She reflected that, in all the weeks she had known the gentleman, he had never before spoken as many words to her in all of their previous encounters combined. She also briefly considered how this new, open, charming and kind Darcy was affecting her equilibrium. This was the first time she had entertained positive thoughts about him. She had always considered the man attractive, a fact that only served to pour salt into her wounded pride whenever she was reminded of his most public denouncing of her physical attributes at the assembly. This offence had only served to keep her distaste for him in the forefront. The more times she met with him, the more she found him proud and arrogant.

She questioned whether, had he not vocally debased *her* beauty, she would have tried so hard not to be affected by *his* by thinking ill of him whenever possible. She saw, that morning, moments of shyness and anxiety that had looked very much like the pride and conceit she had witnessed previously, and wondered whether she had not judged him wrongly.

Smiling at Jane, she decided she could not really change her mind about the man after just one pleasant morning. She also could not tell Jane about necessary (and accidental) embraces, the ride together or the fluttering in her breast she felt even now because she did not know yet what they meant to her. She determined to think no more of it until she could retire to bed and be alone with her thoughts.

Laughingly, she said, "I do not know, Jane. He was quite different, was he not? Perhaps it was the anxiety of it all." With that, she shook off the subject as if nothing.

Jane had her suspicions that Mr. Darcy favored her sister because his eyes were so often on her. She believed this change was nothing more than his weakening resolve to hide his feelings for Lizzy. She also knew her sister held her thoughts to herself quite often, especially whenever she was unsure of her feelings. If she had been decided in one way or another, she would have voiced her feelings without hesitation. Recognizing this, Jane decided a change of subject would be welcome. Sitting down in Mr. Darcy's vacated chair near the sofa, she remembered something her father had said when the family breakfasted earlier.

"Oh, Lizzy, while you were out, Papa had the most surprising news for us."

"And what was it, Jane?" Elizabeth was thankful for the new topic and also amused at the strange, humorous glint in Jane's eye.

"It seems we are to have a visitor to arrive this very day!" The mock excitement in Jane's voice alerted Lizzy that the best of the story was yet to come. But before Jane could continue, Mr. Bennet returned to the room and, after bestowing a loving kiss on Lizzy's cheek, sat down near his two favorite daughters and prompted Jane to continue. "It is our long-lost cousin. He is Mr. Collins from Hunsford in Kent. He is a parson, and he is the man to inherit Longbourn when Papa goes." Jane reached over and patted her father's hand lovingly before continuing, acquainting Lizzy with the particulars of their visitor's situation, his patronage of an illustrious Lady Catherine de Bourgh and his wish to reconcile with the family. Lizzy looked towards her father and saw him pursing his lips in humor during Jane's account.

"He sounds like a peculiar type of man. Do you think he is sensible, Papa?" Elizabeth asked.

"Oh, no, my dear! I am greatly anticipating that he is quite the opposite," he replied with a chuckle that was soon joined by his two daughters.

The remainder of the morning and afternoon was spent conversing comfortably between the sisters as Mr. Bennet returned to his library. Occasionally, one of the other sisters would flit in and out, but for most of the day, Lizzy was left to the enjoyable company of her favorite sister. They had tea and relished in the rare treat of getting to eat and talk sensibly without the wild emotional eruptions of their mother and younger sisters. However, the peaceful afternoon could not go on forever, and when Mrs. Bennet finally had finished her preparations for their soon-to-be-arriving visitor, she came into the room to see to her least favorite daughter and hopefully gain information about what really happened with Mr. Darcy.

"Lizzy, dear, you must tell me what happened this morning." Her mother's abrupt manner immediately put Elizabeth on her guard. She knew she would need to put an end to her mother's imagination if she were ever to have any rest over the situation. Mrs. Bennet did not need one more gentleman to gush over in her attempts at matchmaking. Certainly, Mr. Darcy would thank her for tempering her mother's wild presumptions.

"It is as you know, Mama. I was out walking, and I was near that forest by Mr. Gilmore's property when one of the old oak trees broke in the wind. I was startled, and I fell and injured my ankle." Elizabeth avoided mentioning the gentleman on purpose. If she was going to convince her mother, she needed to make the entire situation seem unimportant—a task made more difficult than she anticipated as she was forced to detach the feelings that were beginning to associate themselves with her memories of the events.

"Yes, yes, I know that, Lizzy. But what about Mr. Darcy?" screeched Mrs. Bennet.

"Oh, no, Mama, you are mistaken. Mr. Darcy did not fall; he was not even near the tree at all!" Elizabeth knew her teasing would infuriate her mother, but she could not help herself.

"Oh, ungrateful child! You know what I mean! What happened with Mr. Darcy? Were you walking together? Did you meet on purpose?" Her mother's presumptions were getting to dangerous levels, and her voice kept increasing with excitement.

Elizabeth knew she needed to stop her and so, with a grave voice, dropped all joking and responded, "Mama, you know Mr. Darcy does not like me. Of course we did not meet on purpose. He was out riding and happened upon me after my fall. He did only what any gentleman would do." Here Elizabeth had to pause and try to find words that would be truthful but not lead her mother on. "In fact, he was quite uncomfortable being alone with me." *There, that should quiet her! And it was true; he had been adorably nervous.*

Mrs. Bennet was clearly disappointed but not yet resigned to give up an eligible match for any of her daughters, and she thought a bit on it. Elizabeth tried to invent some kind of stratagem to cause her mother to erase completely the idea of a match between the two of them. Suddenly, a brilliant idea came to her, and she schooled her features to hide her mischief and spoke conspiratorially to her mother.

"Mama, it has just occurred to me that, as Mr. Darcy is the particular friend of Mr. Bingley, we would not want to upset him, right?"

"Well, of course not! Heavens, child! Why would you think of upsetting Mr. Darcy?" chastised her mother.

"Well it is just that we know he does not find me handsome. Would it not upset him to have a match with me be presumed upon? And if he is made to be upset, could he not persuade his particular friend to give his attentions to another in the neighborhood instead of Jane?" Elizabeth knew she should stop here but could not help herself. "And Mr. Bingley did dance first with Charlotte Lucas at the assembly before he danced with Jane."

Mrs. Bennet was struck still at the thought of losing a most advantageous match between Jane and Mr. Bingley, especially at the thought of forfeiting him to Lady Lucas's plain, spinster daughter. No, it would not be wise to upset Mr. Darcy. She thought that, if Elizabeth were right and the man was not interested in her, pushing him on the subject would not be a good idea. If it were not for his ten thousand a year, she would not even care about the fellow. She determined then that, if he were not to marry one of her daughters, she would continue as she did before and hate the man.

Elizabeth could see that her statements were working. She thought about the previous times her mother had been in contact with Mr. Darcy and realized that her mother had disliked Darcy ever since the Meryton assembly. She really was barely civil to him and quite nearly rude on some occasions. She decided to risk her newly won success by adding, "Mama, I think we should treat Mr. Darcy with all the civility we can, as it would please Mr. Bingley to see his friend so welcome. I know you do not like him, but you are such a good hostess that I am sure you could hide your contempt whenever he were to visit, could you not?"

Mrs. Bennet, not being a particularly intelligent person, was always mollified and convinced by a well-placed compliment and therefore was again persuaded by her daughter to rethink her behavior around Mr. Darcy, if only for the benefit of his friend.

The Bennet family gathered in the morning room to accommodate Elizabeth in preparation for the arrival of their much-anticipated guest and estranged cousin, Mr. Collins. Looking around the room, Elizabeth smiled to herself at the differing feelings on the event displayed so openly by the members of her family. Her mother was agitated, slightly vexed at having to host the man who was no doubt coming to appraise his future property and making plans to evict them all before her husband was cold in his grave. She did not believe for a moment that he could find any way to reconcile the impossible nature of the entail. Elizabeth turned her gaze towards Lydia and Kitty, who were redecorating a new bonnet and arguing over which ribbon to use, obviously uninterested in the arrival of their cousin.

Jane was serene as always, and Elizabeth could tell she was inclined already to like the man as she never seemed capable of finding fault in anyone. She sat, contented, with an embroidery sampler, waiting patiently. Mary was dutifully reading her favorite book of sermons and uncharacteristically fidgeting with her dress. Elizabeth paused a moment to consider this strange behavior in her younger sister. Mary never cared about her appearance and usually ignored any guests with a distinct preference for her books. It was not as if she was showing eager anticipation for their cousin to arrive, but Elizabeth could tell that she had a shade of nervous excitement about her.

Lastly, Elizabeth turned her gaze to her father, who was reclining lazily in his chair with the newspaper held up to his face. As if detecting her perusal, he lowered his newspaper at the corner and winked.

When their guest's carriage could be heard on the gravel drive, Mr. Bennet stood to walk out and welcome him, as the ladies sat up properly in anticipation of their greeting. Within a few minutes, they could hear their father's voice in the entryway with another male voice, and a few minutes more brought the sound of the men's boots coming towards the morning room.

Mr. Bennet stepped into the room with Mr. Collins and began the introductions. Elizabeth immediately scrutinized her new cousin. He was not a handsome man. He wore his flat brown hair a little long on the side in an attempt to disguise his loss of hair by brushing it across his forehead. She noticed he had rounded cheeks and a flap of skin that dangled under a weak chin every time he bobbed his head. Mr. Collins looked gravely solemn in his ridiculous all-black parson's suit, which appeared to be a bit small, especially around his midsection where the buttons and stitches whined with his every move. Elizabeth smiled to herself in anticipation of the great amusement she expected to have from watching such a character as her cousin.

Mr. Bennet presented his wife, who curtsied briefly with a stoic expression on her face as Mr. Collins gave an overly low bow, causing his waistcoat buttons to protest. Her father then began to introduce his daughters in order of age. When Mr. Collins fixed his eyes upon Jane, his hand brought a soiled handkerchief out of his pocket to dab at the sweat on his brow, and then held it to his chest over his heart as he smiled greasily to her and bent for another low bow. Jane politely curtsied, and Mr. Bennet moved towards Elizabeth.

"You will excuse my second eldest daughter, Elizabeth, if she does not rise. She has only lately sprained her ankle and cannot stand at the moment," Mr. Bennet explained.

Mr. Collins bobbed his head in understanding, causing his neck flap to dance wildly and bowed again. With every bow, Elizabeth held her breath with amusement—and a small amount of fear that his clothing would actually lose a button in the process. Mr. Bennet then proceeded to introduce Mary, Kitty and Lydia. The first smiled calmly at her cousin, and the last two gave obligatory curtsies and whispered to each other while stifling laughs. When Mr. Collins bowed lastly to the youngest girls, a soft, gaseous noise erupted from him and he straightened quickly, coloring bright red, while Lydia and Kitty burst loudly with laughter. Covering her own incredulous smirk, Lizzy quickly chastised her younger sisters.

As soon as the room recovered its reserve, Mr. Collins opened his mouth to speak for the first time beyond the small greeting he had given each cousin upon introduction. He had a nasally voice that clashed with the serious expression on his face. "My dear, dear cousins. It is an honor finally to meet you all. Your reputed beauty and grace have gone before you, and I assure you, they have most grievously done you a disservice." At this, Mrs. Bennet huffed, and Mr. Collins rushed to add, "That is, to say, your beauty has far surpassed the report, and I am indeed honored, deeply honored, to make your acquaintance. I am also blessed to bring you the condescension and greetings of my most noble and gracious benefactor, Lady Catherine de Bourgh." Here their cousin paused for dramatic effect, and when nobody seemed moved, continued, "Lady Catherine, if you do not know, is the owner of the great estate, Rosings Park, to which my own humble parsonage is attached. I am most fortunate in my patronage and have come to your home with her permission and condescension." After this, he began to bow again, but thinking better of it, just smiled at the room.

"Mr. Collins, we are, indeed, truly in debt to Lady Catherine for condescending to spare you for a time to visit our humble home." Mr. Bennet spoke with mock gravity, causing his second eldest daughter to shoot him a censuring look before speaking to her cousin herself.

"Indeed, Cousin, we are happy to make your acquaintance." Mr. Collins nodded and made his way to Jane and Mrs. Bennet for conversation. Elizabeth watched Mary attempting to divert Mr. Collins's attention by asking whether he had read the particular book of sermons that she was reading and what his opinion of it was. She mused at the sight as she had never seen Mary take an interest in a guest before. Soon after, the dinner bell was rung, preventing his response.

Everyone exited towards the dining room. Elizabeth was helped to her feet by Jane and was pleased to see that, after resting her foot all day, she could almost put her weight on it. With Jane's assistance, she joined the family in the dining room, biting her lip in anticipation of more entertainment from her new cousin.

After the excitement of the day, Elizabeth found that she desired to retire early because of mounting fatigue and a heavy mind. She and Jane, who would be assisting her, made their excuses before Mr. Collins began reading to the group, much to the dismay of her youngest sisters and the delight of Mary. Upon their exiting the room, Mr. Bennet gave his oldest daughters a look of abandonment.

After readying herself for bed, Elizabeth sat at her dressing table and combed out her long curls. She smiled softly as she remembered sitting in the same place that morning, anticipating her walk. She had thought about Mr. Darcy then, and once again thoughts of the strange man came back to her as she plaited her hair in preparation for bed. He had been so kind and solicitous towards her comfort. She remembered, as a shiver stole through her, how his voice was low and husky with worry when he had hastily embraced her. She was certain that he was very concerned for her, but she could not understand why he would be so moved as to hold her to his chest. *It was as if he was deeply grieved by the thought that I was seriously injured.* It was this topic that Elizabeth found most troubling. She was not a close relation to him—indeed, not even a close friend. She determined that Mr. Darcy must be a man of great feeling. That he was a man of action she knew before, but she had not anticipated that he would combine the two so passionately.

Stretching her limbs, she hobbled to the bed and climbed in next to Jane, who was reading a book by candlelight. She looked up at the movement, smiled while putting her mark in her place, and turned to blow out the light. In the sudden darkness, she whispered to Elizabeth as they settled under the blankets, "Lizzy, I miss him already."

"Who, Mr. Collins?" Elizabeth teased. Her sister elbowed her in the side at her jest, and Elizabeth replied gently, "I know." With that, Jane sighed and rolled over to go to sleep, and Elizabeth again was left to her thoughts. Her sister's words for Mr. Bingley reminded her of the other gentleman in residence at Netherfield, and she sighed to herself as she thought, *me too*! With that realization, she allowed the memory of his embrace to lull her to sleep.

Chapter 3

The following two days found the Bennet household in various degrees of disquiet. Mrs. Bennet was no longer unhappy with the arrival of Mr. Collins due to the gentleman's less than discreet admission that it was his desire to come to Longbourn to search for a wife from amongst his fair cousins and at the specific advice of his esteemed benefactor, Lady Catherine de Bourgh. She went from viewing his effusions about the quality of the furnishings with offense—as she had believed he came solely to calculate the worth of his future estate—to hearing his raptures about the property with a state of regal pride. When Mr. Collins insinuated the previous night after tea that his interests were steering him towards the eldest Miss Bennet as his choice, Mrs. Bennet discretely suggested to him that his cousin, although certainly honored by his attentions, would not likely return them as she was very nearly engaged to Mr. Bingley. Regardless of the fact that her eldest daughter and the gentleman had not reached an agreement, Mrs. Bennet believed it would not be long, and therefore held it as fact in her own mind. At this point, Mr. Collins quickly reviewed his options and was delighted to see that another cousin, Miss Elizabeth, was also quite pleasing to him.

It was on this problem that Elizabeth pondered with much anxiety after breakfast as she sat hiding on the windowsill of her room with a book. It had not taken her long to notice the marked attentions of her oaf of a cousin, and she was far from happy about them. She was constantly accosted by the gentleman to hear all about his humble parsonage and the many delightful improvements Lady Catherine had condescended to advise him to make.

She thought back to the conversation she had with him the previous night. Mr. Collins and his over-tight waistcoat had squeaked their way over to her—yet again—after dinner and sat beside her on the settee.

"My dear Cousin Elizabeth, it gives me great pleasure to see you thus occupied this evening with your lovely needlework. I have often heard from my wise advisor, Lady Catherine de Bourgh, that ladies of small means, such as yourself, must always try to improve themselves through such activities so as to make up for other deficiencies. It honors me to see that you, dear Cousin, are so mindful in your humility, and if I may say so, it does not place you in an unfavorable light. No, it does not indeed." With this, Mr. Collins dipped his head with condescension as he curled his mouth up in a greasy smile, causing the little droplets of sweat above his lip to catch the light of the candle and glisten most unattractively.

"I thank you, Mr. Collins. You are indeed quite the gentleman to remind me of the ways I can improve upon the many disadvantages I bring to matrimony," Elizabeth said bitterly, but with such a saucy smile that he did not catch her tone and only heard her reference to marriage. He was delighted with his progress thus far.

Returning to the present, Elizabeth groaned with frustration as she stamped her foot against the wall of the window seat. She found herself becoming frustrated when she thought of the many left-handed compliments he paid her and his failure to be deterred by her impertinent responses. *That man is so odious!* Her annoyance grew at having to hide herself away in her room just to get away from him, as he had taken to following her around since almost the moment of his arrival two days earlier. However, the irritation soon melted away to amusement as her natural temperament would not allow her to stay ill tempered for long. She reflected with humor at the way her father would goad Mr. Collins in a slightly mocking tone when he would ask about his patronage from Lady Catherine, a topic that Mr. Collins could expand upon for a considerable length of time.

Elizabeth was stirred from her reverie by the entrance of Jane into their shared bedroom. Jane laughed quietly to see her sister sitting with her legs bunched up around her on the windowsill. "So this is where you have been hiding, Lizzy. I have been looking for you since breakfast."

"I am sorry, Jane. Since I cannot yet walk as well as I would like because of my ankle, I could not disappear outside." This was said with such a tone of frustration that her sister immediately felt pity for her.

Coming to her side and placing her hand on her shoulder, she replied sweetly, "I am sorry, Lizzy. I know how much you dislike our cousin, but I think we must conclude he has some cleverness about him as he has singled you out."

Elizabeth laughed without humor. "Yes, I am sure it has nothing to do with the fact that Mama certainly hinted at you being spoken for already by your Mr. Bingley. I have begun to wish I had never deterred Mama from believing Mr. Darcy was interested in me. Our cousin might have then singled out Mary!"

"He is not *my* Mr. Bingley, Lizzy," Jane said shyly.

Elizabeth smiled knowingly and patted her sister's hand. Jane blushed and, seeking a change of subject, turned to her sister and said, "You did not tell me what Papa said to you in his library yesterday. Did he ask you about Mr. Darcy?"

At the gentleman's name, Elizabeth thought once more about the events of two days before. She still had not managed to figure out what her feelings were towards the man. She admitted to herself that she no longer felt offended by his comments at the assembly and was beginning to see his brooding stares in a different light than she had previously. She detected that he was a bit shy and reserved, but still she could not convince herself that he was not a good deal prideful as well. A tingle went down her spine whenever she considered the tenderness he showed her and the unexpected concern for her health. She was embarrassed that she had not considered him capable of such gentle regard as he had shown her most naturally that day. Their conversation during the ride back had surprised her with their compatibility on a number of subjects. She had only managed to conclude that she was much attracted to Mr. Darcy and wanted to know him better. With effort, Elizabeth directed her thoughts to the present and to answering Jane's entreaty.

"Yes, Papa was most curious as to the details of my morning." Elizabeth chuckled to herself at the way her father tried to tease her about being in company with Mr. Darcy and riding his horse. She related to her sister their father's laughing insinuation that Elizabeth had *planned* an assignation with the gentleman.

"NO!" Jane gasped. "Lizzy, he could not think such a thing!"

Elizabeth laughed and reassured her sister. "You are right, Jane. Papa did not think such a thing, but you know how he likes to tease. He was merely trying to stoke my ire by suggesting I had a secret *tendre* for Mr. Darcy and that we had met privately on purpose. It was the same silly suggestion Mama made, only I know Papa was trying to provoke me." Elizabeth remembered that her father's insinuation did raise her ire at the time, and she had most adamantly denied such scandalous ideas until she realized her father's motivation was to tease her. He had wanted to provoke a reaction from her since he knew she would never behave so improperly as to meet a gentleman secretly. His desire in doing so was to see her response to the idea. When she realized his motive, she was disappointed in herself for blushing, thereby revealing her feelings. It was the very thing she did not want her father to know and the very thing he hoped his teasing would tell him. Elizabeth thought that her father appeared a bit disappointed at finding she had developed some feelings for Mr. Darcy, but he tried to hide it behind a strained smile. Elizabeth felt compassion for him as she knew he did not welcome the day she would marry and move away.

The sisters were interrupted in their conversation by the high-pitched squeals of their mother, calling excitedly for Jane as she came down the hall towards their bedroom. Upon bursting through the door, Mrs. Bennet panted heavily and tried to address her eldest daughter. "Jane, dear... you must make haste; he is here!" Pausing briefly to try to catch her breath, Mrs. Bennet pulled out her handkerchief, wiped her brow and waved it around her chest trying to stir the heat of the air around her as she continued, "He is come, Jane — make haste and fix yourself! He will be at the door any minute!"

At this, Jane asked with concern and obvious anxiety, for she was sure she knew the answer already, "Who is come, Mama?"

Elizabeth turned her head sharply to the window when she heard her mother pant, "Mr. Bingley, child! He is come to see you, dear. You must not keep him waiting! He has been seen at the gate!" With this, she turned and left. Elizabeth's eyes were arrested and her whole body froze as she caught sight of two gentlemen nearing the house on horseback. The first was indeed, Mr. Bingley. The second — she recognized the horse immediately, and as her eyes roamed upwards to the rider, her heart nearly stopped as she looked right into the face of Mr. Darcy, who had just then noticed her in the window. Their gazes held for a short moment as neither was able to turn away. Elizabeth gave him a slight smile, and his broad smile in return made her breath catch. She turned from the window with wide eyes and a thumping in her chest.

Elizabeth schooled her features into a calm she did not feel and helped her sister adjust her appearance. She pinched her cheeks to give them color and smiled brightly at Jane in an attempt to reassure her. "Breathe, Jane; he has probably come to see after your health. It was but a few days ago that he saw you at Netherfield."

Jane smiled as she recognized that she did not feel as nervous as her sister evidently did and that Lizzy's words were probably meant more for herself. She had also taken a moment to peek out the window and had seen Mr. Darcy smile at her sister. She smiled inwardly as she considered this another bit of proof that her sister's heart was beginning to be touched by Mr. Darcy. Jane took a few deep breaths in an effort to appear nervous for the benefit of her sister and found that Elizabeth matched her action, which helped to calm her. Jane smiled at the success of her acting. It was not that she did not feel a certain amount of nervous excitement at seeing Mr. Bingley again, but she was a bit more confident in her feelings for the gentleman and his feelings for her.

Mr. Darcy was silent on the ride to Longbourn that morning. He had worried about Elizabeth for the few days since her accident. If he was being honest, he was not really worried about her injury. He knew it was not very serious, but he had tried to convince himself that the reason his thoughts so frequently had turned towards her was merely because he was concerned with the extent of her healing. Considering how often his thoughts were on the crook of her neck when she tilted her head to tease him or the sparkle in her eyes when she looked up at him, he knew that her ankle was not forefront in his mind… well, except for the way it delicately and sweetly curved into her pretty little foot.

Now his thoughts were taking a turn in a more anxious direction. When Bingley had mentioned to him that morning that he thought he might ride out to Longbourn to see how Jane was recuperating after her illness and wondered whether his friend would like to join him, Darcy had wanted to hug him. He did want to go and confirmed he would like to inquire after Elizabeth's recovery from her injury as well. He could not suggest it himself for fear of what it might reveal, and after seeing Elizabeth every day for nearly a week while she was at Netherfield and then the day afterwards as well, he found that her absence in his life was becoming nearly painful. As Longbourn came into view, he wondered at the merits of the idea. He did not know how he might be received by the lady and whether their time together a few days before would be viewed by her with pleasure or pain. It was with this thought that he wondered whether his presence would cause her discomfort and he, instead, should have sent his enquiries by way of his friend. Adding to his anxiety was the fact that, even though he knew he was becoming quite lost to the lady, he was not sure he could do anything about it.

He reasoned with himself that even if she did not look forward to a visit from him with pleasure, he had another reason for accompanying his friend that was quite proper. Bingley had finally decided on a date for the ball, and it was scheduled for a week hence. Bingley wished personally to invite the Bennet family, and as his personal friend and guest at Netherfield, it was quite proper for Darcy to accompany him in delivering the invitation. Darcy was grateful that his friend did not appear to notice the lack of conversation during their ride as he whistled a romantic tune to himself.

Upon entering the gate and courtyard, Mr. Darcy looked around the house with discomfort. Where was Elizabeth and how did she feel about his arrival? He scanned the house as he pondered this and caught a glimpse of yellow at one of the upper windows. Immediately his gaze focused on the color, only to be arrested by one of the most beautiful sights he had ever seen. Elizabeth was sitting with her legs curled up to her chest, her beautiful curls framing her face, and looking down at him. He was so caught by her beauty, which struck him as even greater than he had remembered, that he thought, '*She is beautiful, and therefore to be woo'd. She is a woman, therefore to be won*'. He was stirred from his thoughts—and from the many other words Shakespeare might have used to describe her—by the tender smile she bestowed. All of his previous worries vanished as a glorious smile spread across his face. *Oh, I am beyond hope indeed!* he thought as he dismounted and prepared to enter the house.

Elizabeth, having nearly recovered from her injury, needed only occasional aid. Jane was her constant companion and always available to help. The two of them took a brief moment to take a calming breath before descending the stairs together. As they reached the landing, they could hear their mother's excited chatter as she welcomed the gentlemen to the house. Elizabeth cringed as she neared the drawing room door and prepared for the mortification she was sure to feel upon entering the room where the gentlemen waited with her mother. The two sisters looked at each other, and Jane gave Elizabeth's arm a gentle squeeze for support. Together, they opened the drawing room doors and entered.

Mr. Darcy and Mr. Bingley immediately stood at their entrance, and Mr. Darcy, seeing the slight hobble in Elizabeth's step, moved towards her to offer assistance before he stopped, realizing she did not need it. He and Bingley bowed to the ladies as Elizabeth made her curtsy. He felt foolish for his impulsiveness and wondered why he felt it was his place always to be assisting her.

Elizabeth smiled to herself at the sight of Mr. Darcy coming to her aid. She liked the idea that he felt compelled to help her and enjoyed his protectiveness. She and Jane lowered themselves to the sofa and smiled as the gentleman came over to make their greetings.

"Miss Bennet, Miss Elizabeth, we are come to enquire after your health," said Mr. Bingley as he swept his eyes from Elizabeth and rested them on Jane.

"Miss Bennet, Miss Elizabeth." Mr. Darcy bowed again.

"Thank you, sir," replied Jane, sweetly. "As you can see I have quite recovered from my illness. You are most kind in your inquiry." This pleased Bingley, and after briefly stating to Elizabeth his concern about her injury and his happiness in seeing her moving around so well after such a short time, he took the opportunity to occupy the seat near Jane, and they began conversing.

Mr. Darcy shifted on his feet and, with a slight blush, looked down at Elizabeth's expectant face. "Miss Elizabeth, may I ask how your ankle fairs?"

"Thank you, Mr. Darcy, it is nearly recovered. I very rarely need assistance from Jane and look forward to being quite myself again soon."

Mr. Darcy took the seat next to Elizabeth and replied stiffly, "I am glad to hear it."

The two of them sat quietly for a few minutes, each wondering what they should say and feeling too many emotions to decide on any one particular topic. Mrs. Bennet's loud outburst actually came as a relief. "Mr. Bingley,

Mr. Darcy, we are glad to see you both this morning. Please excuse my two youngest daughters as they have set out on a walk to Meryton to visit their Aunt Philips."

It was apparent that Bingley was too distracted with Miss Bennet to notice her mother's comment. "Yes, Mrs. Bennet," Mr. Darcy replied. "I believe we saw them when we made our way through town on our journey here. We did not stop as they were in conversation." Mr. Darcy felt a twinge of jealousy at the other couple's easy conversation, and he glanced quickly to Elizabeth, wondering what had made it easier for them a few days earlier. Returning to the current conversation, Mr. Darcy recollected that he had seen Miss Lydia and Miss Kitty talking to a group of two officers and another gentleman. He frowned as he thought of their ceaseless flirting and lack of decorum. He remembered now that the gentleman with them was not in uniform and had his back to him, but Mr. Darcy thought his stance and figure looked familiar. He quickly dismissed the thought for another more agreeable one as he turned to speak to Miss Elizabeth.

His efforts were interrupted, however, because at that moment, a stout clergyman entered the room, and Miss Bennet made the introduction.

"Mr. Bingley, Mr. Darcy, please allow me to introduce our cousin Mr. Collins." The stout clergyman bowed to the gentleman and placed himself, much to the astonishment of the guests, on the sofa right between the ladies. Elizabeth and Jane clearly were unhappy with their cousin's proximity and immediately adjusted themselves to occupy the smallest amount of space at the furthest distance away from him. Mr. Darcy was inclined to dislike the cousin as it was obvious that Elizabeth was unhappy and did not welcome his familiarity. This newly developed sense of protectiveness provoked him uncharacteristically to intercede.

"Mr. Collins, would you be more comfortable in my seat? I would be happy to release it and sit elsewhere." Mr. Darcy gestured to the armchair across from the sofa. He really did not want to sit across the room from Elizabeth, but her cousin sitting next to her was desired even less.

"Mr. Darcy, I thank you for your concern, but I assure you, I am quite comfortable," Mr. Collins replied, with a sideways smile at Elizabeth and a tilt of his head in her direction. "Although my dear cousins and I have known each other for only a short time, we are already quite as close as any family."

Mr. Darcy watched as Elizabeth forced a smile in return and attempted discreetly to move even closer towards the edge of the couch. He was not pleased with the proximity of the man to Elizabeth and was even more displeased with the way he smiled at her.

"My cousin has recently come to visit us from his parsonage in Kent," Elizabeth hesitantly spoke to Mr. Darcy. He could see she wished to be elsewhere, and he hoped it was not because of his presence but the other man's. Before Mr. Darcy could comment, Mr. Collins's enthusiastic voice stalled him.

"Indeed, sir. I have just come from Hunsford parsonage, where I am most fortunate in my placement by one of the most illustrious ladies of the land. Perhaps you have heard of her; she is none other than the esteemed and favored Lady Catherine de Bourgh." This last part was spoken with such a reverence as to insinuate the lady was perhaps a deity. Mr. Bingley and Mr. Darcy looked at each other with raised eyebrows. Mr. Darcy's expression to his friend warned him against voicing the connection to the lady.

With an air of indifference, Mr. Darcy replied, "Yes, sir, I have heard of the lady." Mr. Darcy glanced briefly at Elizabeth and noticed the small smirk on her face, and he realized she had seen his strange interaction with Bingley.

Mr. Darcy sat back, stunned, when Mr. Collins erupted in excitement. "I am so glad to hear it, sir. My cousins had not heard of the lady before I arrived, and I am glad to meet with someone acquainted with her. I had not thought I would. Is she not the most gracious of ladies?" Mr. Collins did not pause for a reply and continued, "Indeed, she is! For just last week when I was preparing for my journey here, she condescended to stop her barouche at my gate and remind me as to the proper reading material for a clergyman to bring on such a journey and to advise me in all the particular delicacies that I must attend to in my visit with my relations. Is that not most gracious? I attest that it is, and I said to her, 'Lady Catherine, you are most gracious! I thank you for your solicitous concern over my comfort and your most suitable advice for the cultivation of my mind with your suggestions for my reading. You are everything proper.' I often deem it necessary to pay such compliments to her ladyship as she is always most attentive to me."

Elizabeth coughed into her handkerchief in an attempt to hide her mortification at her cousin's absurdity. She colored in embarrassment until she saw Darcy glance at her and hide a humorous smirk behind his own hand.

Seeing Mr. Darcy's attempt to curb his humor, Elizabeth decided to tease him and shot him a reproachful look but did not hide the laughter in her eyes.

Jane addressed her cousin at that point, causing him to turn towards her and Mr. Bingley and join their conversation, much to the relief and thanks of Mr. Darcy and Elizabeth.

With humor still in her eyes, Elizabeth took the opportunity to speak to Mr. Darcy. "Sir, would you be so kind as to tell me: how is your great black beast?"

It took Mr. Darcy a moment to realize she was referring to his horse and was pleased about the allusion to their morning together. "You are most kind, Miss Elizabeth," replied Mr. Darcy with a hint of a smile at the edge of his lips. "My horse is quite well, though he seems to miss his new favorite rider."

Elizabeth laughed softly and shook her head as she responded, "Oh no, sir, I will not be fooled by that. I am sure we, neither of us, miss each other too much."

Mr. Darcy smiled kindly at her and, after pausing for a moment, leaned in to say softly, "Miss Elizabeth, you look well this morning. I am glad to see you so recovered."

Elizabeth colored beautifully at his comment and murmured a soft, "Thank you."

Mr. Darcy enjoyed seeing her thus affected and, ignoring the stammering of his heartbeat, boldly continued, "Though I must admit you are correct. My horse is not the one who misses riding with you." At this, he sat back in his chair watching her discomposure and savoring the brightness her blushing cheeks gave her complexion.

Elizabeth was momentarily stunned by Mr. Darcy's boldness and could do nothing but try to calm her rapidly beating heart. After a short time, she recovered enough to retaliate in her own attempt at discomposing him. Raising her shoulders and chin, she looked at him with one eyebrow raised saucily and, pausing to make sure she had his full attention, opened her mouth to speak. Her look of flirtatious challenge was delicious to Mr. Darcy, and his eyes lit with excited anticipation of her response. She was so beautiful, and it was that same impertinent look that first put him in her power. *What do you have to say to me, you minx!*

"Mr. Darcy—" she began.

"Cousin Elizabeth, I forgot to mention that I have found a passage in

Fordyce's Sermons that I really must insist you read. I assure you, you will find it most interesting."

The look of fury that Mr. Darcy leveled at Mr. Collins at this interruption could have set ice on fire. His disappointment and subsequent frustration were not lost on Elizabeth, and she smiled to herself at their similar feelings. Mr. Darcy went from disliking the attentions Mr. Collins bestowed upon Elizabeth to wanting to remove the gentleman bodily from her presence. He was imagining with wicked delight the many ways he could physically remove the odious man, including a scenario involving his boot and the gentleman's backside, when Elizabeth's gentle voice interrupted his thoughts.

"Thank you, Mr. Collins. You are most attentive to my education." Although she said this to her cousin, Mr. Darcy saw the flick of her eyes towards him, and he was quieted by the look of disappointment in them.

At that point, Mr. Bingley remembered the other reason for his visit and announced to the room his invitation to them all to attend a ball at Netherfield Park in one week. The raptures that erupted from the ladies were numerous, and Darcy and Bingley both delighted in seeing the warm smiles their particular ladies bestowed at the news. Mrs. Bennet, of course, was beyond herself, and in her delight, accosted Mr. Bingley for some time with compliments to his person and appreciation for the invitation.

Elizabeth turned to Mr. Darcy, her eyes lit with excitement, and asked, "Mr. Darcy, sir, if I remember correctly from my time at Netherfield, some of the party there believed you would not welcome a ball. I hope that is not the case."

"Indeed, no, Miss Elizabeth. While I cannot profess to be overly fond of dancing as my friend is, I do delight in the activity if I am acquainted with my partner. If I may be so bold... as to request... " Mr. Darcy cleared his throat to continue when Mr. Collins yet again interrupted the important moment. It was Elizabeth's turn to glare at her cousin.

"A dance is a splendid idea for the entertainment of young people. And even though I am a man of the cloth and of a nature inclined towards holier activities, I find nothing improper about a dance given by a man of respectability to people of upstanding virtues. I am so far inclined to think the activity not at all unworthy of a man of my profession, as to ask the hand of all my fair cousins for a dance throughout the course of the evening. I would like to take the opportunity, now, to ask my dear Cousin Elizabeth for her hand for the first dance of the evening." Mr. Collins paused for her answer with a smile of great assurance.

Mr. Darcy could not believe his ears! He was about to ask for that very dance from Miss Elizabeth when interrupted by Mr. Collins's ridiculous speech and then thwarted by the precipitous request Collins made to his cousin. Mr. Darcy was now contemplating the very great pleasure that murdering a clergyman could bring.

Elizabeth schooled her face into one of apathy and responded with a low voice that did not disguise her frustration to everyone except the man to which it was leveled. "Thank you, Mr. Collins. It would be my pleasure." The last was said through clenched teeth and she looked away immediately.

The atmosphere in the room was stilted for a moment as people either were still stunned by the abrupt speech by Mr. Collins or by the cold tone of Elizabeth's reply. Mr. Bingley collected himself first and turned towards Jane in a request for her hand for the first set as well. At this, previous conversations resumed, and a delighted Mr. Collins again turned to speak with Jane and Bingley.

Elizabeth's delight in the upcoming ball was significantly reduced after the request from her cousin. Determining to find some enjoyment in the evening, she turned towards Mr. Darcy, hoping to encourage him to continue where he left off before her cousin once again interrupted them. "Mr. Darcy, I apologize for my cousin's intrusion. I believe that you were saying something?"

Mr. Darcy was startled out of his irritated thoughts by the pleading eyes of Miss Elizabeth. He sighed as he was calmed by her look. He felt a wave of compassion for her as he could see the delight she once had discussing the ball had dimmed. "Yes, Miss Elizabeth, you are correct. I was hoping, that is, I was preparing to ask if you would permit me to dance a set with you. As you are engaged for the first set, perhaps the supper set?"

Elizabeth was pleased that he chose the supper set as it indicated to her that he would want to continue in her presence into the meal. Feeling contented again, she smiled at him in response and accepted his hand for the supper set.

"And Miss Elizabeth, if you are not already engaged for the last set, may I apply for that one as well?

Elizabeth was stunned that he would request two dances right away and felt the compliment, as she realized he had never before asked any other lady of the neighborhood to dance. She blushed as she responded with a soft chuckle, "You are most fortunate, sir, for I am not engaged for that set either. I would be most delighted, sir."

They sat in comfortable silence for a moment, thinking with pleasure about their upcoming dances until, with relief, Mr. Darcy noticed Mr. Collins stand and thought, *finally, he is leaving!* But it was not to be, and to Mr. Darcy's horror, the clergyman approached him and began to perform a very low bow so near to him that he had to lean back in his chair to avoid a collision. Elizabeth noticed the shock and surprise on Mr. Darcy's face and once again felt embarrassed by the behavior of her relations. Mr. Collins rose from his bow and began to address Mr. Darcy.

His excitement was evident as the skin at his neck began to flap side-to-side. The low bow had dislodged a few strands of his greasy, combed-over hair, causing them to fold outwards from his head and protrude stiffly above his ear into the airspace beside his head. He rubbed his sausage fingers together as he spoke with a severe reverence and the small movement caused the hair flap to bob in the air. "Mr. Darcy, sir, forgive me for not paying my addresses and respects before now as it has just occurred to me that you are the nephew of my most esteemed patroness, Lady Catherine de Bourgh. Had I realized earlier, you may be sure I would have been most attentive in my discussions with you, and it is my pleasure to assure you that your aunt was in the best of health four days ago, sir." With this, he bowed again, dislodging a few more strands of sweat-soaked hair from their place.

Elizabeth was shocked to hear Mr. Darcy thus accosted and even more amazed that he had not mentioned his connection to Lady Catherine when her cousin first introduced himself and mentioned her. She wondered if the sort of treatment he was now receiving was the reason. She smiled in amusement and was the recipient of a look of feigned reproach from Mr. Darcy before he turned to her cousin.

"Mr. Collins, I thank you for your assurances as to the health of my aunt."

"It is my pleasure, Mr. Darcy. As you may know, I am often in the presence of your aunt and your elegant cousin Miss de Bourgh. It is indeed a treat, a pleasure, to be acquainted now with another of that illustrious and most noble family. In fact, if I may be so bold, I congratulate you and wish you well on your future nuptials to your cousin Anne. You are, sir—and in this I share the opinion with your aunt, her ladyship—taking away one of England's finest ladies."

Mr. Darcy drew in a long breath and held it. *I cannot believe he has presumed to bring up the ridiculous engagement with Anne!* Darcy was furious with the parson and even more so with his aunt, who was obviously making public statements that he would marry his cousin. He had tried to dispel her of this notion as neither he nor his cousin was inclined towards marriage to the other. He also knew with absolute certainty that it was not the favorite wish of his mother as his Aunt Catherine always claimed. *She just will not give up! The audacity of the woman!* Mr. Darcy was beginning to feel his anger cause him to lose composure when he looked over to Elizabeth and his heart stopped. She had grown pale and was looking down at her hands. *Oh no! What must she think now?* He was humiliated that she would think he was trifling with her.

Elizabeth, upon hearing the news that Mr. Darcy was engaged to his cousin, was struck dumb. Feelings of foolishness flooded her awareness as her disappointment became acute. *I should not have allowed my feelings to run away like this.* Three days before, she would have cared little for the news that Mr. Darcy was engaged to another woman. She did not want to think about why it bothered her so much now and, instead, berated herself for trusting his recent, easy affections and for allowing them to creep into her heart and color her feelings towards the man. She knew he was above her in society's station, and she felt embarrassed for having forgotten that and allowing something akin to hope to take root in her heart. She looked down at her hands on her lap and tried to still them as they began to tremble. Suddenly, the air in the room became too stifling for her, and she stood abruptly to excuse herself.

Mr. Darcy could see strong emotions playing in her eyes, but he could not get his mind to work quickly enough to forestall her, so he watched her leave in a state of disbelief. A few minutes later, he heard her go out the front door. He looked towards Bingley, who responded with a look that indicated he did not understand what just happened. Jane looked concerned; having not heard Mr. Collins's speech, she did not know why her sister left so quickly. It was at this point that Mr. Bingley reluctantly made his move towards taking his leave. He addressed Mrs. Bennet, the rest of the ladies in attendance and Mr. Collins on behalf of himself and Mr. Darcy, and the two gentlemen left the house.

Upon their exit, Mr. Bingley turned to his friend. "Darcy, what the devil happened in there? I saw that silly Collins come up to you and say something, and then you looked like you were going to commit murder; Miss Elizabeth looked as if she was going to be sick, and then she left."

"I cannot talk about it now, Bingley." Mr. Darcy was about to mount his horse when he heard a noise from around the side of the house. "Bingley, give me a minute. Go on without me, and I will catch up with you shortly."

Bingley looked questioningly at his friend but shrugged and kicked his horse into movement, turning it towards the gate. Mr. Darcy waited until he could see his friend pass through the gate and then walked slowly around the side of the house. In the distance, he spied Elizabeth sitting on a swing attached to a colossal oak tree. She had her back to him, and she was kicking the ground with her slippers as she rocked back and forth. She looked so young and fragile with her shoulders slumped against one of the ropes. He realized he had never seen Elizabeth look vulnerable. She always had a strength about her that made her seem impenetrable. He took a few silent steps towards her, closing the distance between them.

Elizabeth sat on her childhood swing trying to curb her swaying emotions. She went from extreme disappointment, to anger at Mr. Darcy's attentions, to frustration with herself for setting herself up for an obvious fall. She was lost in her thoughts when she heard a familiar voice call her name softly.

"Elizabeth." Mr. Darcy's voice caught as she stopped her movements on the swing and stiffened at the sound. When she did not turn to acknowledge him, he closed the distance and began again. "Elizabeth, I do not want to assume the reason for your hasty departure. It does pain me, though, to see you upset. I can explain about what your cousin alluded to—"

At this, Elizabeth stood and turned quickly towards Mr. Darcy with her anger rising. Interrupting him, she said, "Pray, Mr. Darcy, stop. You owe me no explanation, and I ask that you do not address me in that familiar way. You have not the right nor my permission to do so."

Her eyes were ablaze with her anger towards him, and her mouth set in a grim line. She stood erect with her shoulders back in defiance, and her hands grasped tightly to the ropes of the swing. Her knuckles were turning white with the strength of her hold. There was a slight breeze that caused the delicate coils of hair near her temples to tremble slightly. The entire image caught Darcy as irresistible. *She is so beautiful!* Her appearance caused feelings of scalding delight in him, even as he felt acutely the pain of her anger. He could not help himself from drinking in her beauty enhanced by the display of passion. He tried to pull his mind back to attend to her words, and he was properly taken aback by her biting remarks. He knew he should not address her as he did but it was beyond him not to. A pain shot through him as he saw the turn of her features; the sweetness that was becoming familiar to him was absent.

"Forgive me, Miss Bennet. I am sorry to have upset you. I will leave you now if it is what you wish, but I must beg you to be allowed to say one thing before I go."

"I do wish it, sir." She spoke firmly, but even though her voice was still cold, she felt the strength of her resolve falter at the gentleness in his voice.

He bowed slowly in acknowledgement of her request for his departure. Straightening to his full stature, he looked at her face and waited until her eyes met his before speaking with a firm but tender tone, "Miss Bennet, I will have you know that I am neither by honor nor by inclination bound to marry my cousin." With that, he bowed again and said only, "Good day, Miss Bennet."

Elizabeth could not tear her gaze from him as she watched him turn and walk slowly out of the garden. His words had touched her. With one sentence, he had set at ease many of the troubling thoughts that had begun to burden her heart. She began to hope again that, by wanting to clarify this fact, he was essentially making a sort of declaration to her about his feelings. She did not think that she was prepared to make a similar declaration but did not want to see him leave with her anger still in the air.

"Mr. Darcy!" she called out to him.

Mr. Darcy stopped at the sound of her voice and hesitated a moment. He was glad to hear her call him back as he had begun to feel an acute sense of loss, but he could not tell from the tone of her voice whether she was still angry with him, and so he turned slowly. He said nothing and tried to keep his face impassive as he looked towards her. Her face was softened, and the tension in his chest lessened somewhat at the sight. He watched as she nodded her acknowledgement of his previous statement and gave him a small smile. The tension fell away completely as he heard her sweet, soft voice address him.

"Good day to you, too, sir."

He smiled softly at her and bowed again before turning to leave the garden. Elizabeth watched until he disappeared around the side of the house and heard his horse's hooves leave the courtyard before she turned and sat back down on the swing.

Chapter 4

Curled up with a book of sonnets in her father's library, Elizabeth tried once again to escape the chorus of her family's voices in other parts of the house. It was still raining, and the north-facing windows of the library took the thumping of the downpour, creating a relaxing hum throughout the room. It had rained heavily since the day after the gentlemen had stopped by Longbourn to extend their invitation to the ball. Everyone was excited about the event, not the least of whom was her mother, and the poor weather only intensified her agitated vocalizations as she dictated this and that for each girl's preparation. Although it was not specified, Mrs. Bennet was certain the dance was held in honor of her sweet Jane, and she was determined that all her daughters were to look their best. Mr. Collins was still eagerly courting Lizzy, and the news that the officers in Meryton were invited to the dance rounded out her hopes for the evening for the rest of her daughters. As the fevered pitch of her mother's voice seeped into the stillness of the library yet again, Elizabeth looked up at her father in the chair opposite her near the fire.

Mr. Bennet rolled his eyes and lowered his head to his book. Elizabeth pulled the blanket tighter around her shoulders and drooped lower into her chair in escape. She loved being in the library. The scents of leather, aged paper and her father's cigars filled her senses with calm and comfort. It was a place in which she rarely had to behave as dictated by society. Even now, she did not sit up properly as a lady ought. She tucked her feet beneath her in the giant, leather armchair, dropping her slippers haphazardly on the floor. Sitting with a most unladylike posture, her shoulders hunched forward and her head leaning against the wing of the chair, she could comfortably escape into the peace of a book. It was *her* chair: the one Mr. Bennet always allowed her to use, sitting opposite to its twin near the fireplace. Mr. Bennet sat in the other with his legs propped up on an ottoman.

However, today Elizabeth could not drown out the thoughts of her mind with a book. Even the comforts of the library, her only chance for peace with the weather keeping her and all her family at home, were not helping her sort out the feelings in her heart. Turning a page in the book that she was not actually reading, she allowed her mind to drift back to the garden a few days before when Mr. Darcy spoke to her last. She was embarrassed that her budding feelings for him had been so apparent in the drawing room and even more concerned that those feelings, which she had believed were only trifling, had driven her from the house at the news that Mr. Darcy was engaged to his cousin. It was not like her to have such a violent, emotional reaction. At least nobody else seemed to notice. Even Jane was persuaded to think she had just needed some air when she asked Elizabeth why she had left so suddenly. She had always been the one to laugh at the follies of others, including herself. She had developed the occasional tender feelings for a gentleman before and, upon hearing his interest was elsewhere, had shaken it off and laughed at her silliness. Not so with Mr. Darcy. *Why must that man continually plague me?*

Before their day in the forest, she had disliked him quite intensely. After, she had found herself intrigued and even drawn to him. She recalled that every reaction she had to him, either good or bad, was rather passionate. That is what confused and frightened her. The weather had served to oppress her into her thoughts, keeping her blocked in without escape.

She recalled his words in the garden. *'I am neither by honor nor by inclination bound to marry my cousin.'* Elizabeth once again tried to determine why such a simple statement produced such a powerful sense of relief in her. She trembled to think that he would feel the need to say such a thing to her. They had no understanding between them and only recently had any civil conversations—well, more than civil if she was honest with herself. A rosy hue colored her cheeks as she thought of the near-flirtatious interactions they had had. His kindness and solicitous concern after her injury brought out a charming side of him that, when combined with his attractive features, had only unbound any attempts she had made not to be affected by the handsome man.

Shaking her head, she turned the page again. The words on the page swam and shifted like her thoughts. She admitted to herself that she had begun to have feelings for Mr. Darcy. That could be the only explanation for the calming effect of his declaration. She decided that his urge to comfort her with the only words that would have done so might be proof that he returned at least some of the regard she felt for him. She was realistic enough to know that a great man with his fortune did not pay his addresses to just anyone. He would have ladies of the *ton* swarming him with eagerness to become his wife, and he would be ever careful not to raise expectations. This thought finally made things clear to Elizabeth as, frowning slightly, she realized that, in all her experience with the man, he had always been honest—brutally so at times. While staying at Netherfield, she had learned that he despised deception.

She now comprehended that, even if Mr. Darcy had developed some feelings for her, he would be a man driven by honor—an honor that required him to clarify the truth of his situation with his cousin. With sadness, Elizabeth realized that he likely did not declare himself unattached to his cousin due to any affection for her but because his honor would not allow the deception, and his natural kindness did not want her feelings burdened. With a pang in her heart, she determined that, at the ball, she would not allow her feelings to be so transparent. They could converse as friends because she did not want him to feel responsible for raising feelings in her that, by honor, he may not be able to return.

"Is something troubling you, Lizzy?" Her father's voice broke through her musing and brought her to the present.

Looking up and smiling convincingly, Elizabeth responded, "No Papa, I am just tired of being indoors. I will be glad when this ball is over."

"You are not looking forward to dancing then?" he teased.

She laughed. "Oh, I am, but I am afraid we will have no peace at Longbourn from Mama until it is over."

"Well, my dear, we have never had peace at Longbourn as long as your mother is at home. But yes, her excitement for the event has seemed to express itself most violently." As if to prove his point, the voice of Mrs. Bennet calling for Hill was heard beyond the door as she walked past the library. Elizabeth and her father broke out in laughter.

Elizabeth covered her mouth to hide the sound when her father gestured with his finger to be quiet lest they attract visitors to their sanctuary.

"Shh, child! Unless, of course, you want your Mr. Collins to find you here."

"Oh no!" She chuckled silently, sinking deeper into the chair. Earlier, when her cousin had been looking for her, he had come into the library to ask Mr. Bennet if he knew where she was. If she had not been curled so tightly in the chair, he would have seen her, and she was thankful that the huge, leather chair had its back to the door. She had shaken her head to her father, begging him not to divulge her hiding place, and he graciously kept her secret, directing her cousin to another room.

"He does seem to have a particular interest in you, Lizzy," her father said suggestively.

"I cannot think why. I never speak to the man if I can help it, and you know that, although I love to read, I have not spent as much time in this library in years as I have since he came to Longbourn. You do not think he..." She could not finish the thought without a shudder.

"Have no fear, Poppet, I will not force you to marry him should he pay his addresses, regardless of the entail and the wishes of your mother."

"Marry him!" she whispered with distress. She shifted uncomfortably as she tried to dispel that thought. "Thank you, Papa; I should not marry such a fool. In fact, I believe I am indebted to my sister Mary for her kind efforts in distracting him. She is often the reason I am able to escape as she always seems to have some topic of great doctrinal import to discuss with him." Elizabeth smiled mischievously.

"Hmm. Yes, Mary has been most kind," Mr. Bennet replied. Although their discussion had been light and teasing, the topic of his daughters' future spouses was of great concern to their father. He could not express to any of them his regrets for not marrying for love. When he met Fanny Gardiner, he was not seeking a wife, but she was pretty, and he was young and foolish. He let the temptations of a great beauty decide his fate and fix him to a silly mate for the rest of his life. He wanted his daughters to marry for love and wanted the men they married to love them in return. He knew that society would not look too closely at his daughters because of their lack of fortune, and he wanted it that way. He wanted them to choose between marrying for convenience and marrying for love, despite their circumstances, and he hoped they would choose correctly. Looking over at his favorite daughter, he felt an uncharacteristic surge of emotion fill his breast.

Speaking with a tenderness not often shown, he said, "Lizzy dear, promise me you will not marry without mutual love."

Elizabeth was caught by the softness in his voice and the feeling of it, and her eyes watered at his urgent concern. "I won't, Papa. I am certain that only the strongest love will ever induce me to marry." She reached over and held her father's hand. He squeezed her fingers gently in response. She had known her parents' marriage was not ideal, and from an early age, she had determined not to marry unless she could hold her spouse in great esteem and mutual respect.

She slowly withdrew her hand as they both settled back into their books in an attempt to clear the suddenly serious air around them. Thoughts of Mr. Darcy drifted unbidden to her mind. He was a good man, and she did respect and esteem him, but there was much she still did not know about him. She should not allow her feelings for the man to continue to spiral out of control without being able to know whether she truly could respect him. The proud way he had spoken at Netherfield on occasion bothered her, and she could not reconcile that proud man with the gentler one she had seen recently. It was either evidence of an unsteady character or one that she did not yet understand. Either way, she should not allow him so much space in her heart until she knew which.

Elizabeth stood smiling at her sister's reflection in the mirror while their lady's maid, Ruth, put the finishing touches in Jane's hair. She was beautifully dressed in an ivory evening gown with gold embroidered patterns around the décolletage and sleeves. She had a matching gold ribbon tied in the front at her waist that extended down to the hem and sent the ribbons in cascades of silky streamers. Ruth had done a marvelous job on her hair and was just pinning the last of the delicate matching ivory flowers into her soft curls.

"You look beautiful, Jane. Mr. Bingley will not be able to take his eyes off of you tonight."

"Thank you, Lizzy. I admit I am excited to dance with him. Did I tell you that he asked to dance the first and supper sets?" She blushed sweetly and smiled.

"Only a few times, but you may tell me as many times as you like. He is a good man, and I give you leave to like him."

"He is everything a man ought to be. He is kind and generous, and I am afraid I am half in love with him already!"

"Only half?" teased Elizabeth.

"Oh, Lizzy, if only I could see you so in love, my happiness would be complete. Tell me: is there such a man?" Jane did not expect an honest answer but hoped that her sister would acknowledge some feelings for Mr. Darcy. He and her Mr. Bingley, as she had begun to believe he was, were best friends, and she had secret hopes that, if she were to marry Mr. Bingley, *her* best friend might marry *his*.

"Well, Jane, perhaps the ball tonight will provide me with such luck. I do have my first dance with Mr. Collins," she replied with pretended anticipation. Both girls laughed and gathered their gloves to make their way downstairs.

The rest of their family waited for them in the vestibule. An excited Mrs. Bennet was physically bobbing with anticipation and scolding Kitty not to trifle with her dress lest it leave wrinkles. Mary was standing serenely next to Mr. Collins holding some sheet music, and Lydia was admiring her looks in the large mirror on the wall.

"Jane! Lizzy! Oh how you vex me! We shall be late with all this dallying. Hurry girls; the carriage is ready." Mrs. Bennet spun in her skirts and hustled the other girls towards the door.

"My dear cousins, how lovely you look this evening. You are as pearls in the sand." Mr. Collins's oozing voice reached them as they were halfway down the stairs. "I trust my dear Cousin Jane will not feel my neglect when I say that you, Cousin Elizabeth, are especially in looks tonight." He smiled sweetly as he walked up the last few steps to offer the sisters his assistance down the stairs.

Extending their hands in acceptance, the two sisters exchanged a quick chagrined smile and murmured their thanks. Elizabeth was grateful to relinquish the damp hand of her cousin upon reaching the landing.

"Mr. Collins, you are most gracious," she responded civilly as he followed them out to the carriage and helped them in.

Once settled in for the ride to Netherfield, Jane and Elizabeth grasped hands as they listened to the cacophony their family made within the small confines of the carriage.

"Kitty, scoot over! You are putting wrinkles in my dress!" Lydia whined.

"I am not, and I am as far over as I can manage!" Kitty responded.

"Girls! Have you no thought for my nerves? Kitty, move over and give your sister some room."

Kitty pouted and stomped her dancing slipper, unfortunately right onto the foot of Mary, who protested loudly and scolded Kitty for her improper behavior. At that point, Mr. Collins began extolling the qualities possessed by a Christian lady—including charity, meekness and a few more—all of which were left unheard as no one in the carriage attended to him. It was to the boundless relief of all when the Bennet carriage finally rolled to a stop in front of Netherfield.

A servant in livery opened the carriage door and unfolded the steps. Kitty and Lydia both made for the door first; their bodies met, jamming the exit. With little grace, Lydia elbowed her sister to the side and exited the carriage first, followed by an angry Kitty, a disapproving Mary, an excited Mrs. Bennet and an imperious Mr. Collins.

Elizabeth groaned and shook her head despairingly at Jane, who breathed deeply and shrugged her shoulders as she turned to exit the carriage. Elizabeth paused a moment to collect herself after Jane stepped out. Taking a deep breath, she tipped her head out the carriage door and stepped down.

Her breath caught at the sight before her. They were standing on heavy muslin laid on the ground to allow the guests to walk into the home while avoiding dirt to their evening clothes on the way. Every room in the home was lit brightly against the night. The walkway to the steps of the house was lined with garlands of flowers on lanterns, their flames flickering in the slight breeze. It was beautiful, and a smile came to Elizabeth's face as her excitement for the evening grew with the elegance before her. Her eyes spotted a movement in the window of an upper floor, and she turned her head towards it, but whatever had been there was now gone.

"Shall we?" asked Jane with a bright smile as she hooked her arm in Elizabeth's and they proceeded towards the house.

"By all means!" Elizabeth giggled as the two girls took the steps to the house and entered the warmth of the entryway.

After divesting themselves of their cloaks to the standing servants, they followed their family through to the receiving line.

"I am glad to see Miss Bingley and Mrs. Hurst again. They were so kind to me while I was ill, and I have not seen them since," Jane whispered as they neared their hostesses. Elizabeth merely nodded. She cared not for the two sisters and did not look forward to their artificial civilities.

"Dearest Jane! How glad we are to see you now in good health!" cried Miss Bingley, as she leaned in to give an air kiss to Jane's cheek before turning to welcome Elizabeth. "Miss Elizabeth! How lovely you look this evening. I believe that gown is nearly in fashion!"

Elizabeth was not offended by her caustic, pretended flatteries and responded with her own thinly veiled compliment. "Thank you, Miss Bingley. And may I say that I have never seen a dress in quite that color before?" Elizabeth covered her smile with her gloved hand and turned towards Mr. Bingley before his sister could decipher whether her comment was praise or not.

"Mr. Bingley, sir, your house is simply stunning. You have outdone yourself," Jane said sweetly, looking up at his smiling face.

"Truly, sir, I must add to my sister's sentiments and say that the evening looks to be quite delightful," Elizabeth remarked.

"Miss Bennet, Miss Elizabeth, I am indeed glad to hear it. It is always gratifying to receive such praise from accomplished ladies such as yourselves," Bingley responded charmingly as he took Jane's hand and bowed to place a chaste kiss on her gloved fingers. Elizabeth stepped around them towards the glamour of the ballroom just as a familiar dark figure took his place next to Mr. Bingley.

Mr. Darcy paced the Venetian rug in his private sitting room on the third floor. He was dressed in his finest evening clothes. His valet would receive an extra bonus in his monthly remuneration for his patience and hard work these past few days. Mr. Darcy knew he had been edgy and ill tempered. He had been uncharacteristically critical of his valet's plans for that evening's clothing and had requested he make a special trip to London for his grey silk waistcoat with the silver pinstriping and white, dress knee breeches. Upon coming to Netherfield, he had brought many suitable dress clothes but none he felt were fine enough for that evening. He had not planned on attending a formal ball when he instructed his valet in packing for Hertfordshire. The evening clothes he brought would have been more than acceptable, but Mr. Darcy wanted to dress his best. He told himself it was out of respect and honor to his best friend and his acceptance in the neighborhood—and not because of a certain lady.

He slowed his pacing, reminding himself he did not want carpet dust to settle on the mirror shine of his dancing pumps. He stopped before a small mirror to inspect his cravat. It was impeccably folded in cascades of bright white silk and held in place with a diamond stickpin. He pulled at the sleeves of his personally tailored, black tailcoat and harrumphed as he began pacing again.

Mr. Darcy took in a deep breath as he considered what he expected from the evening. He was anxious to see Miss Elizabeth and nervous about dancing with her. The thought of having her hand in his, and her body in the near-embrace of the dance was like lightening in his blood. He tried to imagine what she would wear and hoped that she would give him one of those smiles that set his heart beating out of his chest. The last few days bereft of her presence had settled it for him that, although he did not yet know whether he was completely in love with Elizabeth, he at least knew he did not like to consider any length of time spent without her.

He smiled as he thought of the way her face calmed and the angry fire in her eyes stilled when he told her he was not engaged to his cousin Anne. He had not meant to make quite that type of declaration but he could not allow her to think their lovely moments together had meant nothing to him. In the last few days, he had gone from feeling the declaration was premature to feeling that he had not been clear enough in stating his feelings and intentions towards her.

He stopped his pacing to look once again out the window at the incoming carriages. The sounds from below reached his ears as more and more guests arrived. He was apprehensive when he thought about the many people downstairs. He did not like crowds and was not particularly easy with many of the country manners he had encountered in Hertfordshire. His thoughts were interrupted by the arrival of a large carriage that looked to have the Bennet crest.

He took a deep breath and thought, *she is here!* He held his breath as he watched the carriage unload. There was some jiggling of the springs before Misses Lydia, Kitty and Mary exited and walked forward, looking at the house and giggling to themselves. Darcy let out his breath and frowned as he saw Elizabeth's tabby of a mother emerge in an abundance of heavy feathers and bobbles. He watched her plump body skirt after her daughters, none of whom waited for the rest of their party to exit the carriage.

Mr. Darcy had almost forgotten that Elizabeth's cousin, Mr. Collins, was visiting until he saw the man emerge from the carriage. He had a proud and over-bloated air of self-importance about him as he straightened his parson's neck cloth and looked towards the house. Mr. Darcy's hands clenched at his side as he thought of the attentions that man gave to his Elizabeth. He did not like knowing that the first person to have the pleasure of her dance that evening would not be him but her odious and officious cousin. A low growl escaped Mr. Darcy's mouth as he watched Mr. Collins forget to aid Miss Bennet from the carriage. Thankfully, he saw that an efficient Netherfield servant noticed the neglect in time to assist the lady.

There was a pause, and Mr. Darcy drew in an unsteady breath. His heart sank, as it appeared for a moment that nobody else was going to exit the carriage. The idea that she would not come had not occurred to him, and suddenly the evening lost all appeal. He was bombarded with feelings of disappointment and worry over why she had not come until his spell was broken when he saw her dainty little head peek out of the carriage.

The vision of Elizabeth took his breath away. He allowed his eyes to wash over her and drink in her beauty for a moment. Her chocolate curls were piled fashionably in a swirl on her head, and they caught the glimmer of the candles in the lanterns. The light flickered, and the shine of her hair danced in the night. He could see there was a silvery ribbon twirled in and out of the mass of curls. He imagined for a moment that he could run his fingers along the course of that ribbon—in and out of her soft tresses. The thought nearly caused his eyes to close with imagined pleasure, but he could not allow himself to miss a detail, so he forced them to remain open and rest upon the beauty of her face.

His hand came up to steady himself on the windowsill. Her eyes were lit with excitement and danced around the splendor before her. Her cheeks were pink in the coolness of the night, and her lips turned upward in pleasure. His gaze roamed over the beauty of her expressive face until he noticed with satisfaction the color of her dress. Apparently, it had been warm inside the coach, as her cloak was flung behind her shoulders, and he was able to see Elizabeth's gown before the cool outside air caused her to pull it back around her. Her dress was made with a shimmery silver, crushed silk bodice and a broad square neckline leading up to thick straps resting just at the edge of her shoulders. An overlay of grey silk tulle draped over her figure and opened in the front under a pleasing empire waistline to reveal that the main skirts of the dress were made of the same silver silk as the bodice. Her arms were draped in white silk gloves reaching to just above her elbows exposing the creamy white of her upper arms.

His heart beat wildly as he completed his perusal of her gown and returned his gaze to her face. *Elizabeth, you are magnificent!* At that moment, she smiled brightly at the house ahead, and he knew he had to go to her. Spinning away from the window, he walked quickly out the door of his apartment and headed determinedly towards the stairs.

He reached her just as she turned from greeting Mr. Bingley, and he stood next to his friend awaiting her addresses. He pressed his lips together to keep them from turning into a love-struck fool's grin and excitedly waited for her to see him. He watched as she stopped the moment she saw him and slowly lifted her face to him.

"Miss Elizabeth, I hope you will enjoy your evening tonight," he said. *Oh, and I love you!* "Your ankle is restored, I trust."

It took only a moment for Elizabeth to regain her equilibrium after the surprising and sudden appearance of Mr. Darcy. His dimples were peeking temptingly and very nearly wiped her mind free of intelligent thought. Smiling demurely, she replied, "Thank you, Mr. Darcy, it is well. I have every expectation of enjoying my evening."

"I am glad to hear it." He kept his eyes locked with hers as he bowed, captured her hand and placed a soft kiss on her gloved fingers. "Miss Elizabeth."

"Mr. Darcy," Elizabeth replied shakily and curtsied. A shock shot all the way up her arm when he placed the kiss on her hand, and although he had released her, she still felt its tingle.

It was then that she noticed his evening wear. He was handsomely dressed, and the cut of his black tailcoat molded over his broad shoulders perfectly. Her secret inspection of his person stopped when she noticed that the color of his waistcoat complimented her gown. Without thought, she uttered incoherently, "Your waistcoat… my dress… "

"… seem to match perfectly," he finished for her.

"Indeed," she spoke quietly in her surprise. He smiled broadly at her before making his excuses and disappearing into the crowd in the ballroom, leaving her mind spinning with a bit of happiness at the coincidence.

Elizabeth hazily moved towards the ballroom and sought out her dear friend Charlotte Lucas. She shook off the effect Mr. Darcy had on her and smiled at her friend. It had been a long time since they had conversed, and she was happy to have a few moments before the dance started to catch up with her. Soon, she could hear the musicians warming up their instruments and preparing for the first set. It was not long before her cousin came to stand beside her, ready to claim her for the dance.

"Charlotte, allow me to introduce my cousin, Mr. Collins," Elizabeth began. "Mr. Collins, this is my dear friend, Miss Lucas."

Mr. Collins gave a squeaky bow and said, "Miss Lucas, a pleasure."

"Mr. Collins," Charlotte said, as she curtsied.

They spoke together for a few minutes until the band played the opening signal that the set was to begin.

"Cousin Elizabeth, I believe it is time for our dance." He reached for her, and she reluctantly raised her hand to him as he led her to join the set.

She noticed that Mr. Bingley led Jane out to the floor to open the ball. It was quite a compliment, and she smiled in happiness for her sister. Mr. Collins, believing her smile was for him, stepped forward and spoke in a low voice at her side.

"Cousin Elizabeth, I am also pleased with the prospect of our dance." He boldly flicked his eyebrows up and down before stepping back into position.

Elizabeth was shocked and mortified at his statement and barely managed her first steps in time as the music began. Unfortunately, at that moment Mr. Collins, being unfamiliar with the movements of the dance, stepped forward with the ladies and bumped ungracefully into her.

"Mr. Collins!" she shot at him. Her cheeks colored in humiliation and rising anger. To her utter astonishment, instead of rectifying his movements to suit the dance, he began to apologize and missed the gentlemen's next movement. Elizabeth tried her best to complete the turns and movements of the dance with as much dignity as she could with her cousin as partner. He was as disagreeable a partner as could be imagined.

Mr. Darcy, having positioned himself in the location he had determined would afford him the best view of the dancers, and more particularly Elizabeth, stood transfixed at the sight of complete ineptitude on the part of Mr. Collins. He was horrified and angered at the way the parson's stupidity was embarrassing Elizabeth. He fiercely gripped the pillar next to him as he tried to talk himself out of going to her rescue; that would only embarrass her further. But he wanted to—oh, how he wanted to—because it was nearly unbearable to see her suffering so at the hands of her ridiculous cousin.

Just then, he saw Mr. Collins again turn the wrong way and step roughly on her foot, causing the silk flower of her dancing slipper to tear off and glide across the dance floor to rest near the wall to Darcy's right. His jaw was set in a grim line, and he started forward, determined to take her cousin's place in the set. He had seen enough of her suffering and could not handle any more. However, his movements stilled when he saw her limping off the dance floor towards her friend Miss Lucas, who helped her to a chair.

Mr. Darcy turned towards the wall behind him and walked to where he had seen the silk flower slide. He bent over and retrieved it, placing it in the pocket of his waistcoat. He would return it to her later. Looking for her across the room, he could see that she was very angry, but it looked as though her foot was not seriously hurt. Mr. Collins was speaking incessantly to her in what he supposed were repeated apologies. Thankfully, he saw Miss Lucas address Mr. Collins, and he nodded his head and turned towards the refreshment table. Darcy determined then that he would do something to protect Elizabeth from any future attentions by Mr. Collins.

Elizabeth looked up gratefully at her friend for having sent Mr. Collins to retrieve lemonade. She did not know how much longer she could remain civil to the man after his abundant apologies and humiliating dancing. She was thankful, actually, that he had stepped on her foot, because even though it did not hurt, it did give her an excuse to end the dance. She looked down and sadly noticed that her shoe flower had been torn off. She looked around the floor to see if she could spot it and sighed when she was unsuccessful. *What an auspicious start to the evening!* she thought with sarcasm.

Having performed the obligatory dance with Miss Bingley in the second set, Mr. Darcy spent a short while on the terrace breathing in the fresh air. He could not give her the satisfaction of the first set of the night and, knowing that he would have to dance with her at some point during the evening, decided on sooner rather than later so that he could enjoy the rest of the evening. Seeing that Elizabeth would be sitting the set out and that he could not have the pleasure of watching her, he braced himself to dance with Miss Bingley. The warmth of the ballroom had stirred her perfume to unbelievably high levels of torture, and he was glad to escape to the cool, clean air of the night. Perhaps he should suggest to Bingley that he purchase her a new perfume for Christmas in a few weeks.

As Darcy returned to the house, he saw that Mr. Collins was headed towards him. His instinct was to turn and escape before the man could reach his location, but seeing this as a chance to make good on his personal vow to protect Elizabeth from her cousin, he waited for the man's approach. He hoped to discover some way to accomplish the task during the conversation.

Breathless from the short walk across the room, Mr. Collins pulled out a soiled handkerchief and patted at the sweat on his brow as he gave a pretentious bow before beginning his address to Mr. Darcy.

"Mr. Darcy, sir, I have been looking for you as I wish to pay my respects. You honor the people of Hertfordshire tonight with your presence. I had the great pleasure just now to witness your dance with Miss Bingley, and I came directly to tell you personally what a fine figure you cut and how gracefully you moved about the set. It is indeed a great compliment that you would condescend to dance among such humble, country persons as you find here."

"Mr. Collins, it is an elegant ball, held by my friend, Mr. Bingley. I never would do him the dishonor of not dancing."

"Indeed, of course, it is as I would expect from one as generous as you. As I have had the great privilege to be many times in the company of your noble aunt Lady Catherine, for I am often in her company, having been invited to tea four times and to supper twice since the beginning of my patronage, I have found that generosity in your family is part of your nature. Her ladyship is most solicitous in her guidance and often condescends to suggest topics for my sermons that would be most beneficial to my congregation."

"I can easily see my aunt interfere... that is, offer her support in that way." Mr. Darcy was tired of the officiousness of the clergyman and, as his temper was becoming short, hoped to change the topic. "Tell me, Mr. Collins, what brings you to Hertfordshire?"

"I am glad you asked, Mr. Darcy. The reason for my visit to Hertfordshire, and more particularly Longbourn, is yet another example of the great condescension her ladyship has offered me."

"Indeed? Do enlighten me."

"It would be my pleasure, sir. Your aunt the honorable Lady Catherine de Bourgh was just saying to me last Tuesday sen'night, 'Mr. Collins you must find a wife! It is the duty of a clergyman to set the example of matrimony for his congregation, and so you must find a wife.' You see, sir, it is my intention to find a wife at Longbourn. Her ladyship said, 'take heed to make sure she is a humble girl, mindful of the obligations of a clergyman's wife. If you choose wisely, after you marry I will visit her.' Such condescension, such generosity, I have never seen before!"

"Sir, am I to assume rightly that you wish to find a wife from amongst your cousins?" Mr. Darcy was beginning to see exactly how he could save Elizabeth from the attentions of this silly man and was anticipating his moment. He schooled his features into one of disinterest as he listened for the man's response.

"Mr. Darcy, sir, you are astute as ever. You are correct. As you may know, Longbourn is entailed to me, and in the unfortunate event of Mr. Bennet's death, I had thought to amend that poor situation by choosing one of my cousins to be my wife. In fact, I believe I have decided on a most suitable spouse, and if you can keep my secret, I will tell you I plan to pay my addresses to that lovely lady tomorrow!"

After this speech, Mr. Darcy watched his companion's eyes eagerly rake over the dancing form of Miss Elizabeth, and a wave of possessiveness overtook him. He drew a calming breath to ready himself to carry out his plan.

"Mr. Collins, sir, your secret is safe with me, and if I may be so bold, I would like to compliment you on your fine choice as I have seen where your preference lies. I congratulate you on your excellent discernment. The lady is indeed a very superior choice for the wife of a clergyman. She is accomplished but not so much that she is not humble."

Mr. Collins, feeling the great compliment Mr. Darcy was paying him, opened his mouth to agree but was cut off as Mr. Darcy continued.

"She is clever but not too bright as it would not be good to have a wife who questions you or your decisions. It gives evidence to your astute intellect that you would see immediately the value of such a lady in her abilities to make a good parson's wife."

"Mr. Darcy, sir, your approval of my choice is most gratifying, as I know it indicates that Lady Catherine de Bourgh also would approve. As it is my most fervent wish that her ladyship find my wife suitable, I find your words to be most satisfying, indeed—most satisfying."

"Mr. Collins, sir, I can assure you my aunt will approve of your choice. The lady in question will be most honored by your attentions, and she is reverential enough to see her good fortune in receiving such addresses, especially from someone who has been as fortunate as yourself to have the patronage of the great Lady Catherine de Bourgh." Mr. Darcy paused to allow his words to take effect on their recipient.

"Indeed, sir! She is quite perfect; I do not think there is another who would suit as well as she."

"Well, then," Mr. Darcy leaned in conspiratorially to Mr. Collins, and in low tones delivered the final piece of his plan. "Mr. Collins, sir, in that case, may I wish you every happiness and success in securing the hand of your lovely cousin—Miss Mary Bennet!" He gave the man a roguish smile and turned to walk away.

Mr. Collins stood stunned. *Mary Bennet?* He was sure they had been talking of the beautiful Miss Elizabeth, not plain Mary. Mr. Collins hastened to stay Mr. Darcy's retreat and placed a hand on the man's arm. "Mr. Darcy, sir, forgive me but you meant to say Miss Elizabeth, did you not?"

Mr. Darcy had anticipated this reaction, and he gave a jovial laugh. "Mr. Collins! I had not known you were such a wit. Miss Elizabeth, indeed!" He laughed as he shook his head and again turned to leave.

Once again Mr. Collin's hand reached out for his arm. "Mr. Darcy, sir, I beg. I believe you misunderstand me. I thought we were talking of my choice being Miss Elizabeth." His worried voice was exactly what Mr. Darcy had hoped for.

Schooling his features into a serious glare, Mr. Darcy looked down into the face of the nervous clergyman. "Collins, certainly you cannot be serious. Miss Elizabeth? I may have to take back my calculation of your intelligence, for you must see she would not do—would not do at all."

"What do you mean, sir?"

"Mr. Collins, please feel free to be frank with me. Are you not happy in your position under my aunt's patronage?"

"Oh, no, sir. That is, yes, I am very happy. It is a great honor and privilege, and I value it above everything else in this world. If I have displeased you, sir, I sincerely apologize and ask that you forgive me."

"Surely you can see, sir, that making Miss Elizabeth your wife will make her ladyship, my Aunt Catherine, severely displeased. She is outspoken and lively. Such a person would not be humbled by the condescension of my aunt, and her liveliness would be detrimental to the health of my cousin

Anne." He shook his head as if in disbelief at the man.

"Indeed, sir, I can see that you are right." Mr. Collins fixed his gaze at the lady in question just as she laughed at something her dancing partner said. Looking back at his companion, he meekly enquired, "Sir, you said that you presumed my choice was Miss Mary, correct?"

"Yes, for I had presumed you preferred her. She is well read on all things moral and is just the sort of wife my aunt would have chosen for you had you asked her to pick."

Mr. Collins sought out his cousin Mary and finally found her demurely sitting near the side of the ballroom. She was quite plain, and he frowned a little as he resigned himself to her. He wished her figure were more like the pleasing one of her sister. However, as he contemplated the great service Mr. Darcy did in saving him from a most imprudent marriage to his other cousin, he began to see the change as being quite fortunate.

"Thank you, Mr. Darcy, you are quite right. I believe, now, that Miss Elizabeth would be totally unsuitable to hold the position of a parson's wife. I am indebted to you for saving me from a most imprudent choice as she would most assuredly have accepted my desirable offer, and then I would have displeased Lady Catherine—something I assure you I do not want to do. Miss Mary is the right one for me; now that I speak of it, I can see it most clearly. In fact, I believe myself to be falling quite violently in love with her already. If you will excuse me, sir?" With that, Mr. Collins bowed, turned towards Mary's position in the room, and took the seat next to her.

Mr. Darcy bowed and nodded his good-byes to the man and, with a self-satisfied smile on his face, headed to the refreshment table for a much needed glass of wine before the next dance, his much anticipated dance with Elizabeth.

Chapter 5

Elizabeth was standing talking with Jane when Mr. Bingley and Mr. Darcy approached for the supper set. At his near proximity, Elizabeth found it was more difficult than she had hoped to maintain her resolve to be merely friendly and not let him see her feelings. When he stepped up to greet her, his lemony cologne washed over her, and she was shocked into the memory of his strong arms and broad chest pressed against her when he had embraced her after her fall.

Mr. Darcy was delighted finally to reach the part of the evening where he could command Miss Elizabeth's full attention and looked forward to the half hour with great anticipation. The slight blush that overtook her cheeks upon his approach sent his thoughts flying, and he was more eager than ever to have the opportunity to dance with her.

"Miss Elizabeth, I believe this is our dance." He held out his hand to her.

"You are correct, sir. Shall we?" She placed her hand in his and avoided his gaze as it caused a most disturbing feeling inside her.

Mr. Darcy smiled and gave her hand a gentle squeeze as he guided her to the dance floor to join the set beside Mr. Bingley and Jane. The music began, and with great ease, they began their movements. After several minutes of companionable silence, Elizabeth decided that being left to her own thoughts was not helping her keep her reserve, especially when Mr. Darcy's hand captured and released hers, or when his hand occasionally rested on the small of her back as he guided her through the turns of the dance. She determined some conversation would help distract her from the sensations coursing through her body and so thus began.

"Mr. Darcy, I believe we must have some conversation."

She looked at him with that arch smile he loved so much, and he smiled charmingly. "Do you speak during a dance as a rule then, Miss Bennet?"

His smile caught her off guard, and she laughed nervously and said, when they next came together, "Not as a rule, sir, but I find that a little conversation makes a dance more pleasant. But this will suffice for now."

As they separated in a turn and came together again, Mr. Darcy had thought of something to say. "Well, Miss Bennet, if we are to have some conversation, may I say that you look very well tonight—quite handsome, indeed."

He smiled as a blush spread across her face and down her neck and shoulders. *Oh, Elizabeth! You are so beautiful!* He tore his eyes away to continue down the set. When they next came together, he saw her eyebrow raise and her mouth twitch in that becoming way he knew indicated she was about to tease him; he happily readied himself for it.

"Well, since you kept your dance with me, I can assume, then, that I am handsome enough to tempt you." Her eyebrow arched, waiting for his response.

Oh, yes, very tempting indeed... oh, wait... For a moment, Mr. Darcy's mind froze—something about the wording she used. With shocked disbelief, he realized why those words seemed familiar, and the smile on his face instantly dropped. They were the ill-chosen words he had used at the Meryton assembly when he was trying to discourage Bingley from forcing him to dance. He had barely looked at her then—glanced in her direction for only a second really—and spouted out those horrible words without thought. *She heard me!* With mortification, he considered how his proud words could have sounded to her. *It is a wonder she will even speak to me!*

Elizabeth had only wanted to tease him, and seeing that her words were beginning to distress him, she hastened to relieve his worry. "Mr. Darcy..."

"Miss Bennet, please allow me to apologize for my terribly hurtful words that night. I had no right to say such things; it was very ungentlemanly of me."

The dance separated them for a moment, but upon coming together again, Elizabeth gave his hand a gentle squeeze and said, "Mr. Darcy, you are quite forgiven. I did not mean to distress you just now; I was only teasing. You see, it has been some time now since I have found the situation to be quite humorous."

"Eliz— Miss Elizabeth." He cleared his throat, embarrassed again to have slipped in his address towards her. "I do not deserve your forgiveness, but as you have given it, please allow me to also clarify to you my opinion on the matter."

She nodded her assent as the dance moved them apart again. The next movement brought them together with her left hand in his and his right hand on the small of her back as he walked her up the set.

Leaning slightly towards her and speaking in a low voice, he said, "Miss Elizabeth, on this you may be certain: it has been many weeks now that I have considered you one of the most beautiful women of my acquaintance." He punctuated his statement by tracing small circles with his thumb in the small of her back before they separated again.

Elizabeth's heart was racing from the sensations of his touch and from the stunning words he spoke in her ear. Her courage could only allow her to incline her head to his and smile slightly at his words. For the remainder of the dance, they moved in silence, caught in their own thoughts.

At the conclusion, Mr. Darcy led Elizabeth to the dining room, secured a seat for her next to his, and left to fill their plates. Elizabeth was pleased with her dance with Mr. Darcy. He was an elegant dancer, and it was her most pleasurable dance of the evening thus far. She smiled at the thought that they still had another dance left and that it would be the last set of the evening. She blushed as she remembered his compliment, and storing away for future indulgence the memory of his voice near her ear and the feel of it tickling the curls near her temple, she attempted to compose herself for his return.

She decided that, when he returned, she would attempt to get answers to some of the questions she had about him and his family. She did not know him very well and the only way she would learn more was to ask. It was her hope that, the more she knew of him, the better she would understand his behavior.

The supper hour was spent in pleasant conversation. She asked about his parents, his childhood and his hobbies. She was envious of him when he spoke so reverentially of his parents. It was evident that they must have loved each other deeply, and it no longer surprised her that he was such a passionate man, having grown up in that environment. She could barely keep from laughing as he related childhood exploits at his home in Derbyshire. She had never thought the serious Mr. Darcy could be so foolish and silly as a child. She asked about his sister and found it was a topic of great feeling for him. He loved his sister very much, and she understood from his answers to her inquiries that his sister was a sensitive, shy girl. She admired his great concern over her welfare and happiness.

"I have always wished to have a brother, and I can see that you are an excellent brother to Miss Darcy. She is very lucky to have you."

Her words touched him, and he was finding that the bewitching Elizabeth had even more goodness and tenderness than he already thought. He liked that she asked him about his family, and it confirmed her interest in him. He was not usually one to open up to anyone, but he found himself easily conversing and sharing with Elizabeth.

He asked about her life and found an answer to one of his unexpressed questions. She spoke of a beloved aunt and uncle in London who would invite her and Jane to their house for the summers until they had their own children. Since she spent a great deal of her childhood at her aunt's house, he speculated this could be the reason she and Jane were different in temperament from the rest of their family. He could see the tenderness in her eyes as she described this aunt as almost a second mother.

They conversed easily for most of the meal until, at one point, Mr. Darcy's chair was bumped rudely as Lydia and Kitty came skipping by, chased by a couple of officers, causing him to spill a bit of his wine on the tablecloth. She noticed his serious, disapproving face appear immediately, and she apologized for her sisters. Although he smiled at her and nodded his acceptance, he turned and began to focus on his neglected dinner with more effort.

Elizabeth also turned to her meal and, no longer distracted by her conversation with Mr. Darcy, began to realize that her family members were taking turns displaying gross impropriety. To her mortification, her ears now detected a part of her mother's conversation to Lady Lucas several chairs down.

Mrs. Bennet was speaking overly loud and leaning towards her neighbor as she discussed the great benefits the family would have when the much-anticipated and expected marriage between her eldest daughter and the rich Mr. Bingley occurred. Elizabeth dared a glance at Mr. Darcy and closed her eyes in horror as she confirmed he, too, could hear her mother. "And of course once Jane is married, she will be able to throw the other girls in the path of rich men!"

Elizabeth reached for her glass of wine and bit her lip as her shaky hand took the stem of the glass and brought it to her lips. She took an overly long drink and held her glass to her mouth for a moment as she contemplated that their lovely supper was turning into a complete disaster. She scanned the room for Jane and was relieved to see that she and Mr. Bingley, at least, were not witnessing the atrocities of their family. She hoped that Mr. Bingley would not be inclined to forgo his suit with Jane after tonight. Jane was too good and deserved happiness with Mr. Bingley.

Mr. Darcy was indignant with disgust at the lack of decorum displayed by Mrs. Bennet and her youngest daughters. It was like a cold splash of water to the face—a harsh reminder of the folly with which he was playing. He glanced at Elizabeth and noticed the trembling of her hand as she tried to appear poised while taking a drink of wine. He felt for her, and her embarrassment only served to further raise his anger towards her family. He loved her. He knew that for sure now; odd that seeing the mortifying behaviors of her family would drive it home for him. But the realization only served to bring him a shock of pain. He wanted to rescue her from the indignities of her family. However, their actions were so deplorable that he did not know whether he could make them his family.

Lydia and her sister had found their seats a few chairs down from Elizabeth and Mr. Darcy. She was talking animatedly to Mr. Denny and Mr. Saundersen from the militia when a part of her conversation intruded into Mr. Darcy's warring thoughts and caused him to startle.

"It is too bad our charming friend Mr. Wickham could not join us tonight. He is ever so handsome, and I am sure he would have been a pleasant dancer."

"Aye. He said he had sudden business in London, though I cannot think what it could be. He planned to come to the ball until he knew who was hosting it, and then business took him away," Mr. Saundersen added, barely hiding his relief that the gentleman had not come and stolen the attention of the girls as he seemed always to do.

Mr. Darcy listened until their conversation changed topics and he was left to his own thoughts. *Could it be the same Wickham?* The idea that Wickham might be in the area distressed him. He concluded from the conversation that this Wickham had joined the militia a week earlier and that both of the youngest Miss Bennets knew him. The memory of the previous summer returned and angered him as he recalled that sister was only a shadow of her former self because of *that man*.

Elizabeth interrupted his thoughts. "Mr. Darcy, please do not let my family's behavior anger you. If I could . . . " Her voice fell away to a whisper.

The agony in Elizabeth's voice brought Darcy to the present, and he was filled with a sudden concern for her. He turned his head and looked at her for a moment. Her eyes were lowered to her hands resting in her lap, and her lip was trembling slightly. He was not sure he could ignore the behavior of her family, but at the moment, he had a more pressing concern in mind.

"Miss Bennet, are you acquainted with a Mr. Wickham?"

His abrupt change of topic surprised and saddened her. *So he is too offended by my family to allow for my apologies.* She raised her shoulders in an attempt to appear less affected than she felt. "I do not know a Mr. Wickham myself, sir, but my younger sisters have recently made an acquaintance by that name in the militia in Meryton."

"Do you know whether his name is *George* Wickham?"

"I cannot be certain as I do not always listen to the babbling of my sisters, but I do believe it might be George Wickham. Pray, sir, do you know the man?"

Mr. Darcy considered for a moment how to answer her question and rubbed his jaw. "If it is the man I think it is, then yes, I do. I know him very well. He was the son of my father's steward." He paused and then, with more feeling, continued, "Miss Elizabeth, I am almost certain it must be the same man, and I have to warn you, he is not a good man. He has easy, pleasing manners, but his character is seriously lacking, and you should not trust him as he is not an honorable man."

"Mr. Darcy, this is most alarming. Of what are you speaking?"

"Miss Elizabeth, what I know of Mr. Wickham's character is not proper supper conversation, and some of it is indelicate and would upset your sensibilities. Please just trust me and stay away from the man. I will speak to your father, and I hope that what I relate to him will rouse him to keep your sisters away from him, too."

"I see," was all she could mumble in her response to his intense glare. She felt this disclosure must be significant to him as she could see anger and pain in his eyes. She wondered what he could know of the man to make him speak so passionately.

"Promise me, Miss Elizabeth, that you will stay away from him." The earnest concern in his voice made her heart weak, and she dared to look him in the eyes. What she saw caused her to sit back, and she nodded numbly. "I promise."

The heaviness of that moment hung in the air for the rest of the meal, and she breathed a sigh of relief at the end of it. Her mind was quite full, and she wished she could be left alone to sort through the mixed emotions she was experiencing. She had been so happy and contented talking to Mr. Darcy, but then her family's behavior had intruded, and the realization struck that their worlds would be unlikely to combine. She shuddered to think of the intensity in his voice when he warned her of Mr. Wickham. He did not give details of his knowledge of the man, but she knew enough of Mr. Darcy to trust his honorability and believed he would tell her if she asked him to explain.

With a clouded mind, she allowed her first dance partner after supper to claim her from where she stood silently next to Mr. Darcy as he had escorted her from the dining room back to the ballroom.

Mr. Darcy watched her begin the dance and then turned and sought out a conference with Colonel Forster. He soon discovered that the new member of the local militia was indeed his former childhood friend, Mr. George Wickham — the same man who tried to seduce his sister and wickedly persuaded her to agree to an elopement for the sole purpose of gaining her dowry of thirty thousand pounds, thus achieving the ultimate revenge against Darcy.

Ordinarily, he would have considered leaving once he found Wickham was nearby, but this time there were people in the area that he knew and respected. Bingley would likely settle there, especially now that he was nearing a decision on Miss Bennet. And then there was Elizabeth. His heart stopped at the thought of anything happening to her at the hands of Mr. Wickham. He could not let her or someone she loved be hurt. Her pain would then be his. He decided staying quiet about George Wickham would only serve his own sensibilities and could, quite possibly, end up destroying much more. He could not call himself a gentleman of honor if he did not say something.

Upon confirming Wickham's identity, he invited the colonel into Bingley's library for a short conversation. After pouring them both a glass of brandy, he sat opposite the colonel. There he divulged his previous relationship with the man and expanded on the character of Mr. Wickham. He related a history of debts to tradesmen and numerous debts of honor nearly everywhere the man went. He also warned the colonel of Wickham's licentious behavior. He attested that, on at least two occasions, Wickham had abandoned enceinte women with no support.

Finally, with a heavy heart, he related Georgiana's story without divulging her identity. The recent attempt to maneuver an elopement to take a girl's dowry and disgrace her family shocked Colonel Forster. The colonel was concerned and grateful for the information regarding a member of his regiment, and he promised to keep an eye on him. He had suspected a little of it already as he had seen Wickham's constant inclination to play cards with the other officers.

Mr. Darcy, weary from the interview, concluded his speech by giving the colonel the name and direction of his cousin Colonel Fitzwilliam. He asked that he contact his cousin for support if he had any questions or if anything happened of concern as he was familiar with Mr. Wickham's habits.

Mr. Darcy remained a few minutes to finish another glass of brandy after the colonel left the library before returning to the ballroom in a much lighter mood. He was feeling confident that, except for a necessary conference with Elizabeth's father, he had done much to protect the people of Meryton from Wickham's exploits. He strode through the ballroom until he could find a comfortable vantage point that allowed Elizabeth's beauty as she danced to wash through him and rest his mind.

He did not plan to decide tonight on whether or not to pay his addresses to her. He had detected reluctance on her part and wanted to be certain of her regard before he did. He loved her and had never felt anything like this about another woman. The matter of her family weighed heavily on him, but for tonight, he decided that he just wanted to return to the warmth he felt during their dance and the first portion of their meal. So, with his worries forced to the back of his mind, he looked forward to the last dance of the evening with her. He would not contemplate anything else tonight except enjoying her company. He would consider her family tomorrow... or the next day... or the next.

Elizabeth's mind was not so agreeably engaged. She still felt the sting of going from blissfully enjoying his company to seeing him retreat into himself at the impropriety of her family. They had often been a source of embarrassment, but her naturally cheerful disposition had always rescued her from their effect. Now, she could see the very real possibility that their behavior could cost her a love she was only barely starting to grasp with the best man of her acquaintance. When he came to claim her for the last set, she hesitated a moment before addressing him. "Mr. Darcy, I would understand, under the circumstances, if you would prefer to release your obligation to me for this set."

Her sincere, timid, trembling voice caused him to take an involuntary step closer to her. He turned his back to block the view from the rest of the ballroom and, placing a finger under her chin, raised her downcast eyes up to meet his.

She watched his dark eyes as he spoke firmly to her, "I do *not* release you. I enjoy your company, and I asked you to dance this set with me so that I might end my evening on the most agreeable terms possible. I want the image of your smile to stay with me, and I want the music of your laughter and voice to be amongst the last sounds I hear before retiring this evening." He paused and looked at her for a moment before adding, "Miss Elizabeth, will you do me the honor of this dance?"

With moisture gathering in her eyes from the relief caused by his declaration, she nodded her acceptance and bit her lip as he removed his hand from her face to clasp hers and lead her to the dance floor. She was more than halfway in love with him already, and she realized, with worry, that a separation now would cause a most acute pain. She looked at him as the music started and thought, *You, sir, are dangerous to my heart.*

Their dance was spent in silent intensity as neither felt the need to speak as they had during their first dance. Their thoughts and feelings concentrated on the touch and release of the dance, and the quiet privacy it afforded. When the music stopped, both seemed slightly surprised by the people around them, as the room had seemed to grow empty in their private moment.

With gentleness, Mr. Darcy led Elizabeth off the floor and stood near her in an alcove off of the vestibule as she waited for her family to gather and depart. Their silence was made comfortable by the unspoken feelings surrounding them.

The Bennet family was one of the last to leave, and when a servant came to hand the ladies their cloaks, Mr. Darcy retrieved Elizabeth's and tenderly draped it around her, tying the strings under her chin. He rested his hands on her shoulders for a brief moment before returning his arms to his side. She was so beautiful that he had nearly lost control. She blushed and was thankful that her family had already turned towards the door during his ministrations.

After one long look at her lovely face, Mr. Darcy bowed elegantly and said in a soft voice, "Good night, Miss Bennet."

She waited until he finished his bow before smiling serenely up at him. "Good night, Mr. Darcy."

She turned slowly with him to walk to the carriage. He and Bingley helped their particular ladies into the carriage, and if Mr. Darcy held her hand longer than was proper, nobody noticed in their happy musings of the evening. The gentlemen watched the carriage until it turned out of the drive and then returned to the house. Mr. Darcy immediately took the stairs up to his rooms in a deliberate attempt to avoid Bingley's sister.

Mrs. Bennet sat in happy contentment as she mused over the events of the evening. Mr. Bingley was never far from Jane, and Mr. Collins spent most of the evening with Mary, much to her surprise. Mr. Darcy had danced twice with Lizzy, which was more than he danced with anyone else all night. The younger girls had delightful stories to tell of the officers, and she had spent the evening gossiping with the other matrons.

"So, Jane, what of Mr. Bingley?" she asked her daughter.

"Mama!" Jane blushed, but smiled happily while one of her hands reached for Elizabeth's. "He did ask if he could call on me tomorrow."

Mrs. Bennet's excitement could not be contained in the carriage, and she spent the rest of the ride home mentally planning ways to allow the two of them a moment alone the next day. *Certainly all the man needs is a bit of privacy and he will get to the sticking point!*

Mr. Darcy dismissed his valet as soon as he reached his dressing room. He would manage by himself so that he could be alone with his thoughts. He shrugged out of his tailcoat and rested it on the chair. Next, he removed his stickpin and replaced it in the jewelry case. He paused in pulling at the folds of his neck cloth and let his mind drift, bringing forward the sensations of their last dance. He remembered the exquisite twinge he felt as her hand drifted across his shoulders during the turns of the dance. His thoughts led him to the admiration he felt as he watched her pleasing, graceful figure step and turn about the dance floor.

He removed his cravat and loosened the buttons of his shirt as he sank into the chair with a low groan. When he had helped her with her cloak, he had wanted nothing more than to kiss her sweetly. Never had he wanted to kiss a lady good night before, and it had taken all of his control to stop himself. She was just too lovely. Their quiet companionship in the last thirty minutes of the evening had been a balm to his warring, tired mind. His hand drifted unconsciously to lie across his chest over his beating heart. He was pulled from his fantasies when he noticed an irregularity in the folds of the fabric. Curious, he looked down as he reached into his waistcoat pocket and removed the silver flower that had torn off Elizabeth's shoe.

He smiled as he turned it around in his fingers. He had meant to return it to her so that she could repair her slipper, but he had forgotten. Now he was glad to have a piece of her to keep with him that evening since saying goodbye had been near torture. He raised the flower to his face, pressed it lightly to his lips and closed his eyes, returning to his memories.

After a few moments, he resumed his preparations to retire. He took up the small, silk flower again and looked at it happily before taking his pocket watch out of his jewelry case. Opening the lid of the watch, he kissed the flower before placing it tenderly behind the glass screen of the lid, opposite the clock face where a man might put a miniature of his wife or children. Now, every time he wanted to know the time, he would see the flower and think of her and that evening. He planned on checking the time quite often in the future. He liked the idea of keeping a part of her near him and close to his heart. He placed the watch back into its case and blew out the candles as he allowed that thought to lure him into a comfortable sleep.

Chapter 6

Sitting alone in his library, Mr. Bennet looked over the estate's account books. Having been absent from the previous evening's festivities, he relished the rare opportunity to enjoy the quiet of a sleeping household. Mr. Bennet did not usually attend assemblies and evenings out with his family, as he was generally more inclined to prefer the sanctuary of his library than the niceties of society. After settling a column in the book, he sat back in his leather chair, rested his hands behind his head and smiled as he looked towards the bay window and the view of the garden outside. He looked forward to these mornings when his family would sleep long after a late evening and he could enjoy the peaceful sounds of birds chirping and squirrels scavenging outside his study without the brumble of feminine chatter that usually welcomed his mornings.

A knock on the door interrupted his relaxation, and he smiled as he called to his favorite daughter, "Come in, Lizzy."

"Good morning, Papa." Elizabeth grinned as she entered and closed the door behind her before going to him and placing a tender kiss on his forehead.

"Good morning, my Lizzy. Why am I not surprised that you are up early this morning, my dear?"

Elizabeth smiled playfully and shrugged her shoulders. She sat on the bay window bench and looked out the window. Neither occupant of the room felt compelled to converse and instead enjoyed the morning sounds together for a while. Elizabeth smiled to herself as she considered her father a moment. She had awoken at first light as usual and stolen away to the library to share a moment with her father. She had done this since she was a little girl; there they would enjoy the peaceful calm of the morning and talk about whatever came to mind. She heard her father take up his quill to work on the books, and the sound caused her to look over her shoulder towards him.

Mr. Bennet was a man of nine and forty years with soft features that disguised his age. She loved the laugh lines around his eyes and mouth that betrayed him whenever he attempted to look stern. Elizabeth liked that she had inherited his eyes. They were always so expressive, and she often understood more from them than his words would reveal. She also had his dark, curly hair, though the years had turned his to a distinguished gray at the sides.

Mr. Bennet, detecting his daughter's gaze on him, looked up at her and smiled. "Well Lizzy, did you enjoy the ball last night?"

She smiled slightly as she turned her face from him, but not before he saw the blush spread across her cheeks. He wondered at her reaction to such a simple inquiry. Usually, she would laugh and relate the events of the evening. They would chuckle at the foolish antics of their neighbors as she described the humorous scenes from the evening's activities. Mr. Bennet's brows rose and furrowed as he looked expectantly towards his daughter.

A soft, "Yes, Papa, the evening was very enjoyable," came from the window seat.

He waited for more details but nothing more was offered. Elizabeth pretended interest in a particular tree outside the window as she tried to cool her suddenly flushed cheeks after a rush of memories washed over her. If she closed her eyes and concentrated, she could bring to her senses the memory of the pleasant scent Mr. Darcy wore and the vision of his elegant form. The image changed to one of his soft smile with a dimple visible as she sat beside him for supper. Occasionally, their arms had brushed against each other as they ate. The recollection sent a shiver down her spine, and she absently rubbed the goose bumps from her arms. Then she frowned as she remembered the way his dimple had disappeared when her sisters had disgracefully collided with his chair.

Mr. Bennet watched his daughter as a humorous smile played at the corners of his mouth. It instantly faded and his face lost a bit of its color when he caught her whispered question.

"Papa, how do you know if you are in love?"

It was not a question he had anticipated hearing any time soon. He struggled to form an answer as his mind had frozen at her inquiry. She remained turned away from him, and he was glad for it. He shifted in his chair, gathering his thoughts to answer, and looked again at her still form by the window. Immediately, his mind softened and his heart warmed. He stood and walked over to the window seat to sit beside her. Taking her hand, he looked at her until she slowly turned her eyes to him.

"Oh sweetie, I . . . well . . . " He struggled for words and finally, squeezing her hand, said, "Why don't you tell me about it."

As a father, he was not sure he really wanted to hear that his daughter had fallen in love. It was an impossible dilemma. Someday he wanted her to find someone to love and care for her, but he had his doubts as to the possibility of anyone being worthy enough. He was saddened at the thought of his little girl sharing with another man the heart that belonged to her papa.

Elizabeth lowered her eyes and spoke so quietly he had to strain to hear her words. "I do not know. There is this gentleman and . . . " Here she raised her impish eyes briefly to him, indicating she was not yet willing to divulge a name. She continued, her words starting to spill out of her at a quickened pace, "Well, when I am with him, my heart beats wildly, my mind goes from flashing dozens of thoughts to nothing at all and back again, and when I look into his eyes, a tingle surges up and down my spine."

Mr. Bennet wanted to frown, but he schooled his face to remain indifferent, even as part of him was amused at the delightful way she had waved her hands around in front of her while attempting to describe her feelings. Another patriarchal dilemma: he did not enjoy hearing his daughter relate feelings and *bodily* reactions invoked by a gentleman. He breathed deeply and tried to remind himself that it was bound to happen someday. He had just hoped to be dead before finding out his daughters were attracted to the undeserving opposite sex. And in his mind they were all undeserving. He had been a young man once and, well . . . he just would not—nay, could not—go there.

"And, suddenly, the simple moves of a dance set seemed to warm me terribly. Indeed, Papa, I cannot stop myself from blushing! I daresay his touch simply— "

"That will do, child." Mr. Bennet, for the sake of his unsteady composure, rushed to discontinue her descriptions. He patted her shoulder gently, clenched his teeth, and tried to sound unaffected. "It is natural for . . . uh . . . a lady to find a gentleman's features pleasing." He cleared his throat and pulled at his neck cloth. "But do not mistake, dear, the feelings of attraction for love." He knew all too well the consequences of such an error.

Elizabeth colored and kept her eyes downcast. However, as she was accustomed to speaking her mind and heart with her father, she boldly continued. "If it was merely an attraction, and I confess I find him very pleasing to look at..." Elizabeth paused briefly as an image of Mr. Darcy's roguish smile and dark eyes flashed before her mind, causing her to blush and her father to cringe slightly. Her voice softened and she looked towards the window with a faraway gaze. "But it is not just that. When I am with him, I find that his mind and his character are everything pleasing to me. His company is more enjoyable than any other's. I esteem him and value his good opinion. Our conversations are stimulating, and I believe we have many similarities."

Mr. Bennet smiled in response to the soft smile he now witnessed on her face. His heart broke a tiny bit at the idea that, indeed, he was losing his daughter's heart to another man. He told himself it was what he wanted for her. His marriage had not been fulfilling, and he did not relish the thought of the same plight for any of his daughters, especially his Lizzy. Although he suspected the identity of the gentleman she was referring to, he was not quite sure.

"Lizzy, what can you tell me about this 'gentleman' of yours. Shall we call him Mr. Gent?"

His attempt to lighten the atmosphere caused Elizabeth to laugh even as she said, "He is not *my* gentleman. But if you prefer it, Mr. Gent can be his name."

"Well, then, tell me about Mr. Gent."

Chuckling, she said, "He is a kind man, Papa. I think he is often misunderstood. I misunderstood him myself in the beginning. From what I have learned, I think he is rather shy, but I do not think he lacks confidence. He is well read; indeed, we like many of the same books. He has a sister whom he loves very dearly. She is his only family." Elizabeth stopped to admire again the devotion Mr. Darcy had shown when he spoke of Georgiana the previous evening.

"And does this Mr. Gent enjoy his work with Mr. Dennis in town?" Mr. Bennet waited for Elizabeth's reaction to his teasing insinuation that her gentleman was the butcher's apprentice.

Covering her mouth as a peel of laughter burst out, she cried, "No indeed, Papa!" She knew then that his teasing indicated that he had likely deduced the real identity of Mr. Gent, or else he would not have made such an absurd comment. As their laughter quieted, she blushed slightly.

"Do you think Mr. Gent is a good man, Papa?" she asked, quietly.

"I hardly know, Poppet. I have not had many opportunities to enjoy the pleasure of his company to ascertain that." Mr. Bennet paused before asking the question to which he dreaded receiving an answer. "Lizzy, do you believe Mr. Gent returns your affections?"

Elizabeth thought about his question for a few moments. It was clear to her that Mr. Darcy was not indifferent, but whether or not he held feelings more tender was not certain. Since her fall, he seemed much more inclined to concern himself with getting to know her. He had been less distant and forbearing. She could not deny that they had their brief moments of teasing and flirtation. She remembered, with a skip in the beat of her heart, the clear statement he had made about his wishes for their last dance. However, it had only been since her accident that he had been solicitous of her company. At Netherfield, he had only occasionally spoken to her and more than once appeared indifferent to her presence in the room.

"I cannot say for certain, Papa. He does not appear disinterested, and, indeed, at times he is very attentive. I do believe he enjoys conversing with me, but there are times I can tell that my presence near him is discomfiting."

Mr. Bennet was beginning to suspect that Mr. Gent did return feelings for his daughter, and the thought brought mixed feelings. He decided that he would need to brave society a bit more and observe the gentleman. He needed to get a better understanding of the man.

Elizabeth continued, "We have never really voiced our preference for each other. Perhaps if Mr. Gent felt similarly towards me, he would have said something." The thought weighed on her heart as she realized that, although they had many pleasing interactions, Mr. Darcy never indicated any preference towards her other than that statement before their last dance. It was not Elizabeth's nature to open her heart to anyone but her father, and indeed, it would have been improper for her to do so with Mr. Darcy before he indicated something himself. She had given him encouragement with her smiles and teasing conversation and so concluded that his heart must not be touched.

She leaned her head back against the wall and closed her eyes briefly. Her heart spoke that she should still hope, but the reasoning of her mind did not listen.

Mr. Bennet watched the actions of his daughter and, putting his own feelings aside, spoke tenderly to her. "Well, Lizzy, a man like Mr. Gent may not yet know his heart well enough to express his feelings. Do not let this trouble you. We gentlemen usually never know our heart until a lady comes to introduce it to us."

Elizabeth opened her eyes and smiled thoughtfully at her father. He had given her reason to hope.

Voices made their way through the house, indicating the rest of her family was beginning to stir. Reaching for her father's hand, she said, "Thank you, Papa. I believe our peace is about to be disturbed. Do you have much business today?"

"Not much, dear. I plan to go now on a ride about the property. There is a tenant I need to speak with and a fence I need to inspect, that is all."

"Would you care to come with me on a walk, perhaps this afternoon?"

"I look forward to it, dear."

"I, too, sir. I think I will go see Jane now. We did not get a chance to speak last night, and I suspect she will have much to talk about." With a wink and a kiss on his cheek, she left the room.

He watched her exit and remained for a moment looking at the closed door. *Where did the years go?* With a heavy heart and a small sigh, he rose and prepared to leave for his ride.

Mr. Bingley and Mr. Darcy tipped their hats to each other as they parted ways on the road outside of the gates of Netherfield. Mr. Darcy was out for his morning ride and Mr. Bingley was headed to Longbourn.

Mr. Bingley's horse could feel his rider's nervousness. He flicked his head side-to-side, flinging his mane and blowing out a huff of steam from his nostrils in protest of his master's distraction. In response to his horse's protests, Mr. Bingley patted his head and gave in to a faster pace. He was headed to Longbourn to speak to Jane and request permission to court her. He could not understand why his heart was beating so soundly at the thought. He knew that, if he was honest with himself, he really wanted to ask her a different question—one that would bind her to him for the rest of their lives. Although he felt she was partial to him — indeed, he believed she loved him as he loved her — he decided instead to ask to court her. His intentions were honorable, but he did not want to move too quickly. If he knew for certain that she would be amenable to the idea, he would have proposed last night. Thinking of his lovely Jane made him smile and caused his heart to skip a beat. *Oh, my sweet Jane. You are an angel!*

Mr. Bingley spent the rest of the ride to Longbourn imagining how Jane would look when he arrived. Would she wear that pretty yellow dress she wore last Sunday that he liked so much? He tried to formulate plans for getting an opportunity to speak with her privately. *Perhaps a walk in the gardens?*

After discussing a needed repair with a tenant, Mr. Bennet mounted his horse and began his ride back home. About a quarter mile from the house, there was a small rise in the land that provided an excellent vantage point of the surrounding area. It was where he often stopped his horse and gazed at his home, just visible in the distance. Upon reaching the summit, he came upon another rider sitting motionless, with his eyes fixed on Longbourn.

He was surprised to see that the other rider did not acknowledge his approach and was amused when the gentleman turned only as Mr. Bennet's horse moved beside his.

Startled from his reverie, Mr. Darcy shifted slightly at the sudden appearance of Mr. Bennet next to him. He was instantly embarrassed at his distraction and at being caught woolgathering, especially by the father of the woman about whom he was thinking.

"Mr. Bennet, sir. I did not hear your approach."

"Mr. Darcy, good day. No, I believe you were quite otherwise occupied. This rise is a particular favorite of mine as it provides a vast view of the area. Tell me, what particular prospect has caught your interest?" Mr. Bennet could not help the provocation.

Mr. Darcy hid his embarrassment well as he turned to his companion. "Nothing in particular, sir. It is as you say: the area provides a vast view and I stopped to admire it all." He hoped his feigned indifference was convincing. He had been out riding that morning to try to clear his thoughts — and also to avoid Miss Bingley — when he discovered the small hill. To his delight, he recognized that from there he could see Longbourn. He was simply unable for a time to turn from the view, wondering what Elizabeth might be doing and what she was thinking. He had been picturing her impertinent smile, bright eyes and pink lips when his thoughts were interrupted by her father. He cringed inside at the luck of it and attempted to clear his thoughts with a deep breath as he turned to Mr. Bennet.

"Mr. Bennet, sir, are you out for a ride this morning?" He did not know the man very well and decided, since he needed to speak with him about Wickham, he had better begin with some neutral topic.

"I am, sir. I had some business to conduct on the south end of my estate. I came this way to inspect a fence nearby. Would you accompany me, sir? I understand you have an estate of your own, and I would value your opinion." As much as he wished he had no need, Mr. Bennet knew he should try to get to know the gentleman on his right because, if it was as he suspected, the man was in possession of one of his dearest treasures: his Lizzy's heart.

"It would be my pleasure. My estate, Pemberley, is in Derbyshire." He attempted to mimic the levity in Mr. Bennet's voice as he turned his horse to follow him.

Thus began a pleasant discussion of land management, drainage and crop rotation. Though stilted at first, Mr. Bennet's natural, unaffected personality and Mr. Darcy's enjoyment of estate management soon made conversation easy.

Mr. Darcy was surprised to find in Mr. Bennet a man of great thought and less indolence than he had come to understand. He had heard that Mr. Bennet was not a competent property manager, and while the estate had once brought in six thousand a year, it was generally believed that it now produced only two thousand. He could not suppose that the thorough, knowledgeable man he was speaking with could be anything less than an excellent manager of his estate. *Then why the rumors of his diminished wealth?*

At the same time, Mr. Bennet was finding in Mr. Darcy an impressively intelligent gentleman who took the affairs of his estate seriously, unlike many of his generation who left much of their business to stewards as they lived lives of leisure. It impressed him that Mr. Darcy was so knowledgeable at such a young age. As they discussed various details pertaining to typical estate matters, he found Mr. Darcy's forward thinking impressed him greatly. His suggestion for the problem with the fence they had inspected was not only clever but it would cut the costs of the repair significantly without lowering the quality of the workmanship.

After finishing their inspection, Mr. Darcy turned to his companion. "Mr. Bennet, it is fortunate that you came upon me today. There is something I had intended to discuss with you."

Mr. Bennet snapped his teeth together and tried to appear indifferent to the words that had once again set his mind thinking about losing Elizabeth. He hoped that was not what Mr. Darcy wanted to discuss because, although he had come to respect the gentleman greatly in the short half hour they had spent together, he was not yet ready to hear the words that would take his Lizzy away. He simply nodded for Mr. Darcy to continue, fearing his composure might give way if he spoke.

"Mr. Bennet, it has come to my attention that your youngest daughters have made the acquaintance of a certain member of the regiment in Meryton with whom I am also acquainted."

The relief that flooded through Mr. Bennet at that moment almost made him laugh out loud, and he spoke with a slight chuckle in his voice. "Indeed, sir. I am sure they have made many acquaintances amongst the officers. Of whom do you speak?"

"Of a Mr. Wickham, sir." Mr. Darcy's voice was grave, and the sound of it depressed Mr. Bennet's lively demeanor.

With furrowed brows, he replied, "I have heard them speak of him; however, I have not had the opportunity to meet the man. You say you know the gentleman?"

"He is no gentleman." Mr. Darcy spoke harshly but then quickly recovered from his sudden anger. "I apologize, sir. I do not want to presume to tell you what you ought to do with your own household, but I feel it incumbent upon me to warn you that your daughters are not safe with Mr. Wickham."

The steely set of Mr. Darcy's jaw made Mr. Bennet curious at his strong reaction to Mr. Wickham, and he felt it necessary to ask the nature of their acquaintance. Darcy's pain at having to disclose some particulars of his relationship with Wickham became evident to Mr. Bennet, and he was thankful to Darcy for taking the opportunity to warn him. That such a scoundrel could be amongst society and not be known was unbelievable to Mr. Bennet.

Mr. Darcy had not intended to go into specifics with regards to his history with Wickham, but something about Mr. Bennet had reminded him of the wisdom of his own father. Before even realizing it, he had related the whole of his history, including the painful betrayal of Georgiana. It had felt like a purge to his system finally to talk about it. It surprised him that the only other person besides his cousin Colonel Fitzwilliam to know of what happened at Ramsgate would be, of all people, Elizabeth's father.

"Mr. Darcy, I must thank you for warning me about Mr. Wickham. I can assure you that, after hearing what you know of the man, I will not allow him further acquaintance with any of my daughters. You are a good man for being willing to lay out your personal dealings, some of which I can see are quite troublesome to you, in order to protect my family. I assure you that you have my secrecy regarding what you have told me. I will not betray your confidence regarding the pain you and your sister have been dealt at the hand of Mr. Wickham, but I will protect my family. I trust that I may do whatever is necessary with your permission?"

"Yes, sir. I have come to respect Miss Bennet and Miss Elizabeth as our acquaintance has furthered during my stay in Hertfordshire, and I would not wish to see either of them, or someone they care for, pained by the likes of Mr. Wickham. I have already informed Colonel Forster about his character, and he has promised to keep a close eye on the man. It is the most I can do," he added, with frustration.

"You have done more than enough, sir. Let the rest of us take it from here, and do not let it trouble you further." He offered Mr. Darcy his hand and was gratified when it was readily accepted. "Well, Mr. Darcy, my estate business is concluded. Would you care to join me back at Longbourn for a glass of brandy? You look as if you could use one after this discourse."

Mr. Bennet watched as, at the mention of returning home with him, Mr. Darcy's gaze fixed on the direction of Longbourn despite it no longer being in view. He seemed to think about it for a minute and even smiled a little bit.

"I thank you, sir, but I cannot accept for today. Our previous discussion on estate matters reminded me of a letter I must send to my steward at Pemberley regarding a matter of concern we are working through. Perhaps another time." Mr. Darcy pulled out his watch to check the time, and a sudden smile spread across his face as he caught a glimpse of the silk flower hidden in it. He had forgotten about placing it there the night before, and he was sorely tempted to change his mind and accept Mr. Bennet's invitation, but he could not. He had ridden out that morning to clear his thoughts a bit, and seeing Elizabeth would not help that at all—however tempting it was.

With obvious reluctance, he bid his farewell with thanks for the pleasant company and shook Mr. Bennet's hand again.

"I enjoyed our conversation, too, Mr. Darcy. I may pick your brain again sometime about that four-crop rotation plan you say you implemented last year at Pemberley."

"It would be my pleasure, sir. Good day."

"Good day, Mr. Darcy."

Mr. Bennet waited only a moment before turning his horse away and riding in the direction of home. He felt a little less concerned over losing Lizzy to such a man. Although he was not sure whether he would ever find a man truly worthy of his bright and witty little girl, he was beginning to think Mr. Darcy came pretty close. Oddly, Mr. Bennet had begun to think of Mr. Darcy as a son not long into their amicable conversation. Mr. Bennet admitted to himself that if he had had a son, he hoped he would have turned out much like Mr. Darcy. Riding about the estate and inspecting it with Mr. Darcy brought back visions he had had for himself and the son he was sure he would produce but had not. He pondered these strange impressions all the way back to Longbourn and further as he settled himself into his chair in the library with a glass of brandy. His thoughts returned to the discussion earlier with Lizzy regarding Mr. Darcy. *When is a father allowed to stop worrying about the happiness of his children?* The answer was never. He took another drink.

Chapter 7

When the house came into view, Mr. Bingley sat up straighter in his seat and nervously fingered his cravat. He had asked his valet to tie it into a more formal knot than was usually appropriate for a simple morning call. He hoped that it would present him in the most favorable light to his Jane, but as the house came closer, he repented that request, as now the knot began to feel restrictive around his neck.

No sooner had he dismounted than the doors of the house opened and Mrs. Bennet came quickly out to greet him.

"Mr. Bingley, you are welcome to Longbourn. Did you have a pleasant ride, sir?"

"Indeed, I did, ma'am," he replied, smiling widely at her.

One hand instantly rose to cover her beating heart even as the other fanned her face. He marveled at the flush of her face, and he considered it odd that she appeared about to swoon at his smile. He turned his gaze towards the door and noticed Jane standing in the entryway. All thoughts of her mother's strange behavior vanished at the vision of the woman he loved.

Jane was exquisite in a light blue morning dress that matched her eyes perfectly. The yellow dress was forgotten at seeing the way the blue complemented and warmed the ivory softness of her skin. Her smile was delightful, and he could not believe his good fortune that she was, indeed, happily greeting his arrival. He returned a broad smile and broke into a long stride to close the distance to her.

"Miss Bennet, good morning to you." He bowed over her hand as she curtsied.

"Welcome to Longbourn, sir." She blushed slightly at his light touch and stepped aside to allow him access to the house.

A few moments later found Mr. Bingley seated awkwardly in a room full of women. Mary was reading, ignoring everyone. Lydia and Kitty were uncharacteristically silent as they sat boldly inspecting his person. Elizabeth was seated beside Jane on the sofa next to his chair. Mrs. Bennet's gaze, much in the same vein as her youngest daughters, was also fixed on him in a manner that made him want to look anywhere but at her.

For a few minutes, nobody spoke. Finally, Mr. Bingley cleared his throat and addressed Mrs. Bennet. "I hope that your family is well this morning, Mrs. Bennet."

"You are all kindness. We are well this morning. My Jane looks especially well, does she not, sir?"

Jane blushed and shifted a quick, uneasy glance at Elizabeth. Mr. Bingley was not discomfited at all by the comment, enjoying the opportunity it gave him to rest his eyes on Jane. "Indeed, ma'am, she looks exceedingly well this morning."

He watched with a satisfied smile as the blush spread further across her face.

"Thank you, sir," she softly replied.

With the help of Elizabeth and Mr. Bingley, the conversation began with a pleasant recital of the previous evening's festivities. All the ladies had compliments to give on the enjoyable evening at Netherfield. Even Mary voiced an uncharacteristically satisfied opinion of the outcome of the evening.

"I am glad that you all enjoyed yourselves. For myself, I cannot think of a more pleasant time than I spent last night." Bingley glanced significantly at Jane.

At that moment, the door opened, and Mr. Collins entered. He made his usual officious greeting to Mr. Bingley and then took a seat next to Mary. Mr. Bingley noted with amusement the obvious preference each showed in the company of the other.

After another few moments, Mr. Bingley began to feel that his time was running short, yet he had not had the chance to speak with Jane alone. His natural modesty made him question whether Jane would accept with pleasure his request to court her. As he considered the unhappy alternative, his eyes moved to settle on her. As if sensing his gaze, she looked to him and smiled brightly in her shy way before lowering her eyes back to her hands in her lap.

It was enough. He sat up and, with a happy countenance, began to speak.

"It is such a lovely day. I would like to take a walk. Perhaps Miss Bennet and Miss Elizabeth would care to join me?"

He eyed Jane significantly and was happy to hear her acceptance. Elizabeth, having seen the particular way he looked at her sister, knew that her own presence was not necessarily wished for, and she decided that she would find some way to allow them time alone.

Jane and Elizabeth rose to retrieve their pelisses and bonnets. Once they reached their room, Elizabeth turned to Jane and, holding both her hands, smiled knowingly.

"I know that look, Lizzy, and you must not think it."

With pretended offense, Elizabeth responded, "Jane! I do not know what you mean!" Seeing Jane smile and shake her head, Elizabeth gave her another knowing smile.

"Lizzy!"

"Dear Jane, you know my opinion as we spoke at length of it this morning, and you shall not convince me that he is merely a friend to you."

"I only said that I believed him to be *inclined* towards me, but that is hardly being in love—"

Elizabeth's groan interrupted her sister, and she rolled her eyes. "Yes, yes, dear, you did say that. And I said that you could not make him more in love with you if you tried." Elizabeth gave her blushing sister a warm hug. "And furthermore, it is your luck that you are, indeed, hopelessly in love with Mr. Bingley too. At least on this point, I believe we may agree, do we not?"

Jane smiled softly at her sister. "I believe we do."

"Well then, shall we join the gentleman downstairs?"

"We shall, indeed." Jane's smile widened.

The ladies descended the staircase and, upon meeting Mr. Bingley, exited the house towards the gardens.

As soon as the guest and his cousins left the morning room, Mr. Collins decided it was the right time to make a request of his hostess. He turned in his seat and, with an air of confidence that his request would be given ready approval, said, "Mrs. Bennet. I wonder if I may request the honor of a private audience with your daughter this morning."

Mrs. Bennet could not think of happier words to have come out of Mr.

Collins's mouth in the course of his whole visit. She was so lost in the satisfied musings of her luck in the attentions of Mr. Bingley to Jane—and now Mr. Collins's request—that she almost forgot to respond.

"Of course, Mr. Collins, you may have your audience with any of my sweet daughters." She glanced from Lydia to Kitty, whose faces were locked in shocked amusement at their cousin's request. She then briefly looked at her daughter Mary and dismissed the idea. *Elizabeth! Of course, he must mean Elizabeth. Oh, wretched mistake, she has left with Mr. Bingley!* Mrs. Bennet rose quickly and said hurriedly to Mr. Collins, "I will just go get her, sir. You will not have to wait."

"Mrs. Bennet, I would like to speak with Miss Mary if I may." Even as he said this, he turned his head and tilted it with a smile at Mary, who returned his look blankly.

"Mary?!" Mrs. Bennet exclaimed in obvious amazement but recovered quickly. "Of course, sir. Mary, you will stay here and hear Mr. Collins." Not wanting to waste a single opportunity, she turned to her youngest daughters and snapped them out of their shocked state. "Lydia, Kitty—I wish to speak to you; follow me." With giggles, the girls exited the room with their mother.

As soon as the door closed behind the ladies, Mr. Collins slid to one knee and grabbed one of Mary's hands, causing the girl to startle at the familiarity.

He began speaking rapidly. "Miss Mary, you cannot mistake the meaning of my request to speak to you. Indeed, I am sure you are aware of the special attention I have paid you during my visit to Longbourn. Please allow me to impart to you my reasons for seeking your hand. Firstly, it is the implicit request of my noble patroness, Lady Catherine de Bourgh, that I set the example of matrimony to the people of my parish. Indeed, her condescension is most generous. Secondly, I am convinced that marriage will bring me much happiness. And lastly, my marriage to you will resolve the distress your family feels on the subject of the entail of this estate."

"Mr. Collins, are you asking me to marry you?" Mary asked incredulously.

"Indeed, I am, and you have made me the happiest of men!"

"You are too hasty, sir. You forget I have not given you my answer. If you please, I have some questions before I can do so."

"Ask away, Mary, my delight, my sweet!" Mr. Collins brought her hands to his lips and squished them against her knuckles.

"Sir, what is your home like?" she asked, removing her hand from his grasp.

"My home is called Hunsford, and it is a splendid home of modest size in Kent. It is located on the edge of Lady Catherine de Bourgh's great estate, Rosings Park."

"And you say, sir, your income is sufficient to support a wife and children?"

"It is. As you well know, I am greatly blessed with the patronage of her ladyship, and as such, I am never without. Indeed, Lady Catherine often condescends to have me to tea or to dinner at least once a week."

Mary thought on his answers for a moment. As she was not romantically inclined and never had any ambition to marry—indeed, she had never thought she would—she considered the prospect placed before her. It would mean her own home away from the noise of her family, who never seemed to appreciate her moral homilies. If she were to marry, she admitted to herself, the morality of a parson was most suited to her. He would probably want an heir, especially as he was to inherit Longbourn. That was not a happy prospect but she concluded she would make do. Lastly, though it did not mean much to her, she could save the entail of her family's estate.

"I accept, sir," she stated solemnly.

"Mary, angel of my heart, once I have gained the consent of your father, we shall marry as soon as possible!" he exclaimed excitedly as he once again claimed her hand in his.

"How soon did you have in mind, sir?"

"A week, dear, no later. Her ladyship does not wish me to stay away longer than a fortnight. You would not want to upset her; indeed, I know you would not."

Mary shrugged her shoulders and, once again pulling her hand from his grasp, replied, "I cannot see a reason to delay. Do as you wish, sir." With this, she resumed possession of her book and continued reading. Mr. Collins, being too excited to sit quietly, informed her he would just ask her father's consent and be back in her lovely presence as soon as he could. Nodding her assent, she waved him off, and he went in search of Mr. Bennet to relay the happy news.

Mr. Bennet was nursing his glass when an unwelcome knock was heard on his study door. With resignation and no small amount of distaste, he called, "Enter!"

Upon seeing Mr. Collins open the door, Mr. Bennet let out a low groan.

This was going to be worse than he thought. He should not have acknowledged the knock, and now he would have to entertain the oaf. "Good morning, Mr. Collins," he said gravely.

"Good morning to you, too, sir. It is, indeed, a good morning—a most glorious morning!"

"Indeed," Mr. Bennet murmured with no attempt to hide his boredom.

"Sir, I have come here to speak to you on a most important matter. I have asked your daughter Mary to be my wife, and she has accepted. I come here to receive your consent and ask that we be allowed to marry at the end of the week. Lady Catherine does not wish for me to be gone long from my duties, and I wish to return to Hunsford married. Indeed, the thought of being separated from my dear Mary quite breaks my heart," he said, dramatically placing a hand over his heart.

Mr. Bennet's astonishment was great, and he blinked several times before the words spewing from Mr. Collins's mouth registered in his mind. "Mr. Collins, sir, would you care to sit? Before you make haste for the church, allow me a moment to speak with you."

Mr. Collins sat and started to open his mouth to say something when Mr. Bennet stopped him with a raised hand. "Mr. Collins, you say Mary has accepted your offer of marriage, correct?" He rubbed his head when he heard Mr. Collins's eager acknowledgement of the fact. Before Collins could continue with descriptions of his future marital felicity, Mr. Bennet interjected, "Mr. Collins, before I give my consent, I have one question to ask you."

"Yes, sir."

"Mr. Collins, could you tell me why you want to marry my daughter?" He fixed his gaze at the man and held it steady; the answer was very important to him.

"You will be gratified to hear that it was at the insistence of my noble patroness, Lady Catherine de Bourgh, that I marry. I would like to marry your daughter because I believe her ladyship will approve of Mary, and I am convinced that Mary will add to my future happiness, especially when we have her ladyship's approval."

Mr. Bennet hung his head as his company began to extol on the many benefits he was offering to Mary upon their marriage, most notably a long list of satisfactory opportunities to interact with the great lady at Rosings. He tuned out the officious diatribe and, with sadness, realized that at least one of his daughters was not going to marry with real love. He knew Mr. Collins did not love Mary, and he suspected his daughter did not love him. He would need to learn her feelings on the matter.

Abruptly cutting off the parson's speech, Mr. Bennet said, "I give my consent sir. Now be off with you."

Mr. Collins had not noticed the harsh tone or the clear incivility directed towards him, and he eagerly bowed and exited the room, excited to relay the news to the rest of the family.

Mr. Bingley offered an arm to each of the ladies as they entered the garden. There was a slight breeze, but the air was unusually warm for early December. It was so pleasant just to be outside, that for a few minutes nobody in the party spoke. Mr. Bingley stole sly glances at Jane, who was enjoying the feel of his soft coat under her hand.

"You have a very pleasant space here." Mr. Bingley spoke as if to either of the ladies, but Elizabeth saw that his eyes flicked to Jane.

"Thank you, Mr. Bingley. I have often admired the gardens at Netherfield Park, as well, sir. They are quite extensive," Jane replied.

He led them to a small copse of trees, and Elizabeth released his arm, feigning an interest in some wild ferns at the base of a tree. "I believe you said you were from the north, Mr. Bingley?"

"That is correct, Miss Elizabeth. My family is from Scarborough. I have an aunt there still."

"It can be very cold there, can it not?" Jane offered.

This was what Elizabeth had hoped to do, introduce a topic of conversation comfortable for both. She knew Jane found everything about Mr. Bingley interesting, and she figured he would be comfortable discussing something familiar to him. She continued her interest in the ferns as she listened to them continue the conversation.

"The winters are not as mild as they are in Hertfordshire, to be sure. While I enjoyed living there until I went off to school, I find the entertainments of London and the country delights that can be found in Hertfordshire more to my liking." He spoke with a significant glance towards Jane.

Elizabeth turned towards her sister and, with feigned innocence, said, "Mr. Bingley, Jane, I beg you will excuse me. This is such lovely wild lavender, and it is the last of the season. I cannot let it be wasted; I will just take it to the house to be dried."

Jane glared at her sister's obvious excuse and made as if to return to the house too, but Elizabeth forestalled her. "No, Jane, Mr. Bingley, I shan't be long. Do continue your walk, and I will join you again shortly." She smiled sweetly at Jane and curtsied to Bingley before either could protest. Jane shook her head slightly at the mischief in her sister's eyes.

Thank you, Miss Elizabeth! Mr. Bingley silently appreciated this easy solution for getting a moment alone with Jane. They both watched Elizabeth's retreat before turning towards each other.

Mr. Bingley offered his arm. "Shall we continue, then, Miss Bennet?"

"I would like that, thank you." She slipped her gloved hand onto his arm.

Mr. Bingley had anticipated the soft pressure of her hand and smiled when he felt it. He loved that she was so delicate and feminine. In a moment of boldness, he turned towards her with a tender smile as his other hand came up to cover hers. His smile spread as he watched her cheeks blush and the corners of her mouth come up in a small smile.

"Miss Bennet, I have something I had hoped to discuss with you today." His voice was low and so close to her ear that she felt a shiver as it moved the soft curls near her temple.

For a brief moment, Jane felt a little faint and had to swallow before asking, "And what is it you wished to discuss, sir?"

"Well, Miss Bennet, I thought to tell you that I believe you have an admirer." He held his breath for her reaction. His wait was short as he saw her smile broadly and chanced a glance up to him before replying.

"Indeed, sir? I did not know that. Pray, tell me, who might this admirer be?"

My, what a sweet little temptress you are, Jane! "He is an acquaintance of yours and has told me that he has come to find your company most pleasing."

"Is that so?" She bit her lip at their charade.

Mr. Bingley's smile grew even wider as he leaned closer and, with a low voice, responded, "Indeed. In fact, I believe he finds your company more pleasing than any other lady of his acquaintance." He paused to gauge her reaction and happily continued when she looked at him with amusement. "I am certain your admirer has come to believe you are the most beautiful creature he has ever seen."

Jane's breath hitched as she listened to his pleasant overtures. For a moment, she could do nothing but nod slightly in recognition of them. Mr.

Bingley brought them to a stop at a stone bench and helped her to sit before placing himself next to her.

"Do you think you could consent to a courtship with the gentleman?" Mr. Bingley looked at her intently in anticipation of her answer.

The happiness that then filled Jane's heart was beyond what she could have imagined. She looked into his blue eyes and saw a sweetness there that melted her heart. She turned her face away in shyness at the raw feeling exposed in his gaze.

With a slight smile, she teased, "I am sorry, sir. I cannot enter into a courtship with this admirer." When she saw the color drain from his face, she hastened to continue, "For I could not consent to a courtship with any other gentleman than yourself, sir, as my feelings are quite fixed on the matter."

Mr. Bingley felt like pulling her into his arms and placing light kisses all over her face. He was elated at her words and smiled brightly as he said, with a laugh, "Well then, Miss Bennet, it so happens that I see no cause to object to your reasoning." He paused and locked his eyes with hers before saying tenderly, "Miss Bennet, would you consent to allow me to court you?"

"I would like that very much, Mr. Bingley," she responded shyly.

Mr. Bingley reached for her hand and relished in the freedom to do so. "You have made me very happy, Jane."

Jane had long imagined the sound of her name coming from his lips; to hear it brought contentment to her heart. The sound replayed over and over in her mind with an exquisite echo. It was not strictly proper for him to use her Christian name as they were not engaged, only courting, but she would not protest.

They spoke softly to each other for a few minutes longer before Jane suggested that they should return to the house. As they began walking, Elizabeth came into view, and Mr. Bingley leaned close to Jane's ear to whisper, "I will go and ask your father's consent now." When she nodded, he smiled and walked directly towards the house.

Elizabeth smiled as she saw the exchange and waited until he was out of hearing before turning to her sister. "Well, Jane?"

"Oh, Lizzy, how can it be possible to feel so much joy?"

Her sister embraced her quickly and said, as she pulled back, "It is only possible for such a person as you, Jane, for you are too good to deserve anything less. Tell me all."

"He has asked if he could court me, Lizzy; he is even now gone to our father. Can this be real? I feel as if I am in a dream."

Laughing, Elizabeth took her sister's arm and led her towards the house. "It is real, but if you would like, I can pinch you to make sure it is not a dream."

Jane laughed and squeezed her sister's arm. As they walked to the house, the sisters' heads were in close confidence as Jane related the conversation she had had with Mr. Bingley. They entered the house and went towards the morning room to await his return.

Mr. Bennet lowered his head to his desk. The coolness of the wood soothed him. It was not in Mr. Bennet's nature to remain melancholy, though, and soon he began to see the humor in the day's events. This morning had been an intriguing time of discoveries. Lizzy had fallen in love. Mr. Darcy had proven himself to be less proud and more generous. Mr. Collins and Mary had proven greater fools than he had previously suspected. And he had been reminded more than once that time had slipped away from him.

With these thoughts, he laughed slightly in disbelief at the sound of another knock on his door. He grumbled to himself, "By all means, let the whole world intrude upon my sanctuary today!" Laughing humorlessly, he called out yet again, "Enter!"

Mr. Bingley opened the door, walked right up to Mr. Bennet with his usual jovial stride and offered his hand. "Mr. Bennet, I have come to ask your consent to court your daughter Miss Bennet."

Mr. Bennet shook Mr. Bingley's hand and laughed as once again he was taken by surprise. "You are direct, sir!"

Mr. Bingley laughed, too, and took a seat. "I apologize if my manner was abrupt. You see, sir, I have had the great pleasure on many instances of getting to know your daughter over the past few weeks. I find that she is one of the most delightful women I know. My feelings for her have grown over the course of my time in the country. I could wait no longer and have asked her permission to court her so that I may get to know her better. She has accepted, and now I come to you for your approval. I promise you, sir, my intentions are honorable. I wish to further my acquaintance with her and hope, in doing so, that she may come to have the same hopes for the future that I have."

Mr. Bennet sat back in his chair as he listened to Mr. Bingley's speech.

What a difference it made, having a man approach him with feelings and wishes for affection regarding his daughter. Although he was sure this meant that he was likely to lose Jane soon, too, it soothed him a bit to know that theirs would be a love match. He rubbed his jaw and, with humor hidden in his eyes, looked gravely at Mr. Bingley until long after the man ceased to speak. Mr. Bennet tried to keep from smiling as he watched the gentleman become more and more ill at ease at his silence. He knew Mr. Bingley was a kind and unassuming man just like his Jane, and they would be a good match. He waited only another minute to tease the man further before giving his answer.

"Well, sir. As you have been direct with me, I shall be so with you. I consent."

Mr. Bingley's face radiated his sudden relief and happiness, and he abruptly stood to shake Mr. Bennet's hand vigorously. "Thank you sir, you will not have reason to repent of this decision." With that, he turned and hastily left the study.

Mr. Bennet stood and went to the sideboard to pour himself another small amount of brandy. He held it to his mouth and paused. Three daughters going or soon to be gone. Once again, he asked himself as he shook his head, *where has the time gone?* He tipped the glass and swallowed the liquid in one gulp, squeezing his eyes at the burn in his throat. With a disbelieving chuckle, he said aloud to the empty room, "The day is not yet over; perhaps before the end of it, some young gentleman will come for Kitty or Lydia." With amusement, he placed his glass on the table and went to join the others in the morning room to inform Mrs. Bennet of the new courtship.

Upon entering the room, Elizabeth and Jane were taken aback by the suddenly advancing form of their cousin.

"My dear cousins, welcome back from your walk. We have a bit of news to relate to you."

Elizabeth and Jane looked at each other in wonderment and shrugged as they took their seats. Mr. Collins snapped his hands together excitedly, causing his neck to jiggle. His face contorted into a greasy smile as he continued.

"I am not to be cousin to you any longer; indeed, I am to be something much more dear." At the look of astonishment on their faces, his smile grew wider and he looked towards Mary and gave her a small wave of his hand.

"I can see your surprise, but I shall not keep you waiting. I am to be called brother to you now. Your father has given his consent, and your sister, my dear Mary, and I are to be wed at the end of the week!"

If their astonishment was great before, they were perfectly frozen now at the news their cousin related. Numbly looking at Mary, Elizabeth's eyes grew wide upon seeing her sister nod her confirmation. Jane was quicker to recover and offered her congratulations to the couple. After a moment, Elizabeth was stirred out of her disbelief by the slight nudge from Jane's elbow.

With a voice devoid of emotion, she replied, "Congratulations. I wish you joy." Nothing else needed to be said, for Mrs. Bennet then began to extol again and again her joy in seeing one of her daughters find such an excellent match. This allowed Elizabeth to recover herself just in time to see Mr. Bingley enter the room, followed after a few minutes by her father. While Mr. Bingley was informed of the news, Elizabeth glanced to see how her father bore it. She could tell that he was slightly distressed at something, even though he looked at the couple with amusement. When he turned towards her, he smiled sardonically and slightly shook his head. All she could do was shrug her shoulders.

After extending his congratulations to the newly engaged couple, Mr. Bingley went directly to claim the seat next to Jane. He leaned over to her and spoke softly. "So there is to be a wedding in the future," he said, his voice heavy with suggestion.

Jane looked sweetly at him. "So it appears, sir." If she noticed the implication in his words, she did not show it.

He winked at her then and proclaimed with a broad smile, "Your father gave his consent."

When the excitement of the engagement calmed down a bit, Mr. Bennet announced to the room that Mr. Bingley had asked for his consent to court Jane, and he had granted it. This news caused Mrs. Bennet a new wave of excited fits, and Mr. Bennet took the opportunity to exit the room and return to the peace of his study, but not before whispering to Elizabeth that he would not be walking with her that day. She understood his feelings from the expression in his eyes and nodded her acceptance. Once back to the solitude of his favorite room, he locked the door and sat down. He had much to think about.

Chapter 8

Mr. Darcy rested his head against the tall frame of an armchair in the Netherfield library. He propped one of his Hessian boots across the other leg and began absentmindedly brushing the tassel with his fingers. His forgotten book lay on his lap. The more he thought about the letter he received from Georgiana that morning, the more he worried about her. He could tell she was trying to sound cheerful in her accounts of her studies, progress with the pianoforte and outings with Mrs. Annesley, her companion. The letter was just too calm, too perfect. It was not right. Georgiana never hesitated speaking her mind in the past, and those letters usually portrayed a combination of moods. Her most recent ones were mostly insipid, dull accounts of nothing.

Groaning, Mr. Darcy dropped his leg, leaned forward with his elbows on his knees and rubbed his face. His heart pained him every time he thought about the broken spirit of his sister. He felt partially responsible for it. *If only I had been more careful about checking the references of Mrs. Younge before hiring her as Georgiana's companion.* Instead, he had given her papers only a cursory inspection before approving her. He had been in a hurry to get on his way to Cambridge to meet with some former classmates for a few days. In her character, he was seriously deceived, and he blamed himself for not discovering her connection to Wickham.

For six months, she and Georgiana seemed to get along nicely, and he had prided himself in having done well. When Mrs. Younge approached him to suggest that Georgiana could benefit from a holiday away from her studies and perhaps a visit to the seaside would be pleasing to her, he had agreed. He was in the habit of indulging his younger sister.

He anticipated surprising her a week after she arrived in Ramsgate. He had just finished a meeting in Kent with his Aunt Catherine's steward, and as the business had gone well, he was able to leave three days earlier than he intended. As he had frequently since that day, Darcy lifted his head in a solemn prayer of thanks that he arrived when he did, for it was but a day before the planned departure to Gretna Green. Wickham, with the help of Mrs. Younge, had convinced Georgiana that surprising her brother with their marriage *fait accompli* would bring him such joy, especially as it was to an old, dear, childhood friend.

Darcy flinched and closed his hands into fists as he remembered his arrival in Ramsgate, finding his sister on a settee with Wickham—and Mrs. Younge nowhere to be seen. He had opened the door to the sitting room himself, asking not to be announced as he wanted the full effect of his sister's surprise upon his entrance. Instead, his chest clenched and his eyes narrowed in horror at the sight of that blackguard holding his sister's hands.

"Georgiana." His voice was fierce and hard as steel.

Georgiana snapped her head around at the sound of her brother's voice and jumped up from the settee to run into his embrace. Her happiness at his appearance was so evident in her features and her surprise so great that she did not immediately comprehend his hard expression or tone of voice.

"Brother! What a lovely surprise!" She stepped back from him and, in an attempt to appear less like a child and more ladylike, began again. "William, this is such a delight. You remember our friend, Mr. Wickham. We met quite by accident last week and he has been so kind as to visit with me several times." She was confident her brother would be pleased to see his childhood friend and she turned her beaming countenance to her beloved Wickham. Her smile drooped at the stricken look on Mr. Wickham's face as he stared, dumbfounded, at her brother.

"Wickham! What brings you to Ramsgate?" Darcy's voice held an eerie calmness that Wickham recognized as more dangerous than it sounded. He fidgeted with his coat sleeves as he thought of what to say.

Georgiana puzzled at the tension she was now detecting between her brother and Mr. Wickham. As she could think of no reason for it, except perhaps the shock of seeing his friend after such a long time, she turned excitedly towards her brother. "William, as you have surprised us with your arrival, I must share a surprise with you that Mr. Wickham and Mrs. Younge were certain you would like." She paused briefly as her attention was drawn to Mr. Wickham, who had cleared his throat loudly and was giving her a pointed look she did not understand. "You see, we were going to leave for Gretna Green tomorrow, brother. Mr. Wickham loves me and wants to marry me!" She put a gloved hand on her brother's arm and looked up expectantly for his happy reaction to her news. Instead, the guttural sound that came from him made her step back in shock.

"What! Georgiana you cannot be serious!" Darcy blared at her, his displeasure evident all over his face.

By that time, Wickham had recovered from his shock and disappointment at Darcy's unexpected appearance. With feigned calm, he strolled lazily to stand next to Georgiana. She had taken several steps away from her brother, stunned by the sting of his displeasure.

"It is true. My dear Georgiana has agreed to make me the happiest of men," he pronounced, his conceited charm radiating around him.

"Mr. Wickham, let me be clear. Should you marry my sister, you will never see a shilling of her dowry—not one pound of her thirty thousand. What say you now?" Mr. Darcy's glare was ice and his voice even colder.

"Now Darce, that is not fair! As her husband, that blunt should be mine."

"You will get none of it!"

Unsuspecting, Mrs. Younge strolled into the room. "Here I am, Georgiana, returned with that embroidery thread I told you would look nice for your stitch—" Her voice died at the sight of her employer's heated glare descending upon her.

Mr. Wickham looked from Darcy to Mrs. Younge to the pale chit next to him. He knew that Darcy would not budge, and Georgiana's charms were not enough to induce him into a penniless marriage. His charming façade transformed into one of wicked amusement.

"Well played, my friend. You are a lucky bastard for coming when you did. You can keep your thirty thousand and the insipid wench. I care nothing for her."

Georgiana started at his words. "George, why are you saying such terrible things? You said you loved me." Her voice faltered at the last as her eyes began to swim with tears.

"Oh, hush, girl! Nobody likes a watering pot. If Darcy will not grant me my rights as a husband to your scratch, you are not worth being leg-shackled to for the rest of my life."

Darcy saw the hurt register in his sister's glassy eyes and watched as she slowly took a seat. His anger flared, and he turned first to Mrs. Younge, who was still standing dumbstruck at the doorway. "Mrs. Younge, you will return to your rooms, remove all your belongings and quit this house and my employ in fifteen minutes' time or you will see yourself relegated to the magistrate for breach of contract. Do I make myself clear?" His voice was nearly a shout, and the woman physically fell backwards with the force of it, hastily nodding and exiting the room.

Mr. Darcy schooled his features into a barely controlled look of rage as he turned then to Mr. Wickham. His voice was slow and deliberate. "You, sir, will leave this house—and this county if you have any sense at all—and you will never see Georgiana again. If you so much as think of coming near her, so help me God, Wickham, you will pay dearly for the mistake."

Wickham's face contorted into a look of pure hatred as he sneered his acknowledgement of Darcy's words and, without a backward glance at Georgiana, left the house.

As the memories of that horrible day filled his senses, Mr. Darcy stood abruptly and walked towards the terrace doors. He pulled one open and allowed the crisp winter air to roll over his face and calm him. A solitary tear escaped his eye as he thought with compassion of his sister recovering slowly, day by day. After the incident, he had taken her to London. Together with his cousin Colonel Fitzwilliam they had cared for and comforted her. She had come to understand that Wickham was not the man he presented himself to be, but Darcy knew she still held herself to blame for believing his charming display and nearly ruining her family with an elopement. Together with his cousin, they had researched and secured Mrs. Annesley, who was making progress with Georgiana, but the recovery was slower than he had hoped.

Mr. Darcy reached into his waistcoat pocket and pulled out her letter. As he read it again, he thought about what else he could do. The only portion of her letter that held any feeling seemed to be her response to his latest missive about his time at Netherfield. He had written her, finally, about Elizabeth and had told her about their conversations and verbal swordplay. He was careful not to reveal his interest in Elizabeth as he was still not ready to admit his feelings in such a decided way. It was one thing to indulge in it in his mind, but to share it with another was quite different. Georgiana had asked about Elizabeth and seemed interested in knowing more about her.

The thought of Elizabeth, combined with the coolness of the breeze that blew over his face, soothed his spirit, and he was able to reflect more peaceably. His discussion with Mr. Bennet a few days before had gone smoothly. His surprise was great at the amount of enjoyment he had in the gentleman's company. Darcy's mouth turned upwards in a small smile. Mr. Bennet had reminded him a little of Elizabeth. He had a quick wit and a tendency to lighthearted banter. He had not expected Mr. Bennet to be a sensible man when he reflected on his choice of wife or the rumors of the neighborhood regarding his mismanagement of the Longbourn estate, but Darcy did not find him lacking or insensible. He was intelligent, fair and understanding when he learned of Wickham.

Mr. Darcy could not say exactly why, but he felt he could trust Mr. Bennet implicitly with Georgiana's secret. He remembered that, during the moments he spoke with Mr. Bennet about his painful history with Wickham, he had felt an unexpected nostalgia. It now dawned on him with no small amount of surprise and sadness that the feeling was a reminder of the talks he used to have with his father as they rode around Pemberley. *Oh, how I miss you, Father!*

Darcy closed the terrace door and walked over to stoke the fire. He was lonely and wished he did not have so many items of worry. A moment of envy washed over him as he considered his friend Bingley. Two days before, Bingley had returned from his visit to Longbourn radiant and excruciatingly jovial in his mood.

"She is an angel, Darcy! An absolute angel, and soon she shall be mine!"

"Whatever are you talking about, Bingley?"

"Miss Jane Bennet. I asked permission today to court her, and she has accepted." Bingley laughed to himself before continuing. "I was so happy when she said yes that, for a moment, I thought I would just ask her to marry me right then."

"Bingley, are you sure this is what you want? You could secure the hand of nearly any lady of consequence in England. Miss Bennet's connections and wealth are below you, and you could do better." Darcy had been asking himself the same question for many weeks now, and it felt good to voice out loud the concerns that had been assaulting his peace of mind.

Bingley turned on him and shook his head disbelievingly. "Darcy, sometimes you are such a pompous— I will not say it, but really, man, you should listen to yourself!" His mood could not be ruined by his dour friend.

Darcy hid the offense he felt and continued, "Bingley, what about your duty to your family?"

"Duty be damned, Darcy! My father made his fortune in trade and, although I have been raised as a gentleman, it is merely my money that has bought my acceptance into society. Jane is the daughter of a gentleman. She is everything lovely, pure and beautiful. I'll be damned if I let some misguided talk of duty to any person or to society keep me from living the rest of my life in her happy companionship."

Darcy sat silently contemplating his friend's words. "Bingley— "

"No, Darcy, I shall not let you talk me out of this. I have lived with only my sisters and Hurst as family for far too long. I have spent years in London without meeting anyone who suits me as Jane does. I shall have happiness, Darcy. I shall!" He turned and, patting Darcy on the shoulder, left the room with as much enthusiasm as he had entered it. Darcy was left wishing he had the courage to obtain such happiness.

Mr. Darcy took out his watch and opened it to gaze at his stolen treasure. He was supposed to be trying to loosen the strings Elizabeth had wrapped around his heart and ignore their tugs in the direction of Longbourn. He was staying out of her presence so that he could figure things out. But his control regarding her was slipping, and Bingley's happiness was tempting him. He snapped the watch shut and hoped the image of Elizabeth's sparkling eyes would snap out of his mind, too. He was different from Bingley, his duties not so easily forsaken.

Elizabeth folded her letter and heated the wax with a candle before stamping the seal. She had written her aunt a lovely recital of the events of the Netherfield ball and days following. Jane had asked her to include the news of her courtship with Bingley, and Elizabeth happily accepted the charge. She knew her aunt would be interested, and Jane was much too occupied to write herself—what with daydreaming about Bingley when the gentleman was not visiting and spending time with him when he was.

Elizabeth took up the letter and tapped it on her writing desk absently as she frowned. Bingley had come nearly every day for three days now since he had begun courting Jane. Although she was happy for her sister, she was beginning to feel a bit of disappointment that his friend had not accompanied him on at least one of his visits. She had not ventured to ask about Darcy as her courage did not extend that far. Mr. Bingley was lively company, and she enjoyed his conversation, which was fortunate as she was often relegated to chaperone her sister and the gentleman.

However agreeable Mr. Bingley's visits were, they lacked a certain something that had been there whenever Mr. Darcy had accompanied him. Bingley, although intelligent, was not a great reader, and Elizabeth found the range of topics to discuss narrowed in their ability to challenge her mind. She was disappointed in herself for thinking about Mr. Darcy so much. It was not as though the gentleman was at Netherfield pining after her company. If he had been, he had only to call with Mr. Bingley to secure it.

Elizabeth, who prided herself in her independence, was beginning to find the feelings of her heart to be rather irritating at times. Falling in love with Mr. Darcy—and love him she did—was stealing her composure. She did not like the assortment of feelings the man caused in her. At one moment, she would feel shivers of joy pulse inside her when he simply smiled, then in the next moment, her natural pride faltered as she worried he did not return her regard. Now, she was sitting there wishing to see him and disappointed that she had not. *What has happened to me? Elizabeth Bennet of Longbourn does not need the attentions of Mr. Darcy of Pemberley to be content,* Elizabeth thought discontentedly.

When Elizabeth carried her letter down to her father's study to be posted with the rest, she was surprised to see he was not alone. Sitting across from his desk were the unhappy faces of her two youngest sisters and her mother. Elizabeth sensed it was a private meeting and, therefore, just slid her letter on the post tray on her father's sideboard. She had intended slipping out without a word, but her father's voice stalled her.

"Elizabeth, you may stay." It was less of an invitation than a polite request. She recognized this and, bewildered, took a seat at the side of the room.

"Papa, did you really have to throw the man out? La! He was only accompanying us home from Meryton." Lydia's shrill voice caused Elizabeth to sit back in astonishment at her impertinence.

"Lydia Bennet, you had best listen very clearly to what I will say now, because I will not repeat myself. You are not to speak so much as two words to the man or go so far as to be in his company. I forbid it. If you do not adhere to my ruling on this matter, you will find yourself no longer out in society and relegated to the nursery again. There will be no balls, no evenings in company, no assemblies—nothing. This goes for you too, Kitty. Do I make myself clear?"

Elizabeth looked with astonishment, first at the impassioned face of her father, who had never once, thus far, exerted himself in his parental role as to forbid anything of his daughters, and then at the stunned profiles of her sisters and mother. Her interest in the cause for such a display without precedence increased significantly.

Her mother was the first to recover from her astonishment. "Mr. Bennet, surely you are not serious. Whatever can you mean by telling the charming Mr. Wickham to leave and not ever come back to Longbourn? And to demand Lydia not speak to the man? You try my nerves, sir, with your teasing. I met the man, myself, today in Meryton when he accompanied us home. He is everything affable and such a handsome gentleman. He is an officer, too, you know!"

Elizabeth was beginning to understand the import of the moment, but she was confused as to how her father had come to the knowledge of Wickham's character. Mr. Darcy had said he would inform her father about Wickham, but he had not been to Longbourn since before the Netherfield ball.

"Mrs. Bennet, I can, and I will, decide what persons are welcome in my home, and I will thank you to remember that. Mr. Wickham is not to be admitted here, nor are any of your daughters to be allowed in his company. I assure you, I do not jest. The man is a blackguard, a gamester, and a philanderer of the first ranks."

"But how can you know that, Papa? You have only just met him a moment ago! I daresay, he cannot be so handsome and so bad, too," insisted Lydia, undeterred by the steel in her father's voice.

"A gentleman of our acquaintance has known Mr. Wickham his entire life and informed me of his character. I have since spoken to Colonel Forster, and he has confirmed that Wickham already has substantial debts around Meryton. And I will not wound your sensibilities with the rumors of his more personal encounters with more than one member of the serving class in the area." Mr. Bennet appeared suddenly exhausted and aged as he looked towards his daughters and wife once more. "I have said all I will on the topic, and you know my demands. I will brook no more discussion regarding Mr. Wickham; you are dismissed."

Lydia and Kitty flounced out of the room with dramatic wails, followed by Mrs. Bennet, not much more composed. Elizabeth stood to leave.

"No, Lizzy. Stay a minute, please."

Elizabeth went to her father's side and took his hand in hers. After a few moments of silence, Mr. Bennet directed Elizabeth to her favorite chair by the fire and sat down in his.

"Elizabeth, I am sure you are wondering why I asked you to stay. I am tired, so I will come straight to the point." Mr. Bennet then related briefly his encounter with Mr. Darcy. He shared with his daughter an abbreviated version of Wickham's history with the Darcy family and, excepting revealing the identity of Georgiana, related the attempted seduction and elopement of a 'near relation' of Mr. Darcy. "I had planned to make less of a display when forbidding your sisters to be in the company of Mr. Wickham, but when they arrived home today from Meryton on the arms of the man, I wasted no time in informing the gentleman his presence was not welcome now or ever at Longbourn or with any of its inhabitants."

"Mr. Darcy warned me to stay away from the man, but I had not thought that he was as bad as that," Elizabeth said in astonishment at the numerous humiliations and betrayals Mr. Darcy and his family had suffered at the hands of one wicked man. Her esteem for Mr. Darcy rose significantly as she realized the many mortifications he must have endured in exposing his dealings with Wickham to her father in order to protect her and her family.

"Your Mr. Gent is a good man, Lizzy," Mr. Bennet said quietly and tenderly as he watched Elizabeth absorb all he had told her. She looked up at her father but could say nothing. They sat there in silence for some time, lost in their own thoughts until it was time to change for dinner.

Chapter 9

Mr. Darcy was beginning to think he should have accepted the invitation with Bingley to dine at Longbourn that evening rather than give his excuse of business. Now, Bingley was in the company of the woman who would soon become his betrothed and also Miss Elizabeth. Mr. Darcy morosely drank from his glass. Miss Bingley and Mrs. Hurst had already separated to the drawing room after dinner to leave Mr. Hurst and him to a glass of port. Darcy looked at his glass as he swirled the cherry-colored liquid. He frowned as he imagined that, instead of sitting next to Miss Bingley all evening over the never-ending courses of food, he could have been listening to Elizabeth's sparkling laugh, ready wit and enchanting voice. Maybe she would have played the pianoforte after dinner, or they might have played a game of cards.

His resolve kept him from accepting the invitation, and instead, he stayed at Netherfield for the evening. After three courses, the assault on his senses from Miss Bingley's perfume was nauseating. Her endless vitriol about the neighborhood was also irritating. Nor did the constant flattery directed at him help his appetite. *'Oh, how precisely you cut your venison, Mr. Darcy.'* He groaned out a humorless laugh at the ridiculous attempts to catch his attention. He found that, if he kept his head bent to his meal and merely nodded occasionally to her, he could minimize the stirrings of the air and thus marginalize the onslaught.

Moments in which he had been ungallant enough to sport with her had brought a little enjoyment to the evening. For example, when he asked for her opinion on the recently discussed Corn Laws in Parliament, her answer caused him to bite his cheek to keep from laughing until he tasted blood.

"Oh it is infinitely important for one to keep in mind that a varied diet is certainly the most healthful."

The memory brought an unbidden chuckle from his lips, and Mr. Hurst, who had dozed off in his chair after the ladies left, sat up and, after clearing his throat rather rudely, proclaimed, "Quite right, quite right," before leaning back in his chair and closing his eyes again. Mr. Darcy covered his mouth, trying to quench another peel of merriment.

He could not avoid rejoining the ladies much longer, so as if to fortify himself, he drank the rest of his wine in one gulp. When he stood, Mr. Hurst did not rouse at the sound, so Mr. Darcy, with a heavy step, found himself heading alone to the front lines. He slowed his pace as he neared the drawing room doors and signaled to the footman not to announce him. When he noticed the door ajar, he dismissed the footman altogether and stopped to listen to the conversation through the door.

"Really, Louisa, we simply must stop him. He will connect himself to that family, and then we will all be ruined."

"I don't know, Caroline, the Bennets are unlikely to spend any time in town and are unknown there. I cannot see how, if Charles were to marry Miss Bennet, it would lessen your chances."

"Louisa, really. You cannot expect that, with Charles as a son-in-law, silly, improper Mrs. Bennet will keep herself at Longbourn."

"When Charles is in town, he usually stays at our townhouse or at Darcy House. He will likely take up his own townhouse if he marries. and you will not have to see his wife or her family if you do not wish it. Besides, I believe he plans to stay at Netherfield much of the time."

"Of course I will have to see her, Louisa. Oh, really, you are most obtuse sometimes. Charles is Mr. Darcy's closest friend. When I marry Mr. Darcy, I will still spend a great deal of time with Charles, and his wife will likely have members of her family often visiting."

Mr. Darcy's posture stiffened when he heard Caroline talk of being his wife. A shudder stole through him, and he nearly walked into the room to make it quite clear that it would never happen. He hated the machinations so many ladies in his sphere of acquaintance used to try to gain his interest. But his curiosity got the better of him, and he waited to hear what else they had to say.

"I see your point, Caroline."

"If Charles marries Miss Bennet, it is more than likely Miss Elizabeth will come to live or, at the very least, visit often with her sister. I cannot think of the discomfort my dear Darcy will have being constantly thrown into her company as I know he quite detests her. Oh, how he will suffer! My only solace is that I shall be there to comfort him."

The force of Miss Bingley's words struck Mr. Darcy full on, and he took a step back and leaned against the wall. *Why had I not thought of that? If Bingley marries Miss Bennet—no,* when *he marries her, as I am sure it is only a matter of days before they become engaged—I will likely see much of Elizabeth.* It was with a mixture of pleasure and pain that his mind contemplated *that* likely result of the marriage. Although Mr. Darcy had acknowledged to himself that he, indeed, did love Elizabeth, he had also come to the reluctant decision that he could not have her. He owed too much to his family, and they expected him to marry a woman of rank and fortune.

I must be indifferent in her presence if I am to endure living without her. The days since he last saw her at the ball had been torture, but he prided himself that he was surviving it well enough. He only managed to think of her half a dozen or so times a day. If he could survive an extended length of time out of Miss Elizabeth's presence, perhaps he could train his heart to forget his love.

Determining his course of action, Mr. Darcy straightened and walked through the drawing room doors. "I am sorry to interrupt you ladies. I came only to bid you good night as I have planned for an early morning tomorrow and wish to retire early." He bowed his acknowledgement while Miss Bingley gushed her regrets at his retiring early, but turned and left before she could rise from her seat and try to persuade him to remain a moment longer.

Upon reaching his suite, he pulled fiercely at his cravat to untie the knot as he rang for his valet. He made quick work of the silken fabric, removed his tailcoat and waistcoat and tossed them hastily on the chair in his dressing room.

After receiving his summons, Rogers entered the dressing room. He frowned at the disregarded garments as he picked them up and carefully folded them.

"Rogers, pack my things; we leave for London at first light."

"Very good, sir. Anything else, sir?"

"A brandy, please."

Mr. Darcy entered his bedchamber and sank heavily in the chair near the hearth. A moment later, his valet handed him the snifter of amber liquid before exiting to begin packing.

Thinking of returning to London turned Darcy's thoughts to his sister. It was a balm to his already sinking mood to know that he would soon be there to cheer her up. He had been gone nearly two months, and it was time he remembered his responsibilities. He took a sip of brandy and then threw the rest, glass and all, into the fire. He would bury himself in his neglected business affairs and the entertainment of his sister, and he would forget Elizabeth. He would.

The following morning dawned gray and dreary. Mr. Darcy watched through the window as his valet instructed the footmen in securing his trunks on the carriage. He had written Bingley a short missive explaining his hasty departure due to business. He also made reference to spending Christmas with Georgiana so that he would not be expected to return for many weeks. After pressing his signet ring into the hot wax to seal the letter, he handed it to Bingley's butler with instructions to give it to his friend when he came downstairs to break his fast.

Upon exiting the house, he paused briefly and looked around him with a heavy heart and even weightier mind. As he entered the carriage, the weather seemed to match his mood; not an hour into his journey to London, it began to rain. Grumbling to himself, Mr. Darcy felt a fissure form in his heart and a last-minute, panicked wish to turn around—to turn around and go straight to Elizabeth. He drew in a shaky breath and reminded himself of his reasons for leaving. They made sense and were sound. The rain pelting the rooftop seemed to be mocking his decision. He closed his eyes in an attempt to block the traitorous weather and was soon lulled into a restless sleep.

When the continued rainy weather turned into the first snow of the season, the inhabitants of Longbourn were forced to remain at home with few callers for several days. With Mary's wedding only days away, Mrs. Bennet fretted excessively about being unable to go to Meryton to secure the items still needed for her trousseau. Occasionally, Charlotte Lucas would venture to walk the short way to visit Elizabeth, for which she was glad as it broke up the tedious pace of the day and distracted her from the question of why

Mr. Darcy had not come for a visit in the week since the ball. He had even declined an invitation to dinner a few days before with excuses sent through Bingley of business he needed to attend. Elizabeth had been disappointed but had also felt admiration for his dedication to his responsibilities.

Elizabeth could not hide her excitement at awaking after three days of poor weather to see sun shining through her window. It was a beautiful day, and she could see the sun glistening on the blanket of snow. She hummed as she picked out a pretty cream frock with a green sash and did a careful toilette on her hair. After breakfasting, she briefly visited her father in his study to say a cheerful good morning.

"Good morning to you, too, Lizzy. You seem to be in good spirits this morning."

"It is bright and sunny out today. I cannot wait to leave this house and finally get some fresh air. Would you like to come with me on a walk this morning, Papa?"

Chuckling to himself, he declined, stating he would like to remain hidden in his library. He had it on good authority that Mrs. Bennet would be out most of the morning doing last minute shopping for tomorrow's wedding, thus affording him a deliciously quiet home.

Elizabeth bid him good-bye and retrieved her woolen pelisse and gloves from Hill. She departed just as Mrs. Bennet, with Mary and Mr. Collins in tow, exited the house to the carriage, bound for Meryton. The brisk winter air assaulted her lungs in a sting of refreshing coolness. She began in her normal quick pace along one of the lanes near her home.

Upon returning from her walk, she recognized the approach of a single horse and rider. Her excitement quickly faded as her disappointment grew, seeing Mr. Bingley once again arrive at Longbourn without his friend. She closeted her feelings in time to receive Mr. Bingley with feigned cheerfulness.

"Mr. Bingley, welcome to Longbourn. It feels as though it has been ages since you last visited."

"Miss Elizabeth, thank you. The weather has been horrid, has it not? I mean, the snow is lovely and makes the landscape quite beautiful, but I dread being kept indoors." The last of his speech was directed away from her as his head had turned to the sound of the door opening. Jane stood at the doorway to welcome him and the two were soon engrossed in each other.

Once all were comfortably divested of their winter wear and seated in the drawing room with a cup of tea, Mr. Bingley, Jane and Elizabeth settled into a comfortable recital of the last few days spent outside of each other's company.

Elizabeth's thoughts kept returning to Mr. Darcy and his absence. She told herself she should not fret over it but felt an ever-sinking feeling that she could not shake. Bingley had not mentioned Mr. Darcy, and at a pause in the conversation, Elizabeth found herself speaking before she could think what she was about.

"And does your friend enjoy his stay in Hertfordshire, Mr. Bingley?"

"Mr. Darcy? I believe he did enjoy visiting here, he said as much in his note," Mr. Bingley replied but, as he was staring once again at Jane, he did not see Elizabeth's look of confusion.

"Mr. Bingley, you say he *did* enjoy visiting here? Pray, has Mr. Darcy left Netherfield?"

She had hoped to sound a little more indifferent and far less panicked, but the words were out before she could school her tone.

Turning to Elizabeth, Mr. Bingley gave a smile of embarrassment. "Forgive me; with the weather, I had forgotten that I had not the chance to tell you Mr. Darcy left for London three days ago. He had business to attend."

Elizabeth heard her detached voice ask the question that was screaming in her mind. "And when do you expect his return, sir?"

"I know not. He left very early in the morning, and his note did not mention returning, though it did speak of spending Christmas with Georgiana, so I presume not for many weeks at least. They usually spend Christmas and the New Year at Pemberley."

Mr. Bingley turned back to Jane and addressed something to her. As their quiet conversation continued, nobody noticed the color drain from Elizabeth's face and her eyes begin to fill with traitorous tears. Quickly excusing herself, she exited the room, disregarding her duties as chaperone. Upon reaching the stairs, she lifted her skirts and ran up to her bedroom. There, she locked the door and fell on her bed, sobbing heavily.

Mr. Bingley saw Jane blush modestly at their being left alone. She looked so beautiful, and he could not help himself from reaching over to capture her hand in his. He had not planned on proposing so soon after requesting to court her, but the moment presented itself. As he gazed at his beloved

Jane, his heart swelled with emotion; he could not wait a moment longer.

"Jane." His voice sounded like a caress and set her heart beating rapidly.

"Yes, Mr. Bingley?" she asked, shakily.

"Jane, you must allow me to tell you how ardently I admire and love you. Indeed, you are all I think about and all I wish for. I long to wake every morning of my life with you beside me. Please tell me you feel the same and allow me to love you today and every day for the rest of our lives. Jane, will you consent to be my wife?" He looked at her tenderly and waited with a bracing heart for her answer.

"Yes. Yes! I will marry you!" She laughed unsteadily as he took her hand and lifted it gently to his lips.

In the next moment, Mr. Bingley jumped up from his seat in excitement and pulled Jane with him. She laughed at his display of exuberance and smiled indulgently at him. Stepping closer, he placed his hand on her cheek. "Oh, Jane, you have made me so happy!"

"You have made me very happy, too, Mr. Bingley," she replied shyly as his light touch sent tingles down her spine.

"Charles. I am Charles to you now, my love," he said and stepped yet closer to her.

"Charles." She breathed before closing her eyes from the light-headedness she felt at his proximity.

Mr. Bingley could not help himself anymore. He dipped his head to brush her lips softly with his. Pulling away, he watched her cheeks flush beautifully as she opened her eyes. They stood looking into each other's eyes for a moment before a noise from the hallway reminded them of the impropriety of their proximity to each other. Mr. Bingley led his intended to the sofa and placed himself at a respectable distance. They spoke endearments for a few minutes as each relished in the new opportunity to share the feelings they had felt but not spoken for many weeks.

"Jane, I think I should like to go to your father now."

Jane nodded and declared she would go to her sister to share their news while he was in with her father. She walked him to her father's study. After tracing a finger along her cheek, he smiled and knocked on the library door. Upon hearing the summons, he entered with one last glance at her. She smiled and stomped her feet prettily in excitement before calming herself and rushing to find Elizabeth.

After a few minutes, Elizabeth's tears dried up and she laid on her bed as feelings of disappointment slowly turned to fuel a rising anger at herself. She was irritated that she had broken down and cried. She did not cry often and was usually much more reserved and in control of her feelings. She allowed her anger to propel her off the bed and to the basin to splash water over her face. The cool water felt good on her burning cheeks and stinging eyes.

After a few moments, she sat on the windowsill to think about what she had learned. Mr. Darcy had not come to see her, and he had left the country without so much as taking proper leave of his acquaintances in the neighborhood. She was hurt that he would not pay her the respect she felt she deserved. She had come to believe they at least had built a friendship in the recent weeks. Her anger at herself for having become so vulnerable to him was palpable.

Before her encounter with him in the grove of trees, she was nearly unaffected by him. She might have admitted to finding his features pleasing, but she was quite able to dislike him. *Why could I not have kept my reserve?* As she sat clenching her fists in frustration at her weakness, she began to feel a stirring of anger at the man himself. He had been charming and teasing with her. He had said pretty words and flirted with her. She ignored the voice in her heart that said there had been true feeling in his eyes when he acted thus, but instead allowed herself to reason that he had trifled with her feelings and then left the neighborhood without so much as a thought for her. It was in this attitude that Elizabeth heard the knock on her door and Jane's voice from without.

She hurriedly checked her appearance in the mirror above the dressing table and was relieved to see no evidence of her former moment of weakness. She took a few deep breaths and said a small prayer of thanks that she had never shared her feelings for Mr. Darcy with Jane. She would now put them aside and forget him as he had obviously forgotten her. After another quick breath, she opened the door to her sister's smiling face and gave an equally bright smile that, if not felt, was at least convincing.

Chapter 10

Mr. Bennet stood up from his desk as Mr. Bingley's jubilant stride propelled him into the room. He studied the young man and suspected the nature of the interview he was now about to have. It did not surprise him that, so soon after granting his permission for Bingley to court Jane, the man would return with another request of a more permanent nature. He had observed the two of them together when Bingley visited, most particularly the evening when he joined the family for dinner, and it was clear that his shy, eldest daughter did fancy Mr. Bingley. He perched his mouth in a crooked smile of amusement and felt a smug satisfaction that he had judged Bingley's character well enough to know that his impulsiveness would not allow a long courtship.

"Mr. Bingley, good morning, sir. What can I do for you this morning?" Mr. Bennet asked, motioning Bingley to sit across from his desk. He tried to hide his humor at watching Mr. Bingley's radiant face change to apprehension in reflection of the memory of their previous interview when he had mercilessly teased the young man.

"Good morning, sir." Mr. Bingley cleared his throat and felt all the discomfort associated with the task he was about to perform. It was not often that he was uncomfortable in any social setting, but he could not forget the stern countenance of Jane's father when he had asked for permission to court her. The thought occurred to him that Mr. Bennet might not be happy about this new request coming so soon after the last. *The sooner I finish this, the sooner I can return to Jane.*

Thinking of Jane brought back his feelings of joy at her acceptance of his proposal and allowed him to speak more confidently. "Sir, I realize that my business with you today may seem rather precipitous after our previous meeting, but if I may be frank, sir...?" He paused and waited for Mr. Bennet to nod his permission before continuing. "You see, sir, I rather think I have already waited for this occasion far too long. I found I could think of no good reason to delay this next step and thus, when given the opportunity today, I could not help myself."

Mr. Bennet leaned back in his chair and rubbed his jaw in mock seriousness. He could see Mr. Bingley's nervousness and knew what he was trying to communicate. However, Jane was his daughter, and he did not want to give up his residency in her heart so easily. So he continued to bait the young man.

"Mr. Bingley, I apologize, but I do not have the privilege of knowing what it is that you are speaking about."

Mr. Bingley colored as he realized that, in his haste, he had assumed Mr. Bennet would know why he sought his company that morning. His embarrassment soon faded as his thoughts briefly drifted to Jane and the joy she must be experiencing sharing their news with her favorite sister. His features softened into that which only a man in love could express, and he sat up straighter in his chair, his tender regard for Jane giving him a renewed determination. He looked Mr. Bennet in the eye and spoke with a voice of certainty. "Mr. Bennet, I have come here to request your consent and blessing. I have asked your daughter, Jane, to be my wife, and beyond all my hopes, she has accepted me. I am here to ask you to grant me her hand in marriage."

Mr. Bennet settled into his usual contented smile as he listened to his soon-to-be son-in-law request his daughter's hand. He did not have the heart to continue goading the man.

"Mr. Bingley, I give you my consent. Jane is a dear, sweet woman whose compassion and understanding for others is one of her greatest virtues. I know you are a good man who will provide my daughter with the happiness she deserves." Mr. Bennet's voice faltered at the last, but he lifted his chin in an attempt to remain in control of himself.

"Thank you, sir. Today you have given me the most precious gift I could ever hope for in this life." He reached to shake Mr. Bennet's hand as he stood to take his leave.

"Just a moment, Mr. Bingley, if you can humor an old man."

Puzzled, but no longer concerned, Mr. Bingley nodded his acceptance and resumed his seat.

"Mr. Bingley, before I grant you leave to return to my daughter, where I am sure you wish most to be, I have just one more area regarding your marriage that I would like to discuss with you."

Mr. Bingley smiled at the sound of Mr. Bennet speaking of his future marriage. Excitement and impatience surged through him, and he looked eagerly towards his new father-in-law-to-be. "By all means, Mr. Bennet. Pray continue."

"I understand that I am asking you to be rather candid with me about your choice of my daughter; however, I must ignore propriety and ask you to provide for me exactly why it is you wish to marry my Jane."

Mr. Bingley's face lit up in a radiant smile. "Sir, that is an easy question, and I do not mind telling you at all. If you allow me access to your roof, sir, I will shout the answer from atop it if you wish. I love Jane. And as you have granted me permission to marry her, I plan on loving her every day for the rest of my life."

Mr. Bennet returned Bingley's smile with one of supreme happiness at hearing the answer he hoped to receive for each of his daughters.

"Very good, sir. See that you do." Mr. Bennet stood and reached for Bingley's hand.

With a hearty bounce to his handshake and a laugh, Mr. Bingley replied, "I will, sir. I will."

As Mr. Bingley turned to leave, Mr. Bennet asked him please to deliver a request to Jane to come to his study as soon as she was able. Mr. Bingley laughed happily again and confirmed he would deliver the message and return with Jane right away.

"Jane, what is this smile of yours about?" Elizabeth queried, as she stepped aside to allow Jane to enter the room.

Jane sat on the bed and, taking in a deep breath of contentment, fell backwards with a sigh. Elizabeth smiled at her sister's serenity, even as she envied it. She caught the sight of her own tear-sodden handkerchief on the bed, and covertly reached to hide it as she sat next to her sister.

"Lizzy, how am I to cope with all this happiness?" Jane giggled and kicked her legs in the air with excitement. She then turned to her sister with a mock frown. "You should not have left us alone in the room, Lizzy. It was very naughty of you, but I shall forgive you, for you see, nearly as soon as you quitted the room, Charles proposed to me. He asked me to be his wife!"

Elizabeth reached to embrace her sister. "Jane, I am so happy for you. It is exactly what you deserve, and I will not apologize for leaving you alone even if you do not forgive me, for how can I regret a sin when the results of it are so fortuitous?" She laughed as Jane gave her a disapproving face before erupting into laughter again.

Elizabeth lay down on the counterpane next to her sister and they looked at the ceiling for a few moments.

"Charles?" she teased her.

Jane blushed. "Yes, it is Charles now. Though I must say I feel flushed whenever I say his name. I do hope that goes away or I shall be a very silly wife." She smiled and sighed again.

Elizabeth turned on her side and grabbed her sister's hand. "Tell me all, Jane. What did he say?"

Jane faced her and began to relate with as much detail as possible, as is usual with ladies, the scene of his proposal and her acceptance. Abruptly, she stopped speaking and flushed.

"Jane... what happened next? You know you cannot keep this from me," Elizabeth begged, as she watched her sister cover her face with her hands and shake her head with embarrassment.

Elizabeth laughed as Jane mumbled something through her hands. She pushed her sister's shoulder gently a few times.

"Jane, this will not do! I cannot hear you through your hands. You are far too discomposed for me to believe it is nothing, so I must insist you tell me!"

Jane kept her hands on her face but took a deep breath and spoke louder. "Then he kissed me!" She squealed again as her face flushed even redder at the memory the words brought back.

Elizabeth grinned and expressed her delight as the two sisters laughed some more. Despite Jane's initial discomfort, they then began a lengthy discussion of the kiss—what it felt like, how it was achieved and when they thought he might do it again. After exhausting the topic, they rolled on their backs and looked at the ceiling, both sighing in contentment.

Elizabeth was truly happy for her sister. She knew Mr. Bingley was an excellent match and they would both be very happy in their life together. Jane's natural modesty would be met by Bingley's affable personality.

Jane sighed, "If only I could see you this happy, Lizzy, my happiness would be complete. If only there was such a man for you."

Elizabeth remained silent as a single tear rolled down her face. She had set aside her own feelings of distress at Mr. Darcy's departure upon hearing Jane's happy news. Being reminded of the man she now believed was the only man she could ever be prevailed upon to marry, her feelings came back full force. She turned her head away from her sister in an attempt to compose herself and disguise her heartbreak. She swallowed the lump in her throat and, adding a levity she did not feel, replied, "Well Jane, you shall just have to be sure to place me in the path of other rich men after you marry!"

Her sister's laughter allowed her the opportunity she needed to push her thoughts of Mr. Darcy aside and laugh too, though without the same warmth she had previously. "However, I am sure that so much good fortune and happiness cannot be granted twice to one family, and so, I shall content myself to be governess to your ten children. I promise to diligently teach them all to paint and play their instruments very ill, indeed."

The sisters laughed again as Jane protested such a ridiculous statement.

"At least it may be said that the Bingley children will, all of them, be 'excellent walkers'," Jane teased her sister. They both laughed softly before returning to their private reflections.

Elizabeth was relieved to hear a knock on their bedroom door as the weight of the conversation was beginning to task her composure, and she stood to answer it. Hill relayed the message to Jane that her father requested her company in his study.

Jane stepped to the dressing table to check her appearance before turning to her sister with concern. "Do you think Papa will say no to Charles?"

Elizabeth smiled indulgently at her sister and shook her head. "Of course not, Jane. I am certain he simply wants to hear your feelings on the matter. Go to him; you will see all is well."

Jane was reassured and, after giving her sister a parting hug and kiss on the cheek, left her to go to her father. Elizabeth's knees gave way as she sank into the bed. Her thoughts were in a jumble, and she felt the beginnings of a headache. When she reflected on Jane's good fortune, her happiness for her sister was to a degree that she could almost believe the state of her own heart inconsequential. However, her hurt feelings refused to be ignored. She could not understand how she could have misunderstood his feelings for her, but misunderstood they must have been, for he was gone and not to return.

Once again her ire was raised at Mr. Darcy and, nearly equally, at her own silliness. She was no better than Lydia or Kitty, whose understanding in such matters was trifling. They fell easily in and out of love with any number of gentlemen. She was always disgusted at her sisters' lack of self-control over their hearts and had prided herself in her ability not to let her heart be so easily touched without proper consideration and protection.

She shook her head as she came to the ugly truth: she really was no wiser than her foolish little sisters. She had allowed her heart to be touched by Mr. Darcy and had deceived herself into believing that he might have returned her regard. What was even more vexing was that, as angry as she was with herself and Mr. Darcy, she could not disabuse herself of her esteem for him. Nor could she convince herself that Mr. Darcy's personality was not everything she had ever hoped for in a partner. She groaned in frustration that he still had such power over her. She hated him, hated him with all the love in her heart.

Jane met Mr. Bingley outside her father's study. Upon seeing him, she blushed deeply, remembering the long conference she just had with her sister, especially the discussion of the kiss.

"Jane, my love, your father has given his consent. We are to be married, and I can hardly contain my happiness." Mr. Bingley took her hand in his and brushed a light kiss across her knuckles. "You must go to him now; he wishes to speak to you. I will await you out here."

"Thank you, Charles," she whispered, as she shyly stole a look at his face before entering her father's study.

Jane closed the door before turning to her father. Her smile could hardly be contained as she saw his tender expression. She ran to him, threw her arms around his neck and gave him a kiss on the cheek. "Oh, Papa, thank you! He is truly the best man."

Mr. Bennet was momentarily surprised at the exuberant physical display from his usually reserved daughter. His surprise turned to embarrassment as her happiness caused his eyes to gather moisture. He cleared his suddenly thick throat and attempted to express a tone of indifference as he patted her shoulder. "Now, now, Jane there is no need for this. That will do." He gently pulled her arms from his neck and slid his hands down to hold hers. It had been many years since any of his daughters had embraced him, and although it caused memories of pleasant nostalgia, it also caused him to lose his composure a bit.

"Come, child; sit with me a moment, and we shall talk." He led her to the window seat, sat her down and found his seat. He smiled to himself as he realized it was the same place he had talked to Lizzy about love only days before. "Well, Jane dear, your Mr. Bingley tells me he would like to marry you."

"Yes," she replied shyly.

"And he also tells me that you would like to marry him."

"Yes." Her voice was softer still and her cheeks colored slightly.

"Well, I am glad to hear it, dear, as I have given him permission to do so." He waited until she looked up at him before continuing. "Do you love him, Jane?"

Mr. Bennet already knew the answer to his question. Even if he had not seen the way her eyes filled with light and her cheeks turned rosy, her lips had transformed into a serene smile that spoke the answer before she voiced it.

"I do, Papa. I love him. He is everything a gentleman ought to be if he can: kind, generous, happy and handsome." She smiled at her father and then looked at her hands in embarrassment at her effusive praise of the man.

"And rich, too," he added.

"I do not care about his money, Papa." She warned him with her voice firm, her face suddenly serious.

Mr. Bennet gave her small hands a gentle squeeze. "I know, dear. I just wanted to make sure your heart was where it should be, though I should have suspected no less from you, Jane."

"Thank you, Papa."

"I think you and Mr. Bingley will be a good match. You are both so kind you will never fight, so affable, the servants will cheat you, and so generous, you will exceed your income."

Jane laughed at her father's teasing. "No, indeed, Papa!"

Mr. Bennet watched his daughter laugh and felt an overwhelming tenderness come over him. She was his first great love from the moment she was placed in his arms as an infant. Now, she was a beautiful young lady who would soon be in the arms of another. He felt a momentary sting at the upcoming loss and said with feeling, "Jane, sweetheart, promise your Papa you will save a small part of your heart for me. Surely, your Mr. Bingley can spare a tiny portion."

Jane reached up to pat the side of his face. "I will always be your little girl, Papa."

"And for that, I am glad." Mr. Bennet cleared the emotion from his throat, and they sat quietly for a few moments. Mr. Bennet reflected with sadness upon his interview with Mary the day she became engaged. When he asked if she loved Mr. Collins, she had nearly laughed at him. Her response still struck him with regret. *"Love? Really, Papa, I do not see what that has to do with this. He has a sufficient income, we have some things in common, and it is a prudent match for me. I had not cared to ever marry, but Mr. Collins has asked me, and I figured I might as well as not. It would also mean saving the entail, though I confess, I did not really care about that."* Mr. Bennet sighed as he turned to his eldest daughter, who was now thinking of her intended, for it was written all over her face.

"Jane, I have something I would like to speak about with you and Mr. Bingley. I will go get him now." He smiled and went to the door. Upon opening it, he saw Mr. Bingley pacing the floor just outside. Hiding a smile of amusement, he issued an invitation for the gentleman to enter.

Mr. Bingley walked into the study with a bit of apprehension and looked around as to where he should sit. He wanted to go sit next to Jane at the window seat, but there were other chairs near the desk. With Mr. Bennet in the room, he did not know what to do. He looked at Jane; she smiled. It was decided; he went to sit next to her.

Mr. Bennet hid a smile of contentment at the image the future held for this daughter, then closed the door and turned to the couple. "Well, Jane, Mr. Bingley, I would like to be the first to wish you joy."

Mr. Bingley and his betrothed gave their thanks and watched curiously as Mr. Bennet went to his desk and took out a paper from a drawer. They did not understand why he had invited Mr. Bingley into the study or why Jane had not been dismissed, but before they could think long on the subject, Mr. Bennet began to speak.

"Mr. Bingley, I assume you will have your solicitor write up settlement documents for me to sign, am I correct?"

Mr. Bingley sat up straighter and appeared slightly uncomfortable as he looked briefly towards Jane. Mr. Bennet recognized his momentary discomfort for what it was and tried to put him at ease. "Mr. Bingley, I understand it is not generally the custom to include ladies in such a discussion of business and that generally this conversation would be between just the two of us and perhaps your man of business. However, as what I have to say to you will pertain to my daughter, I ask that we continue with her in our company."

Mr. Bingley hastened to respond, "Mr. Bennet, I meant no offense. I am perfectly willing to have this discussion with Jane present, as I intend to have no secrets between us. I had not planned on keeping the settlement decisions from her."

"I am glad to hear it, sir." Mr. Bennet took up his quill, filled in a few spots on the paper he had pulled from the desk, and signed his name at the bottom before looking up to address the couple before him. "When you meet with your solicitor, you will need to give him this. It is a statement of the portion Jane will receive upon the event of your wedding." He stood and handed the paper to Mr. Bingley.

Mr. Bingley began to put the paper in his breast pocket, but he was stopped as Mr. Bennet requested that he and Jane read it. Mr. Bingley furrowed his brow but acquiesced. His eyes went wide, as did Jane's, when he read the figure her father had written in regarding her dowry.

"Papa, this is not funny..."

"Sir, there is a mistake..."

They both spoke at once with matching looks of confusion at Mr. Bennet, who stood gazing out the window.

"It is no joke, Jane, and there is no mistake, Mr. Bingley."

"Sir, I do not mean to be impertinent, but I knew Jane had no fortune, and I have not asked that you provide her with one in order for me to marry her." Mr. Bingley was beginning to feel a little offended at seeing the large number on the page. What might Mr. Bennet assume about him?

Jane was equally worried but for a different reason. "Papa, you must not do this. What about Mama and my sisters. It would not be fair to dispense with so much for me at such a cost to them."

Mr. Bingley's anxiety forced him to speak again. "I know it is yet again impertinent for me to say so, sir, but you cannot afford this."

Mr. Bennet turned from the window and gave the two people waiting for his response a small smile. He took a deep breath and sighed before he began. "Do not worry yourselves. Mr. Bingley, I can, indeed, afford it. What I am about to tell you both must be kept in the strictest confidence. As you will see if you read the bottom portion of the letter, it specifies that if either of you speak of this matter to anyone else, the portion will revert back to the previously stated fifty pounds. Do I have your assurances of privacy?" He looked to his daughter and her intended and, with the incredulous nods of their promise, continued. "Twenty-three years ago, I married a woman and inherited Longbourn. I was not in love with your mother, Jane." He said it almost as an apology.

"I know, Papa," Jane offered, and gave him a small smile to indicate she understood his regrets.

"It was not long before I repented my decision. When you were born a year later, Jane, I decided that I did not want you to marry for convenience as I did. I wished you to marry for love, for I knew I would not always be there to love you and wanted you to be loved all your life. I began to economize and led your mother, and the neighborhood, to believe that I was negligent in my estate duties and that the estate was not as profitable as it once had been under my father's management. Thus, for twenty-odd years I was able to save several thousand pounds each year for dowries for you and your sisters."

"But I do not understand. Why would you want everyone to believe Longbourn was not profitable?" Mr. Bingley queried.

"Mr. Bingley, if it were well known that my daughters each had a dowry of fifteen thousand pounds, do you think I would have men showing up at my door with real affection? The answer is no; I would have to beat back the influx of suitors coming for my girls. Although they might fall in love and marry for love with the knowledge of their true fortune generally known, I believed it more likely that they would find a love match if they were not seen as wealthy. A gentleman who is willing to marry for love, regardless of fortune, is the only kind of gentleman my daughters deserve."

Jane began to see the wisdom in what her father had done and, with astonishment, said, "Can it really be true, Father? Fifteen thousand pounds?" Her voice fell away at the thought.

"Jane, Mr. Bingley, the reason I have asked for your secrecy is not just so that my remaining daughters may have a chance to win the hearts of worthy men but also because I have stipulated that my daughters will only receive the larger sum if they marry for love. If they do not, they will get the publicly acknowledged fifty pounds and an equal portion of five thousand pounds at the death of their mother."

Jane and Mr. Bingley sat stunned for a moment as they took in the news. Suddenly, the reminder that tomorrow Mr. Collins was to marry her sister came to mind. Jane knew that Mary did not love Mr. Collins, nor he her.

She looked to her father, who had been watching the play of emotions across her face. "And so Mary...?"

With a solemn and sad face, Mr. Bennet replied, "Will not get the fifteen thousand pounds." He turned to look out the window. "I wish... "

Jane stood and went to her father. She put a hand on his arm and looked at him as she said, "Papa, you cannot make the choices for them. You are a wise father, and I am proud of you for standing for your convictions. My gratitude for your sacrifice is great. I appreciate the opportunity to find a match based on love."

Mr. Bingley stood to join them. "Mr. Bennet, I too would like to thank you for your generosity and tender love for your daughter. I do not care whether she comes with fifty pounds or fifty thousand. I am grateful for the chance just to love her."

Mr. Bennet nodded his acceptance of their gratitude and turned to shake Mr. Bingley's hand as he said, "Welcome to the family, sir."

Chapter 11

The morning of Mary Bennet's wedding dawned a cloudless, cold, mid-December day. Elizabeth and Jane remained in their bedchamber to minimize exposure to the nervous flutterings of their mother on the first of five of the most important days of her life—her daughters' wedding days. Elizabeth and her sister had talked late into the evening about Jane's engagement to Mr. Bingley and Mary's wedding the next day. Elizabeth thought it strange that Jane suddenly seemed quite disturbed that Mary was marrying Mr. Collins. Jane had always found positive attributes about their cousin; it was in her easy nature to see the good in everyone. She even rebuked Elizabeth a time or two for speaking so ill of him during his stay at Longbourn. Yet now, the idea of the two marrying seemed to sadden her. Elizabeth wondered at the changed perspective as she prepared Jane's hair for the day.

Elizabeth thought about how Jane had always found reasons to view Mary's marriage as a positive event for the family but now seemed to judge her sister as having missed out on the opportunity for a marriage with love. Elizabeth smiled as she considered the reason for Jane's new romantic prospect. Having found a love match herself, Jane simply could not consider anything less as good enough for the rest of her sisters. Elizabeth concluded that Jane's new opinion on the matter must have stemmed from this profound new happiness with Bingley.

A knock on the door and the sound of their Aunt Gardiner's voice brought a smile to the girls' faces as they bid their aunt to enter. Aunt and Uncle Gardiner and their children had arrived late the previous evening from London to attend the wedding. They were to return to London just after Christmas.

"Jane, Lizzy, I see you are awake. I thought I would see you at breakfast this morning, but instead I find you hiding yourselves in your room." She glanced at the empty breakfast trays that indicated they had broken their fast in private.

"Aunt Gardiner!" Elizabeth exclaimed, as she went to her aunt and enveloped her in a warm embrace. "Was your journey very bad? You arrived quite late."

"It was perfectly fine, Lizzy. Your uncle had some business matters to finish, so our departure was later than I had hoped." She turned to Jane to receive a hug and then grasped Jane's arms. "Jane, I have heard of nothing else this morning but weddings. Your mother is in fine form for Mary's wedding, but she also has spoken of another wedding in the future." Madeline Gardiner pinched her lips into a smirk and raised her eyebrow.

Jane smiled radiantly. "Yes, Aunt, I am also to be married soon."

"I am glad to hear it. Your mother has made much mention of the groom, but since I had received Lizzy's letter regarding your courtship, I could easily determine which of my nieces this Mr. Bingley was likely to marry."

They all laughed and sat down together to catch up. Jane again expressed her delight in her engagement to Mr. Bingley and, as her aunt asked many questions about the proposal, courtship and, of course, the gentleman, the ladies were engaged in discussion for much of the morning. Elizabeth prided herself in her relative composure during the course of the conversation. However, as she had detected more than one interested glance from her aunt, she knew that her deception might not be entirely effective in the eyes of the lady who knew her best.

Before long, the time to leave for the church was at hand, and with less fanfare than Elizabeth would have expected, the entire population of Longbourn exited the house into carriages and rode to the church.

As Elizabeth settled herself in the pew to wait for the services to start, she had to marvel at the simplicity of the wedding arrangements. It was clear that time had been a major factor in putting limits on her mother's arrangements, but Elizabeth also knew that Mary had insisted on a simple wedding and, to the astonishment of all, was able to carry her point all the way towards convincing their mother. Elizabeth smiled in amazement at the way her sister had stood up to her mother, and she admitted she was impressed with Mary in this regard.

Elizabeth looked around at the assembled group. A few of their neighbors were in attendance, including Mr. Bingley, who sat with Jane and the Gardiners in conversation. Elizabeth turned her gaze to watch Mr. Collins speaking to the Reverend Watkins. It was obvious that Mr. Collins was attempting to counsel the more experienced man in regards to the wedding ceremony. She bit her lip in an attempt to quell her laughter as she watched the scene. It appeared Mr. Collins was expressing his wish for Reverend Watkins to recognize Lady Catherine de Bourgh's approval of the wedding in his opening statements, but it seemed to Elizabeth that her parson of fifteen years was not inclined to do so.

"Mr. Collins, I understand your wishes in this matter, but as her ladyship is not present, I do not feel it necessary to speak of her in my chapel."

"I respectfully disagree, sir. As she is my noble patroness, I feel it is important that those of my acquaintance recognize the significance of her ladyship's great condescension."

The reverend decided to try another angle. After politely accepting Mr. Collins's statement about his benefactor, Reverend Watkins remarked, "It appears her ladyship must be very selective in her choice of whom she deems to acknowledge in society, is that not so?"

"Oh, yes, Lady Catherine de Bourgh is most cognizant of her sphere," Mr. Collins replied with inflated self-importance.

"Well then, sir, correct me if I am wrong, for surely you know her ladyship better than I, but do you not think she would not wish to include in her *sphere* some of those in attendance today, and that my acknowledgement of her ladyship would grant those persons a claim to this acknowledgement?"

"I had not thought of that reverend, but of course, you are correct. Continue with the services as you see fit without any mention of her ladyship's condescension."

"Thank you, sir, for your solicitous advice. I believe we are ready to begin now if you will take your place."

Mr. Collins gave the reverend a gracious smile and bowed squeakily before resuming his spot just as the processional music began.

Elizabeth turned to watch her father walk Mary to the altar. She was inclined to look at the wedding as an opportunity for amusement, until her eyes rested on her father's face. She could see that, although he was keeping his face expressionless, his eyes were sad. Elizabeth's own heart became full as she remembered the tender talk she had with him over a week ago about love and the promise he compelled her to make that day only to marry for love. She had not considered how Mary's wedding would bother her father. She chastised herself for having only thought of herself that week, between her eagerness to see Mr. Darcy again and then her bitter disappointment upon learning of his return to London.

With these and many other disturbing reflections, Elizabeth spent the entirety of the wedding ceremony and much of the wedding breakfast in thought. Her subdued mood attracted the notice of her aunt. As Mr. and Mrs. Collins departed Longbourn for their journey to Kent, Elizabeth startled at the feel of her aunt's arm encircling hers and leading her towards the garden.

"Come, Lizzy, let us take a stroll in the garden."

Mr. Wickham reclined lazily in a corner booth at the back of Wilson's Pub in Meryton. He had ducked the morning's training maneuvers and was already well in his cups. He angrily swallowed the last of his ale and waved his hand to signal for another. *This venture is proving to be most encroaching on my free time.* He enrolled in the militia only as a means of temporary financial support, but it was not long after that he found Colonel Forster breathing down his neck at every turn. He felt eyes on the back of his neck and it irritated him. The other officers used to be fun to stir up a bit of trouble with, but as his gambling debts began to mount, they were starting to turn on him and report some insignificant infraction or other to the colonel, making his plans to secure a wealthy bride even more difficult.

Wickham kicked the chair next to him, causing it to slide across the wood floor. It was all Darcy's fault, and he knew it. All his troubles with Forster and the village of Meryton started when that man came into the county. *He is so damned selfish that he cannot allow me to be happy*, he thought bitterly. The more he thought about his current situation, the angrier he became, and it could all be laid at the feet of one man: Fitzwilliam Darcy. *He could never accept that his father loved me better. He refused to acknowledge me at every turn. If it were not for his selfish ways, I would be married to Georgiana right now and living the life I deserve instead of sitting in a dirty pub where everyone is looking at me with suspicious eyes.*

A barmaid approached with his requested pint of ale, and Wickham watched her figure as she walked uneasily towards him. He grinned wickedly as she came close enough for him to reach. With a quick motion, he grabbed her arm and pulled her onto his lap.

"Hello, miss," Wickham sneered as she struggled to free herself. "Oh, you're feisty. That is all right; I like a little fight in a woman sometimes."

"I'll 'ave none of dis, Mr. Wickham." The owner of the bar marched up and pulled his niece free of the man. "The likes of yous no welcome no more, sir."

Wickham spit angrily to the side as he said, "Your wench fell on me! I suggest that, if you do not approve of such behavior, you speak with the trollop and leave me be."

The man stood taller and lifted his chin. "I says yous not welcome, sir. Kin'ly leave m' pub."

"Don't mind if I do." Wickham stood and raked his eyes up and down the scared barmaid's body before saying, with disgust in his voice, "She isn't much of a temptation anyway. Flat as a board and plain as the day is long."

The few patrons of the pub began to voice their approvals of the owner's eviction of Wickham as he passed by them to leave. Wickham's ire rose significantly at the disrespectful way he was being treated and determined to find a way to humiliate and ruin Darcy once and for all. He left with a slam of the pub's door and walked towards his barracks. He had never been treated with such malice, and he was sure Darcy was behind it. He nearly had at the altar that Mary King girl with the recently inherited fortune when suddenly her uncle whisked her off to Bath. Then the father of those Bennet chits, who were always good for a little flirtation, refused his admittance into their home.

Ducking behind a wall as he spotted Colonel Forster and his young wife enter a shop across the road, Wickham decided it was time for a change as he was not about to suffer through more of that man's tyranny for having skipped maneuvers. Upon reaching his chambers, he pulled out a paper and writing supplies from the desk and sat to write a letter that would be the beginning of his revenge on Darcy. When he completed the letter, he searched through the possessions of his bunk mate until he found his purse. Gathering his belongings and the sack of coins, Wickham left to frank his letter and catch a ride with the post to London.

Elizabeth happily walked around the garden with her aunt in silence for a few minutes before speaking. "Aunt, I cannot tell you how wonderful it is to have you and Uncle here to visit us. With you here, we shall have a little more sense in the house."

"We are glad to be here, as you know. So, Lizzy, what did you think of the service?"

"Mr. Collins is ridiculous, of course, but it is what Mary wants, so I suppose there is nothing more to say."

Mrs. Gardiner leaned towards her niece as she enquired, "But what did you think about Reverend Watkins' closing counsel?"

Elizabeth thought back to the ceremony and tried to recall what the reverend had said but could not find a single part that she could remember with clarity. She had been more engaged in her own thoughts at the time. She looked at her aunt and recognized that her relation had seen her distraction during the service. With contrition, she said, "I confess, Aunt, I was rather occupied in my thoughts and did not attend the reverend's words."

Her aunt smiled indulgently before giving her a look of concern. "I noticed, Lizzy. Will you not tell me what is bothering you?"

Elizabeth looked away from her aunt as she thought about whether or not to share the feelings in her heart. Her folly in allowing affection to develop for a man of Mr. Darcy's station was great, but she also felt that it was materially lessened in its degree by not being generally known. She needed to put her feelings for Mr. Darcy aside, and that would be easier to do if they were not known to any beyond her own heart. Suddenly, she remembered her talk with her father and colored with embarrassment that he knew her feelings. It was definitely worse to have others know your mistakes, and so she decided she would not tell her aunt what was really troubling her.

"I suppose I am feeling a bit melancholy; that is all. Mary has made a foolish choice in her marriage, but that is done now. Jane will be married soon, and I suspect, with the wedding preparations that will begin now that Mary's is over, I will see less of her than I am used to. All these changes"—she paused and turned her lips up in a forced smile—"are just causing me to be a bit more reflective. But you are here now, dear Aunt, and I am determined to be as happy as ever."

Her aunt could tell she was being a little evasive but determined not to press the point. They continued their walk for a time, speaking of various and safer topics. After a while, they paused beneath a large oak tree and sat on a bench to listen to the birds.

Elizabeth's thoughts returned, as they had frequently in the past few days, to Mr. Darcy. Her anger had begun to burn out, leaving only a few warm embers and pleasant memories of their time together. She accepted that the majority of her unhappiness could not be laid at Mr. Darcy's feet as she was initially inclined to do when he first left the area. Since getting to know him better after her fall, she had found that he was generous and kind. She acknowledged that certain interludes in their acquaintance, especially during the ball at Netherfield, could not be explained as merely friendly but more on the level of romantic. This acceptance forced her to concede that Mr. Darcy probably did have feelings for her. Her heart spoke the truth of it even as she thought it. However, for whatever reason, his regard was not of a degree to keep him from leaving her, and for this she mourned.

With his removal to London, he would be amongst ladies of his own station and significance in the world and would soon forget her as she had nothing to entice him except a few lovely dances and memories. She looked up into the branches of the tree above her, and she was reminded of their day in the grove when she twisted her ankle. She blushed, remembering his tender touch and the deep timbre of his voice as he spoke.

With a touch of sadness, she realized that, with Bingley's marriage to Jane, she would likely be often in his company in the future. Although the thought quickened her heart rate in anticipation, it also reminded her that, for his sake and her own, she should learn to live without him, as he would no doubt marry someday. Her presence might make him uneasy as a reminder of the few weeks he spent in her company in Hertfordshire. Just then, her aunt's voice began to enter her consciousness.

"So what do you think of my idea, Lizzy?"

"Oh, forgive me, Aunt, I am afraid you caught me woolgathering. What is it you were saying?"

Her aunt's face showed concern as she repeated herself. "I was just suggesting, Lizzy, that perhaps a change of scenery might be good for you. How would you like to come to London with your uncle and me for a few weeks after Christmas?"

Elizabeth's mind raced quickly to Mr. Darcy again; she did not need to be pursuing him to the part of the country in which he lived. Then she remembered Bingley's saying that Mr. Darcy usually spent Christmas and the New Year at Pemberley with his sister and so would not likely be in town while she was. She smiled to her aunt with real gratitude for her kind offer. "I should like that best of all, Aunt."

"Then I will speak to your uncle and get your father's permission. And I am sure your mother will consent to spare your help with the wedding preparations if we suggest you could retrieve a few things for Jane's trousseau from the shops in London. What do you think?"

"You are very clever, Aunt. I think we shall manage a clean escape!" She laughed.

They stood to return to the house, and as they walked, Lizzy thought of her upcoming trip to London. Even if Mr. Darcy did remain in town for the holidays, she decided they were unlikely to move in the same circles, and she would be safe. *Certainly, I may enter his vicinity with impunity and rob it of a few of its pleasures without his perceiving me.* She smiled in anticipation of the new distractions that would help her recover from his charms. *A few walks in Hyde Park, perhaps a visit to the theatre, and certainly some happy excursions to the shops with my aunt will do quite nicely.*

Mr. Darcy rubbed his eyes and tried, once more, to focus on the document in his hands. It had been laborious to concentrate on the many items of business that required his attention since his return to London. He had not seen Elizabeth for over a week now, and for some reason, it was becoming harder rather than easier to forget her as he had hoped—especially since it seemed to be one of the few topics of conversation he could have with Georgiana that stirred any animation in the girl. He shook his head in puzzlement; why was Elizabeth such a source of interest to Georgiana, particularly after only one letter about her?

On his return a few days earlier, he had walked straight to the music room to see his sister. He had stood in the door frame and leaned his tired body against it as the sounds of her music washed over him. It was a great relief to be home in familiar and safe surroundings. Netherfield had begun to torture him as his memories of Elizabeth's visit had caused her image to haunt the halls and rooms. He could easily conjure her features, reaching for a book in the library or walking the length of the drawing room. Indulging in those images was his particular choice of self-torture. Now, however, he was home, safe in a house to which she had never ventured before; her ghost could not haunt these halls.

When Georgiana had finished the piece, he clapped his hands softly so as not to startle her with his unexpected presence. She turned at the sound and smiled brightly at him. His heart leapt with hope that perhaps she was returning to her previously happy disposition.

"William! I have missed you." She walked sedately towards him and accepted his embrace. "I did not anticipate your return so soon. Did you not enjoy your time in Hertfordshire?"

"Georgie." He spoke his pet name for her tenderly as he mussed her hair a bit. "I missed you too, dear. Your playing has really improved. I enjoyed listening to it just now as I always do." He leaned back to look at her face.

"Thank you." She shyly lowered her head, and he led her to a sofa in the room.

"Tell me, dear, what have you been doing while I was away?" He listened as she related the same trivial things she had written about in her letters. His new hope for her recovery began to fade a little as he watched her mechanically speak of nothing at all. He reached for her hand and frowned when she flinched slightly. He did not think he would ever understand the workings of the female heart.

"You did not answer me, William. Did you enjoy your stay in Hertfordshire? I did not anticipate your return until just before Christmas."

Her words pulled him from his thoughts; he had been mentally compiling possible solutions to Georgiana's mood. He looked up at his sister when she spoke the name of *her* county and the reference to his stay there.

Clearing his throat, he spoke with feigned indifference. "I had a very pleasant time there. Bingley has let a fine estate, and the neighbors, although a bit provincial, were, for the most part, enjoyable."

Georgiana was quiet for a time before finally deciding to broach the topic of most interest to her. Ever since her brother had written about a Miss Elizabeth Bennet, she had been fascinated. Her brother did not seem to realize that he had never before written of any lady in his letters. Although he had not mentioned having a particular regard for Miss Elizabeth, she recognized that something was significantly different about his relationship with this lady, or else he would not have written of her.

"You mentioned in your letter that Mr. Bingley was courting Miss Bennet.

She is one of his neighbors, is she not?"

He furrowed his brows at her introduction of this new topic. *What is she about?* "Yes, she lives at an estate called Longbourn three miles away."

"I see. So, Miss Elizabeth Bennet is probably going to marry Mr. Bingley?" Georgiana tried to hide her disappointment.

Mr. Darcy smiled slightly at the irony of having left Hertfordshire to avoid Miss Elizabeth, only to come home and have his sister eager to speak of her. "No, Georgie. Miss *Jane* Bennet is the eldest of five sisters and is the one Bingley is courting. Miss Elizabeth is her sister next in age."

Georgiana suppressed a sigh of relief and sat up with a smile in her eyes that her brother had not seen in a while. "I understand now. You wrote in your letter that you had enjoyed talking to Miss Elizabeth. What did you talk about?" She wished she could think of a more plausible way to steer the conversation of Miss Elizabeth in the direction of what she really wanted to know—whether he had any feelings for the lady.

"We spoke of many topics. She enjoys the theatre and reads a variety of books."

"Does she play and sing?"

Mr. Darcy watched her attempt to look disinterestedly around the room as she spoke. He puzzled over her duplicity and answered hesitantly, "She does. I have heard her many times."

"Did you enjoy her performance? Was she very good? What kind of music does she play?" Georgiana's interest was betrayed by her rapid speech and her brother laughed at her excitement.

"Georgiana, why all this sudden interest in Miss Elizabeth?"

Biting her lip, she regained control over her enthusiasm and accessed the familial Darcy talent of hiding her emotions from her face. She shrugged indifferently at his question. "I suppose I am just intrigued by what you have said about the lady. She sounds interesting and unlike so many other ladies I have met."

Mr. Darcy ignored his suspicion for a moment to indulge his sister, as her animation on this particular topic reminded him of her spirit before Ramsgate. "Miss Elizabeth plays and sings very well. Though perhaps not as talented as some, her expression is excellent, and I have rarely heard anything I enjoyed more." He paused, recollecting the last time he heard her sweet soprano voice. "You are right; she is quite singular and unlike any lady of my acquaintance."

Georgiana detected the tenderness that infused his last statement and smiled to herself. "Do you think she is pretty?"

Mr. Darcy started at the rather bold look on her face and the decided impropriety of her question. Frowning at her, he warned, "Georgiana." He watched determination set into her features and her eyebrows rise in challenge. He was not sure whether to rejoice at his sister's budding confidence or reprove her for disregarding his censure. In the end, he relented as her look of determination reminded him a bit of an angry cat trying to be a tiger. He chuckled before answering her with a sigh. "Yes, dear, she is beautiful." He paused as his mind brought Elizabeth's lovely face before him and said quietly and more to himself, although his sister heard, "She is the most beautiful woman I know."

Georgiana felt a sudden happiness such as she had not felt in a long time. When Wickham deceived her, she lost her faith in love. She lost her confidence in many things and still felt frustrated at her poor understanding and choices. She could not quite fathom why this woman, Miss Elizabeth Bennet, held her interest. Certainly, the fact that her brother had written of her was unique and intrigued her, but there was more. The more she learned of Elizabeth, the more she was determined to try to be like her. Watching her brother's peaceful, faraway look as he spoke of Elizabeth made her wonder whether love was not such a terrible thing after all.

Darcy awoke from his spell when she remarked, "And so, she has four sisters. How nice for her. I always wanted a sister."

Darcy frowned at her, even as he was a bit amused by her suggestive tone. All this talk of Elizabeth, although it seemed to make his sister happy, only served to sour his mood, and he determined to change the topic. They talked of other matters for a while longer before he took his leave to change out of his traveling clothes. Since that day, Georgiana had brought up the topic of Elizabeth Bennet a number of times.

A knock on his study door brought Mr. Darcy back to the present. He barely had time to bid, "Enter," before the door swung open and his cousin Colonel Fitzwilliam pushed past the butler, essentially preempting his announcement of the colonel's arrival.

"Darcy, you bore—when did you get back to London? I had to hear it from Mother, who, I can tell you, was not happy to have heard it first from a friend who saw you shopping with Georgiana yesterday."

Mr. Darcy chuckled at his cousin's ribbing and shook his hand. He turned to his chagrined butler and said, "You must forgive my cousin, Mr. Carroll; his manners are deplorable."

Colonel Fitzwilliam feigned offense and turned to the butler while addressing his cousin's barb. "Mr. Carroll and I have an understanding, don't we, man? He knows I prefer to walk in unannounced."

Mr. Carroll gave a proper bow and said, "Of course, sir." Turning to his employer, he asked, "Will you be needing anything, sir?"

Mr. Darcy's raised eyebrow sent a silent question to his cousin regarding refreshments. Upon seeing the colonel shake his head, he turned to his butler and said, "No, thank you, Mr. Carroll; that will be all."

Mr. Carroll gave another quick bow and said, "Very good, sir," before closing the door behind him.

Colonel Fitzwilliam burst into laughter. "I make him so mad every time. I do not understand why he still insists on trying to make it into the room to announce me before I do. But I tell you, Darcy, I have great sport with him over it. Today he nearly ran to stay ahead of me!"

"You are incorrigible! He is simply doing his job, and your deplorable manners are making it difficult for him. Besides, I think you try to annoy him on purpose."

"Perhaps I do." The two laughed as they took their seats. Colonel Richard Fitzwilliam and his cousin Darcy had been the best of friends from childhood. Richard was a few years Darcy's senior and, being of a naturally jovial sort, enjoyed teasing his younger cousin. Darcy's somber personality made him an easy target, yet he never could be angry with his cousin for his pranks. As the two grew into manhood, their relationship remained essentially the same. Richard would tease and laugh at his cousin, who had learned to laugh at himself occasionally but pretended distaste for Richard's behavior.

When the two cousins had settled into comfortable positions, the colonel enquired, "So, Darcy, where have you been these past few weeks?"

Mr. Darcy's smile faded only slightly as he replied, "In Hertfordshire with Bingley. You remember my friend?"

"Ah, yes, the unnaturally happy one." He laughed at his cousin's disapproving face and continued. "What the deuces were you doing in that part of the country?"

"He asked for my advice regarding an estate he is leasing." His answer was so matter-of-fact that Richard, who knew Darcy better than himself sometimes, detected something unusual about it.

"For two months?"

Darcy shifted in his chair uneasily and shrugged his shoulders with indifference. "He has never had an estate, and there was much to consider."

Richard merely nodded in acquiescence but sat staring at his cousin for a few minutes. Darcy detected his gaze and tried to ignore it. Whenever his cousin smelled blood, he was ruthless, and Darcy was proud of himself for appearing disinterested in the topic of his recent trip. He hoped his cousin would see nothing amiss.

"Well, I am glad that you could lend your experience to your friend. Does he stay in Hertfordshire?"

"Yes, he enjoys the area tremendously; in fact, he has recently begun courting a local gentleman's daughter." Darcy flinched slightly at his mistake. Knowing Richard was always interested in hearing about ladies, he should not have brought up Bingley's news. He held his breath for a moment, hoping his cousin would uncharacteristically ignore the chance to enquire about the lady. His hope was for naught, for when Richard had seen his cousin's sudden discomfort, he could not help himself and decided to pry deeper.

"You don't say! Well, good for him. Does Hertfordshire boast of many good-looking ladies?"

"There are a few handsome ones, yes." Darcy nonchalantly brushed an invisible speck of dust off his trousers.

"I had not known Hertfordshire was the place to meet fine ladies. It has been a while since I have been in company with Bingley; perhaps I ought to pay him a visit." Richard watched his cousin squirm and realized that a lady was behind his discomfort. The idea was completely fascinating as he had never before seen his cousin enamored by any lady. This lady must be something special, indeed, to have caught his cousin's interest.

Mr. Darcy, on the other hand, was trying desperately to keep his composure at the thought of his handsome and naturally charming cousin traveling to Hertfordshire and possibly making the acquaintance of Elizabeth. She was so witty and delightful when she teased and stunning when her laughter brought a sparkle to her eyes, that he knew his cousin would immediately take to her. *What if he is able to win her affections?* The idea boiled inside him, and for a moment, he could do nothing but torture himself with the image of Elizabeth as his cousin's wife.

With a serious tone, Richard looked at his cousin and asked, "Who is she, Darcy?"

A startled Darcy looked up and said, "What?" He realized his abruptness was telling and so added, "I am sure I do not have the privilege of understanding your question."

Richard laughed. "I am sure you do not." His laughter grew more unrestrained when he looked at his cousin, who was frowning seriously at him.

"Richard, was there a particular reason you came to my home today?" Mr. Darcy's temper was beginning to chafe at his cousin's discovery, and he desperately desired a change of topic.

Richard decided to humor his cousin but by no means planned to leave this intriguing subject alone. He would certainly revisit it—and soon. He chuckled, though, at the stern look on his cousin's face. "I see you cannot be deterred. As a matter of fact, I did have a reason. I received a missive from another colonel in a regiment stationed in *your* lovely Hertfordshire regarding Mr. Wickham. He tells me you informed him of Wickham's character upon learning the man had joined his regiment and that you invited him to contact me."

"I did. Wickham has joined the regiment for God-knows-what reason, and just my luck, it was the very regiment stationed in the town near Bingley's new home."

Richard was now quite serious. "What is the man up to now, do you think?"

Darcy shook his head and ground his teeth together before speaking. "I have no idea. I am sure I have not heard the last of him after Ramsgate. He was pretty angry for having his plans spoiled to get Georgiana's dowry, and I shall never forgive him."

Richard stood and helped himself to a glass of his cousin's fine port. "Nor shall I. I am glad you contacted his superior officer. I wrote back to Colonel Forster to confirm that, should Wickham misbehave, I would be more than happy to lend my assistance." He laughed a dry, wicked laugh. "But to be honest, I am glad that Wickham has joined the militia. It will give us the ability to watch his moves. I only wish he had been stupid enough to join my regiment, for I sorely wish to teach him a few maneuvers."

A knock on the door interrupted the conversation, and Mr. Darcy went to open it. Mr. Carroll stood with a tray in his hand. "This letter has just arrived, sir, by way of express."

Mr. Darcy took the letter, saying, "Thank you, Mr. Carroll," before closing the door and returning to his seat by his cousin. He looked at the letter and saw that it was posted from Meryton but without a return address. He wondered who would have sent him something anonymous from Meryton, and for a moment, a delightful image of Elizabeth writing to him secretly entered his mind. A smile came unbidden, and before he could hide it, his cousin spoke.

"I see you have a letter from Hertfordshire. Forgive me, your distraction allowed me to spy at the envelope."

Darcy frowned at Richard then stood and walked towards the window to open the letter. He almost stopped himself as he considered whether or not he wanted to read Elizabeth's letter in front of his cousin. However, he could not help himself or wait any longer, so he broke the seal and frowned at the familiar male handwriting.

Darcy,

It was delightful to have moved in the same circles as you again in Hertfordshire. I imagine neither of us expected such a pleasure. I could relate news of our common acquaintances here, but I shall not bother with that for now. You have done a pretty trick on me here, Darcy. I am certain it was you who gave Colonel Forster his distaste for me, and now many of the families in the area are refusing my company. It made me realize it has been ages since you and I talked. I believe it has been too long, and I look forward to meeting with you soon. Give my regards to Georgiana. She is such a darling.

G.W.

Mr. Darcy's fists clenched in anger, and he turned to his cousin. "Perhaps, I was too hasty. It appears Wickham is up to something." He shoved the letter in his cousin's hands and huffed at his confused face.

Richard began to read the letter, and Darcy listened as his cousin let out a few decidedly ungentlemanly words before asking, "What are you going to do, Darcy?"

Darcy spun around to face his cousin and barked, "What am I to do, Richard? The man will never stop until he makes me absolutely miserable. You read it. He means to contact me, and he mentioned Georgiana. Do you think he is planning a second attempt with her?" He paced the room in agitation.

Richard shook his head. "Actually, no, Darcy. I think even Wickham knows that chance is lost to him. He knows you are here and that Georgiana is, too. She is perfectly safe from him. I think he has something new in mind, and I wish I knew what it was. I suppose there is nothing you can do for now. Let me know if you hear from him again."

With frustrated resignation, Darcy sank into a chair. "I will let you know."

"Well, I should be going. Is Georgiana in the music room? I wish to say hello to her before I leave."

"I believe she is."

"You know my mother was unhappy to have learned of your arrival in London from that gossip mill, Miss Varner. You know she considers you like a son, Darcy."

Mr. Darcy looked at his cousin and smiled. "Yes, I know. Tell Aunt Ellen I would be delighted if she and Uncle Henry would join me for dinner later this week. Any day is fine. You may come too, Richard."

"How kind of you, Darcy!" Richard feigned offense and added, "I will let her know. It will make her happy to see you again. She worries about you, but you know that."

Darcy sighed. "Yes, I know."

Darcy stood to walk his cousin to the door and bid him goodbye. He stopped when Richard turned to speak again.

"Say, Darcy, when are you and Georgiana leaving for Pemberley for Christmas?"

Darcy paused a minute as he considered his cousin's question. With Wickham's letter causing him worry, he wondered whether staying in London might not be better. He would be closer to Richard if he were needed. The idea of removing to Pemberley after spending so many weeks imagining Elizabeth there was also a deterrent. Besides, if he was honest with himself, he did not want to put so many miles between himself and Elizabeth just yet.

"I believe we may stay in London this year for the holidays."

Richard eyed his cousin suspiciously but said calmly, "That will make my mother happy. Can I tell her you will be in town?"

"You may—unless you want her to hear it from Miss Varner."

They both laughed, and Richard patted his cousin on the back as he made his good-byes. Darcy watched him walk towards the music room, closed his study door and leaned his back against it. He suddenly felt very tired, and he knew Wickham's letter had everything to do with it.

Chapter 12

With her aunt and uncle present at Longbourn, Elizabeth's time was so engaged during the day that the troubles of her heart usually were successfully set aside. Between visiting with her aunt, shopping for last minute Christmas gifts for her family and the ever-constant discussion of Jane's wedding details, Elizabeth, who usually found solitude preferable, was grateful for the diversions. When evening came, however, her troubled thoughts were her only company. At night in her bed, she found sleep eluded her until the early morning hours as she spent most of the night in a flux of emotions.

There were moments when she nearly turned to wake Jane and confess all to her regarding her feelings for Mr. Darcy. In those moments of weakness, she had nearly convinced herself that sharing her burden would lighten it as she had always experienced in the past. However, the peacefully sleeping form of her sister always made her pause. She considered what the revelation would do to Jane, who was so compassionate; she knew Jane could not help but feel a bit of her pain if she knew. Elizabeth would then roll over and stare at the ceiling as she changed her mind. Jane did not deserve to have anything weigh down the lightness of her heart during her engagement. Furthermore, the knowledge of how Elizabeth loved and missed Darcy would forever make her sensitive sister uncomfortable after her marriage whenever they were forced into company together.

It was after a particularly trying night that Elizabeth rose at dawn, having only experienced a few hours of restless sleep. She quietly retrieved her dressing gown, pulled its soft wool around her shoulders and sat on the windowsill.

With unseeing eyes, she looked out the window and played with the frost that had accumulated on the windowpane. Her dreams for the past week had one principle element—Mr. Darcy. She would have peaceful dreams of their encounter in the woods, only to have a different ending with her alone and unable to escape as a fierce wind blew trees down around her. In other dreams, she spoke to Mr. Darcy, but he was angry at her, his features twisting in rage, as she stood stunned.

The night before, she dreamt they were dancing at Netherfield again and nobody else was in the room. The music seemed to flow around them like a current; their gazes never left each other. Just as the dance ended, the door to the ballroom opened, and Miss Bingley walked in. Darcy looked at Elizabeth and, without a word, shrugged his shoulders and left her standing alone in the empty room as he exited with Miss Bingley on his arm.

A noise from the bed startled Elizabeth from the remembrance of her dream, and she looked towards her sister. Jane was still sleeping peacefully, but as Elizabeth turned back to the window, she noticed that in her absent mental wandering, she had drawn several sets of his initials in the frost. She hastily rubbed her palm across the surface to erase the letters. She stood up and, with a sigh, began her morning toilette. After she dressed and sat down to un-plait her hair to put it up for the day, she noticed her reflection in the mirror.

Her eyes held dark circles, and her face was pale. She finished her hair and went to splash cool water from the basin on her face to help bring some color to her cheeks. When she returned to the mirror, she noticed a slight improvement, but the rest could not be helped. With another sigh, she quietly left her bedchamber and descended the stairs in hopes of getting a cup of restorative tea before the rest of the house woke. When she neared the door to her father's study, she was startled and let out a gasp when the door suddenly opened, revealing her father.

"Papa! You scared me, I did not expect…" Her voice died away as she laughed uneasily at the pounding of her heart.

Mr. Bennet reached his hand out to his daughter and, upon obtaining possession of it, spoke to her as he led her into his study. "Forgive me for startling you, Lizzy. I had not meant to. I heard you coming down the stairs and did not want to miss the opportunity to speak to you. Won't you come in and visit with your Papa a while? It has been some time since you did."

Elizabeth colored in embarrassment and guilt as she considered how she had tried to avoid any conference with her father since learning of Mr. Darcy's departure. She did not want him to broach the topic most close to her heart and so had busied herself with their guests and other ventures.

"Yes, Papa, let me just pour myself a cup of tea." She went to the tea things at his sideboard as he closed the door. "Can I pour you one, too?"

"I believe I will have some tea. Thank you. You know how I like it, I trust."

Elizabeth smiled. "Yes, with more sugar than you ought." She shook her head in mock reprimand but heaped another spoonful into his cup.

"Well, one never knows. You have not had tea with your old, boring father in such a time; I began to wonder if you would forget how I take it. Perhaps you have been too much in raptures over wedding lace and ribbons, like your mother, to have noticed your neglect."

Elizabeth smiled apologetically as she handed him his cup and took hers to her seat across from his at the fire. "I have not forgotten your preferences, nor am I in raptures over lace. That I can assure you, sir." She tried to chuckle lightheartedly.

For a moment, they warmed themselves quietly by the fire, and Elizabeth allowed the heat from her cup to soothe her. She breathed in the calming aroma and realized how much she had missed being in this room with her father.

Mr. Bennet pretended to relax in his chair and watch the flames of the fire lick the logs in the hearth while surreptitiously surveying his favorite daughter. She had been in low spirits for a while now, and although she often laughed or teased with her siblings, he had detected the occasional distracted look or abrupt turn of her features. The dark circles under her eyes indicated she had not been sleeping well. What had bothered him most, though, was her decided absence from his study and near avoidance of him for over a week. It was most unusual, as she had always spent time with him there. Sometimes it would be a quick hello, and other times she would sit and stay for a few hours to talk or read.

He watched one of her slim hands reach up to adjust a curl near her ear and then rub at her temple slightly. He frowned and asked, "Are you feeling well, Lizzy? You do not look like you slept well last night."

Elizabeth started and sat straighter in her chair. "I am perfectly fine, Papa, but you are right, I did not sleep well."

"Why not?" he asked, with evident concern in his voice.

Elizabeth looked up and gave a reassuring smile. "I suppose with the wedding planning, Christmas in a few days and our guests, I had too much on my mind to sleep."

"Was that all that was on your mind, Lizzy?"

Elizabeth colored, and her eyes flashed to her father's. His face was kind and patient, but she knew, as with her Aunt Gardiner, that she was not likely to fool him. She bowed her head for a moment and spoke quietly, "No, that was not all."

Mr. Bennet put his cup down and leaned over to rest his hand on her knee so that she would look at him. "Would you like to talk about it, dear?"

His tender voice and gentle entreaty nearly shook her reserve regarding her feelings. "I do not know... that is to say... I have been so foolish, Papa." Elizabeth placed her tea on the table and covered her face with her hands as she felt the hot sting of tears.

Mr. Bennet furrowed his brows and thought of what he could say. He began to understand the reason behind his daughter's strange behavior possibly having something to do with the removal of a certain gentleman from the neighborhood.

"Dear girl, do not lose hope. It is not as bad as it now seems, I am sure."

Elizabeth looked at her father and saw, from the look on his face, that he knew what was troubling her. He seemed to believe everything would work out. His kindness and faith comforted her even if she was not sure she could accept them. She smiled in thanks, and they sat back in their chairs to return to their private thoughts.

Having spent some considerable time in conversation with Mr. Darcy on their ride about the estate, Mr. Bennet had seen ample evidence of the regard the man had for his daughter. Therefore, he was not worried about the reason for Elizabeth's distress. During their ride, Mr. Bennet had purposely made casual mention of Lizzy or 'his daughters' as he pointed out a view or prospect here and there. Each reference caused a slight change in Mr. Darcy's countenance.

But the moment he knew for sure that the gentleman was in love with his daughter was when they had stopped to rest briefly under a large maple tree. Mr. Bennet had chuckled as he recalled the specific tree they were under. Mr. Darcy was then forced to question the source of his humor. Mr.

Bennet's eyes filled with laughter as he related the memory that had come to him regarding their location.

"I do not know if I should tell you, sir. I think my Lizzy would be quite upset with me if I did."

Mr. Darcy's head turned abruptly towards his companion, and his eyes went wide with poorly hidden interest as he said reluctantly, "Then perhaps you had better not say, sir."

Mr. Bennet could clearly see that Mr. Darcy did not mean his words. As the memory was washing fresh through his thoughts, he could not help but share it. "She will, no doubt, wish that I not reveal this to anyone, but if I have your promise of secrecy, sir, I will share it with you."

Mr. Darcy struggled a bit with indecision. He wanted to know anything he could about Elizabeth but did not want to raise her ire. In the end, curiosity won over ethics. He smiled mischievously at her father and nodded his consent to continue the story.

Mr. Bennet reached for a low-lying branch and held it for a moment as he considered where to begin. "When Lizzy was a little girl, she was quite . . . shall we say, enthusiastic in her ventures, as I am sure you can imagine." Mr. Bennet smiled, and Mr. Darcy chuckled to himself at the way her father gently suggested that Elizabeth was a bit wild and passionate. It was something he could easily picture, and the image brought a smile to his face.

"When she was eleven, she had somehow procured a pair of boy's breeches. Now, how she had come to obtain such an article of clothing in a house without brothers, I still do not know and she has never admitted. However, obtain them she did, and one day she came down to breakfast wearing them instead of her usual dress." Mr. Bennet had to stop to chuckle again at the memory.

Mr. Darcy raised his hand to his mouth to cover his own amusement as Mr. Bennet collected himself to continue.

"I apologize; I had forgotten this story until now, and I can easily recollect the scene of that morning in the breakfast room. As you can imagine, Lizzy's mother was quite upset over the state of dress of her second eldest daughter and demanded she return to her room and change. Lizzy refused, and the two quarreled over the issue until Lizzy ran from the house. I was summoned by Mrs. Bennet to retrieve her before any of the neighbors saw how scandalously she was dressed."

Mr. Bennet and Mr. Darcy both erupted in chuckles at this point, and Mr. Bennet watched as his companion's eyes not only were filled with mirth but also touched with obvious admiration and feeling for his Lizzy.

"I ventured out in search of her and found her at the top of this very tree." Mr. Bennet pulled at the limb he held as he looked through the branches to the top. "When I came to her, she was quite upset and told me, quite vehemently I assure you, that she was never going to come down from this tree and that she would live up there for the rest of her life." The two men burst into laughter again.

"Of course, I tried reasoning with her, but she would not come down. She declared she would rather wear breeches than the frilly gowns her mother chose for her. I still remember her passionate response when I told her if she did not wear gowns, she would not grow up to be a lady. She looked me in the eye and, with a boldness I have yet to tame, declared, '*Then I shall not become a lady. I shall cut off all my hair and join the Navy, where I can wear breeches every day and travel anywhere I want.*'"

Mr. Darcy's rich, deep baritone laughter surprised Mr. Bennet as it came from the usually sedate man. When his amusement calmed a bit, he turned to Mr. Bennet and asked, "What happened then, sir?"

Mr. Bennet shrugged his shoulders and smiled at the memory. "I gave her my consent to join the Navy and went home. Eventually she got hungry, and as Mrs. Bennet had refused to allow her to eat if she was not properly attired, she changed her clothes and ate her dinner with a pout on her face. The breeches did not make another appearance and disappeared as mysteriously as they arrived." Mr. Bennet looked towards his companion with a smile. "Though I suppose Mrs. Bennet had something to do with that."

Mr. Darcy chuckled quietly as Mr. Bennet watched him. It was at that moment he knew that the gentleman was in love with his daughter. His face was filled with an unconcealed adoration and contentment as he sat quietly in thought over the revelation regarding Elizabeth.

Now sitting in his study with the same daughter who nine years before had passionately declared her intentions to join the Navy, Mr. Bennet, too, was filled with love and adoration for her. She was still just as beautifully defiant, passionate and devoted to the voice of her heart, and he felt for her as she obviously struggled with her feelings for Mr. Darcy.

He stood up to replace his teacup on the tray table. He patted his daughter's back and spoke tenderly to her as she looked up at him. "Give him time, Lizzy. Give yourself time."

Elizabeth's brows twitched as she pulled her legs up under her and leaned against the side of the chair. Mr. Bennet moved to his desk and began looking over his correspondence and estate matters. Before long, he could hear Elizabeth's quiet breathing. Turning around in his chair, he found she had fallen asleep. He sat there a moment considering her sleeping form. After a short while, he stood up, carefully placed a blanket over her and returned to his desk with a sigh.

After his butler closed the study door, Mr. Darcy turned to his cousin and invited him to sit. He shook his head in rebuke for a moment before saying, "That was hardly fair, cousin."

Colonel Fitzwilliam laughed and propped his feet up on the ottoman as he shrugged his indifference.

With barely concealed amusement, Darcy continued his rebuke. "You know, if I begin to lose valuable members of my staff to your charades, I shall not be amused. Mr. Carroll's wife is my housekeeper and essential to the smooth running of my household. If you drive away my butler, she will go too!" Mr. Darcy could not maintain his serious mien at the chuckle Richard gave to his speech.

"But Darcy, you should have seen the man's face when I handed my hat and gloves to *him* instead of the footman and left to find you. He had only time to unceremoniously dump the items on the man before trying to catch up with me."

"Well, temper yourself a bit if you can. The only reason he stays on under my employ is that I have it on good authority from Mrs. Carroll that it is as much a game to him as it is to you. She believes he tries to provoke you into behaving badly by pretending his frustration."

Richard's eyebrows shot up at this revelation. "Is that so? Well then, I might have to reconsider my next move."

Mr. Darcy poured his cousin a glass of wine, and after procuring one for himself, he sat down opposite to him. It was a signal that the intended purpose of the visit was about to begin.

With new seriousness, Mr. Darcy thanked his cousin for coming. "Last night when you and your parents dined here, you said you had a matter of importance to discuss with me."

Richard's jovial face instantly drew to a frown as he put his feet on the floor and leaned towards his cousin, matching his gravity. "Yesterday, I received a letter from Colonel Forster." He saw Darcy frown with frustration. "He informed me that Wickham has left the regiment—deserted the militia. He has not been seen in the area for several days."

Mr. Darcy stood abruptly and began to pace the floor in front of the fireplace. "Do you think he is coming here?" His voice rose in anger. "Coming for Georgiana?"

"Calm yourself, Darcy. I do not think he is so stupid as to try to come for Georgiana, but perhaps you should tell the household she is not at home for visits and require a footman to accompany her and Mrs. Annesley on their outings."

"I will accompany her myself from now on. I cannot let Wickham get near her," Mr. Darcy said resolutely.

"Very well, do as you wish, but there is more." Richard watched as his cousin stopped his pacing and stared at him.

Before he could continue, Darcy nearly shouted, "What other news, Cousin! Go on with it for heaven's sake!"

"I am just getting to it, Darcy. Colonel Forster's man reported that Wickham was witnessed leaving on the London post coach the day you received his letter."

"He must be planning something, Richard. What is the militia doing to recover him?"

"I have sent word throughout my regiment and those in the surrounding areas, but there is no place he can be so well hidden as in London. Believe me; I want to find him as well."

Mr. Darcy simply nodded his head distractedly as he walked to his desk and wrote a quick note to his housekeeper, informing her of the new policy regarding Georgiana. "Excuse me a moment, Richard," he said as he briefly left the room to deliver his note.

Upon his return, he took his seat across from his cousin, and the two sat quietly for a moment. Richard looked to him and said, "Perhaps it is good you are in London for Christmas, even if Wickham is here too. It is certainly easier to coordinate efforts this way." When Darcy simply nodded, Richard decided a change of topic might be useful. It was not in *his* nature to brood like his cousin. "Does Bingley stay at his estate for the holidays or will he come to London?"

Mr. Darcy looked to his cousin at the change in topic and said, "He is staying in Hertfordshire. Christmas is only days away, and his intended's family is there." After a pause, he added distractedly, "Miss Bennet does have an aunt and uncle in Cheapside, now that I recollect, but I suppose they would have gone to Hertfordshire for the wedding last week and will remain there for the holidays."

"Wedding? Intended?" Richard looked to his cousin in confusion.

Mr. Darcy nodded his head. "I suppose I forgot to mention I received a letter a few days ago from Bingley. He has proposed to Miss Jane Bennet of Longbourn, and they are engaged. The wedding I referred to is that of a younger sister, Miss Mary Bennet, who married our Aunt Catherine's clergyman."

Richard surprised Darcy with his sudden burst of laughter. "What a small world, eh, Darcy? Bingley is going to be related to our Aunt Catherine's rector. What kind of man is this parson? I cannot recall his name from our visit to Rosings last spring."

Mr. Darcy smiled mischievously as he remembered the odious Mr. Collins. He allowed himself a moment to let his thoughts drift back to the Netherfield ball and his orchestration of that man's future. "He was not there when we were last. His name is Collins, and he is as ridiculous as they come, Cousin." Darcy laughed lightly. "And our aunt takes prodigious care of him."

Both men broke into laughter as Richard said, "She takes prodigious care of everyone she can get her claws on."

Richard then recalled his cousin's uneasiness when he had previously provoked him on the subject of ladies in Hertfordshire. Finding in this current topic an avenue in which to return to that one, he studied his cousin closely and said, "Tell me about Bingley's girl."

Mr. Darcy swirled the contents of his glass around for a moment and, without looking up, said, "I am not sure what there is to know. She is a gentleman's daughter, and their estate, Longbourn, is a few miles from Bingley's. He met her at an assembly held in Meryton."

Richard's apparent lack of interest put Darcy a little at ease but did nothing to slow his now rapidly beating heart. "And has she any brothers?"

Darcy tried to match his cousin's bored tone as he answered, "No brothers, only four sisters. In fact, Mr. Collins is their cousin and will inherit Longbourn as it is entailed from the female line."

Richard watched the brief gleam pass across his cousin's eyes and his renewed interest in the contents of his glass. "Four sisters! That is singular. Knowing Bingley, he will have taken the most beautiful one. Mr. Collins has married another and that leaves only three to choose from for you and me, Cousin. What say you; shall we be brothers to Bingley?"

Although his comment was made in jest, it had hit an unexpected mark. Richard was delightfully surprised to see his cousin's eyes dart up to his. Darcy's face first displayed shock but soon turned into one of embarrassed confusion as if he had been caught at something. Richard knew that face well, because as boys, the two of them had often been caught in various ill-conceived schemes.

"Whoa-ho, Darcy! What is this you are hiding from me? I believe I have found the location of the lady who has caught your eye in Hertfordshire."

"I have no notion of what you are speaking, Richard," Darcy shot back.

"I am sure you do. Tell me about her, Darcy. She must really be something if she has caught your interest."

"I have nothing to say to you." Darcy swallowed the contents of his glass and stood to refill it from the decanter.

"Very well, then, Cousin. I shall know how to act. If you will just allow me some ink and paper, I shall write Bingley directly and ask him if he knows of any particular lady in residence at Longbourn who might have caught your attention."

Darcy turned around to face his cousin. "You shall do no such thing, Richard!"

Richard smiled. He now knew it was just a matter of reeling his cousin in; he had already gotten Darcy stuck on his hook.

"Why do you not tell me who this lady is then, Darcy? What are you afraid of?"

Darcy glared at his cousin and fumed at his challenge for several long minutes. After a lengthy battle of wills, his shoulders drooped, and he folded himself into his chair again, saying in defeat, "Her name is Miss Elizabeth Bennet."

Richard smiled in triumph. He marveled at the sudden drop in his cousin's countenance, as it looked as though he were about to relate that the lady had died or something equally horrific. "Why the long face, Darcy; what is wrong with the lady?"

Darcy looked up briefly at his cousin as Richard sat himself down in the chair across from him. He lifted his chin and said defensively, "There is nothing wrong with her."

Richard sat back and raised his eyebrows at the suddenly fierce tone of his cousin's voice. "I did not mean to imply that something was *wrong* with the girl. But you look as if you are not happy talking about her." He laughed as Darcy gave him a sarcastic expression that said he, indeed, did not wish to speak of her.

"What does Miss Elizabeth look like? Is she handsome?"

Shaking his head at his cousin, Darcy again submitted in defeat. "I should have known you would not give up. I shall tell you all now, and then you must leave me be on the matter." His eyes took on a faraway look as he began. "Yes, Miss Elizabeth is pretty. She is amongst the most handsome women of my acquaintance. She has lovely chestnut brown hair and sparkling, expressive, brown eyes. She is funny, passionate, lively and warm. She loves to read and walk about the countryside. She mocks me whenever she can, and I cannot seem to get enough of it. She is irresistible." Mr. Darcy smiled, lost in memory for a minute, before adding, "She used to despise me, I am sure, but we met once under... unique circumstances... and I believe we understand each other better now."

Richard sat back in awe while listening to his cousin. He had never heard Darcy say anything beyond a slight compliment about a lady. Never had he expressed such admiration. Richard watched, fascinated, while his cousin spoke about Miss Elizabeth Bennet. Darcy absentmindedly took out his pocket watch and, after opening it, continued to speak while he stared at it. The action confused Richard, and he wondered why his cousin felt the need to check the time while speaking of Miss Elizabeth.

When Darcy finally finished, he sat quietly looking at his watch. Richard was puzzled about his cousin's continued distraction but pushed the thought away and asked, in a serious tone, "Do you love her, Darcy?"

Mr. Darcy snapped the lid of his watch shut and lifted his head to look at his cousin in alarm. He could not speak anymore of Elizabeth. The fact that his feelings were so obvious to his cousin spoke only of the great distance he still needed to cover in order to forget his feelings for her. Speaking the words out loud would brand their truth into his heart, and he could not do that.

He pulled his face into one that brooked no argument. "I do not wish to speak of this, Richard."

His cousin put his hands together and stared at him in mocking challenge as he raised one eyebrow and again questioned with equal fervor, "Are you in love with her, Darcy?"

Mr. Darcy glared at his cousin and fumed in anger at his blatant disrespect for his privacy on the matter. After a while, he could not handle his cousin's mocking countenance and finished his drink in one gulp. The warm burn down his throat nearly caused him to cough, and he stood abruptly and walked away from his cousin to the window. Holding his arms rigidly behind his back, he looked angrily out the window, trying to ignore his cousin's challenging gaze.

Richard watched him for a moment before asking yet again, this time in a softer, more brotherly tone, "Are you in love with her, Darcy?"

He watched his cousin's anger slowly melt away and his jaw relax as he dropped his head as if in shame and moved his arms up to support himself against the windowsill. Richard was amazed that such a simple question could turn his cousin into the broken man before him. The sound of his cousin's strained voice captured his attention.

Mr. Darcy spoke barely above that of a whisper, "Yes. Yes, I am in love with Miss Elizabeth Bennet; irrevocably, incandescently and thoroughly in love with her."

Richard's face spread into a huge smile at his cousin's declaration and he stood up jovially to join him. Placing a hand on his cousin's shoulder, he said spiritedly, "Well then, Cousin, when will I be wishing you well?"

Darcy turned pained eyes to him. "You do not understand, Richard; it can never be." He dropped his arms to his side and went back to his chair, sinking into it and once again pulling out his watch. Richard watched his cousin's actions with confusion.

"I do not understand, Darcy," Richard stopped when he saw his cousin look up at him and shake his head. He sat down and offered sympathetically, "Ah, I see, she is already spoken for. I am sorry, Darcy."

Darcy simply shook his head slowly, as he continued, absently looking at his watch. "No, she is not."

"She is not?!" Richard puzzled that for a moment. "Then she does not return your regard? That is difficult, but not hopeless. Perhaps with time—"

"No!" Darcy interrupted and lifted his head as if in thought for a moment. Richard watched as some memory flitted across his brow and turned his expression into one of momentary happiness, the likes of which he had before never seen on his cousin. But his face fell again into sadness as he spoke. "That is to say, I do not know for sure. She may return my feelings. If she does, it is that much worse, for it can never be."

"Why ever not, Cousin?" Richard was losing his patience, and he reached out to grab his cousin's watch.

Darcy pulled it away just in time and returned it to his pocket before looking at his cousin with frustration. "You want to know why? You want to know why I cannot have the only woman I have ever loved? I shall tell you." Darcy's sudden, heated passion surprised Richard as he rushed on in his frustration, "Because of my duty to my family, to Georgiana, to my station! That is why!" He sank back in his chair as his sudden ire burned away just as quickly as it had begun.

"Your duty to your family? To Georgiana? What is this nonsense, Darcy? You cannot be speaking of Anne, can you?"

"No, I am not speaking of Anne," he shot back angrily.

"Thank goodness for that! I never anticipated you were ever serious about Aunt Catherine's nonsense that you must marry Anne." Richard shuddered.

"Richard, you do not understand. Elizabeth may be a gentleman's daughter and a lady, but she has no fortune and no connections."

Richard huffed in disbelief. "You do not need her fortune, Darcy."

"I know that, and I really do not even care about it. But what of her connections? What if I were to marry her and the *ton* did not accept her? What if Aunt Ellen and Uncle Henry reject her and she is shunned? I could not subject her to that, and I owe it to your parents and Georgiana to marry well." He pulled his watch out yet again and held it in his hand.

"My parents will not shun you for your choice of wife. You are a gentleman; she is a gentleman's daughter; so far you are equal."

Darcy stared at his cousin as his mind registered his words. When put so plainly, it made it seem that the mountains between him and Elizabeth were as nothing.

"I do not know, Richard. What if you are wrong and I marry Elizabeth and they do reject her. I do not know if I can take that risk," he said dejectedly.

The fact that Darcy had now twice referred to Miss Bennet by her Christian name was not lost on his cousin. Richard's anger began to rise at this ridiculous reasoning. Darcy was totally in love but ready to live a life of unhappiness merely because of a few convoluted notions of duty.

"I cannot and do not believe that, Darcy. Your reasoning is not sound. Lord and Lady Matlock, the elite of the *ton*, your illustrious aunt and uncle, *love you*. They want only for your happiness, and you know that. They will accept anyone you choose and will champion that person against the rest of London—hell, England if need be! You are the one holding yourself back because of some convoluted, inane notion of duty. Go right ahead then, Cousin. But I will not support you in this foolishness."

He stood abruptly and grabbed at his cousin's watch, this time successfully taking it from him. "And what the deuces is so fascinating about the time?" he asked as he opened the watch and caught sight of a little silver silk flower. He looked questioningly at his cousin regarding the strange object as he turned the watch to show Darcy.

Darcy just looked back at him offering no explanation at all.

Richard pinched his lips together as he realized that the object must belong to Miss Elizabeth and somehow his cousin had obtained it, most likely by suspicious means. He burst into laughter as he tossed the watch back to his cousin and strolled towards the door, calling back over his shoulder, "You are absolutely hopeless, Darcy!"

Mr. Darcy pinched the bridge of his nose as he heard his cousin's laughter all the way down the hall and listened, as it did not stop mocking his ears until after Richard had exited the house. His mind was heavy with the words his cousin had said. He did not know what to think but could not ignore the inkling of hope that sprang into his chest. It had felt good finally to declare aloud the love he had for Elizabeth. A weight lifted even as a new burden fell upon his shoulders. *Do I dare hope?*

Chapter 13

Mr. Darcy looked up from the letter in his hand at the knock on his study door. He folded the sheet and placed it under a book on his desk as he went to open it.

"Hello, William. Am I disturbing you?"

Darcy smiled at his sister and pulled her into an uncharacteristic embrace. He took her hand to lead her into the room. "Not at all, Georgie. Is everything all right?"

"I am well, thank you. I wished actually to speak with you for a moment if you are not otherwise engaged."

Darcy's eyes flashed to the book on his desk with the letter he had just received from Wickham hidden underneath it. *There is no need to worry*, he kept telling himself. *Georgiana is here, and she is safe.* Wickham was just trying to goad him as always. Darcy saw his sister's concern and realized he had not answered her.

"No, Georgiana, I was not working on anything important. What is it you wished to speak to me about?"

Georgiana played with her fingers in her lap as she worked through the words she wanted to say. Usually he was the one caring for her but now she worried for him. "Did you and Cousin Richard have a fight, William?" A direct approach seemed like the best idea until she looked up to see her brother's sour expression.

Darcy sat in the chair next to her and took her hand. "No, dear."

Georgiana's brows came together in confusion. "But he has not been back to visit since before Christmas a week ago. Have I offended him?"

"No, Georgiana, you must not worry. I suspect he has been busy with his regiment, and you remember, we saw him just days ago at Aunt Ellen's Christmas dinner."

"Yes, we did. However, I also saw that whenever he spoke to you, he walked away chuckling while you were frowning."

"Richard always finds things to tease me about, dear, you know that. He has just found something particularly interesting this time; that is all."

Darcy looked at his sister as she simply nodded her head. It was not like her to approach him about something like this, but it made him happy that she felt confident enough to do so. When he thought about it, he had noticed other times when she asserted herself more in their conversations, even challenging him. He was far from unhappy about it as it made him hopeful that she was recovering, growing into a stronger version of herself. He looked towards his desk again, remembering Wickham's words. He was not going to let that man control him or dictate their lives.

"Georgiana, how would you like to go shopping today? There is a bookstore on Brook Street I would like to visit, and it is near several of the shops I know you enjoy. Would you accompany me?"

Georgiana's face lit up at the offer, and she smiled brightly. "I would like that very much, William. When would you like to go?"

"Will a half hour be sufficient for you and Mrs. Annesley? I have just a small amount of business to attend, and then I will be ready."

"That will be fine. I will meet you in the vestibule then." She leaned over and hugged her brother tightly around his neck. "You are the best brother!" She kissed his cheek and skipped happily out of the study, closing the door behind her.

For a moment, Darcy was stunned by her enthusiastic approval of his proposal. It made him feel guilty that he had not offered to take her out more often since his return to town. If doing a little shopping were all it took to make her happy, he would gladly spend the money.

With renewed determination, he strolled over to his desk and took out a sheet of paper to write to his cousin.

Richard,

Received this note from Wickham today. He says he is watching us. I will have my men look out for him near our house. –F.D.

Darcy retrieved Wickham's letter and folded it within his own. After sealing it, he took it to Mr. Carroll to post with the rest of his correspondence and went up to his chambers to prepare to go shopping with Georgiana.

Elizabeth had just finished placing the last pin in her hair when she heard giggles outside her door. Her little cousins had taken to trying to frighten her whenever she left her room in the morning by hiding behind the door. She had been in London for a week now and was enjoying herself. The change of scenery was, indeed, helpful for her, and she relished in the undivided time with her aunt.

She smiled as she heard whispering and giggling in anticipation from the hallway. She quietly donned her slippers and tiptoed to the door. Carefully, she turned the handle, waiting to see if her young cousins had heard her, but they were still whispering and giggling. Swiftly, Elizabeth pulled open the door and roared, causing them to shriek and laugh as she chased them down the hall.

"Come here, you little urchins! I am going to get you all!" She laughed as she grabbed one little squirming body and ran to catch up with the other. Just as her arm came around the small waist, the youngest cousin, Peter, appeared in front of her.

He took his thumb out of his mouth, stood as tall as his four-year-old self could get and put his hands out menacingly. "Boo!"

Elizabeth loosened her grip on the other two and pretended to be frightened as she stumbled backwards onto a bench with her hands over her heart. The children wiggled away to stand next to their younger brother. They all laughed and then the little ones came to hug their favorite cousin.

"Good mornin', Cousin Lizzabet. I sure scared you," Peter said.

"You most certainly did, Peter!" She laughed as she mussed his hair. The other two children took her hands to lead her down the stairs.

Her Aunt Gardiner turned towards them as Elizabeth entered the breakfast room, escorted in a most gentlemanly fashion by her nine-year-old son.

She gave her cousin a proper curtsy. "Thank you for escorting me, Master Edward."

This appellation caused the younger boy to stand proudly taller as he performed a perfect bow. "It was my pleasure, Cousin Elizabeth."

Madeline Gardiner laughed softly and reached for her niece's hand. "I hope they did not come too early this morning, Lizzy. They did not wake you, did they?"

Elizabeth smiled indulgently at her cousins. "Not at all. I was awake."

Her aunt studied her for a minute and then smiled. "You look well this morning, dear. You must have slept better than you have been, for your cheeks are bright, and you seem in good spirits this morning."

But Elizabeth had not slept well. Her thoughts of Mr. Darcy had followed her to London. Before she left Longbourn, Jane mentioned that Mr. Darcy was standing up with Charles at the wedding, now just over three weeks away. Knowing that she would see him again caused a mixture of feelings. She was excited and nervous at the same time. She did not know how he felt about her, and she was afraid to hope in that regard. However, she was convinced, regardless of his feelings for her, that she would forever love him.

"I slept well enough, I suppose. Perhaps I am just excited for our shopping trip today, Aunt. Where are we to go?"

Her aunt laughed at her enthusiasm. "I have a friend from school whose husband owns one of the finest milliner's shops in London. It is on Brook Street. Would you like to go there?"

Elizabeth squeezed her aunt's hand and shot her eyebrows up as she nodded her head and smiled.

"Very well, then, have your breakfast, and I shall order the carriage."

Wickham adjusted the newspaper he held and lowered the brim of his hat when the front door to Darcy House opened. He had been sitting on a bench in the park across the street for a while. In frustration, he turned a page of the paper. An entire week had passed, and he was still not completely able to work out enough of Darcy or Georgiana's schedules to determine the best time to surprise and accost them. He especially wanted a chance to speak to Georgiana alone and have her deliver his final threat to Darcy.

Darcy was everything loyal and predictable when it came to those about whom he cared. Wickham snarled to himself and let out a low chuckle. It was this predictability that had always given Wickham the upper hand. He knew well enough that, when it came to those he cared about, Darcy was willing to protect them at any cost. Wickham had sent Darcy the notes in hopes of familiarizing his old friend with a bit of fear, so that when the time came for Wickham to lay his final claim on the table, Darcy would do anything he demanded.

Wickham peeked slyly over the edge of his paper to see first Mrs. Annesley and then Georgiana exiting the house. He began folding the paper while he watched. *Today may be my day to speak with Georgiana*, he thought with satisfaction. A moment later, he frowned as Darcy exited the house and handed the ladies into the carriage.

He watched Darcy look down both sides of the street. Wickham dipped his head as Darcy's gaze briefly washed through the park and passed over him. He smiled to himself at the obvious effect of his most recent letter. Darcy was at least taking him seriously, which was a good sign. Wickham raised his head when he saw Darcy enter the carriage and leave with his sister.

In frustration, Wickham finished folding the paper and slapped it across his leg. Once again, Darcy had accompanied his sister, and he would not get his opportunity that day. He walked apace to where he had tethered his horse near a tree and rode off through the park. As long as Darcy was with them, he knew he would have no chance of finding Georgiana alone.

ELIZABETH AND HER AUNT ENTERED the milliner's shop with happy determination. They had enjoyed their discussions so far that morning as they went from shop to shop.

"Well, Lizzy, this is my friend's shop, and we have saved the best for last, I daresay. What is left on your mother's list for Jane's trousseau?"

Elizabeth laughed softly as she reached into her reticule and retrieved the paper her mother had sent with her to London. Her eyes scanned the lengthy list as she read, "A few pairs of evening gloves, a parasol, and plenty of ribbons and lace." Elizabeth looked up with a smile and scanned the shop. "I believe we shall find all we need here and perhaps a bit more."

Elizabeth laced her arm through her aunt's, and they smiled at each other as they ventured down the aisles of the large establishment.

"Are you jealous of Jane, Lizzy?" her aunt asked with a feigned indifference when they stopped to browse a rack of ribbons, as if she were merely commenting on the weather.

Elizabeth gave her aunt an impertinent rise of her eyebrow. "Well, Aunt, you seem most direct this morning." She laughed and continued, "Of course I am not jealous. Mr. Bingley is perfect for Jane, and she could not be happier. Her felicity is mine."

Her aunt studied her and said, doubtingly, "You do not always appear happy to hear her say she loves him." She turned to inspect another ribbon. "You always look away or your smile seems to freeze on your face."

Elizabeth tried to deflect the import of the subject with humor. "Aunt Gardiner! I did not know you were such a studier of persons. Pray tell, are you hoping for a career as a Bow Street runner?"

Her aunt turned to her with a serious look. "Lizzy, tell me you have not also developed feelings for Mr. Bingley. Is that why you seem uncomfortable when Jane speaks of her love for him?"

Elizabeth's heart melted at the sincerity in her aunt's voice. Her concern was obvious and touching. She never could speak to her own mother about her feelings, and although she often spoke of such things with her father, not having another woman to consult was difficult. Elizabeth rested a warm hand on her aunt's arm.

"Dear Aunt, do not be troubled for me. I do not love Mr. Bingley; he is to be my brother, and a brother's love is all I would wish from him." *His friend, however, is a different story.* She smiled at her aunt to reassure her.

After scrutinizing her niece's face for a few moments, Madeline gave a sigh of relief and patted the hand on her arm. "I cannot tell you how glad I am to hear you say so, Elizabeth. I had begun to worry for you."

Elizabeth laughed softly to dispel the serious nature of their conversation. "Well, you need not be worried, Aunt. I hear Mr. Collins might have a cousin for me."

Her aunt gave her a censuring look before covering her mouth to stifle a laugh, and they began browsing again.

Outside the shop, Mr. Darcy helped his sister and her companion down from the carriage. He again scanned the street around them and smiled at her.

"Would you like me to come with you?" he asked, kindly. But Georgiana could see the subtle distaste in his tone and she laughed.

"William, I know how much you dislike browsing the ladies' shops with me." She laughed again at his chagrined frown and acknowledging nod at the truth of her words. Georgiana lifted her chin and smiled cheekily at him. "Though, why, I do not know. There are always lovely ladies inside, and I am sure you can learn much more about a lady in a shop than on the floor of a ballroom."

Darcy smiled at her and kissed her forehead. "Perhaps you are right. I shall go in this one directly, and if cupid is on my side, I shall find a wife *and* a pair of slippers for her all at the same time. What a time saver that shall be!"

Georgiana laughed cheerfully at her brother's silliness and then abruptly stopped and covered her mouth. She looked around to see if anyone had witnessed her most unladylike show of amusement. Upon seeing no one around, she smiled at her brother and said, "No indeed, Brother. You would have no such luck. Your taste in lady's fashion is something atrocious, and I am sure you will not find yourself a wife. But even if you should, the slippers you choose would drive her away just as quickly."

Darcy smiled broadly, revealing his dimples and causing his sister's smile to widen. Neither had seen the other smile so genuinely in quite a while, and both were glad for it. Darcy looked at his sister with affection and continued to tease her. With a dramatic pose of his hand over his heart, he said, "You wound me, Georgie! How can you say I have poor taste when, just days ago, you were so delighted with the gloves I gave you for Christmas?"

Georgiana looked at her brother with a guilty smile. Twisting her reticule strings in her hands, she mumbled, "Well . . . "

"You did not like them?" Darcy asked with astonishment. When he saw her guilty face lower again at his discovery, he said in a softer tone, "Georgiana, I am not offended." He lifted her chin with his finger and said with a smile, "Perhaps you are right, then. I will have no such luck finding a wife in this establishment."

The smile on his face disarmed Georgiana and she spoke softly, but with humor. "Leave it to me, William. I will find you a wife and some slippers for her as well. Go to that bookstore across the street that you always eye longingly whenever we shop together. Leave the ladies' business to me."

Darcy was chastising himself for ruining their happy banter, so he sighed in relief at Georgiana's response. "You are a most clever girl, my dear. I wanted to speak to Mr. Jenkins anyway about a book I ordered last week. Now look how efficient we are! Do be sure to choose a pretty wife for me, dear."

Georgiana laughed and shook her head at her brother as she turned to enter the shop. Darcy waited until she and Mrs. Annesley were safely inside before turning to his groomsmen on the carriage and asking one of them to sit inside the shop to watch over the ladies. He dismissed the carriage and headed across the street to the bookstore.

Elizabeth looked up automatically when she heard the bell of the door. She noticed a young girl and an older lady enter the shop before returning her attention to examining a few more ribbons.

She and her aunt had long since found many of the items on their list and were just enjoying looking through the shop's abundant merchandise. Their conversation was companionable and happy as they moved throughout the shop. Elizabeth stopped briefly at a table of folded handkerchiefs and fingered their fine fabrics and embroidery. She looked up when a bit of color came into view on the other side of the table. It was the same girl she noticed enter a few minutes before.

Elizabeth watched as the girl and her companion quietly exchanged comments about the items on the table. Her eyes then caught sight of a most unusual but beautiful pattern embroidered on one of the handkerchiefs in the center of the table. Wanting to examine it closer, she reached for it just as the other girl did. Their hands nearly touched before Elizabeth realized they were reaching for the same item.

She looked up and smiled at the girl, who returned a shy smile and indicated to Elizabeth to claim the item. An expression in the girl's eyes caught Elizabeth momentarily, and she felt drawn to her. She seemed timid, so Elizabeth smiled sweetly and said, "No, you go ahead." She motioned towards the cloth and continued, "But I must say, you have excellent taste." Elizabeth smiled again before leaving the table.

Georgiana's lips twitched in a brief attempt at a smile and hesitated before reaching for the handkerchief. She watched as the lady who complimented her walked down the aisle and then began speaking with another lady while they held out various types of lace to compare. Georgiana admired her confident stride and the engaging smile she gave her companion. She looked down at the cloth in her hand and closely examined the embroidery. It was a combination of Lavender blossoms and Sweet Williams wrapped together with a twisting vine of leaves. It was prettily done and Georgiana turned to show Mrs. Annesley.

"Which lace do you think Jane would like for her veil, Lizzy?"

Elizabeth examined the fabrics. "I think this one would suit her best; do you not agree, Aunt?"

Her aunt pulled out the folded lace and lifted the tissue paper surrounding it. "I believe you are right, Lizzy. Though I wonder..." She unfolded the fabric a little and frowned. "I do not believe there is enough here for what we need. I will ask the clerk if there is more in the stockroom if you will just excuse me."

Elizabeth smiled. "Of course. I am going to go try and select the gloves Jane needs. Our hands are similar in size."

Elizabeth walked towards the back of the shop where there was a small alcove devoted to various types of gloves. She admired the soft feel of a pair of leather outdoor gloves for a few minutes. She turned her hands around to inspect their stitching and fit before removing and returning them to their place. When she turned around towards the table with the evening gloves, she noticed the same shy girl from the handkerchief table examining a pair of white silk ones.

She walked up next to the girl and her companion and gave her a wink. "My compliments again on your taste." She gently reached for the gloves in Georgiana's hand. "May I?"

Georgiana looked at the pretty woman next to her and acknowledged her kind smile before handing them to her. "Of course."

"These are quite lovely. I like the way they taper here at the edge." Elizabeth leaned a bit closer to show Georgiana what she meant.

Georgiana marveled at the easy nature of the stranger next to her. She had a confidence about her that was genuine without the self-absorbed way of the ladies Georgiana usually encountered while shopping. She gave a hesitant smile and replied so softly Elizabeth had to strain to hear her. "Yes, I liked that, too."

Elizabeth gave Georgiana a sweet, satisfied smile. She handed the gloves back and picked out a pair she thought Jane might like. To Georgiana's surprise, Elizabeth then turned to her to continue the conversation as if they were well known acquaintances.

"I am shopping for my sister who is getting married soon. I am having all the fun picking out items for her while she is forced to sit all day planning with my mother." Elizabeth smiled conspiratorially and gave Georgiana a wink.

Georgiana giggled before quickly covering her mouth in embarrassment. To her further surprise, Elizabeth laughed as well. She smiled to herself and thought a moment while she pretended to examine another pair of gloves. The lady next to her was most peculiar. She was friendly and cheerful, and she did not adhere to the normal societal rules regarding speaking to strangers. There was nothing improper about her speaking to Georgiana, but the easy manners she displayed were surprising.

Georgiana thought of all the things her brother had told her about Miss Elizabeth Bennet. Her description appeared, to Georgiana, to be similar to this lady. Both ladies seemed to have qualities Georgiana admired, and she decided it was time to try to practice them herself. She leaned slightly towards Elizabeth and said in her own conspiratorial voice, "I am here shopping for a new pair of gloves to replace the horrid ones my brother got me for Christmas."

Elizabeth drew back in surprise, and for a moment, Georgiana froze, fearing she had gone too far. She relaxed when her anonymous friend smiled broadly and said with mock seriousness, "Men have no taste."

While Elizabeth laughed heartily, Georgiana giggled softly.

"You are lucky, though, to have a brother. I have only several sisters and no brothers."

Georgiana smiled in return. "I have only my brother. And although I should have liked to have a sister, having him does grant me many opportunities to shop."

Elizabeth chuckled. "To replace the items he purchases for you?"

Georgiana nodded her head, and they laughed quietly together for a minute. Elizabeth tried on the gloves she had selected for Jane and stretched her arm out to pull one up above her elbow. As she turned her arm about to look at it, she said to her friend, "What do you think of these? They are pretty, are they not?"

Georgiana reached over to feel the fabric and tentatively took Elizabeth's wrist in her hand as she turned it around to inspect a bit of embroidered lace on the underside of the glove.

She smiled softly and said, "Yes, they are quite beautiful. I like the lace right here."

Elizabeth smiled at the boldness of her new friend in touching her arm. She seemed less shy and reserved than she had been earlier, and Elizabeth was enjoying her company while waiting for her aunt to finish with the clerk.

Georgiana suddenly began laughing and covered her mouth in a futile attempt to hide her amusement. When Elizabeth turned to her questioningly, she said, "Forgive me," before erupting in another bout of laughter.

Elizabeth found her amusement contagious, and even though she did not know what her anonymous friend was laughing about, she could not help but laugh a little as well.

"You must tell me what you find so funny about these gloves!"

Georgiana took a deep breath in an attempt to regain her composure. "It is not the gloves that I find amusing. I caught sight of that rack of slippers over there and was reminded of my task here in the shop today." She pointed to the rack of slippers.

Elizabeth's eyebrows rose in amusement and confusion. "And what is that, my I ask?"

Georgiana had become so comfortable with Elizabeth that she momentarily forgot she was speaking with a stranger. "You will think me most silly, but I had teased my brother that I would shop for a wife for him today and choose a pair of slippers for her as well. He was so pleased to get out of coming in here with me that he laughed and went along with it." Georgiana then frowned as she realized her silliness.

Elizabeth laughed at the unusual declaration and said, as she glanced around the shop, "I did not see the 'wife aisle'."

Elizabeth smiled as her jest had the intended effect of bringing a smile back to her friend's face, and they began giggling again.

Darcy walked across the street to the milliner's shop after retrieving the book he had hoped to obtain. Upon entering, his level of discomfort rose immediately as all the ladies' fashion accessories surrounded him. He had never really been comfortable in a shop for ladies and was suddenly very glad that Georgiana had given him leave to go to the bookstore instead.

He turned to the bored look of his groomsman who sat in a chair next to another gentleman, most likely waiting for his wife. Their faces clearly revealed that their discomfort matched his. He asked about Georgiana's location, and the groom pointed towards the back of the establishment. Darcy began walking in that direction.

As he neared the back of the shop, he heard the most delightful and beautiful laugh. His heart stopped, and he instantly ducked behind a rack of bonnets upon hearing the very familiar sound. *It cannot be—my ears deceive me! Elizabeth?!* His heart raced as he again listened for the sound. He began to think he had certainly imagined it and was losing his mind.

Just then, the tinkling sound again drifted to his ears, and he sighed as he allowed it to melt through him.

He had to concentrate to get his muscles to obey him and walk towards the sound as it had paralyzed him in place. He turned the corner towards its source and quietly walked along another tall rack of bonnets. Once again he heard the laugh, followed by another softer one that he recognized as Georgiana's. Immediately, his curiosity got the better of him, and he hesitantly lifted a bonnet from its rack and peered through the opening.

The sight momentarily stunned him as he discovered, with wonder and delight, Elizabeth, *his* Elizabeth, talking animatedly with Georgiana. It was so much like the nature of his dreams that he closed his eyes and rubbed them just in case the scene was imaginary. When he dared to look again, they were still there smiling and talking to each other.

How can this be? He watched with wonder as they examined and compared various gloves before them on a table. His breath caught in his throat as he watched Elizabeth delicately try on a glove and pull its length all the way up her small arm. She was stunning, and he realized then that, for all the weeks he had not seen her, his mind had not done her justice, for she was beyond beautiful; she was exquisite. He stood, transfixed, looking at her as she splayed her hand and twisted her arm about to examine the length of the glove.

His heart beat faster as he watched his beloved sister reach for Elizabeth's wrist and turn it around in her hand. He was momentarily filled with jealousy at the act, at his sister's touch on Elizabeth's arm. He wanted nothing more than to be the one holding her small hand in his while giving soft kisses to the lace on her wrist.

He could not hear their conversation, but as he tore his eyes away from Elizabeth, for the first time, he saw his sister more animated and confident than he had ever before beheld. He watched her laughing as she leaned towards Elizabeth. She said something as she pointed in another direction in the shop. Elizabeth gave Georgiana a look of surprise and again laughed before saying something in return. He quickly replaced the bonnet in the opening in the rack when he saw Elizabeth's gaze roam the shop before the ladies' laughter again reached his ears.

He stood taller and prepared himself to make an appearance, but as he took a quick peek behind the bonnet again, he saw another lady come up and say something to Elizabeth. Elizabeth turned to Georgiana and excused herself. Darcy realized, almost too late, that they were walking towards where he was hiding, and he moved the bonnet again to hide his location, just as their conversation reached him from the other side of the rack.

"Who is that you were speaking to, Elizabeth?" the lady asked. Darcy leaned closer to the bonnets to hear Elizabeth's lovely voice for the first time in weeks.

She laughed as she said, "I cannot tell you, Aunt. I do not actually know her. We were just having a pleasant conversation over the gloves."

The astonishment in the voice of the lady, who Darcy now knew to be Elizabeth's aunt, was easily heard. "You do not know her? I thought perhaps you had a previous acquaintance with the lady. You seemed to be enjoying a familiarity with her."

Darcy could imagine the smile he heard in Elizabeth's voice. "Yes, she is quite lovely. We just happened to come upon each other a few times in the shop and began talking."

"She looks to be a very nice young girl."

"Did you find out what you needed from the clerk?"

"Yes, and I apologize for taking so long. My friend, who owns the shop, came out from the back and we began talking. Unfortunately, there is not enough of the lace we wanted for Jane, but she said she could get more from a warehouse outside of town tonight, and it will be ready with the rest of our purchases to pick up at this time tomorrow."

"Well that is good news; I know Jane would like the one we chose better than any other."

"Would you mind very much, Lizzy, if we had to go shopping again tomorrow?"

Darcy smiled to himself at the obvious teasing tone of Elizabeth's aunt.

"Somehow I think I shall survive!" She laughed and then said, "Here are the gloves I have chosen for Jane. I will meet you at the front in just a moment. I want to say goodbye to my new friend."

"Very well, dear, I will see you in a moment."

Darcy let out a breath he had not realized he had been holding and looked around him. He realized a few elderly matrons had been observing his strange fascination with the bonnet in front of him and he colored as he bowed to them and looked away. He stepped away from the rack in time to see Elizabeth say goodbye to Georgiana and walk up the aisle towards the front of the shop. He was too transfixed to move from his spot.

He watched as she stopped briefly at a table of handkerchiefs and examined one of them with obvious admiration before replacing it on the table and joining her aunt at the front of the shop. Now that he could see her aunt more clearly, he was surprised and impressed at her fashionable attire. He was slightly embarrassed at the assumption he had made about her aunt and uncle in trade and realized his mistake immediately.

When they were no longer in sight, he turned and walked towards his sister. When he reached her, she gave him a bright smile and warm welcome.

"Well, Georgiana, have you enjoyed your shopping this morning?" His heart was light, but he could not be too obvious in his interest yet.

"I had a most enjoyable time, William. I met a lady, and we had a pleasant conversation."

"Indeed?" Darcy looked around as he asked, "And where is this lady?"

"She left with her aunt."

"And what is the name of your new acquaintance, Georgie." He knew she did not know or she would have immediately said, but he wanted to see what he could find out about their conversation.

Georgiana's brow furrowed. "Actually, now that I think of it, I do not even know her name. We did not introduce ourselves."

He led her down the aisle and, with as much indifference as he could manage, enquired about their conversation.

Georgiana laughed a little as she remembered their conversation about men and their poor taste as well as her confession about finding William a wife. She turned an impertinent smile towards her brother that caught him momentarily in its similarity to Elizabeth's. "We ladies must have our secrets, Brother."

He stopped, stunned by her teasing words and sassy smile. He watched as she walked up to the counter with her purchases. He quickly caught up with her and shook his head as he winked.

"Go with Mrs. Annesley to the carriage; I will make your purchases and be with you shortly." He motioned to his groom at the door to accompany them as he turned to the clerk to pay for his sister's items.

"Will that be all, sir?"

Darcy looked at the clerk and paused a moment before answering. "I would like to add one more item." He quickly walked to the table of handkerchiefs and, picking up the one he knew Elizabeth had admired, returned with it to the counter.

When the purchases were made and the clerk began to wrap the items in paper, Darcy took the handkerchief and said, "I will take this one with me," and tucked it in his coat pocket.

"As you wish, sir."

Chapter 14

The next morning, Georgiana was interrupted in her practice at the pianoforte when her brother came into the room. She smiled at him and continued playing the rest of the piece. She watched with interest as he kept shifting uncomfortably in his chair, seemingly agitated by something. Normally, when she played, he was very calm and sedate as he enjoyed the music. Today it seemed he was impatient for her to finish.

Before the sounds of the last notes left the air, she was startled by his sudden appearance at her side.

"Georgiana, dear, I thought I would like to take you shopping again today."

Georgiana's eyebrows shot up, and she sat back in disbelief. "There is no need for that, William; I do not have anything I wish to buy. I went yesterday, or do you not remember?" she teased.

She pursed her lips in amusement, watching him fumble with his watch chain and shift from foot to foot. "Yes, dear, but do not all ladies enjoy shopping?" he asked, looking at her hopefully.

She laughed at his obvious impatience and could not understand his sudden interest in shopping.

"William, do you have some shopping you would like to do?"

Darcy smiled and thought perhaps he could convince her by agreeing. "Yes, I should like to browse the bookstore again."

"And you would like me to accompany you?" she asked incredulously.

"Can a brother not wish for his sister's company from time to time?" he countered, exasperated.

She laughed at him as she responded, "Very well. I will be happy to accompany you this afternoon if you wish." She then turned back to the pianoforte.

"No, Georgie!" Darcy checked himself before adding, more sedately, "I have some business to attend to this afternoon, can you not come with me this morning?" He had debated how he could see Elizabeth again, and since he was not acquainted with her relations, he concluded seeing her at the shop would be his only opportunity.

Georgiana shook her head at her brother's strange behavior. "Very well, this morning will be fine."

She watched as her brother pulled out his pocket watch and looked at the time. The sudden smile on his face caught her by surprise, and she barely heard what he said next. "I will see you in fifteen minutes then, Georgie."

She regained her composure in time to shout to his retreating figure, "Fifteen minutes? What is the rush?" She shook her head again as he simply waved behind his back and continued out of the room with a quick stride.

Darcy went straight to the housekeeper's office. "Mrs. Carroll, if all goes well this morning, I hope to have some guests for tea this afternoon. Please inform Cook and make sure the necessary arrangements are made. See that she includes lemon tarts on the tray." Darcy turned from the room after hearing his housekeeper assent to his orders and smiled to himself. He remembered Elizabeth had preferred lemon tarts at Netherfield.

Thirty minutes later saw them pull up in front of the same milliner's shop Georgiana had patronized the day before. After securing her arm in her brother's, Georgiana was surprised to be led towards the milliner's shop instead of crossing the street to the bookstore.

"William, I do not have any need to come to this shop. I told you as much this morning."

Darcy looked down at his sister and smiled widely enough to show his rarely revealed dimples before he begged, "Please Georgiana, humor me."

She looked at him a moment, considering his perplexing behavior, then shrugged her shoulders and shook her head. "As you wish, Brother, but I cannot see why you would wish to spend any time in a shop for ladies." She laughed before adding, "Unless you have developed a sudden interest in ladies' fashion."

Darcy smiled to himself. "Perhaps I have." He opened the shop door and ushered his sister inside. She watched as he quickly scanned the establishment while they walked the aisles. She could see a moment of disappointment pass over his features before he led her towards a display of bonnets near the front.

They were standing at the display for a few minutes when Georgiana noticed her brother kept looking towards the door and around the shop. After a minute, Darcy realized he was getting strange looks from his sister and tried to act naturally.

"What do you think of this one, Georgiana?"

She narrowed her eyes at his odd behavior and turned to examine the bonnet he indicated. "It is tolerable but not handsome enough to tempt me."

She was surprised when his eyes went wide and he seemed to choke after hearing her statement. "Is something wrong, William?"

He stared at her a moment but then started to laugh softly and shook his head. She rolled her eyes at him but then another bonnet caught her eye and she quickly moved to examine it. Vaguely, she heard the chime of the doorbell just as she turned to show her brother the bonnet.

"I do, however, find this one quite beautiful, what do you think—" She frowned as she realized she was facing her brother's back. He had turned around and was suddenly interested in something on the other side of the shop. Before she could gain his attention, however, she felt a slight touch on her arm.

Georgiana was delighted and surprised when she turned around to see her friend from the day before looking at her with a bright smile.

"Well, hello, my anonymous friend! What an interesting coincidence that we should meet again in this shop!"

"Hello to you, too!" Georgiana placed a gloved hand over Elizabeth's and leaned towards her. "I realized, yesterday, that I did not get your name. Would it be too presumptuous to request an introduction?"

Elizabeth laughed. "No, indeed, we, neither of us, are ill-qualified to recommend ourselves to strangers."

Georgiana smiled and opened her mouth to introduce herself, when her brother turned around suddenly and said, "Georgiana, would you do me the honor of introducing your friend to me?"

Elizabeth blanched and stood frozen as she looked up at the face that had haunted her dreams and stood permanently in her heart for so many weeks. Her heart stuttered to a stop and then began to beat wildly as her voice uttered in complete astonishment, "Mr. Darcy!"

Georgiana looked from her brother to her friend in confusion. Neither one seemed inclined to speak; instead, they just stared at each other. She could tell her friend was in shock and slightly embarrassed. When she looked at her brother, she realized he was smiling like a love-struck fool, and she marveled at the sight for a moment. *Who is this woman, and how does she know my brother?*

"Excuse me, but do you know my brother?"

Elizabeth was startled out of her spell and reluctantly moved her eyes from Mr. Darcy's handsome face to that of her friend. Suddenly, the words broke through the fog in her mind and she colored deeply in embarrassment. "Your brother?"

Mr. Darcy's smile of affection and adoration turned into one of smug satisfaction as he turned to his sister. "Georgiana, it seems your friend and I are already acquainted. May I introduce to you, Miss Elizabeth Bennet? Miss Elizabeth, this is my sister, Georgiana Darcy."

Elizabeth and Georgiana looked at each other, each replaying their conversation from the day before. Georgiana remembered how much her friend had seemed similar to the Miss Bennet her brother had described and now thought it amazing that they should be the same person. She and Elizabeth seemed to recollect at the same time their conversation about finding Georgiana's brother a wife. They both burst into laughter and began to speak at once.

"I cannot believe—"

"This is astonishing—"

They laughed again as Georgiana reached to clasp her new friend's hands. "I cannot believe that yesterday I had such a pleasant conversation with one of my brother's acquaintances from Hertfordshire. He has told me so much about you."

Elizabeth and Georgiana looked briefly towards Mr. Darcy, who was now feeling slightly uncomfortable at their conversation and obvious familiarity. Elizabeth smiled and colored beautifully. "I hope you have not listened to a word he has said, for I am sure it will ruin your good opinion of me."

Darcy smiled, but Georgiana panicked and rushed to relieve her friend. "Oh, no, Miss Bennet, my brother only expressed the highest of opinions about you."

Elizabeth looked towards Darcy, whose dark eyes seemed to turn liquid as he returned her gaze. She swallowed and tried to regain her composure.

Georgiana realized why her brother was in such a state to come shopping this morning. *How did he know she would be here?* She laughed to herself at the antics he was displaying. *He cannot claim to be indifferent to her after this.*

Elizabeth's aunt, who had been silently observing the entire exchange, could not help but find the greatest of interest in the way her niece was obviously affected by this gentleman and pleased to see him. She could also see that Elizabeth was quite uncertain of herself and his reception in a way that was uncharacteristic of her normally confident niece. She was even more interested when she heard her niece's next statement.

Elizabeth smiled mischievously at Georgiana and winked before speaking just loudly enough for Darcy to hear. "Have you come back to browse the 'wife aisle' this morning for your brother?" Georgiana's eyes went wide, and they both stole a glance at Darcy, who had obviously heard the exchange and was nervously adjusting the buttons of his coat with embarrassment.

Georgiana gave a soft giggle and put her fingers to her lips to quiet her friend.

Mr. Darcy cleared his throat. "Miss Elizabeth, what brings you to London?"

"I came to visit my aunt for a few weeks after Christmas." Suddenly remembering her manners, she turned and gently pulled her aunt forward. "Mr. Darcy, Miss Darcy, please allow me to introduce my aunt, Mrs. Gardiner."

Mr. Darcy bowed over the proffered hand of Elizabeth's aunt. "Mrs. Gardiner, a pleasure."

Georgiana curtsied properly. "Mrs. Gardiner, a pleasure, indeed."

The four began exchanging pleasantries about their mutual acquaintances and news from their friends in Hertfordshire, including details on the upcoming wedding of Jane and Mr. Bingley. After fifteen minutes, in which neither Mr. Darcy nor Elizabeth could remember doing much beyond memorizing each other's features again, Mrs. Gardiner excused herself to see about their orders from the day before, leaving Elizabeth with the Darcys.

When Mrs. Gardiner returned to Elizabeth's side, Mr. Darcy whispered something in his sister's ear. Georgiana smiled as she nodded to him before turning to Elizabeth and her aunt.

"Miss Bennet, Mrs. Gardiner, my brother and I would like to know... that is, we would be honored if you would consent to have tea with us today. If you do not have any other fixed engagements that is..." she stammered with a sudden lack of confidence.

Elizabeth colored and was grateful for the obvious condescension on the

Darcys' part. Her heart beat wildly at the idea. *Could he really be seeking my company?* She cautioned herself not to read too much into the idea and to keep her emotions in check. She did not need to make things more difficult for herself later on when their acquaintance remained unromantic.

Mrs. Gardiner looked to her niece to ascertain her opinion on the matter, and when it became apparent that an opinion was not forthcoming but that the suggestion was not unwelcome, she turned to Georgiana. "We would be glad to accept your invitation, Miss Darcy. We have no fixed engagements."

Mr. Darcy's face changed into one of complete satisfaction. "If you are finished with your purchases, would you like to accompany us back to our home now?"

Although it was obvious he was addressing Mrs. Gardiner, he was looking at Elizabeth for a reaction. He hoped the idea of spending time with him was not unpleasant to her, and he was already more than pleased with the budding friendship she had with Georgiana. Seeing her again had confirmed that he simply could not live without her.

Mrs. Gardiner smiled as she watched his obvious interest in her niece and wondered if this was the reason for Lizzy's low moods in the past few weeks. She knew Mr. Darcy had been staying with Mr. Bingley at Netherfield when she arrived for Mary's wedding and that he and Elizabeth had often been in company together.

"We would be happy to, Mr. Darcy. I will just call for our carriage."

"Mrs. Gardiner, please allow me to escort you and your niece to my home, and you can dismiss your carriage. We will be happy to arrange for your transport back to your home after tea."

"You are too kind, sir."

Mr. Darcy bowed and left the shop to call for their carriages and dismiss the Gardiners'. When he returned, he escorted the ladies out to his carriage and handed Mrs. Gardiner and Georgiana inside. When he captured Elizabeth's hand to assist her ascent, he felt a shock pass through him. When he released her hand, he had to open and close his own to dispel the tingling sensation before stepping into the carriage.

He sat next to his sister, directly across from Elizabeth and her aunt. Mr. Darcy offered the ladies a blanket for their legs and was happy to see Elizabeth blush beautifully when he handed her one.

Georgiana turned to her brother with a sly smile. "Brother, did you not want to visit that bookstore. I am sure I remember you saying as much this morning?"

Elizabeth quickly said, "Mr. Darcy, do not let us keep you if you have other errands to attend."

Mr. Darcy shot his sister a warning glance. "No, indeed, Miss Bennet, I have no other errands."

WICKHAM KICKED AT A STONE in the gravel beneath his feet as he once again placed himself in the park across from Darcy House. He had watched Mr. Darcy leave that morning with Georgiana. He seemed to be in a hurry and uncharacteristically excited about something. Wickham looked up when he heard the carriage wheels over the cobblestoned street between his position and Darcy's home.

He watched with interest as the carriage stopped and Darcy assisted first Georgiana, then an older woman he did not recognize, and then another, younger lady. Something about the younger lady struck Wickham as familiar, and he stepped around the tree to get a better look.

When she turned her head to thank Darcy, Wickham got a full view of her face. His lips turned upwards in a wicked smile when he recognized the lady. She was one of the Miss Bennets, one of the brainless chits at the house he was thrown out of by their father. He also recognized her as the one the other officers mentioned Darcy had danced with twice at the Netherfield ball.

Suddenly, Wickham realized he did not need to speak to Georgiana at all. From the way Darcy was looking moon-eyed at the other young lady, Wickham could tell he had feelings for her. All he would need to do was confirm his suspicions and get to Miss Bennet somehow. *So it seems your heart of ice has finally been captured, eh, Darce! We shall see how you like it when I ruin your happiness the way you ruined mine.*

Wickham settled himself onto a bench and again took up his newspaper to wait.

ELIZABETH WAS TREMBLING SLIGHTLY AS she ascended the steps into Darcy House. She removed her outerwear and handed it to the waiting servant as she looked around the grand hall. It was the most beautiful home she had ever seen. The grey marble was elegantly presented with splendor next to the warm tones of the cherry wood walls and ornately carved wooden railing lining the wide marble staircase.

Darcy watched Elizabeth as she looked around. His lips turned into a satisfied smile as he recognized her admiration for his home. He had a sudden feeling that she belonged there, and he contented himself to think on that for a few moments.

"Mr. Darcy, Miss Darcy, you have a very beautiful home," Mrs. Gardiner said.

Elizabeth could only nod her head and add, "It is truly very beautiful."

Mr. Darcy stepped closer to Elizabeth and said, significantly, "I am glad you like it, Miss Bennet."

Elizabeth colored, and Mrs. Gardiner's eyebrows rose in interest at what she was seeing. Her eyes caught those of Miss Darcy, and Georgiana smiled as she raised her shoulders up in obvious excitement.

They were led into a large sitting room where Elizabeth again admired the fine taste of the owner. The furnishings were elegant and expensive but without any ostentation or false grandeur. She and her aunt sat together on a settee, and Georgiana took the chair next to Elizabeth.

Before long, Mrs. Gardiner revealed her connection to Lambton in Derbyshire and its proximity to Pemberley. An easy discussion followed as the tea things were brought in. While Mr. Darcy and Mrs. Gardiner spoke of Derbyshire, Elizabeth and Georgiana quietly got to know each other better. Elizabeth was embarrassed to hear Georgiana give her praise, especially when told it was first spoken by her brother.

Georgiana was determined to learn as much as she could about her new friend, as it was more than obvious that her brother preferred Elizabeth. She also found a great deal of pleasure at the teasing comments Elizabeth directed at her brother and was astonished at the good-natured way he received them.

Darcy was more than thrilled to have Elizabeth in his home and in his company again. Whenever he looked at his sister and Elizabeth conversing happily together, he was filled with such contentment as he had never before experienced. He marveled at the easy way Elizabeth helped to move Georgiana out of her shyness, and gratitude filled his breast at the way she brought light back into his sister's eyes. It had been her influence all along that had begun the changes seen in Georgiana. Ever since learning about Elizabeth, Georgiana had started to become more independent, less despondent and more confident.

It was with these happy thoughts that Darcy was interrupted by the opening of the sitting room doors and the entrance of Richard and Aunt Ellen. Elizabeth and Mrs. Gardiner immediately stood as the new guests arrived and looked to each other.

Georgiana exclaimed, "Cousin Richard! Aunt Ellen! What a lovely surprise to see you here this afternoon!"

Darcy stepped towards his aunt and bowed after kissing her gently on her hand. He then shook his cousin's hand, giving him a knowing smile that Richard did not understand.

"Aunt Ellen, Richard. I have the pleasure today to introduce an acquaintance of mine from Hertfordshire. May I introduce to you, Miss *Elizabeth* Bennet, and her aunt, Mrs. Gardiner. Miss Bennet and I met during my stay with Bingley this fall." He turned to wink at his cousin's astonished face as he continued with the introductions. He turned to Elizabeth and her aunt, and said, "Miss Bennet, Mrs. Gardiner, this is my aunt Lady Matlock and her son Colonel Fitzwilliam."

Colonel Fitzwilliam gave Darcy a hardy slap on the back and spoke under his breath, "Tallyho, Darcy!" before taking a few steps towards the ladies and bowing properly to them. "A pleasure to make your acquaintance. Miss Bennet, my cousin has spoken most highly of you and his time in Hertfordshire. I am very pleased to finally meet you."

Elizabeth smiled sincerely at his easy manners and engaging address. "Colonel Fitzwilliam, you are most kind."

Lady Matlock, who had come with her son with the express purpose of speaking to Darcy regarding his affections towards Miss Bennet, was more than astonished to find herself in company with that very lady. When she had sequestered her son the evening before to manipulate him into sharing the reason for Darcy's recent reticence, she had not anticipated hearing that her nephew was in love with a girl from Hertfordshire. Richard had related Darcy's fears about the girl's lack of connections and her acceptance by society.

Lady Matlock was only concerned that Darcy did not fall in love with a fortune hunter. She determined, then, to speak with him immediately and decide for herself that the lady was not merely interested in his wealth. If she found that to be the case, then she would give her nephew a good peel over his head for his ridiculous and pompous notions of familial duty. Therefore, she listened with interest to her son's conversation with Miss Bennet.

"Miss Bennet, I pity you for having to put up with my cousin's presence for so long in Hertfordshire." Colonel Fitzwilliam chuckled and shot Darcy a teasing smile.

"Indeed, Colonel, he was most dreadful in the beginning." She also gave a teasing smile to Darcy and lifted her eyebrow in challenge, the way he loved.

"Do tell, Miss Bennet, I should like to know how my cousin behaves amongst strangers."

Elizabeth smiled at Colonel Fitzwilliam, and Darcy found he did not like seeing her smile at another man. He shifted uncomfortably in his chair as Elizabeth responded.

"Prepare yourself for something dreadful, then, sir. When I first saw your cousin, it was at an assembly in Meryton where he danced only two sets though gentlemen were scarce. I suppose he did not want to give consequence to women who were 'slighted by other men'."

Mr. Darcy clenched his jaw and heard his cousin say, "Now *that* I can easily see, and it surprises me not at all. My cousin does not like to dance."

Elizabeth smiled at the colonel again and continued. "But I believe your cousin improves upon further acquaintance." She directed a smaller, more serene smile at Darcy.

Darcy's eyebrows rose in challenge, and he surprised her with his address. "However true that may be, further acquaintance did not prevent *you*, Miss Bennet, from refusing my hand to dance on two separate occasions thereafter."

Elizabeth sat back in astonishment. "I do not know what you mean, Mr. Darcy. I cannot recollect these two instances."

Darcy smiled as he folded his hands together at his chest. "As I recall, I asked you to dance at Sir William Lucas's house shortly after that assembly."

Elizabeth bit her lip enchantingly as she thought back to the occasion to which he referred and began to laugh. "I stand corrected." She chuckled as she turned to the rest of the group. "I did refuse him then." Turning back to Darcy with a saucy smile, she said, "However, sir, I believe that is only *one* instance. You spoke of two."

At that moment, Darcy wanted nothing more than to stand up, march over to Elizabeth and kiss that smug smile off her face. She was so delightful, and he knew he was making a fool of himself by displaying his feelings for her openly to her family and his, but he did not care.

"The second time you refused me was at Netherfield when you came to care for your sister Jane when she was ill. I asked you one evening if you would care to dance while Miss Bingley was playing a lively tune on the pianoforte." He watched as recollection of the evening dawned on her, and her smug expression turned into one of disbelief.

"Mr. Darcy, your memory, I see, is better than mine. However, in my defense, I am sure at the time I thought you to be insincere in your request."

Colonel Fitzwilliam laughed heartily at the exchange along with Georgiana and his mother. "To have refused him twice! I wish I could have been there to witness the phenomenon. I do not believe I have ever known any lady to refuse Darcy's request for a dance."

Lady Matlock listened to her son's words and realized the truth of them. Her fears regarding Miss Bennet's status as a fortune hunter began to dwindle, and she enjoyed seeing the liveliness the lady brought to her usually somber nephew as well as to her niece.

"I wonder, Miss Bennet," Darcy paused to gain her full attention, "if you had known I was sincere in my request, would you have accepted my hand?"

Elizabeth turned her face into one of mock seriousness and pretended to think about his comment. She tapped one slender finger on her bottom lip, and the action nearly drove Darcy to distraction. She turned sparkling eyes on him, bewitching him even further, as she said, "Probably not."

The whole room broke into laughter, including Darcy, much to the astonishment of his relations.

Lady Matlock then turned to address Elizabeth. "How long are you visiting London, Miss Bennet?"

"My aunt, uncle and I will return to Hertfordshire in a week, milady. My elder sister is to be married in about three weeks."

"Have you had an opportunity to attend the theatre or an opera since you have been in town?"

"I have not had that pleasure, Lady Matlock. I hope very much to attend before I leave."

"Well, when you do, I should be happy to accompany you and your aunt and uncle in my box."

Elizabeth was stunned with the condescension and, for a moment, did not know how to respond. She collected herself and replied demurely, "Thank you, your ladyship, it would be an honor."

Darcy, too, was amazed, but pleased, at the civility his aunt showed to

Miss Bennet. He glanced briefly at his cousin and was surprised to see a knowing smirk on his face. *So, Aunt Ellen knows of my feelings for Elizabeth.* He gave his cousin an answering look of recognition with a raised brow and was not surprised to see Richard's smug smile in response.

Shortly thereafter, Elizabeth and her aunt indicated it was time for them to take their leave and for Darcy to order his carriage. As they waited, Darcy made a request.

"Mrs. Gardiner, if you are not otherwise engaged, my sister and I would like to invite you, Mr. Gardiner and Miss Elizabeth to be guests at our home for dinner."

Elizabeth's aunt smiled politely at Mr. Darcy. "It would be an honor, sir. Is there a specific evening you wished?"

"Would the day after tomorrow suit your schedules?"

"That would be fine, Mr. Darcy. Thank you."

When the carriage arrived, Mr. Darcy left his relatives in the sitting room to see his guests out. He handed Mrs. Gardiner into the carriage first and said to her, "Thank you for coming today; your visit has been most enjoyable."

"The pleasure was all ours, Mr. Darcy. Thank you for your hospitality."

Mr. Darcy then turned to Elizabeth and looked at her in a soft and tender way that she had never seen from him before. She could not quite look into his eyes, for doing so did strange things to her insides.

"Miss Bennet, I cannot tell you how happy I am to have made your acquaintance again." She accepted his hand, and he brought her fingers to his mouth and kissed them. "I look forward to seeing you again in a few days."

Elizabeth's courage rose, and she finally allowed herself to look Darcy in the eyes. "Thank you, Mr. Darcy. It was a surprise seeing you today, but I assure you, a most pleasant one."

Mr. Darcy merely nodded as he assisted her into the carriage and closed the door behind her. He stood watching until the carriage rolled out of sight before he turned and went into the house.

Across the street a gentleman watched the exchange closely. He grinned with a wicked glint in his eye as he mounted his horse and prepared to follow Darcy's carriage to wherever it conveyed Miss Bennet. He finalized his plan for his revenge on Darcy all the way to a Cheapside residence, where Miss Bennet and the other lady descended the carriage and entered the house.

Chapter 15

Elizabeth stretched her limbs across the expanse of her bed and sighed in contentment. For the first night in many weeks, she had slept most contentedly. Her night was still filled with dreams, and they still contained one similarity to her previously horrid dreams: Mr. Darcy. But this time, the dreams were pleasant, and she awoke that morning refreshed and happy.

She replayed the events of the day before in her head. She could not believe she had seen Mr. Darcy. He was obviously not staying at Pemberley for the holidays. She laughed to herself and shook her head in disbelief that she had actually met and became acquainted with his sister without even knowing it. She thought about Georgiana for a few minutes and compared her new friend to the many things she had learned about her from Mr. Darcy when they enjoyed supper together at the Netherfield ball. Elizabeth could see that Georgiana was every bit the sweet, shy girl he had described.

She remembered her father had told her about Mr. Wickham's attempt to seduce and elope with a 'near relation' of Darcy's. Elizabeth wondered whether, perhaps, this near relation was Georgiana. Darcy had seemed worried about his sister's state of happiness, and she was, indeed, his nearest relation. Now, having made Georgiana's acquaintance, she was filled with renewed distaste for Mr. Wickham and was glad her father had acted to protect her family from him.

Elizabeth heard a knock on the door and then a multitude of giggles. She sat up in bed and pulled her robe around her as she called to her cousins to enter. The door flew open, and three little children ran to her bed and climbed on. Elizabeth laughed as the oldest ones reached her first and gave her big hugs around her neck. Then she reached over and helped Peter, who was having trouble with the ascent, up into her embrace.

"Are you awake, Cousin Lizzabet?" Peter asked.

"Of course she is. Can you not see her eyes are open and she is laughing?" Margaret, the middle child and only girl, answered smartly to her little brother.

Elizabeth laughed again and gave them all squeezing hugs until they groaned to be released. "How are my favorite cousins this morning?"

"Good!" they said in unison.

"Would you like it if I escorted you to breakfast again this morning, Cousin Elizabeth?" Edward asked.

Elizabeth pressed her lips together to keep from smiling and nodded her head politely. "I should be honored if you would, but I cannot go down to breakfast dressed like this." She indicated her nightclothes, and the kids laughed as they slipped off the bed and left the room, closing the door behind them.

Elizabeth smiled as she quickly dressed for the day. She might have slept well but she did not necessarily know the state of her feelings yet. Seeing Darcy again and having him give her such polite attention, made her wonder at the state of his regard. It seemed that his current actions were very similar to his behavior in Hertfordshire.

She considered briefly whether, perhaps, Mr. Darcy was naturally affectionate in his addresses to ladies he knew well and felt comfortable with. That would explain his behavior as simply an innocent expression of his personality. She shook her head as she rejected that conclusion. If he was so naturally charming to every lady he was on familiar terms with, he would certainly be married by now or, at least, even more pursued by ladies of the *ton*. Besides, he knew Miss Bingley quite well and never seemed to be as warm with her.

But as soon as Elizabeth began to conclude that Mr. Darcy might actually return her regard, she could refute that conclusion based on one question: *Why, then, did he leave Hertfordshire without so much as a by-your-leave?*

Elizabeth finished preparing for the day and grabbed her bonnet and warm winter cloak before exiting her bedchamber. She decided a walk after breakfast would help to clear her thoughts and to understand her feelings better, both of which were essential if she was going to know how to act the next night when she dined at Darcy's home.

She opened the door and smiled as she saw her cousin sitting on the bench in the hallway, swinging his legs and waiting for her. He looked up and quickly assumed the pose of a proper gentleman as he offered his arm. She curtsied and took it with a smile.

"You will be quite the gentleman someday, Master Edward, with all this practice."

WICKHAM WAVED THE SHEET OF paper he held in his hand to dry the ink. His plan was now fully in motion, and if everything worked as he hoped today, by the evening he would be a rich man. He folded the letter for Darcy and placed it in his coat pocket.

Wickham fantasized about the look of pure pain he hoped to see on Darcy's face. Certainly, Wickham needed the money, but in the end, he knew it was not about the money with Darcy. He was raised as a near equal, educated as a gentleman and then denied what he felt was a just portion of the wealth George Darcy left to his son. Instead, the old man, for whom he had pretended affection nearly his whole life in hopes of gaining something in the will, gave him only a lousy position as a clergyman.

At every turn of his life, Wickham saw a Darcy trying to make him miserable. *Today this is going to change, and Darcy will feel it for the rest of his life.* Wickham pulled his boots on and left Mrs. Younge's boarding house. He borrowed her horse once again and rode towards his destination in Cheapside. On the way, he reviewed the plan in his head. All he needed to do was be patient.

"GOOD MORNING, LIZZY," HER UNCLE cheerfully offered as he came in to break his fast.

Elizabeth stood, as she had just finished her meal, and smiled. "Good morning, Uncle."

"Where are you off to this morning?" he asked, placing another cinnamon scone on his plate.

Elizabeth smiled sweetly at him as she took the second scone off his plate and returned it to the tray. When he protested, she merely raised her eyebrow in challenge. "You are lucky I do not tell on you. You ought not to have the sugar, Uncle, and you know it. And to answer your question, I think I will go on a walk to Moorsfield this morning."

"All right, Lizzy, just take a maid with you. I do not want you getting lost."

Elizabeth gave her uncle an indulgent smile and placed the scone back on his plate before leaving the dining room. After putting on her bonnet and gloves, she draped her cloak around her and walked out the door with one of her aunt's maids trailing behind. The maid kept a respectable distance, allowing Elizabeth the freedom to walk briskly through the neighboring streets towards the park that was her destination.

Wickham rubbed his hands together when he saw Elizabeth emerge from the house. He watched for a few minutes to ascertain her direction and then led his horse that way. Soon he had surpassed her, and when he was far enough ahead, he turned his horse down an alleyway and dismounted. He crept closer to the edge of the buildings to wait for her to walk by.

Elizabeth was just beginning to feel warm from her exercise, despite the cold winter wind, when, suddenly, the air was knocked out of her and her neck jarred backwards as a hand grabbed her cloak and pulled her into the alleyway. Her head was shoved violently against the rough brick wall, the force of the blow causing her vision to blur.

Fear arrested her heart as she tried to comprehend what was happening. A man was holding her neck firmly against the wall while his other hand pressed painfully into her side. Her vision focused, and the face of Mr. Wickham came into view. She tried to scream but his hand was cutting off her air.

He leaned in menacingly, and she could feel his body press against hers. She again tried to call for help, but the sound of his sickeningly sweet voice made her freeze in terror. "It is nice to meet you this morning, Miss Bennet," Wickham crooned maliciously. "You really are quite a lovely piece. I can see why he fancies you."

Wickham ran his hand behind her back and aggressively pulled her closer. His other hand moved from her neck to cradle her chin.

"You do not mind giving your dear Darcy a message for me, do you, sweetie?" Wickham tightened his hold on her jaw so she could not respond. "I did not think so."

He released her just long enough to retrieve a letter from his pocket. "I have it right here, Miss Bennet. Be so kind as to see he gets this."

Elizabeth closed her eyes in an attempt to shut out the feel of his hand as he slipped the letter down the neckline of her dress. A tear escaped her eyes, and she struggled to free herself from the fear that gripped her. She opened her eyes as Wickham's evil gaze rose from her neckline up to her face. She watched in horror as he leaned in towards her again.

Elizabeth finally awoke from the grip of fear in time to twist her face to the side. His lips reached her but missed their intended target, instead touching hot against her cheek. She turned and spat in his face. He angrily wiped the spittle, raising his arm to strike her. Before he succeeded, she executed a maneuver her father taught her to use if ever she found herself in such a situation.

With as much force as she could manage, she lifted her knee firmly between them, making contact with Wickham. Instantly he released her and doubled over to the hard cobblestone ground. She stood transfixed for a moment, watching him roll on his side and clutch himself in pain. She was brought back from her stunned state by a tug on her arm.

"Miss! Miss! Come, you must run now!" It was the maid from her uncle's house. She had been frantically looking for her mistress since her sudden disappearance and found her standing over a man in an alleyway. The man was obviously in pain and the maid could see bruises forming on Elizabeth's face.

Elizabeth took a few shaky steps backwards, never taking her eyes off Wickham. Then, she turned and quickly walked with the maid back to her uncle's house.

Upon entering the house, the maid called for Elizabeth's aunt and uncle and escorted her to the sofa in the sitting room. Elizabeth sat numbly, staring at nothing, until the frantic voices of her aunt and uncle reached her ears. She listened as the maid related what she had seen when she came upon Elizabeth in the alley. Her aunt watched in horror as Elizabeth mutely reached into her dress and pulled out the note Wickham had placed there.

"Elizabeth, what happened?" her uncle asked, worriedly.

Her aunt's gentle touch caused her to look up. "Lizzy, tell us what happened. What is this note?" She took the paper from Elizabeth's hand and read the address. "Mr. Darcy?"

"He told me to give it to Mr. Darcy," Elizabeth mumbled.

Her aunt looked towards her husband with shock. He said he would send an express to Mr. Darcy's home immediately, requesting his presence as soon as possible.

"Who attacked you, Lizzy?"

Elizabeth moved her eyes slowly to the concerned face of her uncle. She swallowed and grimaced at the pain she felt from her bruised neck. She could barely whisper the name as bile began to rise in her throat at the recollection of his loathsome face. "Wickham."

Her uncle left the room to write the express, and her aunt pulled her gently up off the sofa as she said, comfortingly, "Come, dear, you must rest."

She nodded her head and walked slowly with her aunt up the stairs to her bedchamber. When she reached her bed, she climbed on top of it and lay on her side, staring blankly. She felt her aunt place a blanket over her shoulders and kiss her forehead before leaving.

When Elizabeth heard the click of her door, she took a deep breath and, pulling her knees up to her chest, allowed her tears to flow freely.

Richard was visiting with Darcy, discussing the surprising turn of events of the day before, when Mr. Carroll knocked and delivered an express.

Richard watched Darcy open and scan the letter and then stumble backwards into a chair as his face blanched.

"Darcy! What is wrong?" The colonel was alarmed as he watched his cousin mutely read through the missive again and then quickly open another that was enclosed.

Mr. Darcy stood abruptly, his face filled with anger as he called loudly for Mr. Carroll. When the man entered, Darcy nearly roared at him, "Saddle my horse!"

"Darcy! What is going on? Who is the letter from?" Richard was now shouting in his concern.

"He has gone too far this time, Richard. I swear I will kill the man with my bare hands."

Richard took a step towards his cousin in shock. He had never before seen Darcy so upset, pulling his hands through his hair and pacing the floor. Richard grabbed his shoulders to stop his pacing.

"For God's sake, Darcy, tell me what is going on!"

"Wickham!" Darcy spat the word and tossed the letters at his cousin.

Richard quickly read the first one: *"Mr. Darcy, I request your immediate presence at my house on Gracechurch St. A man named Wickham has attacked my niece Elizabeth. He gave her this note to give to you. –Edward Gardiner."*

Richard cursed under his breath and looked at his cousin. Upon seeing the pain in his eyes, he whispered, "Darcy."

Darcy looked away and demanded, "Read the next one." He strode to the study door and shouted towards the footman near the front door, "Where is my horse?!"

Richard pulled Darcy's arm and led him to sit on a chair. "Darcy they are working as fast as they can. Yelling at your staff is not going to get the horse saddled faster."

Too agitated to sit, Darcy stood again and paced the perimeter of the room as Richard read the second letter, this one from Wickham.

Darcy,

By now you will have learned that I have met your lovely Miss Bennet. She is a delightful little thing. How does it feel to know that I have compromised the two women you love most in this world? I know you would not want my almost elopement with Georgiana to become public, but what would you do to save your Miss Bennet's reputation, I wonder? For the reasonable price of twenty thousand pounds, you have my word that I will tell nobody of either lady's unfortunate circumstance. I will be waiting for you by the center statue in Hyde Park at 10 this evening. Bring a bank note and, Darcy, do come alone.

Sincerely yours, George Wickham

Richard let out a low whistle and a few decidedly improper oaths. He turned to his cousin, waving the letter in the air. "What are you going to do about this, Darcy?"

"Exactly what I have to do—pay the man!"

"You cannot be serious! When will it ever end? If you pay him now, he will just come back for more."

"What the hell am I supposed to do then, Richard?! He has hurt Georgiana before, and I cannot let him do it again. And now… now… " Darcy fell onto the couch and raked his hands through his hair as he rested his elbows on his knees. "Now he has hurt my Elizabeth. That man's evil has permeated every part of my life."

Richard sat in the chair next to Darcy. He spoke calmly and softly. "Darcy, you cannot keep paying him." Richard sat quietly, thinking for a minute, before turning confidently to his cousin. "I know what we can do."

Mr. Carroll knocked and announced Darcy's horse was ready. Darcy shot off the couch.

"Darcy, I will meet you here at 7:00 tonight to discuss with you what we will do about Wickham."

Darcy merely nodded as he left the room and put on his riding gloves and coat. Richard followed him to the grand hall and asked, "Where are you going now?"

Darcy looked at his cousin as if he had grown a third eye. "I am going to Elizabeth, of course." Darcy turned to Mr. Carroll and ordered that nobody but his cousin be allowed entrance into the home and Georgiana was to stay inside until further notice. He shot Richard another quick look before taking the steps, two at a time, and mounting his horse. He kicked the animal into a full gallop as he turned towards the street.

When Darcy reached the Gardiners' home, he was led into their sitting room, where he was asked to take a seat. After he was introduced to Mr. Gardiner, a formality that struck him as oddly out of place given the circumstances, he immediately asked the man to relate what happened.

"We do not know the full details, Mr. Darcy. Elizabeth was too stunned when she arrived home to describe much of what had taken place. The maid who had accompanied her on her walk said that she lost sight of Elizabeth after turning a corner. She began scanning all directions looking for my niece and finally found Elizabeth standing, quite distraught, in an alleyway. She was staring at a man writhing at her feet, obviously in pain. I believe Elizabeth may have assaulted Mr. Wickham and incapacitated him temporarily, which allowed her escape."

Darcy groaned and his head fell into his hands.

"Elizabeth did say that Mr. Wickham gave her the note I sent to you and asked her to deliver it. I do not know what other liberties he may have taken or words he used with her."

"Is she . . . is she all right?" Darcy could barely manage the words.

"She is resting right now. Mr. Darcy, I have to ask you — who is this man and what does this have to do with my niece?" Mr. Gardiner spoke firmly but kindly.

"It is a long story, sir. Suffice it to say, he wants to hurt me and my family."

"What does that have to do with Lizzy?"

"It is because I..." Darcy's voice faltered and he took in a deep breath. "Mr. Gardiner, may I see her? May I speak with Miss Elizabeth?" He looked up pleadingly at the man.

"I am sorry, Mr. Darcy, but she is resting. She was quite upset after..." He looked away to hide his own discomfort.

Neither man noticed that Elizabeth had entered the room. She stood, resting her back against the door. She watched Darcy rub his face and let out a shaky breath. He raked his hands through his thick curls and hung his head as he pulled at the hair on the back of his head.

Elizabeth's soft voice broke the stillness in the air. "Mr. Darcy."

Darcy immediately rose and rushed to Elizabeth's side. His heart broke as he saw the discolored skin around her neck and jaw. Elizabeth had to turn away when she saw his anguished expression. Mr. Darcy closed his eyes and took in a deep breath to steady his emotions.

Mrs. Gardiner entered the room and, seeing the silent exchange between her niece and Mr. Darcy, spoke softly with her husband before they both exited the room to allow the couple a few moments to talk.

"Elizabeth..." Mr. Darcy's voice was unsteady as he reached out gently to examine her bruised face. He stood there silently for several minutes, carefully turning her head.

Elizabeth naturally flinched as his hand approached her face in anticipation of the tenderness of her injury. She was then surprised by Mr. Darcy's gentle touch. He held her face so carefully that she could feel no pressure from his fingers as he turned her face towards him.

She looked up into his eyes and saw them brimming with emotion. Her own eyes began to fill with tears. She had determined to come downstairs when she learned of his arrival. When left to her own thoughts, she had been tortured by the continued replay of the assault. All she wanted was to see Mr. Darcy and feel his arms around her again as they had once been in the grove. She needed to hear his tender voice and feel his warmth chase away the nightmare. Standing in front of him now, looking into his eyes so filled with a similar pain to hers, she could not utter the words she wished to say.

She was mortified and humiliated at the thought of what he must now think of her, but the tenderness of his touch and the concern in his face testified that her worries were unwarranted.

Darcy forced himself to see all her bruises. He felt personally responsible for each injury and for the anguish he saw in her eyes. Her perfect little face was discolored because of him. He blamed himself for Wickham's actions; he was the one who caused Wickham to notice Elizabeth and target her. It was Wickham's hate for him and wish to seek revenge that caused Elizabeth harm. *You did not deserve this. I do not deserve you, Elizabeth,* he thought with anguish as he once again settled his eyes on hers. At that moment, all he wanted to do was pull her into his arms and hold her—to comfort her, tell her everything would be all right and that he would protect her. But he could not. She would not want him to. *How she must despise me!*

Darcy wiped away the single tear that fell from Elizabeth's eye. Reverently, he said, "Oh, Elizabeth, I am so sorry."

His wretched voice broke through her barriers, and she stepped forward to grasp onto the lapels of his jacket, burying her face in his chest. He slowly, gently wrapped his arms around her small frame. He bit his cheek as he heard her quiet sobs and rested his head on hers, trying to breathe deeply. He never hated himself more than he did at that moment. After a few minutes, he led her to the sofa and sat down with her, never releasing her from his embrace.

"Elizabeth, I am so sorry," he said again. "You are safe now; he cannot hurt you anymore. I will not allow it." His voice gained a raw conviction in the end.

He barely heard her muffled voice through her tears and his embrace. "Why did he come for me? What did I do?"

Mr. Darcy gently brushed back the matted hair at her temples. He closed his eyes to block the view of her tear-stained face, and her eyes squeezed shut. He could feel her hands gripping his coat tighter, and his heart broke yet again.

"You did nothing, my dear. Wickham wants only to hurt me, and he knows the best way to hurt me is to hurt those who are important to me."

Elizabeth's mind barely registered his words, and she froze for a moment to comprehend them. His endearment and subsequent declaration echoed through her mind. '*The best way to hurt me is to hurt those who are important to me.*' She could not fully grasp what he was saying, but her heart slowly began to feel lighter.

Mr. Darcy had not realized the confession he had made nor its importance to Elizabeth; he simply spoke from his heart. He noticed when her body stiffened and wondered whether she wished for him to release her from his embrace. Reluctantly, he loosened his arms from around her, and she leaned back far enough to look at his face. She closed her eyes when she felt his gentle hand cup her cheek.

Darcy smiled slightly as she leaned her head into his hand, and he spoke softly to her. "Elizabeth, will you tell me what he did? I know it may be painful to speak of, but I must know. I must..." His voice trembled.

She opened vacant eyes and turned her face from him. The words came in a detached manner. "He held me against a wall and tried to kiss me. He was quite angry when I turned my face. I think he was getting ready to strike me when I brought my knee up and... well, then he fell to the ground, and I was free. Only I was so scared, I could not move for a moment. The next thing I knew, the maid was pulling me away, and we were walking home." An involuntary shiver ran down her spine.

She bowed her head against his chest and could feel his hands clench into fists behind her. She listened to his labored breathing before speaking again.

"What did he want from you? His note..."

Darcy considered for a moment not telling her but then decided she deserved to know it all after what she had been through. "He wants to meet with me. He wants me to pay him to keep quiet over what he attempted to do to you and the intended elopement with Georgiana."

She pushed against him to sit up in panic. "But you cannot meet him! What if he tries to hurt you, too? What about Georgiana? Is she all right? Did he come for her, too?" Elizabeth rubbed her hands in worry.

Mr. Darcy was washed anew with love for her as he saw how, mere hours after her own attack, she was already more worried about the welfare of him and his sister.

"She is well and safe at home," he replied, reassuringly.

A moment later, he became conscious of the elapsed time they had spent together and did not want to cause the Gardiners or Elizabeth any more discomfort, so he slowly withdrew his arms the rest of the way from around her. He took out his handkerchief and handed it to Elizabeth, who took it gratefully to wipe her tear-stained face. His timing could not have been better because, not a moment later, Mr. and Mrs. Gardiner gingerly entered the room and sat opposite them.

"Mr. Gardiner, Mrs. Gardiner, I am most sincerely grieved, and I ask that you accept my apologies."

Elizabeth turned to Darcy and, with fervor, declared, "Mr. Darcy! What have you done today that you should apologize for? Wickham is to blame, not you."

"I beg your pardon, Miss Bennet, but I would have to disagree. I was Wickham's ultimate target, and as such, I must take responsibility."

Elizabeth crossed her arms in frustration and angled her body away from him. "That is the most ridiculous— " She stopped and pressed her lips together to keep the words from coming out.

"Mr. Darcy, I have to agree with my niece," said Mr. Gardiner. "As unfortunate as Elizabeth's attack was, it was by no means your fault."

Mr. Darcy merely nodded at him. "Regardless of culpability, we should speak about Miss Elizabeth's safety now. I do not think Wickham will attempt anything further, and I certainly will not allow anything to happen to her again." He turned to Elizabeth and repeated adamantly, "I will not let anyone hurt you again." She lowered her eyes from his intense gaze, and he turned back to address her aunt and uncle. "I think it may be best, however, that Miss Elizabeth returns to Hertfordshire."

Mr. Gardiner nodded his head. "We are planning on leaving in a week's time. Unfortunately, my business does not allow us to leave before that."

Mr. Darcy looked at Elizabeth and then at her relatives. "Sir, with your permission, I would like to offer to take Miss Elizabeth back to Longbourn myself. I have no fixed engagements after this evening. My sister will be accompanying me to Hertfordshire for the wedding, and we can leave as early as tomorrow."

Mr. and Mrs. Gardiner looked towards their niece to see how she felt. She looked to Darcy before speaking. "I should like to see Jane."

Mr. Gardiner nodded his head. "Then I thank you, Mr. Darcy, for your generous offer. What time shall you leave tomorrow?"

"If we leave by noon, we shall arrive in the afternoon. I do not want to leave too early in case Miss Elizabeth needs to rest in the morning."

"Thank you, Mr. Darcy." Elizabeth turned to her aunt and uncle. "May

I have permission to speak to Mr. Darcy for a moment in private before he takes his leave?"

Mrs. Gardiner looked towards her husband, who looked at the two of them. "I suppose you may."

Elizabeth waited until the Gardiners left before turning towards an expectant Mr. Darcy. He did not know what she wished to speak about, but he was silently glad for the opportunity to converse privately again. He watched as she nervously folded and refolded her hands in her lap.

"Mr. Darcy, I wished to thank you for the comfort you provided me today." She held up her hand to forestall a response. "Please, sir, allow me to say what I wish to say before my courage leaves me." She looked for his nod of agreement and breathed deeply as she dared to look him in the eyes. "Mr. Darcy, earlier you said that Wickham targeted me because he knew that he could hurt you that way. You said he always tries to hurt those who are important to you."

"That is true, Elizabeth." He spoke with soft conviction.

Elizabeth looked down at her hands and spoke as if to them, "You said you will be meeting Mr. Wickham tonight. I just wanted to be certain you will take care." She swallowed and continued barely above a whisper, "because you are important to me too, sir."

Mr. Darcy's lips spread into a broad smile, exposing his dimples, and his eyes filled with tenderness. He could hardly believe what he was hearing.

He brought one finger to raise her chin up gingerly so that she could see him. Again, he glanced briefly at her bruised face and said, "Elizabeth, I will be careful. There is much more for us to say—even if all we say are the same things over and over again."

Chapter 16

Richard walked into his cousin's study, expecting to find him in as irritated a state as he left him hours before. Instead, he found Darcy sitting calmly—too calmly—watching the dance of flames in the fireplace. He closed the door to the study behind him and walked quietly up to his cousin.

Darcy looked up at him lifelessly when Richard placed a hand on his shoulder. Their eyes met briefly before Darcy returned his unseeing gaze to the fire.

"Talk to me, Cousin," Richard said as he took a seat next to Darcy. He watched his cousin take off his cravat and unbutton the neck buttons of his shirt.

"He hurt her, Richard." Richard understood the pain behind those few words, and he reclined back into his chair, loosening his cravat.

"Did he... his letter said..." Richard struggled for words to ask the delicate question. He had begun to respect and esteem Elizabeth from the moment he learned of her. As he loved his cousin so dearly, any woman who caught his eye would immediately gain Richard's approbation. Having also met Elizabeth in person and having seen the natural liveliness and warmth she brought to both Georgiana and Darcy only caused Richard to esteem her more. The idea that Wickham had hurt her pained him nearly as much as it did Darcy for not only what she went through but also the extent to which his cousin suffered for it.

Darcy shook his head slowly and rubbed his face. "He did not. Thank God, he did not!"

Richard breathed a sigh of relief and confirmed the sentiment.

Darcy's face took on a humorless smirk. "He did not get the chance actually. Elizabeth did not let him."

"Indeed? What do you mean?"

Darcy turned to his cousin with the beginnings of a proud smile. "She assaulted him before he could so much as kiss her. She left him writhing on the ground at her feet, dastard that he is."

Richard smiled to himself before falling into quiet laughter. Darcy looked at him questioningly, and he said between chuckles, "Where did you find this woman? She has the power to compel the best and worst of men to fall at her feet." Richard saw his cousin frown and continued, "She broke through your wall, Darcy! Made you fall in love with her despite yourself. I would even venture to guess she did nothing to encourage you. Then she has the strength and courage to outplay the biggest cad in England. She is simply brilliant. A '*Phantom of Delight*'."

Darcy smiled slightly. "I have often thought of her as such. Sometimes I wonder whether she is truly real. I still cannot believe that I have been so fortunate as to gain her esteem."

Richard leaned forward with interest. "Her esteem? Care to elaborate?"

Darcy smiled smugly at his cousin. "She told me to be careful tonight —that I am important to her."

Richard whistled and sat back again. Darcy smiled as he heard his cousin mumble under his breath, "Lucky bastard."

For a few minutes, they sat in silence. Darcy replayed the sound of her voice speaking the words he had so longed to hear. She cared for him. He was important to her. For now, it would be enough. He did not know if she loved him yet, but he determined that not a day would go by that he would not try to make her fall in love with him. If it took a lifetime to earn her love, he would do it. And when he was sure she loved him, he would ask her to be his wife: his beloved companion, partner, lover and friend for the rest of his life.

He closed his eyes and leaned his head back in the chair to remember better the feel of her in his arms. She had sought *his* embrace—her actions a declaration that he was not lost to her even after what Wickham had done. She had thanked him for his comfort. His heart swelled at the thought that she drew comfort from him. Thinking about holding her reminded him of the tears she shed—tears that still stained the silk of his cravat.

He opened his eyes and reached for the discarded fabric. Turning it around in his hands, he watched the light catch the water marks. Anger again rose in his chest. *I will not allow another person to bring tears to her eyes like this again!* He turned to his cousin who was watching him quietly.

Richard noticed the moment Darcy had prepared himself to face whatever needed to be done that evening. "Are you ready to hear my plan?"

Darcy sat up straight in his chair and looked his cousin in the eye. "Tell me what I need to do."

Darcy walked briskly through Hyde Park towards the place he would meet Wickham. The cold winter air was chilling, and the frost was beginning to remove the feeling from his feet. When he reached the statue, he placed his lantern down and began pacing restlessly in front of it.

Darcy needed to look the part in order to convince Wickham, but he tried to remind himself it was not necessary that he actually *feel* nervous. Wickham was going to get what he deserved, and Darcy finally would be free of him. Footsteps on the path behind alerted him to someone's approach. He swung around to see the shadow of a man a few feet away.

In the darkness, Darcy could not make out all the man's features, but his jaw clenched and his eyes narrowed when he heard the familiar voice.

Wickham casually strode up to Darcy and said tauntingly, "Good evening, Darcy. It was so good of you to come."

Darcy stood still, ignoring the mocking tone of his old, childhood friend. "Wickham."

"What? No greeting for your old friend? 'Tis a pity, for we have so much in common."

Darcy clamped his teeth together and ignored the attempt to raise his ire. He needed to appear indifferent to Wickham's threats.

"Perhaps we can dispense with the pleasantries, Wickham." He turned to face him. "Your note said you wished to speak with me?"

Wickham laughed derisively. "You are such a bore, Darcy—always quick to get down to business and never willing to have a little fun. Perhaps that is why your father loved me better."

Darcy opened his mouth to retort but quickly closed it again. He forced himself to count to five—and then again three more times—before he was calm enough to speak indifferently. "You should know, Wickham, that you will not see a pound of my money. I have had enough of your evil."

Darcy saw Wickham's easy, charming façade fall away and his face twist in anger for a moment before he composed his features and gave him a mocking smile. "Very well, Darcy. It is your choice to make." Wickham saw that his friend appeared unconcerned by the threat. Never had he imagined Darcy would not agree to his terms. It worried him a bit, and he decided to dig in where he knew it would hurt. He sneered at his old friend and said provokingly, "Georgiana deserves what she will suffer when her reputation is ruined after I tell all of London, stupid girl that she is. But see here, old friend, I am not one to carry a grudge. When you cannot find a suitor in all of England who will want to take her off your hands, you can give her to me. She was not half bad to look at, after all."

Darcy took a step towards Wickham but then shook his head and swallowed hard to regain his control. "I am not afraid of you or your threats."

Wickham's mouth fell open slightly, and he turned his head to think. Things were not going as he had planned. Darcy was still irritatingly in control of his emotions. He leaned causally against the statue, and the two looked at each other. Darcy could see that Wickham was planning his next tactic and knew it would be even more difficult to restrain himself. He was barely able to keep from throttling him.

Wickham laughed, spitefully. "My compliments on your choice with Miss Bennet, Darcy. She is a nice piece of muslin — responsive, passionate, just my type. Would you like me to tell you what her kisses tasted like?"

Darcy laughed once and turned amused eyes to Wickham. This reaction was not what Wickham had expected, and Darcy could see his companion begin to lose composure. Wickham obviously did not expect Darcy to know what really happened. It increased Darcy's amusement, and he laughed again. "Now how would you know what her kisses taste like, Wickham? From what I hear, you were too busy crying in pain at her feet to experience any."

Wickham snarled at Darcy, his humiliation fueling his long-held rage. He lunged at Darcy with his fist pulled back to strike. Fortunately, Darcy was expecting some form of aggressive behavior and was not unprepared. He deftly reached for Wickham's fist and pulled it behind his back. Wickham yelped in pain.

Darcy held onto Wickham's arm and leaned in to whisper menacingly,

"Wickham, you have always said you deserved more from my family. On this subject, I think you will find, we agree." He pulled Wickham's arm up higher on his back, causing the man to cry out again. "That, Wickham, is what you deserve for hurting Georgiana." He jerked his arm up again, this time breaking his wrist in the process as Wickham screamed. "That is what you deserve for hurting Elizabeth."

Wickham managed to sputter with feigned bravery, "What are you going to do, Darcy, gentleman that you are? Are you going to take your fists to me? That will not save their reputations, for I can still speak."

Darcy leaned closer and spoke slowly and so calmly that a chill ran down Wickham's spine. "I do not believe you will have the chance where you are going."

All of the blood ran from Wickham's face when, at that moment, Colonel Fitzwilliam emerged from the surrounding area with several members of his regiment. The men surrounded Darcy and Wickham.

Richard pronounced, "Lieutenant George Edward Wickham, Esq., as a member of His Majesty's Royal Armed Forces, and under the parliamentary Incitement to Mutiny Act of 1797, I hereby place you under arrest for the willful abandonment of employment and duty to your regiment in violation of your legal obligation."

Wickham sputtered in disbelief.

Darcy again pulled his arm, giving him another shot of pain. "I will speak slowly so you understand. Desertion, Wickham. You left the militia without permission when you came to London."

Richard smiled briefly at Wickham's horror-stricken face and then resumed his formal address. "As such, Lt. Wickham, you are hereby required, under civil law, to be tried in Martial Court."

Darcy spoke in a low tone directly into Wickham's ear. "Desertion is a felony, Wickham, and the sentence is death."

Wickham's eyes went wide, and his mouth opened as if to speak, but no words came out. Richard covered his mouth in amused disbelief when the light from a lantern held by one of his men caught the evidence that Wickham had soiled his breeches.

Richard indicated to his men to take the miscreant away. "Darcy, you can let him go now." When his cousin did not release Wickham, he stepped forward to intervene. "Darcy, let us take him from here."

Darcy finally pushed Wickham into the waiting hands of two officers and stepped back as they placed restraints on his arms. A wave of relief mixed with exhaustion washed over him. He took another few steps back until he bumped into the statue and leaned against it. He could not believe it was over. Nearly fifteen years of suffering the cruelties and slanderous evil at the tongue of Wickham, and it was over.

After Colonel Fitzwilliam ensured Wickham was securely in custody on a carriage between two of his officers, he returned to Darcy. Placing a hand on his cousin's shoulder, he leaned in and said, "It is finished, Darcy."

Darcy turned to look at his cousin as his lips turned up slowly into a smile. "Indeed, it is, Cousin!"

Richard patted him on the back. "I will meet you at your home as soon as I see Wickham safely secured at Newgate to await his trial. Then we shall have a drink. What do you say, Cousin?"

Darcy nodded his head. "I will wait up for you."

THE NEXT MORNING, DARCY WATCHED his groom secure Elizabeth's trunks onto the carriage as he waited with Georgiana in the Gardiners' parlor for her to come down the stairs. He tapped his fingers against his leg in worried anticipation. He had informed Georgiana that morning of the events of the previous day—from Elizabeth's attack to Wickham's arrest. He had wished to spare her the pain of knowing there was ever a threat from Wickham, but once he realized she would certainly notice and question Elizabeth's injuries, he knew he had to reveal it all.

He was surprised at the calm way that she listened to his news. He was worried at first that her serenity was hiding a more distressing reaction, but when her only real concern was for Elizabeth's well-being, he knew she had not been set back by Wickham's attempt. He was grateful and pleased to see her strength.

Georgiana's greeting to Elizabeth caused him to turn from the window and look at them.

"Miss Bennet! How are you feeling today?" Georgiana's voice was infused with concern, and her eyes showed all the understanding she felt.

Elizabeth pursed her lips and captured her friend's hand in hers. "I am well, thank you." She wrapped Georgiana's arm around her own. "If you do not mind, I would like you to call me Elizabeth. After all that has happened,

'Miss Bennet' sounds too formal, do you not think?"

"I would like that very much, Elizabeth, and please call me Georgiana."

Darcy's lips turned upwards in a small smile, and he walked over to his two favorite ladies. He bowed to Elizabeth and tried to maintain his smile when he noticed her bruises were a deeper color now that they had set in.

"Good morning, Miss Bennet." He swallowed.

Elizabeth smiled to herself as she curtsied. As always, her heart started beating faster as soon as she heard his voice. "Good morning, sir."

Their eyes locked in a long gaze until Elizabeth's aunt and uncle came into the room. Elizabeth gave each of her cousins a warm goodbye and hugged her aunt and uncle. Shortly afterwards, Darcy, Georgiana and Elizabeth exited the house.

Darcy handed Elizabeth and Georgiana into the carriage and sat opposite them as their journey began. Immediately, Elizabeth and his sister began talking quietly to each other. Darcy sensed their need for a private moment after all that had happened, so he turned to look out the carriage window.

He happily amused himself with a new mental picture of Elizabeth as mother to his children after having seen the affectionate way she interacted with her young cousins. His slight smile and contented look soon garnered the attention of the ladies, who whispered and giggled to each other about it.

Darcy became aware of their amusement and inspection not long after it began, but pretended ignorance as he settled into the soft cushions and closed his eyes. Rest did not come, however, as the enchanting sound of Elizabeth's laugh reached his ears repeatedly. Her lavender scent permeated the small carriage space and tickled his senses. He fought the urge to open his eyes to look at her and drink in her beauty, but he felt his ability to survive the journey with equanimity would be in jeopardy if he did.

An hour into their trip, the voices of his sister and Elizabeth ceased altogether. When the carriage became quiet for several minutes, Darcy wondered whether the girls had fallen asleep and decided to investigate. He carefully opened one eye to scan the carriage. Georgiana was asleep, but as he adjusted his view to include Elizabeth, he caught her looking at him with a smirk on her face.

He immediately closed his eye and pressed his lips together to keep from smiling. Her soft giggle was his undoing, and he opened his eyes to look at her.

"You did not fool me, Mr. Darcy. I knew you were not asleep."

His eyebrows rose at her statement. "Indeed? And how did you know that, Miss Bennet!"

She laughed softly and looked quickly to see that Georgiana was not disturbed before turning a delicious smile on Darcy. She looked down at her skirts and smoothed them as she shrugged confidently. "I have never known anyone who spent their time *sleeping* while constantly trying not to smile." She looked up at him with that impertinent grin he loved.

Darcy tried to hold his face in the stern mask at which he was so adept but could not maintain it for long. He smiled at her and shook his head. They sat silently looking at each other for a while as Georgiana slept. His eyes roamed over her bruises, and he frowned before forcing himself to look out the window.

Elizabeth watched as his hands clenched into fists. "Will you tell me what happened last night?"

Darcy looked over to her and thought for a moment. He nodded and began recounting what he had told Georgiana that morning about Wickham's arrest. As with Georgiana, he left out the vile insults Wickham had spat at him about both ladies.

"So that is it? He has been arrested; now what will happen to him?"

"His desertion is punishable by death when they find him guilty."

"How do you know he will be convicted?" He could hear panic begin to rise in her voice. "What if they let him go?"

He gave her a comforting smile. "He will be convicted. Colonel Fitzwilliam has documents from Colonel Forster detailing numerous acts of insubordination prior to his desertion, and of course, he did leave his regiment. Besides the fact that he left without leave to do so, I have proof that he did not intend to reenlist or return to his regiment."

"What proof do you have?"

"He wrote me several threatening letters." Darcy swallowed and clenched his jaw again.

"I am sorry." Elizabeth was quiet for a minute, leaving them to their thoughts. "So, it is over." She spoke more to herself than to him, but he responded with a sigh.

"It is finally over."

A few minutes later, they felt the carriage begin to slow as it neared the coaching inn where they would stop for a short rest and some refreshment.

When they reached the inn, Darcy gently woke Georgiana, and the three of them left the carriage to stretch their legs and have a cup of tea while the horses were changed.

As they approached the carriage to resume their journey, Georgiana requested, "William, could you get my valise? I should like to read a book that is packed in it."

He assisted the ladies into the carriage as he replied, "Of course, dear, I will ask the groom to retrieve it, and I'll bring it to you."

After handing her the bag, he stepped up to enter the carriage. As his head ducked inside, he noticed Georgiana had placed her bag on the seat next to her and opposite Elizabeth. Realizing that the only place left for him was next to Elizabeth, he shot a disapproving look at his sister, who gave him an innocent look in return. He saw that Elizabeth was oblivious to the situation and only interested in the book she was reading.

He hesitated briefly and, after giving his sister another scowl at her blatant machination, stepped into the carriage and placed himself in the seat next to Elizabeth. Her head shot up when she noticed him, and she blushed.

Darcy tried again silently to censure his sister and reached for Georgiana's bag to switch places with it. As the carriage jolted forward and jarred him back into the seat, he gave up the effort. He turned an apologetic face to Elizabeth, who smiled demurely before returning her attention to her book. Georgiana smiled widely at him before lowering her head to her own book with a look of satisfaction.

Darcy held his hands tightly in his lap and looked out the window. With Elizabeth so near, her perfume was all the more disastrous to his composure, as was the occasional brush of her arm or leg against his when the carriage wheels rolled along a rut in the road.

Elizabeth was not managing to keep her composure any better. Every time Mr. Darcy's leg or arm brushed against her, it left her skin feeling as if it were on fire. She would just gain command of her senses and try to resume reading her book, when the carriage would jerk again and their limbs would collide. Her only consolation was the fact that she could see that he was just as affected. She saw him trying to remain impassive, but whenever they brushed against each other, he would nibble his bottom lip and clutch his hands together tightly, making his knuckles turn white.

Eventually, the quiet sway of the carriage, combined with the previous night's tumultuous sleep, caused her eyelids to become heavy, and despite the sensations coursing through her when they touched, she was lulled into a restful slumber.

Darcy was relieved when he noticed Elizabeth had fallen asleep, as it gave him the opportunity to relax his tight jaw and let out a deep breath. When she was awake, it had taken all his control not to pull her into his arms and kiss her. Instead, he had to force himself to hide the effect her proximity was having on him. Now that she was asleep, he could relax a little without her seeing the state he was in.

His momentary relief vanished when a bump in the road caused the carriage to jerk and Elizabeth to slide nearer to him, her head falling to rest on his shoulder. His eyes went wide as he glanced at her sleeping face. He looked across the carriage to his sister for help and then shook his head in exasperation as she smiled happily at him and resumed reading her book.

It was exquisite torture to be so close to Elizabeth, feeling her soft breath as she inhaled and exhaled. Her hair piled high on her head was tickling his face, and her lavender scent was even more intoxicating. He turned his head towards her and closed his eyes as he allowed himself the indulgence of one deep breath. He was reminded, suddenly, of their horse ride after her fall. He smiled at the memory for a minute.

Georgiana giggled softly from across the carriage, and he looked to her at the sound. She whispered, "You are welcome, William."

He frowned at her briefly for good measure before breaking into a brilliant smile and winking at her. He settled in next to Elizabeth and determined to enjoy the dream as long as he was allowed. Eventually, he became aware that Georgiana had dozed off, which allowed him unabashedly to admire Elizabeth's beautiful, sleeping face without the amused smiles of his sister. To see her sleep was an image he had dreamed of and hoped never to forget. He spent a long time memorizing every curve of her soft face and delicately splayed eyelashes. Her features were relaxed in such a contented manner that he decided she had never looked more beautiful.

The temptation to bend his head to kiss her soft curls the way he had in the grove so many weeks before, became too much, so Darcy turned his head away to look out the window for a long while. The time had passed quicker than he realized as he began to recognize the surroundings of Hertfordshire as their carriage neared Meryton.

Reluctantly, he nudged Elizabeth awake as their journey was coming to an end. Her eyelids fluttered for a moment before she opened them and looked around. When she realized she had been resting on Mr. Darcy's shoulder, she sat up straight and apologized, blushing in mortification.

"Do not worry, Miss Bennet; it was no sacrifice on my part." He smiled triumphantly, and she raised her eyebrows at his brazen speech. "I am sorry to wake you, but we are nearly there." He pointed out the window.

Elizabeth looked out the window and, with astonishment, exclaimed, "I cannot believe it! It has always taken my uncle's carriage four hours to reach Longbourn from London. Your carriage, sir, must be well sprung, as I did not think the horses were going so fast."

"I beg your pardon, Miss Bennet, but it *has* been nearly four hours. I would like to accept your compliment to my carriage and horses, but they have been no faster than your uncle's would have been."

Elizabeth shook her head in disbelief. "You are too modest, sir. It cannot have been so long."

Darcy laughed at her look of skepticism and, without thinking, pulled out his watch and handed it to her. "Check for yourself. I assure you, it has been nearly four hours."

He smiled at her defiant look as she took up his watch. "I will, thank you very much."

The moment she opened the watch, he realized his mistake. He saw immediately that she recognized his memento, and he quickly tried to retrieve his watch from her possession.

She pulled it out of his reach and began to laugh. "Oh, no, Mr. Darcy! You may not have this back just yet."

Georgiana woke to the noise and opened her eyes to see a laughing Elizabeth holding her brother's watch out of his reach as he tried to retrieve it without leaning too close.

"Miss Bennet, you have already discovered my thievery, so returning my watch will not lessen your triumph, I am sure." Completely embarrassed, he reached again for the watch.

Elizabeth laughed as she moved his watch to hide it behind her back. "Sir, is it a new fashion among gentlemen to carry silk flowers in their pocket watches?" she teased.

"Minx!" he cried, as he tried once more to reach behind her and take the watch. Elizabeth was quicker and turned to hand it to Georgiana.

Georgiana opened it and, seeing the silk flower, began to laugh at her brother. Darcy sat back, defeated, and crossed his arms, pretending to be more upset than he was embarrassed.

"William! What are you doing with such a feminine item in your watch?"

Elizabeth explained with amused satisfaction and a sideways look at Mr. Darcy. "The silk flower is mine, Georgiana. It came off my shoe at the Netherfield ball nearly six weeks ago. I suspect I know where it has been located ever since."

Darcy eyed Elizabeth sideways as his pretended frown broke, and he gave her a guilty smile. She laughed endearingly at him. "Mr. Darcy, may I have my flower back now?"

Darcy leaned forward and surprised them both as he quickly retrieved his watch from his sister and replaced it in his pocket. "No."

Elizabeth's eyes widened, and her brows rose at his statement. "No? Sir, I do not believe it belongs to you."

Darcy shrugged indifferently but maintained a slight smile. "Regardless, it is mine now. I do not plan on returning it."

Elizabeth laughed at his proud demeanor and thought a moment, tapping her finger on her lips. Mr. Darcy swallowed. *If she only knew what that does to me...*

"I believe, sir, that it is only fair that I have some sort of compensation for your thievery."

Mr. Darcy looked at her in challenge, nodding his head for her to continue.

Elizabeth accepted the challenge and reached into her dress pocket to retrieve the handkerchief he had loaned her the day before when she was crying. "Well, seeing as I was going to return this to you, sir, after it was laundered, I believe it is only just that I should keep it now. What say you to that?" she asked, saucily.

Darcy's pressed lips turned upwards in a smile. "I accept your terms." His smile widened when Elizabeth and Georgiana began to laugh.

Elizabeth stretched her hand out to him. "Then it is agreed?"

Darcy took her hand, laughing at her unladylike proposal to shake hands to seal the agreement. After shaking it gently, he pulled her hand to his lips and kissed it softly before releasing it. "Agreed." He smiled smugly when he saw her turn in her seat and blush.

Georgiana watched with fascination at the way Elizabeth was able to tease her brother and the way he responded so charmingly to her. It was clear that their affections were engaged and mutual. She bit her lip with excitement as hope rose in her heart that she would soon get the sister she had always wished for.

Chapter 17

Elizabeth drew in a slow, deep breath. The clear, country air was invigorating, and she felt refreshed and glad to be home. Not only was the air cleaner than sooty London, but even the frozen, sleeping land of Hertfordshire in January made Elizabeth feel like she was breathing in new life. She pushed with her boots and swung backwards on the tree swing. She swayed sideways slightly as the air blew past her, tickling the small curls escaping her bonnet.

The day before, she had arrived back at Longbourn amid laughter and smiles within the carriage and concerned chaos without. Her father came to the carriage first after Mr. Darcy had handed her out. Elizabeth's eyes moistened remembering the concerned, tired face of her father. He looked as if he had not slept at all since receiving their express the night before, detailing the attack and change of plans in their travel arrangements. She could see on his face the worry he must have suffered, and as she looked into his eyes, she knew she saw a bit of guilt, too.

When he stepped up to the carriage, he looked as if he wished to speak but then engulfed her in a father's embrace, whispering, "Oh, my Lizzy."

Jane, too, was nearly in tears as soon as she saw the bruises on Elizabeth's neck and face. She immediately pulled Elizabeth into the house to care for her. Lydia was uncharacteristically silent and grave. Kitty did not come to greet Elizabeth as she was attending Mrs. Bennet, who had taken to her rooms in a fit of nerves as soon as she learned of Elizabeth's attack.

Elizabeth kicked the ground, sending the swing higher as she continued to reflect on the previous day. As soon as the entire party was inside, Mr.

Darcy made introductions for Miss Darcy to the rest of the Bennet family. Mr. Bennet requested a moment with Mr. Darcy in his study, and Elizabeth declared she would go to her mother.

"Come and join us when you have seen your mother, will you Lizzy?" her father requested.

Elizabeth smiled and nodded her head before removing the hand he still held in his. Jane attended to Miss Darcy, making sure she felt comfortable.

Upon Elizabeth's entrance into her chambers, her mother was immediately in raptures over her safe arrival home.

"Oh, my dear Lizzy! How afraid we were to hear that you had gotten attacked by Mr. Wickham. I am sure I thought you would die and then my brother would have to fight Wickham!" Mrs. Bennet fanned herself and fluttered her other hand around anxiously. Before Elizabeth could say something soothing, she continued, "And Mr. Wickham! I am sure I did not think he was so bad, but then again, as I told Mrs. Phillips this morning, I never quite trusted him. No, I did not."

"I am well now, Mama, as you can see. Wickham has been arrested, and he cannot hurt anyone again."

Mrs. Bennet ceased her movements for a moment to assess her daughter and, for the first time, noticed the injuries to her face.

"Oh, Kitty, get me my smelling salts!" Kitty rushed to bring her a vial of salts, and she huffed into them before falling back into her mass of pillows and moaning. "Just look at yourself, Lizzy! I am sure no man will have you now. Whatever will we do?"

Elizabeth turned her face to roll her eyes and then sat on her mother's bed. "Mama, my face is perfectly fine. It is only a little bruising and will be gone in a few days," she said reassuringly.

Mrs. Bennet waved Elizabeth away. "I pray it will be so, child, for what man will have you with such ugly colors all over your face? Let me be, I am very ill, very ill indeed."

Elizabeth gladly exited and headed to her father's study.

Mr. Bennet held the door open to usher Mr. Darcy into his study before closing it and heading solemnly to sit in his desk chair. Mr. Darcy, who had expected such an interview, took a seat across from him.

"Well, Mr. Darcy, you have rescued my daughter and returned her home twice now," Mr. Bennet began.

Mr. Darcy grimly declared, "Unfortunately, I must take the blame for her need to be rescued this time. Wickham was after me, sir. As you are familiar with the particulars of our history, you can see he has made it a life-long habit to choose his victims from among those I hold in regard."

Mr. Bennet considered his companion for a brief moment before saying, "I think you take too much upon yourself, Mr. Darcy."

Mr. Darcy's lips turned up in a half smile. "So says your daughter as well, sir."

Elizabeth's father chuckled lightly. "Mr. Darcy, I must thank you for the help you have rendered this family with regards to Elizabeth. I thank God she was not more seriously injured physically or emotionally." The two men sat quietly, nodding in agreement. "I also wish to thank you, more particularly, for bringing my Lizzy home to me today. Even without a more serious injury, I do not think I could have waited to see her until her uncle brought her later this week."

"It was my pleasure, sir." Mr. Darcy's words were solemnly spoken, but as soon as they were out, he was reminded of their pleasant banter over her discovery of the silk flower in his watch, and he smiled secretly to himself.

Witnessing his expression, Mr. Bennet said, "Elizabeth has an uncanny ability to recover quickly. It is not in her nature to be grave and forlorn. As worried as I was for her, I was more than relieved to see her emerge from your carriage, sir, with laughter in her eyes and a smile on her face. Thank you for that, too."

"I deserve no such gratitude. Your daughter is a remarkable lady who seems to lift the spirits of those around her quite naturally, sir," Darcy boldly stated, looking Mr. Bennet in the eye.

Mr. Bennet nodded his head in consideration. "So she is." After a moment, in which Mr. Darcy studied his clasped hands in front of him and Mr. Bennet studied Mr. Darcy, Elizabeth's father asked, "So, what is to become of Wickham, then?"

Darcy shifted in his seat, thankful for the change in topic and the businesslike tone of Mr. Bennet. He related the events of the previous evening in the park: Wickham's being detained and arrested under charges of desertion.

Mr. Bennet listened to the recounting and let out an audible sigh. "I cannot say that I am sorry for him. It may not be Christian of me, but I would not wish to know that man was anywhere on this earth and still breathing."

"And, so, he will not be, soon." Darcy replied.

They were interrupted by a soft knock on the door. Assuming it was his favorite daughter, Mr. Bennet's mood lifted as he called her to enter. Elizabeth gingerly opened the door to join the men. The familiar smell of books and old cigar smoke came upon her, and she nearly began to cry at the unexpected relief she felt from it.

Darcy, having determined that Mr. Bennet and his daughter might want a few moments alone, decided to take his leave, but only after securing her permission to call the next morning. Having received her consent, he left and gathered his sister before traveling the short distance to Netherfield.

A tear rolled down Elizabeth's cheek as the cold January wind cooled its path down her face. After Mr. Darcy took his leave, she went to her father's side. Without a word, he escorted her to the window seat and sat them both down. She had expected him to talk about the attack but, instead, he had wished only to hold her, and so they sat for many moments, Elizabeth being comforted by her papa or the other way around.

Not for the first time since stepping out of Mr. Darcy's carriage, Elizabeth breathed in a sigh of contentment at being home. She smiled at the irony of how she had felt relief at being away from home only a week before when she left Longbourn for London. Now, she was returned to the country and feeling relief for having left London. The realization hit her like the force of a push from behind. *I feel most contented when in the part of the country where Mr. Darcy is.* Elizabeth smiled to herself as she kicked her leg lazily, causing the swing to twist and turn. Later that morning, Mr. Darcy would be visiting. The anticipation made her giddy with excitement.

Mr. Darcy looked down at the letter in his hands, letting out a frustrated breath and uncharacteristic oath. He was really beginning to hate letters. This one had just arrived that morning and from a quarter of the country from which he had not anticipated receiving anything. It was from his Aunt Catherine, requesting his immediate presence in Kent. *Can I not have even a day to enjoy Elizabeth's company?* As soon as the thought materialized, though, he felt guilty for having had it. More than likely, the letter was due to Cousin Anne's health or the Rosings Park estate. As there was still three weeks until Bingley's wedding, he certainly had time to see to whatever the urgent summons was about.

He folded the letter and secured it with the other business correspondence he had brought with him from London. He sat back, lacing his fingers behind his head. He had awoken early and readied himself for his visit to Elizabeth. Pulling out his watch, he checked the time and chuckled to himself at the sight of the silver flower. *Still too early for a proper visit,* he thought, glumly.

Checking the time was a lot more fun now that she knew he had her flower hidden there. Before, it was only secretly satisfying, a private indulgence and reminder, allowing him to think of her. Now, when he glanced at the flower in his watch, he knew that she was aware of his thievery and, instead of being upset about it, seemed to find great pleasure in it. He was also enormously thrilled at her desire to own something of his in return. For a moment, when she had extended her hand to shake on the business agreement, he had wanted to say, "*If you will give me your hand now, you can have all that I have.*"

He breathed in deeply at the thought. He wondered what she would have said to his sudden proposal. Before the ride from London, he only hoped that she held him in high esteem. Now he wondered whether God and luck had granted him his greatest wish: her love in return. Today he wished to speak privately with her and perhaps plant the suggestion of a future life together—in vague terms, of course, just to gauge her reaction to the idea. If it seemed she was favorable, he would send his valet to London for his mother's ring, and as soon as it arrived, he would ask her to be his wife.

He checked his watch again, and although the act was still satisfying, he frowned that only fifteen minutes had elapsed and it was still much too early to visit. Too restless to sit any longer, he decided, instead of leaving for Kent in the morning, he would leave that day after his visit to Elizabeth. Then, hopefully, he would be able to return that much sooner. He called for his valet and informed him they would be leaving in a few hours and he should begin packing his bags. The journey to Kent could be accomplished in just over six hours with the fair weather. He was satisfied.

After waiting another excruciatingly long hour, Darcy exited his chambers, eager to visit Elizabeth. He found Bingley and his sisters just finishing their breakfast.

Miss Bingley walked quickly towards him, purring, "Mr. Darcy. We are so glad you have come. You have rested late this morning; can I fix you a plate for your breakfast?"

Darcy spun on his heels and headed for the breakfast sideboard. "Thank you, Miss Bingley, but I have already breakfasted in my room and need only a cup of coffee." *To use as olfactory defense.*

Her perfume caught up with him before she did. Noticing his riding crop, Miss Bingley asked flirtatiously, "And where do you go off to so secretly this morning, sir."

Darcy raised his cup to his nose and breathed the cleansing brew in deeply. Keeping it close to his face, he crossed the room towards Bingley. "It is no secret, Miss Bingley. Your brother and I are calling at Longbourn this morning."

Miss Bingley's face fell in a pout before she deftly transformed it into an artificial smile. "Oh, yes, of course. How is dear Miss Eliza?" she asked insincerely. "Though, if you ask me, it serves her right in a way. She was always giving off airs, and"—she paused conspiratorially— "it would not surprise me in the least if she led Mr. Wickham to believe she wished for his attentions."

She tapped her fan satisfyingly on the edge of a chair to make her point as she looked to her sister, who nodded in agreement.

Darcy's jaw clenched in anger, and he nearly gave her a well-deserved set down. He was glad that Georgiana had decided to sleep late after traveling the day before and was not present to hear Miss Bingley's slur against Elizabeth. When Bingley placed his hand on his shoulder, he turned his look of daggers from Miss Bingley towards her brother, who gave him a pleading look before saying, "Well, Darcy, shall we go? It is still early, but I daresay if we take a longer route we shall arrive at a respectable time."

Darcy let out his breath and nodded at his friend before putting his coffee down and exiting the room without so much as a word regarding Miss Bingley's ill-tempered comment.

When Darcy arrived at Longbourn, he noticed Elizabeth swinging at the side of the house and, without a word, left Bingley to enter the house alone as he strolled over to see her. She was deep in thought and did not hear his approach. When the swing came back towards him, Mr. Darcy gave her a small push forward.

Elizabeth squealed in surprise as she turned her head quickly to see the source of her sudden exhilaration through the air.

She laughed as she said, "Good morning, Mr. Darcy," before facing forward again.

He gave another push. "Good morning to you, too, Miss Bennet."

Mr. Darcy circled the path of the swing and rested casually against a tree truck beside her. He folded his arms across his chest and watched her swing back and forth.

Elizabeth was somewhat unsettled by his steady gaze and cocked her head to the side. "It is still a bit early for a visit, is it not, Mr. Darcy?"

He smiled with humor as he tipped his head and, while maintaining eye contact with her, made a show of pulling out his watch. "Well, let me see." He glanced down at the time and then closed his watch, replacing it in his pocket. "Perhaps a little early. Do you mind?"

Elizabeth pressed her lips into a tight line to keep from smiling at his antics before saying pertly, "I suppose not if you promise to be pleasant company."

Darcy raised his eyebrows at this remark. "I shall do my best, Miss Bennett. What shall we talk about then? What say you to books?"

"Oh, no, Mr. Darcy, I can never talk of books while on a swing," she said sternly.

Darcy chuckled softly and shook his head. "Of course not, what was I thinking? Books and swinging—preposterous!"

The tinkling laugh that came to his ears was delightful, and he found himself watching her with pronounced admiration.

"You surprise me, sir. I did not always think you had such a sense of humor or could behave so charmingly." Elizabeth smiled at him.

"Oh, no? I suppose not. As you unashamedly declared to my relations, my behavior was... ah, yes, I remember, 'most dreadful'."

Elizabeth smiled but blushed with slight embarrassment. "Yes, well, I believe we already covered that topic, sir. What say you to a discussion of poetry this morning?"

Mr. Darcy's lips turned upward slightly. "I believe it has been said that poetry is the food of love."

Elizabeth laughed lightly as she shook her head. "A stout, healthy love, perhaps, but I am certain that if only a vague inclination, one good sonnet will starve it away."

Mr. Darcy smiled at this, and the two began an easy discussion on various authors in vogue and the merits of each. Before either of them had realized it, an hour of pleasant companionship had passed, and Mr. Bingley and Jane walked outside to greet them.

Mr. Darcy realized the passage of time only as Mr. Bingley suggested they take their leave. Reluctantly, Mr. Darcy offered his hand to aid Elizabeth off the swing and led her towards the house to say goodbye. They walked slowly, allowing the others to outstrip them. Darcy stopped, and Elizabeth looked up at him, smiling as she gave his arm a gentle squeeze.

"Miss Bennet, unfortunately, I have also come to take my leave of you for more than just today. I received a letter from my Aunt Catherine requesting my urgent presence at her estate in Kent. I do not know what she requires, but I hope to return as soon as possible. My sister will remain with Bingley and his sisters. May I ask that you look in on her while I am away?"

Elizabeth frowned in disappointment but responded cheerfully, "Of course, I will take good care of her in your absence."

"There is one more thing I should like to request of you Eliz— Miss Bennet," he said slowly and with significance.

Elizabeth's heart faltered, and she swallowed carefully as she looked up to his face. "And what is that, sir?"

Her breath came more rapidly, and her heart was speeding in anticipation, especially when she saw a tenderness in his eyes that made her toes curl in excitement.

Darcy allowed his eyes to wander from her beautiful hair to her brow—so often turned up at him in challenge—to her liquid brown eyes and rosy cheeks. His gaze slowly lowered to her pink lips, now pressed slightly together as she waited for him to speak.

His voice came a little more shakily than he had hoped as he said, "When I return, Miss Bennet, there is a matter of great importance I should like to speak about with you." He paused for significance and watched her slowly nod her head. He continued softly, "I have a question I should like to ask you."

Elizabeth's slow smile eventually reached her eyes as she replied, "I will look forward to your return, then, Mr. Darcy."

Mr. Darcy grasped her hand on his arm and brought it to his lips to kiss softly. "So will I. So will I."

Chapter 18

As soon as his carriage rolled across the grounds of the Hunsford parsonage, Mr. Darcy could see Mr. Collins waving ecstatically from his threshold. He leaned back against the seat — and away from the window — with a sigh. He hoped that his time at Rosings would be brief and he could soon be back with Elizabeth. A moment later, the carriage swayed to a stop in front of his aunt's great manor house, Rosings Park.

A servant in brilliant livery opened his carriage door, and another held a lantern to give light to the evening as he descended the carriage and walked up the steps into the open doors of the home.

He was greeted by the butler, who commissioned a footman to retrieve his outerwear and hat. "Where is my aunt this evening?" he asked.

"She is resting, sir. If I may be so bold, sir, it is good that you have come. We had begun to fear you would not be in time."

Darcy stopped short in the process of removing his gloves and looked at the butler with furrowed brows. "Excuse me, but is my aunt unwell?"

It was his cousin Anne's weak voice that answered as she entered the entryway from the parlor. "She took suddenly ill, Cousin. We fear for her life."

Darcy immediately assumed his serious, grave demeanor. "Has a doctor seen her?" He walked towards his cousin with a determined stride and carefully assisted her back to the parlor and out of the drafty entryway.

"Yes, Mr. Putnam was here to see her last evening and again this morning."

Darcy rubbed his face after depositing his cousin gently on the sofa. He began to pace as he enquired further, "And what is his diagnosis?" He had never known his aunt to have so much as a cold, and for her to be so gravely ill was unsettling.

"He does not say. He is as puzzled as we are. He prescribed some draughts for her and gave the nurse some laudanum in the event that she should be in pain in the final hours." Anne's voice broke with the last, and Darcy stopped his pacing to sit next to her.

A servant came in and said that the mistress was awake and asking for him. Darcy turned towards Anne after acknowledging and dismissing the servant. "Do you come with me, Cousin?"

Anne's shaky voice was barely audible. "No, I think I will retire. I only stayed up to receive you this evening."

Darcy tenderly helped his cousin to stand and placed her securely on the arm of her companion before making his way to his aunt's bedchamber.

He knocked softly, and a nursemaid opened the door for him. Immediately, he was aware of the stale smell of the sickroom and resisted the urge to pull out his handkerchief to cover his nose. As he approached the bed, he had to squint to see his aunt's form on it. There were very few candles lit, and they, along with the roaring fire, gave the only light to the room. The heat from the fire was stifling, and Darcy pulled at his neck cloth.

As soon as his eyes adjusted to the darkness, he could see the pale form of his aunt lying in her bed. Her face was white and had a ghostly pallor.

He spoke softly so as not to disturb her. "Aunt Catherine, it is your nephew."

Lady Catherine turned her face towards him and croaked, "Fitzwilliam?" She pulled one of her hands from under the covers and reached weakly to him.

Darcy took her hand in his and startled at the frigid coldness of it. "Yes, Aunt, it is I. How are you feeling?"

Lady Catherine gave a hacking cough that caused Darcy to lean back slightly. Her raspy voice said, "Horrid. I am most seriously displeased."

Darcy almost smiled at his aunt's trademark statement. "Is there anything you wish for your present relief? A glass of wine? Shall I get you one?"

Darcy could feel her hand warming slightly in his, but she removed it limply to return it under the blanket. "No, Nephew. I am just glad that you are here to see after Anne. I cannot think what will become of her should I... should I..." Her voice faltered, and she turned her head from him.

"Hush, Aunt Catherine. Nothing is going to happen to you. I will have my doctor from London summoned right away. He is an expert, you know.

I can have him here by tomorrow evening, and he will find out what is ailing you and have you feeling well in no time."

"No!" Darcy sat back in surprise at the sudden strength of her voice, but then she continued, more raspy than ever, stopping to cough occasionally. "That is not necessary, Fitzwilliam. I am resigned to my fate."

Darcy frowned and said, gently, "Where is my Uncle Henry? Have you sent word to the Fitzwilliams?"

Lady Catherine croaked, "Let us not worry them for now. Perhaps you are right and this is only a passing folly. I should not like to intrude unnecessarily upon their lives."

Darcy's brow furrowed at the comment. He could not remember a time when his aunt had not willingly intruded on the lives of her relations, but immediately he dismissed it and felt guilty for his ungrateful thought. Perhaps in her last days, she was softening.

"I should like to rest now, Fitzwilliam. Visit me tomorrow, if you can spare a moment for your invalid of an aunt."

"Of course, Aunt. What time shall I come?"

"I will send my nurse for you. I never know when I am well enough for visits. I am much too weak sometimes, you see." She coughed violently before adding, "You are a good boy to come to my sickroom to see me."

"I would do no less, Aunt Catherine." He reached for the hand she had again taken out from her blanket to give it a squeeze. It was cold as ice again, and he rubbed it gently to warm it before placing it on the bed and standing to leave. "Good night, Aunt. Rest well."

She weakly waved him away, and once Darcy had reached the outside of her room, he collapsed upon a bench in the hallway. He ran his hands through his hair and thought a moment. His aunt was really quite ill, and now he was beginning to fear for her life. He remembered the freezing feel of her skin and the whiteness of her face. Amid all that heat from the fire, he could not believe she felt so cold. It sent a chill through his spine, and he stood up to walk it off.

Reaching his bedchamber, he rang for his valet who was already in his dressing room unpacking his trunks. He decided to retire early and dressed quickly for bed. He knew Rosings would pass to Anne upon his aunt's death and that his cousin would be well taken care of. As much as he had hated his yearly visits to Rosings every Easter, he was beginning to wonder whether the previous Easter was to have been his last with his aunt. He never enjoyed her company, as she was always so sanctimonious and demanding. All that seemed to matter little now, seeing her frail form in the sickroom.

Darcy rolled over, blowing out the candle next to his bed and lay staring at the canopy above him. The stresses of travelling and hearing the news of his aunt's illness were taking a toll on him already. He breathed in deeply and brought his mind willingly to Elizabeth. Thoughts of her always calmed him. He allowed himself to imagine what she was doing or how she would look when he saw her again. He fell asleep recalling their pleasant morning together and her obvious pleasure at his request to speak to her upon his return.

The next morning, Darcy awoke and asked the housekeeper how his aunt was doing. She could not give a favorable reply, saying only that his aunt would allow no one but her nurse in the sickroom, and the nurse had reported that Lady Catherine was no better and, perhaps, even worse. He informed the housekeeper where he could be found should his aunt summon him, and he left for his aunt's study where he decided he would look over her estate books as he had always done.

Darcy busied himself all morning with estate business, trying to keep his mind off the lack of news or updates from his aunt's sickroom. Twice he asked the housekeeper for news, and twice she had given him the same reply: "She remains unwell and is resting."

When Anne came down later in the afternoon, he spent a few minutes visiting with her before she declared she wished to rest. In the early evening, once it began to darken outside, he was summoned by his aunt. He eagerly went to her room and entered when the nurse opened the door for him. He was met with the same unpleasant aroma of illness and the same sickly appearance of his aunt as the evening before. The room was even more stifling in its heat, yet his aunt's hand remained cold.

Darcy breathed a sigh of momentary relief as it seemed, at least, she was no worse, and they conversed for a short while. Mostly, Lady Catherine made him promise to see to this or that upon her demise. He consented and promised her that, should she go, even though he was sure she would pull through, he would take care of all that was necessary.

"You need not worry, Aunt," he said tenderly.

Soon, however, she tired and wished to rest, so he left her sickroom with a mixture of relief and growing concern. The doctor came the next day and pronounced the situation no better and could offer no solutions.

The routine of Darcy's day was the same for three days as he worked feverishly in the morning and afternoon at the estate books to distract his growing concern. He met and visited briefly with his cousin at least once during the day and then, in the evening, he was summoned to his aunt's sickroom to visit for a half hour before she retired.

On the fourth night, his aunt's voice and pallor seemed much worse as she said, "Fitzwilliam, promise me you will see after Anne."

For most of his life, he had disliked his aunt, but in the past few days, she had seemed to be so changed, so weak. He felt compassion for her and, for the first time in his life, thought, perhaps, he had misjudged her. "Of course, Aunt Catherine. Do not trouble yourself over Anne. I will take care of her."

She seemed satisfied and dismissed him for the evening. He left her chamber with a heavy heart and went straight outside for a moonlit walk around the gardens to clear his mind. He wished Elizabeth were there with him to comfort him during these strange, stressful days. He looked to the sky; it was a clear night, and he could see the stars.

The next morning Darcy did not go down to the study to work on estate business. He was worried and stressed from the decline he had seen in his aunt the evening before. Instead, he tried to occupy his time with a book and by writing letters to Elizabeth. Of course, he could not give them to her as that would be improper, but the process was cathartic to him, and it soothed his mind a bit.

Late in the morning, he decided to go for a ride to exercise his mount and release some tension. He gathered his riding crop and gloves and walked down the hallway from his bedchamber. Nearing his aunt's room, he slowed his pace as he heard a voice from within.

He quietly walked closer to the door, and his eyes grew wide with astonishment. He could hear Lady Catherine's voice clearly through the door, as strong and imperious as ever, and he was completely confused. A surge of relief flew through him at the thought that she had recovered overnight. He quickly opened the door and walked into the room.

Nobody noticed his entrance, and he watched with amazement and growing anger at the scene before him. His aunt, sitting upright and rigid, was commanding servants all around her with as much power as she ever had before her illness.

"Remove those buckets of wet towels, I do not need them until tonight, and the smell is putrid. Add a little more vinegar tonight before you return. These things must be attended to!"

Darcy erupted. "What is the meaning of this, ma'am?!"

Lady Catherine immediately sunk back against the pillows as if exhausted and pulled the covers over her body. "Fitzwilliam," her voice raspy again, "Thank God you are here, these servants are incompetent—they have left the towels in here from when they washed the floor, and I am sure it is aggravating my illness—" Her voice was cut off by her nephew's.

"Aunt Catherine!" He went to her and felt her forehead. "Are you well?" Pulling back his hand, he saw that it was covered in a white powdery substance. His eyes came together in anger as he realized it was chalk powder that gave the pale color to her cheeks. "Are you even ill? I suppose your cold hands were the work of ice under the blanket!" he shouted disbelievingly.

Lady Catherine blanched at his discovery. Resigned, she sat up and immediately dismissed all of the servants, who had been standing paralyzed at the sight before them.

"Fitzwilliam Darcy! You will stop this immediately!"

"Excuse me, Aunt, but why with so little endeavor at civility, am I thus refused an answer to my question?"

"Darcy, you can be at no loss as to why I would pretend illness."

"You mistake me, Aunt. I have not the pleasure of knowing why you would subject me to such trickery," he growled.

"I did it to prevent an alliance of monumentally disastrous proportions. I heard last week from my rector, Mr. Collins, that you spent much time with Miss Elizabeth Bennet while in London and you escorted her back to her home in Hertfordshire. Tell me this is a scandalous falsehood! Her arts and allurements must have caught you. I set straight away to bring you here to prevent such an impossible folly."

"I wonder, Aunt, if you thought it a scandalous falsehood, why you took the trouble of appearing ill. What could your ladyship propose by it?" Darcy seethed.

"To garner your promise, of course, to Anne as I received last night."

"I made no such promise to Anne!"

"You did, indeed, Fitzwilliam!"

"I promised to support her—to make sure she was taken care of! I did not promise to marry her," he said incredulously.

"This is not to be borne, Darcy! I insist on being satisfied. Have you made Miss Bennet an offer of marriage?"

"You have declared it to be impossible, Aunt."

"Let me be rightly understood, Nephew. This match to which you have lowered yourself can never take place. You are engaged to my daughter, Anne. Now what have you to say?"

"Only this, if that were true, you could have no reason to worry that I would propose to Miss Bennet. Besides, I have made no such promise to Anne."

"Darcy!" Lady Catherine was shaking with anger. "Your engagement is of a peculiar kind, you know that. It was the favorite wish of YOUR mother as well as myself. While you were in your cradles, we planned the match, and now when the dreams of both your aunt and your mother could be realized, you wish to destroy them by allying yourself with a woman of inferior birth and connections? Are you lost to all feelings of propriety and delicacy?"

"I never heard my mother speak of such a wish. Furthermore, being the husband of Miss Bennet must bring its own sources of extraordinary happiness that would make such disadvantages seem trifling."

"Obstinate, headstrong boy! I am not in the habit of being disappointed!"

"That will make your position more pitiable, Aunt, but will have no effect on me."

"Tell me at once; are you engaged to Miss Bennet?"

Darcy hesitated; he wanted to tell his aunt that he was and walk out of her room—nay her house—with a slam of the door, but he could not dissemble. "I am not."

Lady Catherine breathed a sigh of relief. "And will you promise not to enter into such an engagement?"

"I will not and certainly never shall. You have insulted me and the woman I hope to make my wife beyond all accounts. I must take my leave now." He turned to go but stopped upon hearing her next sentence.

"Not so hasty, Nephew. I have one more objection. Do you think I am not aware of the distasteful dalliance Miss Bennet has engaged herself in with the son of your former steward? Is such a woman of low morals and no virtue to be the mistress of Pemberley? Are its shades to be thus polluted?"

Darcy spun around and glared at his aunt with such disgust and anger that she sat back involuntarily. "Enough!! I will not allow another slanderous word to be spoken by you against the woman I love. I WILL marry Miss Elizabeth Bennet if I have to wait my entire life for her to accept me. I will beg on my knees if she so requires, but I will not listen to you speak of her in this manner. Until such time as you can speak with kindness and respect to the woman of my future life, all connections between us are henceforth at an end. Goodbye, madam."

Darcy strode out of the room angrily and slammed the door behind him as he walked to his chambers and pulled the bell for his valet. When Rogers entered, he blared, "Pack my trunks, Rogers; we leave in an hour."

True to his word, Darcy entered his carriage with his belongings an hour later and left Rosings Park, perhaps forever. His mind reeled at the presumption of his aunt. To fake an illness and to trick half the staff, her own daughter and him into coming and playing court at her sickbed was inconceivable. He had told her many times he did not wish to marry Anne. Long ago, he had spoken to Anne and found she had no such expectations. She had no wish to marry as she knew she was not well enough to do so.

Lady Catherine's disgraceful comments and assumptions about Elizabeth angered him further, and he swore under his breath as he remembered her presumptuous words and actions. He was filled suddenly with only one desire: to take Elizabeth as his wife and damn anyone in the world who opposed him. He tapped on the roof of the carriage, and as soon as it rolled to a stop and his groom came to enquire at the door, he said, "Make a stop at Darcy House; I have something to retrieve."

"Very good, sir."

Chapter 19

Darcy stood near the window in his chambers at Netherfield watching the sunrise. Although he had arrived late the evening before from Kent, he could not sleep any longer, and so he had risen early and dressed. His mind was filled with Elizabeth. He knew it would be a long while before enough of the morning had elapsed to allow him to go to her. He decided he would spend the time pleasurably running through each of his memories of her, one by one.

Not unlike the changing colors beginning to show across the horizon, his memories stirred within him an array of feelings. The sun rose slowly into the sky and turned the grey shadows of the ground below into pale shades of landscape and then to a brilliant glistening tapestry of color. The sun caught each patch of frost and melted it into crystal dewdrops, like tiny stars all over the ground. While he watched the transformation over the hills, he realized that Elizabeth had been like the sun to him. She transformed him, turning his life from a dull grey to fill it with vibrant colors—defrosting his heart and demeanor and warming him to feel the shimmer of love throughout.

He reached inside his pocket and pulled out his mother's ring, a ruby surrounded by tiny diamonds. He gently brushed his finger across the top of the ring as he had always done when it graced the slim finger of his mother. She had given it to him just before she died. He remembered her frail hand holding it out for him, and he did not want to take it. He did not want to believe she would not be around to wear it. When she was gone, he kept it locked in his safe in London, hidden away so he could not be reminded of its existence. It had been in the family for generations and was now his to give to his future wife.

Before he met Elizabeth, he had begun to suspect he would never marry. He could simply not imagine disgracing the memory of his sweet mother by presenting the ring to anyone less deserving than its previous owner. He turned it around in his fingers as he looked at it. Now, he could not imagine it gracing anyone else's hand but Elizabeth's. The thought of it on her finger brought a smile to his face, and he serenely placed it back in his breast pocket and resumed his vigil at the window.

AT LONGBOURN, ELIZABETH, TOO, WAS up early. She pocketed Mr. Darcy's handkerchief and left her chamber before sunrise to visit with her father before going on a walk. She had missed Mr. Darcy since he left her in the garden several days before and had taken to carrying his handkerchief with her as a reminder that he was coming back. It frustrated her that she was so discomfited due to his absence even though she was now convinced of his affection. However, after another long night and still no word from Bingley of his return, she had decided a little exercise would help calm her impatient spirits.

She knocked and entered her father's study to see him sitting peacefully by the fire with a book. He smiled at her before dipping his head back to his book. She poured herself a cup of tea and put some toast with jelly on her plate before joining her father at the fire.

They sat together in silent companionship, and Elizabeth was glad for it. The wonderful thing about being in her father's study was that neither felt compelled to converse all the time. It was the only room in the house in which she could be left to her thoughts if she wished to be. She sipped her tea and leaned her head back to savor the warmth, wondering what Darcy was doing at that moment. Mr. Bingley mentioned that he had written a few days before with news of Lady Catherine's serious illness. Elizabeth hoped that he was not suffering too much under the worry for his aunt's welfare.

By the time Elizabeth had finished her tea, the sun had begun to rise and bring more light into the study windows. She decided it was bright enough for her walk. and so she stood to leave.

"Going for a walk this morning, Lizzy?"

"Yes, Papa; would you like to come with me?" She smiled.

Mr. Bennet laughed quietly. "Not today, dear. I am afraid these old bones would slow you down. Come to see me when you return, will you?"

"Of course, Papa." Elizabeth leaned down and placed a kiss on her father's head before leaving the room. She languidly put on her warm cloak and gloves before stepping out into the crisp, January morning. She paused for a moment on the portico and looked around, deciding which path she wished to take that morning. She turned her eyes to the distance and decided a long walk would be just what she needed. She moved briskly to keep warm as she headed to the grove of trees that reminded her most of Mr. Darcy.

Mr. Darcy turned in response to the knock on his dressing room door. He bid the visitor enter, and the door opened to reveal his valet.

"Mr. Darcy, sir, your horse is ready."

"Thank you, Rogers."

Darcy turned and gathered his hat, gloves and crop from his valet after pulling on his greatcoat. He had decided that a ride about the countryside would serve the purpose of occupying the time before he could visit Elizabeth. He stood beside his horse on the mounting block and swept his gaze around to determine where he would ride. His memories from a morning many weeks earlier gave him only one choice. If he could not see Elizabeth yet, he, at least, could go to where he felt her memory. He mounted Salazar and prompted him into a quick pace, heading in the direction of a certain patch of trees.

When he finally reached the grove, he took the same footpath as he had on that day and slowed his horse to a walk as he tried to relive that morning in his mind. He smiled as he neared the bend in the path where he had first spotted Elizabeth. Stopping his horse, he dismounted to walk for a while.

When he came around the bend, he stopped abruptly. He would not believe his eyes; he had conjured up that memory so often in the past weeks that now he was not surprised his mind had created the form of Elizabeth before him. She was sitting on the same log, tapping her foot as she hummed a tune. As he looked upon her, he was surprised and impressed with himself for imagining her so clearly. It was as if she were really there. About the moment he realized it was no dream, she turned to look in his direction and smiled.

He dropped the reins and walked right to her. She was really there before him! As he neared her, she made to stand, but he forestalled her.

"Miss Bennet!" he exclaimed. "No, do not stand. May I?" He indicated the space beside her on the log.

Elizabeth could not believe her good fortune and wondered whether she, in fact, was dreaming. But her dreams were never *that* good, and Mr. Darcy was there in the flesh, standing before her. Her mind was swimming and her heart beating so wildly that she did not immediately acknowledge his words. She was still just looking at him with amazement when his smile started to fade and she realized she had not answered him.

"Oh, yes, by all means, sir." She shifted her position, allowing him more room beside her. Her hand unconsciously came to her chest as she willed her heart to slow. "This is a pleasant surprise. I did not expect you today."

Darcy folded himself beside her and looked at her with open admiration. "I returned from Kent just last night."

Elizabeth smiled and tipped her head in the direction of his horse wandering towards its master. "And you were out for a ride this morning, I presume." Her smiling face then turned to one of concern. "But, sir, Mr. Bingley said your aunt was gravely ill. How is she?"

Elizabeth was taken aback by the sudden fierceness on Darcy's face as he scowled. "I daresay she is herself again."

She could not understand the sudden dark cloud passing across his countenance, so she tentatively placed a comforting hand on his arm. "That is good news, is it not?"

As Darcy looked down at her hand, his face softened and his lips turned upwards slightly. He placed a hand over hers and said, "Miss Bennet, I cannot believe my luck in finding you here this morning. Let us not sour the dream by speaking of my aunt. I will explain later, but for now I wish only to dwell on happy topics."

Elizabeth puzzled over his words but nodded as she gave him a gentle smile.

Speaking of his aunt and the still surreal reality of Elizabeth sitting beside him reminded him of his long-awaited purpose in his wish to see her. He had planned to think through his words carefully and then request a private audience with her later that morning if his reception was what he had hoped it would be. Now he was struck with the blessed truth that he was already with Elizabeth—in their patch of woods, no less—and her hand was resting on his arm.

He looked at her beautiful face and smiled as he noticed her bruises were nearly gone, leaving only a few light yellow discolorations. He reached a hand to her face and gently touched each spot.

Elizabeth's breath caught in her throat at the sudden intimacy of his action. She held herself very still to savor the feel of his hand on her face. Her eyes nearly closed with pleasure at his touch, and she had to will them to stay open.

"Your bruises are nearly gone," he stated quietly before realizing what he was doing. He pulled his hand away and looked down in embarrassment.

Elizabeth smiled at his reaction and turned a playful voice to him. "I have a confession to make, Mr. Darcy."

Darcy smiled as he recognized the tone of her voice and saw that her face was set in a serious and contrite manner. He laughed softly at her attempt to keep the smile that played at her lips from destroying her repentant façade.

His lips twitched as he forced his own expression to match her serious look. "Is that right, Miss Bennet? And what is this confession?"

Elizabeth peeked guiltily through her lashes, and he bit his lip in amusement. "I am afraid to say it, sir."

Darcy laughed spiritedly before resuming a serious demeanor. "Now, I will not be baited like this, Miss Bennet. You said you have a confession to make; now out with it, girl!"

Elizabeth's mouth betrayed her with a sudden smile and quick laugh before she could cover it with her glove and try to wipe away the smile. "Very well, sir. I confess that I came to this very spot because I missed you and it reminds me of you."

Mr. Darcy smiled down at her and leaned in so that their shoulders brushed as he said conspiratorially, "I confess that was my purpose, as well, in coming here this morning."

Elizabeth gave him a playfully surprised look. "Indeed!"

He leaned a bit closer and took her hands in his. "However, if I had known I would be fortunate enough to encounter you here, I would have had another purpose in mind."

Elizabeth raised her eyebrows. "Is that so?" Her breath suddenly caught at the intense look he gave her. She watched as his dark eyes turned liquid and his smile softened.

Darcy looked at her while he sorted through the emotions running through him to find the right words to say. He broke their gaze as it was doing nothing but churning those emotions further. He began speaking while his head was lowered, looking at her small hands in his, but soon the words sparked a need to see her face.

"Elizabeth . . . dearest, loveliest Elizabeth. Words are insufficient to express the love that dwells in my heart for you. I cannot mark the moment or the hour or the look that first laid the foundation. I was in the middle before I knew I had begun. I love you, Elizabeth! I think I might have waited my whole life to love you. Will you . . . will you consent to allow me to continue to love you every day for the rest of our lives? Will you be my wife, Elizabeth?"

Elizabeth sat transfixed as her heart began a steady increase in its rate until she was sure it would burst. His words washed through her and claimed her. Her eyes filled with moisture, and she had only command enough of herself to softly whisper, "Yes."

Darcy smiled brightly, revealing his beautiful dimples. He pulled her hands up to his lips and kissed each one. His actions served to break her from her dream-like state, and she realized with a sudden skip to her heart that he had just proposed! She exclaimed with more strength and a laugh, "Yes! Yes, Mr. Darcy!"

He laughed at her sudden enthusiasm and smiled at her again.

Elizabeth then felt tugging at her fingers and she looked down to see that Mr. Darcy was removing her left glove. "What are you doing, sir?" she asked playfully.

Darcy shrugged as he said, "You just gave me your hand, Elizabeth, and I am inspecting my acquisition. Do you object?" He gave her a look of challenge.

Elizabeth opened her mouth to speak but then could not when she felt the exhilarating touch of his skin against hers. *When did he take off his gloves?* she wondered briefly before again being swallowed up by the sensation. Never before had she felt an unrelated man's bare hand touch hers. Tingles ran up the length of her arm and back down again to the spot where he was tenderly turning her hand in his.

She swallowed in an attempt to compose herself before saying, "I hope you approve of your recent acquisition, sir."

Darcy smiled. "It is quite lovely. However, I cannot approve just yet. There is something missing."

His words surprised her and she looked down at her un-gloved hand in puzzlement. At that moment, he reached into his greatcoat and pulled out an object. Before she could say anything, he slipped the most beautiful ring on her fourth finger.

She slowly pulled her hand out of his for a closer look at the ring. She whispered to herself, "It is so beautiful." Looking up at his serene face, she said, "Are you sure, Mr. Darcy? This is too much!"

Darcy reclaimed her hand and shook his head, laughingly. "Elizabeth, you have just consented to be my wife. Do you not think you can address me less formally now?"

Elizabeth bit her lip before giving him a playful smile. "And how would you have me address you?"

Darcy pulled her closer to him. "My name is Fitzwilliam, but many of my family call me William. You may address me anyway you wish, Elizabeth."

Elizabeth thought about it a moment. She looked up at him and said, "Very well, William."

Darcy had not imagined that hearing his name fall from her lips would have such an effect on him. Unconsciously, he placed one hand on the small of her back as he brushed the other through the hair at her ear, coming to rest upon her cheek. He looked down at her and could not help himself. He whispered, "Forgive me, Elizabeth," before lowering his head and pressing his lips gently against hers for the first time.

His lips were warm and she nearly melted in his arms at the touch. All too quickly, he pulled back and rested his forehead against hers. His eyes were closed and his breathing was shaky.

Elizabeth was just as affected by the kiss but managed to say, playfully, "I will forgive you, sir—only if you do that again."

Darcy smiled before again gently brushing her lips with his. After another too short moment, he pulled away and leaned back to take in a deep breath.

"Sir?"

Elizabeth laughed breathily and said, "It is now you who must forgive me. I am afraid this will take some time to get used to, *William*."

Darcy laughed and swooped in to kiss her cheek quickly before sitting up, thrilled to be able to do so.

Elizabeth looked at him with an arched eyebrow as she said impertinently, "Am I to expect this reaction every time I say your name, my love."

Darcy's smile widened significantly at her endearing appellation. "I am afraid you may have to depend on it, madam."

His bright smile transfixed her for a moment, and she hesitantly raised her hand to his face. She paused briefly just before her hand made contact, and she looked at him as if to say, "May I?"

Darcy nodded, and Elizabeth touched her hand to his face. She brushed the tips of her fingers lightly over his eyebrows and down the side of his temples to trace the dimples she loved and then finally to cup his jaw. She said in wonder, "I have wished to feel your face since we were last here in this grove."

Darcy reached his hand up to cover hers and leaned into it. "If you had, then I am sure I would have scared you away, for I do not think I could have helped myself from doing this." He turned his face to kiss the inside of her palm and then her wrist.

A soft murmur came from her throat at his caress, and she pulled her hand away from his face in embarrassment. Darcy recognized his own slipping self-control and said, "Elizabeth, may I walk you home? I should like to speak to your father as soon as possible."

"I think that would be wise."

Darcy gently guided her fingers back into the warmth of her glove before putting on his own and standing to assist her. He retrieved the reins of his horse and came back to offer her his arm. She smiled brightly as she tucked her hand in the crook of his arm.

"I cannot believe my good fortune, Elizabeth, to have received your acceptance."

Elizabeth smiled playfully at him. "Can you not, sir? I should have guessed you would know I would accept. For how can I do anything else when I love you as I do?"

Darcy stopped as they both realized it was the first time she had voiced her love to him. He looked at her so tenderly that she could only smile sweetly in response.

"Elizabeth . . . " he whispered.

She squeezed his arm and indicated to the road ahead. "Shall we?"

He nodded slightly, drew in a long breath and took her hand to place a kiss on her fingers before resuming their walk. After a few minutes of quiet reflection, he turned to her with unexpected nervousness.

"Elizabeth, there is something I wish to speak to you about."

She looked at him with concern at the edginess in his voice.

He looked ahead, trying to fix his words, and finally said, "I wonder whether you would be willing to marry me soon. When I was traveling through London, I procured a special license. I thought, perhaps, we could marry in a double wedding with Jane and Bingley. I feel like I have waited so long already, and I did not want to wait any longer." He paused to see she was surprised and hastened to add, "But, Elizabeth, if you wish to wait longer, I will understand. I do not want to rush you."

Elizabeth turned towards him, and the smile on her face did much to take away his worry that she was upset at his presumption. "Do not trouble yourself, dear. I was only surprised by your request. When I left this morning, I had no thought of coming back engaged, and now, to think I will be married in a fortnight… It is all a little astonishing, that is all."

"If it is too hasty for you, my love, I can wait. If I try very, very hard, I am sure I can even smile while doing so," he teased.

Elizabeth laughed. "You mistake me, William. I believe I should also like to marry soon."

"Hmmm," he groaned, "perhaps it is a prudent choice, for if you are to call me 'William' now, I do not think any further delay would be wise." He winked at her.

She blushed beautifully, and they walked quietly for a moment. By the time they reached Longbourn, though, they were laughing as they discussed various aspects of their future together. Their playful banter continued until they reached the entryway to the house.

Mr. Bennet heard Elizabeth's laugh through the window of his study, and he stood up from his chair to see its source. He smiled serenely, with only a small amount of sadness, when his gaze rested upon his daughter being escorted on the arm of Mr. Darcy. Their level of familiarity was obvious, and he suspected that he shortly would be granting the man an interview. He watched as they walked up to the house and strolled over to his study door to receive them.

Just as they reached the door to his study, he startled them by pulling it open. "Mr. Darcy, sir, Elizabeth, won't you both join me for a moment?"

He smiled with amusement as he watched them look at each other with surprise and then a bit of nervousness before nodding to him as they entered the room.

Darcy led Elizabeth to a chair adjoining his near her father's desk. Mr. Bennet took his seat at the desk and laced his hands across the expanse of his chest as he leaned back and smiled mischievously.

"Thank you, sir, for inviting me—us—into your study. I was actually coming to request a moment of your time when you opened the door. There is a matter I would like to discuss with you." Darcy spoke with a smile and a quick look at Elizabeth, who blushed and took a sudden interest in her hands on her lap.

Mr. Bennet pressed his lips together and chuckled. "I should imagine so. Tell me, did my Lizzy make you beg?"

Elizabeth's father laughed aloud as he watched both heads of the young people in front of him snap up in surprised alarm. His daughter gave him an endearing frown before laughing herself. At her reaction, Darcy's apprehension faded, and he, too, began to laugh.

"Then I suspect you know why I am here. Thankfully, Mr. Bennet, she did not make me beg, though I assure you, I would have if she felt it was necessary," he said playfully.

"Papa, you are incorrigible." Elizabeth laughed.

"Well then, as we all know why you are here, Mr. Darcy, why do you not begin by telling me why I should grant you my blessing to marry Lizzy?"

Mr. Darcy's smile faded into one of passionate feeling as he resolutely declared, "There is no other man in the world, sir, including yourself—if you will forgive me—who will dedicate more of their life or can promise you more definitively to love and honor your daughter better than I. That is why, sir."

Mr. Bennet leaned back into his chair, impressed and, with a smile, turned to his daughter who was blushing at the declaration made by her betrothed. "And you, Lizzy, why should I allow this man to take you away from me to the wilds of Derbyshire?"

Elizabeth, at first startled to be addressed, and still a little surprised to have been invited into attendance for such an interview, looked at her father and said, "Because I love him, too, Papa." Smiling playfully, she continued,

"And because Pemberley, I am told, has a very impressive library in which, I can assure you, you will be welcome at any time."

Darcy chuckled and was pleased to hear her speak of Pemberley as her own. He reached for her hand and confirmed, "You will be as welcome as any, sir."

Mr. Bennet laughed. "Well then, how can I refuse my blessing or the chance to visit your library, sir?"

They all laughed softly, and while Elizabeth and Darcy were caught momentarily in their own little world of happiness at having their wedding condoned by Mr. Bennet, he pulled out a paper from his desk and, for the second time in as many months, filled out the form and signed it. With satisfaction, he began to address his daughter and her new intended.

"Mr. Darcy, Lizzy, there is one thing you ought to know." Mr. Bennet handed the paper to his son-in-law-to-be and began explaining its import. He told them about his wish for his daughters to marry for love and the extent to which he saved and thereby provided them the opportunity to do so by pretending diminished wealth. He expressed his gratification to Darcy and Elizabeth for choosing this course for their future life and thanked Darcy for loving his daughter well enough to overlook her lack of fortune. He finished with his requirement of their secrecy and watched as astonishment and disbelief played across their faces.

Elizabeth stood and circled the desk to embrace her father. "Thank you, Papa!" she said, through tears.

Darcy folded the paper and placed it in his pocket. "Mr. Bennet, I, too, wish to thank you; however, you have already given me so much in granting the hand of your daughter. I understand the reasoning behind your motives and secrecy, and I commend you for your bravery. You have quietly endured censure amongst your neighbors for your apparent poor management of your estate. You have my respect, and if I may be so bold to say"—he paused and looked back at his betrothed as she held her arm around her father—"I am honored to become your son. It has been many years since I had a father, and I feel fortunate to have garnered one so wise."

Mr. Bennet hid the warm feeling that swelled in him at Mr. Darcy's statement and calmly responded, "I appreciate what you have said and wish only to add that you are a most welcome son to me."

Both men then cleared their throats to dispel the sudden tenderness they felt, and Elizabeth chuckled to herself as she watched the two men she loved most in life pretend indifference to the bond they felt.

"Well, you can at least shake hands; nobody will question your masculinity with such a gesture," she teased them.

They laughed with chagrin at her jest, and each reached to shake the other's hand.

Chapter 20

Elizabeth sat at her dressing table and watched as their ladies' maid, Ruth, put the final flower at the base of her neck. She looked in the mirror and tried to convince herself that today she would, indeed, marry William. The previous two weeks had seemed as much a dream as the day he proposed. After having received her father's consent, they announced their intended wedding date. Elizabeth could tell that her father was a little unhappy with the early date but only because she knew he wished to keep her home longer.

Elizabeth had then gone to her mother's room and told her the news in private while Mr. Darcy stayed with her father in the study. She was worried about her mother's reaction to the news but, instead, found something totally unexpected.

"You are joking, Lizzy! Engaged to Mr. Darcy? No, no I do not believe it!"

"Oh, this is a retched beginning, indeed! I am depending on you, Mama. Nobody will believe me if you do not," Elizabeth laughed.

Now, reflecting back to that conversation, Elizabeth smiled again at her efforts to convince her mother that she was actually engaged to Mr. Darcy. *Perhaps I was too convincing in the beginning when I told her he did not care for me.* Her mother's reaction was nothing like Jane's, though, who sat stunned and quiet for some time before exclaiming excitedly how happy she was and how Charles would now be a brother to his best friend. She was ecstatic about the double wedding, which had initially worried Elizabeth. The two spent some time in conversation while Elizabeth finally told her sister of her long-held feelings for Mr. Darcy and how they had come about.

Elizabeth turned her head to examine her maid's work. "It is beautiful, Ruth! I have never seen this style before. Where did you learn of it?"

Ruth patted a straying curl back into place and replied, "Thank you, mum. I's seen it once in one of Miss Lydia's London magazines."

Elizabeth turned her head side to side to better view her coiffure. Ruth had twisted her curls into a cord on either side of her head; coming together to create a bun at the base of her neck where she placed many tiny beads and flowers. Her veil, she could see, would pin directly behind it to flow down her back.

"It is absolutely perfect, Ruth. Thank you."

At that moment, Jane and Aunt Gardiner came into the room. Elizabeth's aunt had already helped Jane into her dress, and Elizabeth turned in her seat to look at her. Ruth had styled Jane's hair elegantly as well, with a silky braid around her hairline and the rest of her hair stacked beautifully in curls. A soft yellow ribbon woven through the braid matched Jane's dress, which was white with embroidered yellow flowers cascading down the length of it. The bodice was white silk accented only with a thick yellow ribbon beneath her breasts.

Elizabeth reached out her arms to her sister and they took hands. "Jane, you look so beautiful. Charles will hardly know what he is about when he sees you."

Jane blushed and said, "Oh, Lizzy, you look very beautiful as well. My happiness on this day is only increased by sharing it with you and Mr. Darcy."

"You do look very happy, Lizzy," Aunt Gardiner observed, "but perhaps a little underdressed for the occasion."

Elizabeth looked down at her stays and chemise and chuckled. "Do you think so, Aunt?" She laughed. "Perhaps I ought to put on my dress now. I would not want to scandalize the town."

The three ladies laughed as Elizabeth's aunt lifted her dress from where it lay displayed on the bed. Elizabeth paused as she watched her and briefly thought how blessed she was to have her aunt helping with this process. She had never really been close to her mother, and as it was, her mother's voice could be heard throughout the house in a fit of nerves as she spoke with cook over last minute directions for the wedding breakfast and scolded one of her sisters over her manner of dress. Elizabeth was grateful to have this tender moment with her aunt instead and smiled her thanks.

She gingerly stepped into her dress and allowed her sister and aunt to pull it up as she eased her arms into the sleeves. She turned to examine herself in the mirror as they fastened the tiny buttons up her back. Elizabeth had chosen a dress entirely of ivory silk. The top had the most beautiful matching Brussels lace overlay that her aunt had found for her in London. The dress fit snugly to her figure until her hips, where it flared elegantly. She smiled as she smoothed the silk skirt and took a deep breath.

I am going to marry William today, she kept telling herself. No matter how many times she said it, though, it still felt too wonderful to be true. Her aunt finished with the buttons and rested her hands on Lizzy's shoulders as the three of them looked at each other in the mirror. A knock on the door brought Hill with a bundle in her hands.

"A package come for ya', Miss Elizabeth." She curtsied and handed over a small, tissue-wrapped item.

Elizabeth smiled as she recognized the handwriting on the attached letter. She looked up at her aunt and Jane who politely excused themselves but not before Aunt Gardiner reminded her not to be long, as it was almost time to go to the church.

Sitting carefully on the bed, she opened the letter from Mr. Darcy. Her smile was soft and happy as she read the missive.

Dearest Elizabeth,

Today you are granting me my greatest wish. Thank you once again for consenting to be my wife. For as long as I have had your acquaintance, I have often wondered whether you are not a 'Phantom of Delight,' unreal in your beauty and loveliness. The day you said you would marry me gave me such pleasure, and I knew, then, that you were real, for I could not dream something so wonderful. I hope that we share more than a mere inkling of love, for I do not wish to starve ours away with this sonnet. The words have always reminded me of you. I will see you later today, my love. I will be the one smiling like a love-struck schoolboy at the front of the church.

Most sincerely yours,
Fitzwilliam Darcy

She was a phantom of delight
When first she gleamed upon my sight;
A lovely Apparition, sent
To be a moment's ornament;
Her eyes as stars of Twilight fair;
Like Twilight's, too, her dusky hair;
But all things else about her drawn
From May-time and the cheerful Dawn;
A dancing Shape, an Image gay,
To haunt, to startle, and way-lay.

I saw her upon a nearer view,
A Spirit, yet a Woman too!
Her household motions light and free,
And steps of virgin liberty;
A countenance in which did meet
Sweet records, promises as sweet;
A Creature not too bright or good
For human nature's daily food;
For transient sorrows, simple wiles,
Praise, blame, love, kisses, tears and smiles.

And now I see with eye serene
The very pulse of the machine;
A Being breathing thoughtful breath,
A Traveler between life and death;
The reason firm, the temperate will,
Endurance, foresight, strength, and skill;
A perfect Woman, nobly planned,
To warm, to comfort, and command;
And yet a Spirit still, and bright,
With something of angelic light.
— *Wordsworth*

Elizabeth wiped a tear from her face as she set the note aside and opened the tissue-wrapped package. A soft and silky fabric fell into her lap. She picked it up and recognized the handkerchief she had admired at the shop in London. *But how did he know?* She kissed both the letter and the handkerchief when she heard her mother's frantic call that it was time to leave. She placed them both in the top of her packed trunk. After the wedding breakfast, she would be leaving Longbourn with William.

Darcy stood serenely at the front of the church watching Bingley pace back and forth across the floor in front of him. He smiled at his friend's nervousness and wondered why he did not feel the same. *It is because this is not just a beginning for me. It is the end of loneliness and the end of solitude.* He breathed deeply in contentment. The day had finally arrived. If Darcy was feeling anything, it was impatience that the two weeks of their engagement had not gone more quickly and that this morning was not going fast enough, either.

"Charles! Calm yourself, man! This is the greatest day of your life, is it not?"

Mr. Bingley stopped and gave a glorious Bingley smile. "That it is, Darcy! I am just nervous for Jane. I know how much stress her mother can cause, and I am sure Mrs. Bennet is in fine form this morning."

Darcy nodded his head and wondered for a moment whether he should worry about Elizabeth. He shook his head as he thought that, as soon as her aunt had arrived in town, Elizabeth had been spared much of her mother's effusions over the wedding planning.

The reverend came up to the two grooms and gave them some last-minute instructions, letting them know the service would begin shortly and they should resume their spots. Bingley quickly took his place beside his friend and fidgeted with his hands instead.

Darcy looked over the crowd of people. His eyes fell upon his Aunt and Uncle Fitzwilliam, his cousin the colonel, and his other cousin James, who was Richard's older brother. The members of his family were all in one row and smiling brightly at him. His aunt gave him an indulgent smile, and his uncle gave him an encouraging one. James nodded his head, and when Darcy turned his gaze to his cousin Richard, he groaned quietly to himself as Richard was bobbing his eyebrows up and down and making kissing faces. Darcy smiled and shook his head. He would have to remember not to look at *this* cousin during the service.

When his eyes caught those of his sister, both his happiness and hers could not be expressed clearer than the expressions on their faces. Over the past few weeks, Elizabeth and Georgiana had continued their relationship, and they were now very fond of each other, giving Darcy a calm sense of contentment.

He looked away from his family and was not disappointed at the obvious absence of his Aunt Catherine and, by consequence, his cousin Anne. The former had been outraged by his letter informing her of his wedding and had written a scathing response. He could not allow that kind of treatment towards Elizabeth and so had chosen to cut off Lady Catherine.

When his eyes rested on Miss Bingley sitting with her sister, he pressed his lips together in humor. All those around her were discretely fanning themselves or constantly needing their handkerchiefs while she sat completely unaware. Looking at her reminded him of the moment she had learned of his engagement.

Bingley had convinced his sister to extend an invitation for tea to Elizabeth and Jane, and she had entered the room reluctantly to greet her guests. He, Bingley and Georgiana were already there, sitting next to the ladies.

Miss Bingley immediately noticed Elizabeth's ring. "Miss Eliza! What is this that I am seeing? Am I to wish you joy?" she asked in utter astonishment and disbelief.

"Yes, Miss Bingley. It is as you see; I am engaged to be married."

Miss Bingley's eyes narrowed and she said insincerely, "How nice for you. Do I know the gentleman?"

"Yes, I believe he is among your acquaintance." Elizabeth secretly eyed Darcy, who had resolutely kept silent.

"Indeed! Tell me, who is this gentleman who has been so fortunate as to secure you?" She sneered in barely concealed sarcasm.

"It is I, Miss Bingley. I am most fortunate, indeed. Thank you," Darcy had then spoken as he took Elizabeth's hand and kissed it.

Miss Bingley had sputtered a few words of congratulations and remained unusually silent for the rest of tea. After a while, she had claimed a slight headache and excused herself.

Music began to fill the church, and Darcy was brought back from his memory. He looked around, noticing that Elizabeth's family had found their pew and everyone was now standing and looking towards the back of the church as the music drifted and changed to indicate the beginning of the services.

He pulled at the sleeves of his jacket and glued his eyes to the church doors, willing them to open and Elizabeth to appear.

Mr. Bennet blinked his eyes to keep away the tears as he felt each of his daughters intertwine a delicate arm with one of his. It was not an easy task for Mr. Bennet to give away his two most sensible daughters at once. The music could be heard through the doors and he noticed when the tune changed, indicating it was his time.

He turned to Elizabeth and gave her a kiss on the cheek. "I could not have let you go to anyone less deserving, Lizzy." He turned to Jane and kissed her too. "Or you, either, Jane."

"I love you, Papa" Jane said.

"Me, too." Elizabeth laughed as she leaned in to kiss his cheek.

Mr. Bennet shook his head as if to dispel their affection and grumbled as he cleared the emotion from his throat. "Now, now. Enough of this. I believe it is time."

With his nod to the two altar boys, they pulled the great doors open, and he began escorting his daughters down the aisle to their waiting grooms.

Darcy was lost to all other thoughts as his eyes captured the scene of his Elizabeth walking down the aisle to him. She was exquisite and ethereal in her beauty. Everything else in the room disappeared, and he was aware only of her. As he finished his inspection and met her gaze, her beautiful smile beckoned him. Before realizing it, he had walked the last remaining steps to her instead of waiting for her to come to him. He heard a few of the guests snicker or swoon at his impulsiveness. Outside his awareness, he barely registered the distinctive chuckle of his cousin. He did not care; she was his, and he had to go to her.

Mr. Bennet relinquished Elizabeth to her betrothed, and Darcy escorted her the rest of the way to the altar. After placing Jane's arm on Bingley's, Mr. Bennet solemnly took his place next to his wife in the family pew.

The reverend began the services with a prayer. In turn, each couple repeated the required promises. The words of the vows flowed around them as Jane, Bingley, Elizabeth and Darcy each spoke them reverently, binding themselves to their partners.

When prompted, Darcy and Bingley turned to their brides.

Darcy held Elizabeth's hand as he placed the ring on it. He looked deeply into her eyes as he said his part reverently. "With this ring I thee wed, with my body I thee worship, with all my worldly goods I thee endow: in the name of the Father, and of the Son, and of the Holy Ghost. Amen."

They continued looking into each other's eyes while Charles made his oath to his bride and placed the ring on her finger. After another solemn prayer by the reverend, he pronounced to the witnesses they were man and wife.

"May I present to you, Mr. and Mrs. Charles Bingley and Mr. and Mrs. Fitzwilliam Darcy."

Darcy looked down at his bride and kissed her lovingly. "Hello, Mrs. Darcy."

Elizabeth smiled happily at her husband and replied, "Hello, William." The words were barely out of her mouth before he bent to kiss her again.

Elizabeth walked on the arm of her new husband into the cottage he had reserved for their first evening as man and wife. The next day, they would travel the last of the distance to Pemberley and stay there for many weeks. Elizabeth left her husband's side as he went to instruct the footman where to place their trunks.

She ran her fingers along the back of an elegant sofa in the small sitting room as she reflected on the last few hours. After the wedding, the newlyweds and all of their guests went to Longbourn for the wedding breakfast. Elizabeth smiled as she remembered the happy hours of last good-byes extended to lifelong friends. It was also the first time she had met William's uncle and other cousin.

She was pleased they were so friendly and kind to her. She felt blessed to have joined such a loving family. Elizabeth brought her hand to her mouth as she thought of the easy way Colonel Fitzwilliam was able to bring a smile to her husband's face. If only for that ability, she would be appreciative to his cousin for a lifetime, for she loved to see William smile.

Elizabeth was not surprised, though, after having learned from her husband what happened in Kent, to see that Mr. Collins barely spoke to either of them upon his arrival with Mary in Hertfordshire. They had arrived soon after she became engaged as Lady Catherine's displeasure had induced them to travel early to avoid her rants. Mr. Collins was as displeased with Elizabeth and Darcy as was his patroness.

Elizabeth was startled out of her reverie by the feel of her husband's arms slipping around her waist from behind.

"What are you thinking about, Mrs. Darcy?" he whispered in her ear, sending a tingle down her spine.

Elizabeth smiled. "I was just thinking of today."

"Hmm. Yes, we got married today, did we not?"

She laughed as she leaned back into his embrace. "I believe we did. However, I must admit I paid more attention to the groom than the reverend."

"That is good, for you were marrying the groom and not the reverend."

Elizabeth laughed as she disentangled herself from his arms and turned to face him. He immediately captured her hands in his and said, "Come, wife, I have something for you."

Elizabeth's eyebrow rose in question at the mischievous glint in his eye as she allowed him to lead her by the hand into the other room.

"And what is so funny, sir?"

"I am sure I do not know what you mean, my love." He looked at her with pressed lips trying not to smile.

She looked around her and, realizing they were in the bedchamber, immediately colored and turned her head to laugh uneasily.

Darcy recognized her embarrassment and stepped closer. "Elizabeth, I brought you in here to give you this." He reached behind her to the table near the wall and handed her a rather large package.

Elizabeth looked at the package with puzzlement. It was too big to be a book or jewelry but too small to be any kind of gown. She looked up at him with a question in her eyes.

"And what is this, William?"

She watched as her husband fought a serious battle to keep from smiling. She narrowed her eyes at him before turning around, and placing the package back on the table, she began to loosen its strings. After untying the cords, she carefully opened the paper and looked at what was inside.

She held up the garment and turned to her husband with a confused look. "Mr. Darcy, I believe your valet has made a mistake." She lifted and showed him the pair of breeches in her hands.

Mr. Darcy smiled. "It is no mistake, Elizabeth. Many weeks ago your father told me a charming story about you as a child."

He watched with amusement as her confused face froze in recognition of the story he was referring to. She turned wide eyes at him, and her jaw dropped, unladylike. With embarrassment and a bit of amusement, she said, "But... William..."

She bit her lip to keep her composure as she saw her husband erupt in what started as a gentle laugh but grew to a hearty bounce of his shoulders in humor. She began to laugh, too, as she stepped towards him. Putting her palm on his chest, she pushed him backwards, pretending to be displeased. "You, sir, are in trouble. And to think you have only been married a few hours." She shook her head at him.

Darcy covered his face to try to calm his amusement and play along with her for a moment. He schooled his features into a repentant face before saying, "If you promise not to cut off your hair or run off to join the Navy, you may wear those anytime you wish around Pemberley." He burst into laughter again and could barely manage to add, "There are many fine trees to live in there, but I hope you will consent to live with me."

Elizabeth could not contain herself any longer. She laughed and continued to push him backwards until he edged up against a piece of furniture. "I will not cut my hair if it pleases you, sir. But I make no promises about the Navy, William," she teased.

Her use of his name once again captured his interest, and he gathered her into his arms. His chuckles softened to a pleased smile. "You are so beautiful when you are angry, my dear wife."

"Is that so?" Elizabeth asked charmingly. "I hope you will not often make me cross just to see me thus."

Darcy brushed a stray strand of hair away from her face as he kissed her brow. "I will try my best to please you, Elizabeth," he said, laughing softly against her skin, leaving her breathless. "If only to keep you from the Navy."

Elizabeth boldly encircled her arms around his neck and watched with amazement as the simple act seemed to make his eyes grow darker. "I am glad to hear it, William."

Darcy smiled at his wife and thanked the heavens she was his. He leaned down and kissed her lips tenderly. Pulling back only slightly, he whispered, "*Now*, Elizabeth, I wish to demonstrate just how seriously I take one particular vow I made today." He kissed her lips again.

Elizabeth's heart was beating nearly out of her chest, and she was barely able to manage a whispered, "And which one was that, William?"

He kissed her sweetly on the cheek and then on the ear. "'With my body, I thee worship,'" he said, before returning to kiss her lips again.

The End

CPSIA information can be obtained at www.ICGtesting.com
Printed in the USA
LVOW041004020512

279994LV00002B/45/P